THE SECRET WAR

A WORLD WAR TWO NOVEL

STACY LYNN MILLER

Copyright © 2025 by Stacy Lynn Miller.

All rights reserved.

No part of this book may be reproduced in any form or by any electronic or mechanical means, including information storage and retrieval systems, without written permission from the author, except for the use of brief quotations in a book review.

NO AI TRAINING: Without in any way limiting the author's and publisher's exclusive rights under copyright, any use of this publication to "train" generative artificial intelligence (AI) technologies to generate text is expressly prohibited. The author reserves all rights to license uses of this work for generative AI training and development of machine learning language models.

Severn River Publishing
www.SevernRiverBooks.com

This is a work of fiction. Names, characters, businesses, places, events and incidents are either the products of the author's imagination or used in a fictitious manner. Any resemblance to actual persons, living or dead, or actual events is purely coincidental.

ISBN: 978-1-64875-649-8 (Paperback)

ALSO BY STACY LYNN MILLER

Hattie James WWII Novels
The Songbird
The Rio Affair
The Secret War
The Nightshade

Lexi Mills Thrillers
Fuze
Proximity
Impact
Pressure
Remote
Flashpoint

Sign up for the reader list at
severnriverbooks.com

To Leslie and Allison.
My daughters and keepers of my heart.
They teach me every day that love is unconditional and enduring.

1

The Brazilian Jungle, May 26, 1941

Last chances and Strom Wagner were no strangers. He had dispensed a few in his twenty-one years with the Nazi Party, but today, being on the receiving end, was a novel experience. The urgent communique from the German Embassy in his hand made it clear that Brigadeführer Jost, the chief of foreign intelligence for the Sicherheitsdienst, had reached his tipping point. By failing to sink a yacht and assassinate Brazil's president fifteen days ago, Strom had failed his primary mission as ambassador. He did not fracture diplomatic relations between Brazil and the United States or stop an American naval base from being built in the strategic coastal town of Natal. His childhood friendship with Jost no longer mattered. Strom's neck would be in a noose if he was unsuccessful again.

He swirled the ice cubes in his cocktail, admiring the brandy's dark umber hue, and brought the glass to his nose. The inviting scent of oak, spices, and a hint of chocolate made him take one more sip. The harmonious blend of vanilla and caramel balanced the alcohol's subtle bitterness, adding to its smoothness. Swallowing, he grappled with the prospect that he might not get to finish his prized bottle before his luck ran out.

Strom pushed from his leather desk chair and glanced out his study's west-facing window, where his last chance awaited him. The sun had nearly completed its slow descent behind the jungle treetops on the horizon, which meant preparations for tonight's critical test flight were underway. After returning the glass to its proper place on his credenza, he smoothed the flaps of his tailored linen jacket and walked to his newly built hangar.

The smell of petrol fumes and machinery grease was particularly hardy in the evening's warm, humid air. An intricate grid of lights strung from the rafters illuminated welders and machinists scampering around the latest plane being built. The whirring sound of compressor drills punctuated the frenzied pace his teams had to maintain. They were ahead of schedule in manufacturing engines and fuselages, but issues experienced during two previous test flights threatened to eat away the production days they had banked.

As the pilots visually inspected the aircraft, its designer caressed the fuselage and whispered to its metal hull as if it were a lover. Creatives who treated their designs like their children were commonplace after dedicating endless hours to their birth. Still, Reinhart Hoffman, Germany's most well-respected aeronautical engineer, took his attachment to an odd level. Of all the engineers Berlin could have sent for this project, Strom supposed Hoffman was his punishment. His string of failures had started with Heinz Baumann losing Karl James and his lists of spies. Whichever side located those rosters first would undoubtedly have the upper hand.

Until James surfaced, Strom would focus on the task Jost and Herr Göring had assigned him personally, labeling it vital. Both had explained it was only a matter of time before President Roosevelt got his way and Congress voted for war. And it was a loosely held secret that the United States had been working on a more robust strategic bomber since Germany occupied Poland. This aircraft would tack on another sixteen hundred kilometers to its furthest reach and, in some cases, cut ferry times around the globe in half. This endeavor required a bold response. Operation Amerika was the Luftwaffe's answer—a warplane with twice the range of any American plane that could carry five hundred kilos more of armaments. Unfortunately for Strom, the craft's design was Hoffman's brainchild.

"Are we ready?" Strom asked in German, startling Hoffman into standing straight and adjusting his glasses square on his nose.

"Yes, she's all set." Hoffman stroked the plane's outer skin once more. "Aren't you, girl?" The pitiful display made Strom sneer. Hoffman joined him and addressed the mission captain. "Drop your speed below four hundred before entering your first bank. The new welds and longer bolts should eliminate the shuddering you felt during the previous test flight."

The pilot slipped on his leather flying helmet and gloves. "I hope so. Last time, I nearly didn't make it out of the turn."

Hoffman bored the pilot with a death stare, ready to defend someone's honor—the plane's, not his. "Just keep it under four hundred."

Hoffman gave the signal to wheel the plane out. A flurry of activity followed once the pilots boarded. The hangar doors were slowly pushed open, revealing the twinkling glow of the evening stars. A heavy-duty tow truck backed up to the opening. Workmen attached the hitch to the fuselage.

The large steel doors closed as the aircraft moved into position on the darkened runway. Strom and Hoffman entered the control room, where an assistant sat at the desk with a binder of papers in front of the communications radio.

Strom settled into his favorite seat near the large picture window. It offered the best view of the airstrip and the horizon, where the maneuvers would take place. He checked his watch. It was seven, time for the test to begin.

Hoffman went to the corner station and poured a cup of coffee, stirring in an unhealthy amount of sugar. It was no secret why this man hurried through his tasks like a wind-up toy. He would fiddle and fiddle until the energy high wore off and then crash for hours on the cot beside his desk.

Strom observed Hoffman and his assistant meticulously aligning their papers as they had during previous tests. They seemed to believe that perfectly aligned documents were crucial to the success of the trials. He glanced out the window, noting the plane was now positioned at the end of the tarmac.

Hoffman picked up the radio microphone and ordered the operation to begin. Moments later, each engine sputtered and rumbled to life, one at a time, until all four thumped in rhythm, creating a steady, throbbing hum. He flipped a switch, and the runway glowed between two lines of blue.

The pilot's voice squawked over the air. The craft accelerated down the strip, and its nose rose from the ground. It disappeared into the darkness except for the three flashing red lights defining its tail and wingtips.

The test's monotonous first runs, varying speed and altitude while conducting smooth, wide turns, dragged out for an agonizing hour. The results remained unchanged from the previous runs or the ones before that. Hoffman's design performed like any other aircraft during normal flying conditions, but the mission Göring intended for Operation Amerika went well beyond the parameters of a traditional bombing run. This plane would have to fly under American radar defenses, drop its payload, and climb steeply to avoid enemy artillery fire. It would have to dodge high-rise buildings to escape the range of the artillery before returning home. All without stopping to refuel. It was an impossible feat for any current warplane in the German arsenal, let alone any other operational bomber in the world. Hoffman had sworn on his mother's grave, however, that his brainchild could exceed expectations.

Hoffman, now on his second cup of overly sweetened coffee, swallowed the last of it before lifting the radio mic. He ordered the captain to begin the next phase of the test—a steep, low-level banking maneuver mimicking the mission conditions they would contend with after reaching the United States.

The pilot acknowledged.

Strom stepped closer to the window to get a broader view of the horizon. He located the three dots defining the plane's outline and tracked them as they moved across the sky. The specks accelerated, as did the chatter between Hoffman and the craft. Hoffman was impatient for feedback, requesting a report on engine speed, temperature, and altitude every ten seconds. The captain replied with increasing irritation in his voice, but his reports indicated no signs of the vibration that nearly ended last week's flight in disaster.

The pilot reported he was at the proper altitude and had reached the maximum recommended speed. "Starting turn."

"Keep it under four hundred kilometers per hour." Hoffman's tone sounded more like that of a chiding parent than a professional working on Germany's most secret engineering project of the war.

The pilot kept his composure and pressed on, reporting data. "Heavy shudders coming from engines three and four. Straightening and dropping speed."

Hoffman clutched the microphone stiffly. "Negative! The welds will hold. Maintain heading and speed."

The dots in the night sky continued to rise at an angle. This marked the test's crucial point. Hoffman's design needed to be strong enough to withstand the force of a banking maneuver while in a steep climb. Otherwise, half the required pilots for Operation Amerika would be on a suicide mission.

"Vibration increasing." The pilot's voice cracked with tension.

An orange gleam sparked in the air, signifying a disastrous turn of events.

"I can't hold her. Bail out! Bail out! Bail out!"

The bright spot on the horizon burst larger for a moment before the three dots turned in direction and began a speedy descent toward the jungle canopy. In the shadow of the moonlight and the glow from whatever ignited into flames, a single silky parachute billowed in the plane's wake a hundred meters above the trees.

"No, no, no!" Hoffman slammed the microphone on the desk and tore at his graying, oily blonde hair, matting it into a stringy mess. The man chanted his disbelief like a petulant teenager.

A fireball the size of the Hindenburg, accompanied by a piercing explosion, momentarily rocked and lit the area. The test and Hoffman had failed. However, Strom was determined not to be remembered for failure. He grabbed Hoffman by the collar and slapped him across the face twice.

"Get a hold of yourself." Strom paused until Hoffman finally looked him in the eye. The man panted, and beads of sweat rolled down his forehead from the exertion.

A half dozen trucks, including a fire suppression team, rushed toward the accident site. In seconds, the only activity visible outside the picture window were the bobbing cones from the headlights and a faint orange glow in the distance.

"I've never had a plane crash before. Not one of my designs has ever failed." Hoffman appeared dazed and confused.

Strom shook him once more to stop the babbling. "I suggest you and your associate hop in a truck the moment the flames are out and comb through the debris to determine what went wrong. Berlin has no need for engineers who build planes that crash."

Hoffman nodded, the fear of an execution swirling in his eyes. "Yes, yes, of course. I must isolate the flaw."

"Yes, you do that."

Hoffman gestured for his assistant to follow him out the control room door leading to the flight line. They sped off toward the burning wreckage in a pickup.

Strom stayed inside, watching for the first headlights from the site. He assumed the first person back would have picked up the parachutist who'd jumped out before the crash. He went outside once the orange glow had disappeared, suggesting crews had extinguished the fire. Minutes later, a vehicle stopped in front of the primary hangar. He stepped closer. A crewman was sitting against the side of the truck's bed, his legs stretched flat, cradling his left arm. It was the copilot, and he looked like he was in pain.

"Did the other pilot make it out?" Strom asked, more concerned about extracting the root cause of the accident than about the captain's survival.

"There wasn't time." The pilot shook his head. "It bent."

"What do you mean it bent?"

"The wing." The man wiped the sweat from his brow. "We told Hoffman the surface was too large, with too much load, but he wouldn't listen. He said he knew his child inside and out. It literally snapped off as I jumped."

"I see," Strom said, withholding his dislike of Hoffman. He could excuse the man's eccentricities but not his arrogance. An inflated ego too often, as it did tonight, led to sloppy work. Anyone who believed they could do no wrong and make no mistake was dangerous. With the mission and his last chance at stake, he couldn't tolerate such pomposity. But he needed to handle this with delicacy. Hoffman was Göring's golden Luftwaffe child— the man who had designed the bulk of Germany's airborne arsenal. The more trained eyes he had on this flaw, the better.

The Secret War 7

He had less than two hundred days to correct the flaw, so Operation Amerika would coincide with what only a few officials in Germany knew the Japanese intended. The Axis powers recognized the United States as the biggest obstacle to their global conquest. They believed neutralizing the Americans before they entered the war was essential for their success. This campaign would do precisely that—simultaneous attacks on military, industrial, financial, and government sites significant enough to cripple the country for decades. But timing was essential. He had to be ready for a Japanese attack on the US so the Americans would blame them and direct their resources to the Pacific, not Europe.

Strom returned to his office and wrote a message outlining the problem. He hoped to strike the right balance, asking for assistance while avoiding any language that could earn him a firing squad. He placed it in a diplomatic pouch and dispatched a driver to deliver it to the embassy in Rio by sunrise.

He poured another glass of brandy, savoring its full-bodied richness in slow, exploratory sips. If the right minds did not come together to tame Hoffman's arrogance before the deadline, he might not finish that bottle after all.

2

Rio de Janeiro, Brazil, the same day

Maya Reyes was the only one in Hattie James's inner circle for whom she felt, in her bones, that her life was an open book; Hattie kept nothing from her. After the FBI thrust her into the world of espionage and her father's secret life was exposed, it was inevitable that she would develop a suspicious mind.

It had opened her eyes to a cold, hard truth: Few people were as they seemed. Not Heinz Baumann, the SS officer who had kidnapped and killed women in his hunt for Hattie's father. Not Swiss Ambassador Frederick Ziegler, the secret Nazi agent who tried to assassinate the Brazilian president in order to pit Brazil and the United States against one another. Not her mother, who had hidden the reason she cheated on her father and divorced him. Not her father, who had concealed from her his life as a clandestine spy. And not her pianist David, who had masqueraded as her fiancé and protected her secrets.

Not every lie told to her engendered mistrust, though. Whether out of love or loyalty, no matter how many lies her father told, she believed him. Her mother, too. David was a different story. Since she and David had arrived in Rio three months ago, something had gnawed at her about him, telling her that whatever he was hiding needed watching. What she had discovered last night hidden in the lining of her steamer trunk had reinforced that feeling.

Sitting on her bed the following morning, she retrieved Baumann's logbook from the trunk and flipped through its pages, considering the implication of finding it there. Two months ago, her father had secured the logbook from the plantation the night of the massacre. The same night Baumann and his men kidnapped and hunted Hattie and Maya for sport. The night Baumann had shot and killed Maya's sister Anna. Days later, Hattie had given it to the FBI agents operating out of Cohen Dry Cleaners. It had gone missing along with them. Hattie refused to believe that Baumann's book, detailing his intelligence operations in Rio, was unrelated to the disappearances and probable deaths.

The big question was how this book, missing for weeks, had turned up in a slit in the trunk Hattie shared with David. Few had access to it, but anyone, including Ziegler's operators, could have planted it there. But why? She assumed the book had been stolen to keep the information in it from getting into American hands. That wasn't the case, however. Unbeknownst to anyone, she had taken photographs of the book's pages before handing it over to the FBI, photos she had just given to the US Embassy.

She had spent the night lying awake, developing two likely scenarios. Either someone close to her had killed Agent Butler and Nala Cohen for it or somebody intended her to think they had. At present, David was the prime suspect.

A knock on the door startled her.

"Yes?" Hattie scrambled to return the book to the precise position where she had found it.

"Ready to go?" David asked from behind the door. "I want to say hi to the band before your performance tonight."

"Almost. I'll be right there." Hattie placed the stack of clothes inside the trunk and gingerly closed its lid to not make a noise. Until she knew who had hidden the book and why, only those she trusted with her life should be aware of her discovery. That list was short, with Maya at its top, and did not include David. Nor her mother, notorious for her inability to keep a secret.

After grabbing her purse, she opened the door. David was in the hallway, sporting an impatient look behind his round eyeglasses. He had put on his dark suit and slicked back his short brown hair for tonight's visit to Rio's elegant Golden Room nightclub.

"In a hurry, are we?" Hattie put on her best happy face, acting like last night had not happened and that she had never found the logbook. However, the possibility that David had killed Butler and Cohen for it made her regard him in a different light. She had always considered David a gentle man. It took a kind heart to enter a lavender relationship with her, knowing he was attracted to both sexes, particularly her, but could never have her. But her trust in him had taken a beating in recent weeks. She had attributed it to her irritation with his overprotectiveness, but now she had begun to think it was something more. Could he have killed Butler for the book in some misguided effort to protect her?

"I'm going stir-crazy sitting at home every night. The doctor said not to work for another few days but didn't say I couldn't go out," David said. It had been two weeks since he had taken a bullet in the leg while thwarting the bombing attempt on President Garza's yacht. Being in otherwise good health and great shape had helped his recovery, though he still needed a cane to support his injured leg. This allowed his leg muscles and tendons to heal properly.

"I don't want you to overdo it and set your recovery back."

He rolled his eyes. "If I get tired, I can rest in your dressing room."

Hattie narrowed her eyes, jabbing him in the chest with her index finger. "And no drinking. The doctor said you need to lay off it until you're fully healed."

He crossed his heart. "I promise."

"All right. Give me a second. I want to say good night to Mother." Hattie found it odd that her mother wanted to stay at the house on a Saturday night. Eva Machado never passed up an opportunity to make herself the center of attention at the Golden Room, South America's trendiest and most sought-after nightclub.

Hattie turned down the hallway and continued through the living room, finding her mother adding notes to student files in her home office. Hattie had

The Secret War

believed for a decade that her mother had taught music in order to make ends meet since she divorced Karl and returned to Brazil. But while working with her mother to prepare for a gala the previous month, she had seen how masterful Eva was as a musician. She was not merely an incredible performer with a flawless singing voice. She instinctively knew how to attack any song to create the perfect performance, and she conveyed her techniques with clarity and compassion. Eva did not teach for the money. She did it for the love of music.

Hattie knocked on the doorframe. "Hello, Mother."

Eva looked up. Except for her dark hair and slightly darker skin tone, she and Hattie looked much alike. She had put on a little weight since her performing days, but not much, and kept fit by spending hours in her garden and teaching her music students at her studio. Hattie, at thirty-one, hoped to have half her energy when she turned fifty-five.

Only last night, thanks to her ex-husband's encouragement, Eva had taken the first step toward accepting their daughter for who she was and who she loved. However, Hattie could see that she was struggling. Acceptance meant going against the church's teachings. It might be a long time before she could accept who Hattie invited into her heart and bed and not judge her as immoral and unnatural. This would be an arduous journey for Eva, and Hattie would not push.

"I wanted to say goodbye before David and I headed to the club."

"No matter how much he begs, don't let him play for you this evening." Eva wagged her index finger at her playfully.

"I've already reminded him about the doctor's orders, but I don't think I can hold him back for the entire month."

"He's like your father, stubborn and quietly resilient." Eva chuckled.

"He certainly is." Hattie turned to go but stopped. "I'll leave an extra seat for you if you change your mind."

A struggle manifested in Eva's eyes before she spoke, her voice brittle. "Not tonight, sweetheart."

"Nevertheless, it will be waiting for you. I'll see you after church tomorrow."

"Yes, church. I'm not sure if I'll make mass in the morning."

"Really?" As long as Hattie could remember, Eva had never missed the weekly service, rain or shine, sick or healthy. Likely, another factor was at play, but Hattie refrained from probing.

Eva pursed her lips as if fighting a smile or a frown. "Don't look at me like that."

"Like how?"

"Like hell has frozen over."

"Sorry, it's just—"

"Just nothing," Eva said. "No promises, but I need time to work through things."

Hattie smiled with her eyes and took a deep breath, full of hope. "Thank you, Mother."

She picked up David in the hallway and drove toward the Copacabana Palace Hotel with him squirming in the passenger seat. He had recovered well enough to drive, but Hattie had insisted on getting behind the wheel. Though she knew being carted around like an invalid made him uncomfortable, driving gave her more independence. The experience was exhilarating, much like performing on stage, and she was resisting giving it up.

After parking in her reserved spot, they went into her dressing room through the private patio entrance. Hattie tossed her purse on the couch, picked up the phone on the end table, and dialed the club's reception desk. "Yes, can you send in my tea and honey?"

"Of course, Miss James," the server said. "I'll have it sent right away."

After thanking him, she sat at the vanity to begin her pre-show preparations with her makeup and hair.

David kissed her on the forehead. "Thanks for the ride. I'm gonna check on the fellas."

"They're not all men, you know."

"Always Zoya. You remind me how good she is every chance you get." He added a smidge of resentment into his voice.

"I do not." Hattie spied him in the mirror. He looked cross. "She's good, but you're much better. You have nothing to fret about. I'm not replacing you."

He harrumphed. "Sure." He walked out the hallway door with a barely noticeable limp, using his cane minimally. The door closed behind him.

"Great." Hattie resumed her hair routine, thinking the last thing she needed was him acting insecure about his job on top of his jealousy over Maya. She had more important issues to worry about. Besides revealing her relationship with Maya to her parents and the logbook resurfacing, something she hadn't yet told anyone about, the FBI had sent Agent Samuel Knight. His job was to continue pressuring her into flushing out her father, who was wanted by the government for treason and the murders of two federal agents. She had a particular dislike for the man. He had leveraged her sister's freedom and Hattie's love of family to get her to travel to Brazil to do his bidding. David's childish behavior only complicated things.

After fixing her makeup, Hattie went to her walk-in closet and picked out a stage dress that would make her sparkle tonight. She wanted to catch Maya's eye and start testing the water for them to spend the night together again.

A knock on the door drew her attention.

When Maya had brought her tea last night, they kissed. They had also talked about Hattie's offer to front her enough money to rebuild the Halo Club, the business that had been burned down in early March, presumably by Nazi agents. Maya was running out of time to do something with the property before the city took over the land.

Maya had said she needed time to consider the proposal—a good sign. But Hattie was focused more on the heart-pounding kiss Maya had initiated. She had let it linger much longer than Hattie expected, stirring memories of the time they shared bodies. But Hattie was letting Maya set the pace. She was still grieving the loss of her sister and still assigned Hattie some level of blame for it, but Hattie could tell she was inching her way toward forgiveness.

Hattie forced back an insistent grin on her way to the door while hoping for a repeat of that kiss. She opened it, but immediately, disappointment settled in. "Monica."

"Good evening, Miss James. I have your tea and honey." She held the tray higher for emphasis.

"It's good to see you here, Monica." Hattie moved aside to let her place the items on the coffee table.

"Yes, Javier and I are very grateful to you and Miss Reyes. The hotel kindly schedules us together so we see much more of each other."

"I'm so glad the jobs are going well."

Hattie had seen Monica, a valued employee at the Halo Club before it was destroyed, and her husband when they were working at Ziegler's gala. Monica had worked as a server, and Javier had been a valet. They were a young, sweet Brazilian couple, and she was pleased to have had a part in getting them well-paying positions at the Palace.

"Is there anything else I can get you, miss?"

"No, thank you." As Monica turned to exit, Hattie asked, "Oh, one more thing. Is Miss Reyes in yet? She usually delivers my tea."

"Yes, but she's in the kitchen. The cook is throwing a tantrum."

Hattie laughed. "He certainly has quite the reputation. If she's busy after my show, can you ensure the bar sends me a fresh cup?"

"Of course." Monica excused herself, leaving Hattie alone with her hot beverage.

After putting the finishing touches on her makeup and tucking in the waves in her hair, Hattie took to the stage. The packed crowd offered several roaring ovations and finally allowed her to leave after two encores. The band performed well, but Zoya was exceptional on the piano, not missing a single note.

As Hattie left the spotlight and toweled the sweat from her brow while exiting through the wings, she caught up with the pianist. "You did very well tonight. Why didn't you tell me you were one of my mother's students?"

Zoya blushed. "I didn't want you to think I dropped her name to get the gig, so I let my performance speak for itself, Miss James."

"I know what you mean." While making her mark in the music business, Hattie had gone out of her way to hide the fact that she was Eva Machado's daughter. She had refused to live in her shadow. "You're quite talented. I understand from Miss Reyes that you've had trouble finding work before this job."

"Yes, most won't hire a woman pianist."

"Well, I'd like to help you find regular employment once Mr. Townsend returns to the piano."

"That's kind of you."

"Nonsense. Women should stick together. Someone with your skills should have offers lined up."

Zoya's face lit with gratitude. "Thank you, Miss James. If you need anything, just ask."

"I'll keep that in mind."

Hattie tossed the towel on a tray and went to the dining room to say hello to a friend she had spotted during the show. Nearing David's table, she eyed Maya speaking to a couple nearby. They were all smiles.

David and Leo Bell stood politely. Leo was about four inches taller and fifty pounds heavier than David, but it was all muscle. He wore his suit tonight, not his navy officer's uniform, but, in his forties, he would look handsome in just about anything with his chiseled features.

David held out a chair for her before saying, "You were wonderful tonight."

"Thank you." She focused on Leo. "I'm still mad at you for last night. You should have warned me that Agent Knight was my new contact."

Leo snorted. "Would you like me to call him out like I did in high school to my little sister's bullies and beat him up behind the hotel?"

"If that will get him off my back, I'm all for it."

Leo laughed. "I can make that happen."

Hattie lifted the glass of ice water that was waiting for her. "I'll drink to that." She took a sip.

"Knight said you two had a history in DC and New York, but he failed to mention how much of a jerk he had been to you."

"Yeah, well, everyone keeps secrets," Hattie said, suddenly realizing how true that statement was. She had secrets of her own, certainly. She wondered what the two men across from her were hiding from her or from others.

Leo raised and tilted his cocktail glass. "Nothing truer. If Knight gives you any grief, let me know. I'm sure I can find many ways at the embassy to make his stay in Rio miserable."

"I appreciate that, but Knight blames my father for the death of two FBI agents. He'll dog me as long as he thinks he's guilty."

"Then I might do it just for fun," Leo said.

Hattie took a bit of comfort in Leo's protectiveness. After everything they went through with the attempted bombing and rescuing Eva from Nazi abductors, Lieutenant Commander Leo Bell was a good man to have in her corner.

Monica approached. "Excuse me, Miss James. Miss Reyes has asked that you join her at the table over there."

"Of course. Tell her I'll be right there."

"Would you prefer your tea here?" Monica asked.

"No, I need to change after seeing what Miss Reyes needs. Could you send a fresh cup backstage?"

"I'll see to it." Monica scurried away.

Hattie pushed back her chair. "Gentlemen, duty calls."

Both men stood.

"I'll come to your dressing room soon," David said.

Hattie chanced a long look at Maya. She wore a tasteful black dress to blend in with the waitstaff. It was gathered at the waist, showing off her trim figure, and hit an inch below the knee. The neckline was cut low enough to tease the prospect of an alluring cleavage. But her most captivating feature was her hair. She had done something entirely different with it tonight, pulling her long black strands into an updo that hit low at the nape of her neck. It was a sophisticated and elegant look that had Hattie fantasizing about undoing it, one loose knot at a time.

"Take your time," she said in a wistful tone.

Hattie joined Maya, who acknowledged her with a nod and a subtle caress to her arm. She greeted the guests. "Good evening. I hope you enjoyed tonight's show."

"We did," the man said, glowing with a bright smile.

"Hattie," Maya said, "I'd like you to meet the Harrisons. They are on their honeymoon from Los Angeles and came to Rio to see you perform."

Hattie perked up at meeting someone from the States. She shook their hands. "I'm honored. Are you staying at the Palace?"

"Yes," the woman said. "The accommodations are wonderful, and so was your performance. My cousin has raved about knowing you for years, so I had to see you sing."

"Oh, who is that?"

"Helen Reed."

The Secret War 17

Hattie stiffened at the name that sent her into a tailspin whenever she heard it. Her stomach tightened, and her knees felt weak. The recorded music playing in the background and a hundred conversations in the room were all muted by the pounding in her temples.

Maya touched her arm. "Hattie, are you okay?"

"I'm fine." Hattie shook off her malaise and focused on the couple. "Yes, Helen is an acquaintance." She swallowed to keep her shock, anger, and heartbreak from bursting forth in a scene-making rant. "Please enjoy a bottle of champagne on me, and congratulations on your nuptials. If you'll excuse me. It's been a long evening."

Hattie marched across the dining room, willing herself to keep it together for a few minutes longer. Two guests tried to get her attention, likely for an autograph or photo, but she waved them off and continued at a fast pace. She pushed through the employee-only door, where band members lingered in the corridor. Several greeted her with "Hey, Hattie." Others nodded to her with a jut of their chin. She kept calm until Zoya furrowed her brow and eyed her with a concerned look.

"Are you okay?" Zoya asked.

"I'm fine." Hattie's voice quivered as she turned the knob, escaped to the sanctuary of her dressing room, and closed the door. She plopped against it, her pulse racing like she had seen a ghost.

And she had.

Helen Reed had haunted her for nearly three years after breaking her heart. Every time she caught a whiff of Chanel No. 5 in a nightclub or on the street. Every time she taxied through the Upper East Side after sunset. Every time she found the bottom of a vodka bottle, she thought of Helen Reed. Thought of how their bodies had fit together like sandy beaches and hot summer afternoons. Thought of how they would make love for hours, stopping only when sleep took over. Thought of how Helen had made her feel like the most beautiful, desirable woman in the world with a single steamy, piercing stare.

Hattie's hand shook as she brought it to her breastbone and traced a line across her skin the way Helen used to do to make her weak in the knees.

A knock on the door startled her.

"I'm fine, Zoya. I need a minute alone."

"Hattie, it's Maya. I have your tea. May I come in?"

"Damn," Hattie whispered.

She was a mess after fantasizing about the ex-lover who had ripped her heart to shreds, driving her to drink herself to oblivion for nearly six months. A glass of vodka was what she craved at the moment, not tea. The alcohol would help her forget how devastated she had been upon discovering another woman's lipstick on Helen...on a place where only Hattie's fingers and lips should have been. Hattie reminded herself that she had put Helen Reed behind her and cleaned up her act. She was much stronger now, and she had an amazing woman in her life.

"Hattie? May I come in?" Maya repeated.

"Yeah. Hold on." Hattie pushed off the door. Surprisingly, she had not shed one tear. That was a good sign. She opened the door and ushered Maya inside before closing it. After Maya placed the steaming cup of tea on the table, Hattie spun her around and pulled her into a tight embrace. She drew strength from her until the boiling desire to drown herself in a bottle of cheap vodka eased to a simmer.

When Hattie finally loosened her grasp, Maya looked her in the eyes and traced a fingertip down her cheek. "Whoever Helen Reed is, she's a damn fool."

Hattie shook her head. "I was a fool for falling for her."

"Opening your heart is never foolish. It's why we exist." Maya searched her eyes. "Please tell me she's in the past."

"Very much so."

"That's all I need to know."

The urge to say "I love you" nearly burst Hattie at the seams, but Maya still had to untangle the grief and anger wrapped around her sister's death. She had to be the one to say it first. Hattie settled on, "How did I ever find a woman like you?"

"I've been wondering the same thing." Maya paused and lowered her gaze. "But—"

Hattie briefly placed an index finger over Maya's lips. "I will wait for you."

"Okay."

The Secret War 19

"Okay."

"No, I mean, okay, I'll accept your offer of becoming business partners to rebuild the Halo Club."

A smile slowly built on Hattie's face.

"Well? Are you going to say something?"

"I have plenty to say, but you're not ready to hear it yet."

"You might be right." Maya took Hattie by both hands, guided her to the couch, and urged her to sit. "But I'm ready for this." She hooked a finger under the strap of Hattie's dress, lowered it, and ran her lips across her shoulder before pulling her into a searing kiss.

Hattie's body tingled with the desire that had built since that desperate night when they made love for the first time. However, her dressing room was not the place for this. She wanted to savor every inch of Maya until sunrise. Pulling back, she whispered, "Take me home with you."

3

November 25, 1941, six months later

Soft light filtered through the gauzy curtains, and the rumblings of Rio morning life began to stir outside. Hattie stretched across the mattress, a self-satisfied grin for the ages on her face, marveling at her perfect life. Her climb back to stardom had been a steady rise; a ticket to one of her performances at the Golden Room had become a coveted prize in the Western Hemisphere, more sought-after than her mother's shows ever had been. Her love life was even more extraordinary, as the sound of trickling water in the shower in the next room attested.

She threw the covers back, intending to join Maya there. However, the faucets squeaked, and the flow of water abruptly ended, taking with it a first-rate opportunity to continue last night's passion. After gathering a change of clothes from the dresser, she padded down the hallway, meeting Maya at the bathroom doorway.

"I'm sorry. Did I wake you?" Maya said. She looked sexy in her flannel robe, drying her shoulder-length black hair with a towel. She was inviting dressed in almost anything because Hattie knew the delicious curves beneath whatever she wore were reserved only for her.

The Secret War 21

"I needed to get up, anyway." Hattie gave her a brief but deep kiss, earning a contented smile.

"Mmm, I'll put on some coffee." Maya turned sideways to let Hattie in before stepping toward the kitchen.

Hattie swatted her on the bottom. "Don't start breakfast without me again. I love cooking with you."

Maya glanced over her shoulder, forming a tempting smile. "Then don't take all morning and use up all my hot water."

"I can't help myself when I'm here. I think of you in that shower—"

Maya swung around and kissed Hattie, bringing her into a tight, toe-curling embrace.

They prepared their meal much later than expected and sat at the table, eating and chatting about the progress of the Halo Club's resurrection. The project was taking longer than Hattie had envisioned, but the war in Europe had made it impossible to source many of the design elements they had picked out.

"Instead of Italian marble," Hattie said, "we can switch to granite from the United States or travertine from Mexico."

"I don't know." Maya sighed. "Both are expensive. Why not tile like we had before?"

"We can do that, but if you want to compete with the Golden Room like we planned when we started this venture, we shouldn't cut corners with the bathrooms. They're public spaces. Besides, money isn't an issue."

Maya let out a bigger sigh. "Maybe not for you, but I need to watch every penny."

Hattie squeezed Maya's hand. "We're partners, remember? In business and in life. I meant it when I said what's mine is yours. We"—she wagged a finger from her free hand back and forth between her and Maya to emphasize their dynamic as a couple—"aren't even close to needing to pinch pennies."

"Still—"

Hattie shushed her with that finger over her lips. "Uh-uh. Partners."

Maya relented with a nod. "Okay. I trust you to pick the right materials, but we still need to open in time for Carnival."

"That gives us eleven weeks. No matter what, we will be operating for Brazil's biggest celebration. Eva will entice the country's elite to attend. Maggie Moore will invite all her Hollywood and New York friends. We're a guaranteed hit with the three of us headlining those five days. By March, the Halo Club will be *the* place to go in Rio."

"Are you certain you want to give up your lucrative deal at the Palace?"

"For us, yes. I'll play it close to the vest at my meeting with the owner later today, but I'll make sure I have an out to my contract."

"I'm not as confident as you are." Maya took an unsteady breath. "We have yet to find a head chef."

"My mother is on that. She's narrowed the slate of candidates and will start her wining and dining after the holidays. Trust me, no one on that list will turn down Eva Machado."

"I'm glad she's helping us."

"I am, too," Hattie said.

Eva's journey to acceptance of Hattie and Maya had been long and rocky. However, her invitation to dinner tonight and offer to lead the hunt for a top-rated chef signaled a significant shift. While she had only given Maya a stiff, awkward hug before, this marked the first time Eva had gone out of her way to help them with their business.

After clearing the dishes and cleaning Maya's kitchen, Hattie gathered her purse. "Do you want me to check on the Halo Club after the contractor has left since you've been called in to work the lunch service today? They start the floors this morning."

"No, I'm sure he'll do a fine job. Besides, it's Tuesday." Maya placed both hands on Hattie's hips and pulled her closer until their abdomens touched. "You should go."

They had discussed what Hattie did on her Tuesdays off months ago. Just the basics, though, and just once. She had also told Maya about finding the logbook and her suspicions about David. And explained about the encoded lists of spies embedded in the sheet music and why the photos of them were so important. That had been enough for Maya to decide she did not want to hear the specifics of what she did on Tuesdays. It had become solely her business, as well as a game between her and Agent Knight.

So, Hattie wasn't keeping secrets from Maya anymore. Not really. Though, admittedly, she hadn't told her why she had been putting off formalizing an agreement with Maggie Moore, something that would affect Maya.

"All right. I'll go. I'll stop by to see you after I meet with the hotel owner this afternoon. And don't forget our dinner tonight."

"I won't. I've been looking forward to it. Now, go." Maya kissed her. "Before I make us both late."

Hattie hopped in Eva's small coupe and drove north. The streets of Rio were bustling with activity, and the vibrant colors and sounds of the city were a constant reminder of its energy and spirit. After some time, she noticed a black sedan trailing her. She grinned. To her surprise and pleasure, Agent Knight was behind the wheel today. Whoever had been following her last week, either on behalf of the FBI or Nazi Germany, had not been particularly skilled at avoiding detection. Knight, though, was decent at hiding his presence. However, since starting her Tuesday activities, Hattie had gotten better at spotting a tail. No one could track her for long.

She could have acted like she had not recognized him following her and waited to make her move at the right moment, but there was no fun in that. She enjoyed the chase and wanted to let Knight know she had spotted him and could beat him any time.

Hattie downshifted gears and punched the gas pedal to pick up speed quickly. At the next intersection, she took the corner from the middle lane, making the vehicles around her honk and slam on their brakes. The result added a few more car lengths between her and Knight. She was familiar with this part of downtown and knew the perfect spot to throw Knight off her scent.

After she made another series of turns, her target was fast approaching. The alley where she wanted to turn down was blocked by another car. Then the light ahead flashed green, and the line inched forward enough for her to turn into its narrow opening without stopping.

The passageway was wide enough for Eva's small coupe, with a few inches to spare on each side, but not for the four-door sedan following her.

She shifted gears again, steered straight, and glanced in her rearview mirror. Knight turned but crashed into the building wall. Lacking sufficient space to straighten his car out, he hopped out of the driver's door and pounded a fist against its roof.

Hattie rolled down her door window, waved her hand out the opening, and laughed. "Maybe next time."

Once out of the alley, she made more turns, checking her mirrors until she was sure no one else was tailing her. Only then did she resume her route north out of town. Three miles after the jungle started, she turned west on a dirt road and drove another mile. Nearing the road's end, she slowed to a crawl and stopped at a small house. The structure was run-down, stained by years of tropical storms and splintered by an equal amount of neglect. The shingled roof and windows were newer, signs of recent investment to make the place livable. The rocking chairs on the front porch were unoccupied, but the fishing pole leaning against the wall beside the door was a sure sign someone was there.

She exited the car, grabbed the crowbar from behind the passenger seat, and eased the door shut to minimize the noise. Scanning her surroundings, she noted nothing unusual, only the half acre cleared of the lush jungle brush and a sliver of the outhouse at the edge of the clearing.

She ascended the three steps up to the deck, carefully staying near the left handrail, the only section where the wood didn't creak. Once near the door, she touched the fishing line on the pole. It was wet, suggesting someone had placed it there under an hour ago. Twisting the doorknob, she eased the door open without stepping through, waiting to see if whoever was there would try to jump her. Expecting an ambush, she checked the sliver-sized opening between the door hinges and the frame, but saw no one.

Walking inside cautiously, she scanned the room, but it appeared to be unoccupied. A coffee cup was on a small table beside the easy chair. It was warm. Knowing she was on the correct trail, she smiled and entered the kitchen. It was empty. She pivoted to go down the hallway to the bedrooms and bathroom, but a man's firm hand slipped over her mouth, preventing her from screaming. At the same time, he wrapped an arm around her torso, pinning the hand holding the crowbar to her body.

The Secret War 25

Hattie's pulse picked up as her fight-or-flight instinct kicked in. She immediately dropped her weight by bending her knees and lowering her center of gravity, making it harder for her assailant to lift or move her. She swiveled her head to the side to generate breathing space and prevent him from smothering her. With her free hand, she reached up, grabbed the hand that was covering her mouth, and pulled it away from her face as much as possible. She used her elbow to strike backward into the man's ribs, a sensitive area, to cause pain and create an opportunity to escape. She readied to stomp her heel on her opponent's foot, but he loosened his grip and dropped his hold.

"All right. All right. I can do without a broken bone." Karl laughed.

"Damn. I forgot to check the broom closet." Hattie shook her head in disappointment. "I'm getting lazy. I was expecting you in one of the back rooms."

"Never turn your back on a potential hiding place until you've cleared it. Always expect the unexpected, but you did well fending off my attack. Remember to twist and rotate toward your free arm after stomping his foot. That should let you escape."

"I remember your lesson last week."

"Coffee?" Karl lifted the kettle from the stove.

"Please." Hattie grabbed the empty mug in the sink and extended it to her father.

They went to the living room and sat in the easy chairs. He eased into his gingerly. During her childhood, Hattie always considered him big and strong, but two decades of espionage work had taken its toll on his nearly sixty-year-old athletic body.

Karl sipped from his cup. "Any change?"

"No. The logbook was still there last night."

Hattie had told her father months ago about discovering Baumann's original ledger in her trunk. Karl had said if David had killed Butler to keep the book from going to the States, he would have destroyed it, not hidden it away. David must have other plans for it, he had said, or someone had planted it there for some reason. Either way, they needed to be patient in order to unravel the truth. They decided to watch David and check on the book's location every day or so. They would question him if it went missing or moved."

"And the sheet music?" Karl asked.

"Your lists of spies are safe. Are you ever going to tell me who the Professor is?"

"Not unless I have to."

"You're stubborn."

"That stubborn streak has kept me alive." He took another sip. "And you."

"I know it has, Father. Thank you." Hattie also sipped. "What's on the agenda today? More firearms training? Self-defense?"

"Surveillance. A good operative must know how to watch a target without being seen."

"What are we going to surveil in the jungle? A toucan?"

Karl laughed. "Unlike humans, they wouldn't let us get close enough. No, we're heading to the docks."

"Is it okay for you to be in town during daylight?" But Hattie already knew the answer.

Her father, as she had come to learn over the past six months, was a master at the spy game. They met every Tuesday, initially at his shack in the Rio slums. Once he bought this cabin, they continued their meetings here. He taught her a new skill each week, aiming to make her as talented as he was. She quickly learned he would be safe in Times Square, standing in the middle of a police parade. He had a way of blending in and acting like he belonged there. How else could he have sneaked into Hattie's place of work time and again without being seen by the FBI agents and assets surveilling her?

"Never mind." Hattie downed her coffee and pushed up from the chair. "We can't stay all day. I meet with the hotel owner at two."

Karl left his sedan a ways away, hopped into Hattie's car, and directed her to park near an intersection several blocks from the wharf entrance. "When on an op, always park for a quick getaway. A corner is accessible from

The Secret War   27

multiple directions and there's no chance of getting blocked in. No jockeying back and forth to get out of a slot."

Each moment with her father on a Tuesday was a learning experience, and Hattie soaked up every bit of his teaching. She found an ideal spot and joined her father on foot, heading with him toward the docks.

"When possible, stick to areas available to the public so as to not raise the suspicions of workers or the police."

"What if the target goes to a restricted area?"

"That depends on whether you're watching or following. Watching means precisely that. Observe and remain in the shadows. Spying is a long game. The most important aspect is not being seen."

"And if my job is to follow?"

"Try to blend in and keep your gun ready. Always assume you're walking into a trap."

"Like the broom closet."

"Yes, like the broom closet," he repeated.

After picking up a copy of today's newspaper, Karl led them to a small café with outdoor seating across from the dock's main gate. They bought two coffees and an order of pão de queijo and sat at a table facing the entrance, their backs against the wall. Hattie noticed a pattern in how her father positioned himself in a room or when setting up surveillance. He never exposed his back to danger.

Karl taught her to always expect the unexpected.

While snacking on the tasty cheesy bread, he pulled out a pencil and turned to the crossword page. "This gives you a reason to write something down if you need to note a license plate or something important, but it shouldn't merely be a prop. Glance at it and fill in the blocks from time to time to make it appear like you're actually working the puzzle."

Hattie understood. "Blending in."

"Exactly."

Karl passed along more tidbits on surveilling without being detected and evading enemy surveillance. They had been there for nearly half an hour when a caravan of four black sedans drove past and parked outside the marina's main entrance. Karl perked up. Minutes later, a seaplane landed and disappeared somewhere in the marina. Hattie presumed it was docking at the same place where she and David arrived nine months ago.

"What do you think is going on?"

"The American vice president is on that plane."

Hattie laughed. "That's why we're here today. How did you know he was coming?"

"Jack Lynch's garbage cans in front of his house."

Hattie grinned. "The US Embassy chief of security is not very secure."

"Lynch is a bureaucrat, not an operator. He leaks secrets like a sieve."

Hattie had gotten a better picture of what her father actually did for the State Department of late. She also realized she still had to learn much about him and the life he had led for two decades.

Fifteen minutes had passed when a marina security vehicle pulled up inside the main gate. Doors from the caravan flew open, and a half dozen men stepped out. One was in an American navy uniform.

"It's Leo," Hattie said.

"I figured he'd be here since he's on Lynch's team."

Lynch exited one of the cars. He was shorter and heavier than Leo and had much less hair. The effect of those two standing beside each other was cartoonish. Leo was fit and dashing in his uniform, and Lynch...well... Lynch looked like a bureaucrat.

The doors to the marina vehicle opened inside the gate, and four people got out. Two appeared to be security officers, and one Hattie recognized as United States Vice President Henry A. Wallace.

"I'll be damned," Karl said.

"What?" Hattie asked.

"The short, thin guy next to Wallace. I know him."

"Who is he?"

"The Professor's son. You met him once at her house when you were about nine."

Hattie squinted to get a better look at the man. He seemed to be about her age, maybe a little younger. She flashed on the disturbing possibility that her father and the Professor seemed to have a close relationship and that the Professor and he might have—

Stop, Hattie told herself. *That man is not and could not be your half brother. He looks nothing like you.* "I don't remember him."

"This can't be a coincidence," Karl said. "The Professor must have sent him."

"Why would she?"

"To get a message to me." Karl glanced at Hattie. "Can you have Leo meet with me? You know the location."

"Yes, Father. I know where. I'll make the call."

4

Hattie had stayed too long at the docks with her father. She would need to hurry to make her appointment with the hotel owner. Instead of parking in her reserved spot at the other end of the building from where her meeting was, she pulled into the main entrance. When she stopped short of the valet stand, a man dressed in a black tux, the hotel's uniform for male employees serving the guests, jogged up to the driver's door.

"Good afternoon, Miss James. It's a pleasure to help you today."

Hattie recognized the voice as she shifted the coupe into park. She gave him a brief hug. "Javier, it's good to see you. Still enjoying working at the Palace?"

"Yes, very much so."

She squeezed his arm. "Sorry, but I must rush off. We'll catch up soon."

"Of course, Miss James. I'll take special care of your vehicle."

Hattie offered him a grateful smile before turning on her heel and darting through the main doors. The hotel lobby was an exposé in grandeur with its glistening marble floors, gold and brass trim polished to a shine, and a bold chandelier larger than her car. Walking through the space, she compared it to the soon-to-be resurrected Halo Club, which would be grand but not on such a large scale. It would offer luxury and

The Secret War

convenience on an intimate basis, though. Exclusive and sought-after, that was the goal.

She spotted her business agent standing near the registration desk, dressed in a crisp dark suit and carrying a leather briefcase. She shook his hand. "Hector, thank you for accompanying me today. I thought it prudent to have you with me."

"That's why you pay me, Miss James. To represent your best interest."

"I'll agree to any length deal, but I must have a termination clause with either side giving two weeks' notice." The nightclub manager, Mr. Costa, had accommodated Hattie on everything but this point, which necessitated this meeting with the owner.

"Either side? Are you planning to sign Maggie Moore's recording contract and return to New York?"

Hattie could not say it, but she intended to sink her roots wherever Maya Reyes's were. Signing Maggie's contract would commit her to studio time and doing American tours to promote their music. It would mean spending half the year in the States. Hattie was unsure whether their relationship could withstand the separation. Not until Maya finally said the three words Hattie was waiting to hear.

The termination clause gave her an out to concentrate on building their business at the Halo Club, something she and Maya had kept as a closely held secret. No one at the Palace knew Hattie and Maya were behind the club's reconstruction. Neither did her agent. They had filed all the paperwork under their partnership name, JR Ventures, and the contractor had signed an agreement to keep their identities hidden.

"I don't know yet, but make sure he agrees, just in case."

"All right. Let's present your terms." Hector gestured toward the hallway and the owner's private office.

Once they were through the suite door, a secretary offered them refreshments and asked them to wait until Mr. Guinle was off the phone. The room embraced the same grandeur as the main lobby, a workplace befitting Brazil's richest billionaire.

When a light flashed off on the secretary's phone, the woman announced Hattie's arrival and invited her and Hector back.

The owner circled his mahogany desk, extending his hand. "Thank you for meeting with me, Miss James, and you as well, Mr. Marquez." Following introductions, he gestured for them to join him in the seating area's over-stuffed leather chairs. "I understand from Mr. Costa that you have yet to come to terms with a new contract. Are you not happy performing at the Golden Room?"

"On the contrary, Mr. Guinle, I'm quite content. The club is first-class, and the staff is amazingly attentive."

"If it's a matter of money, I'm sure we can sweeten the pot."

Hotel bookings had risen dramatically since Hattie signed on to sing, and tickets to her shows now had waiting lists. There was no doubt that Hattie James was the draw.

"It's not the money. It's about security." Hattie did not lie. War was a concern, and her involvement with the FBI always had her looking over her shoulder. Knowing she could leave at any time without taking a substantial financial hit was reassuring, no matter what she intended with the Halo Club.

"Is six months not long enough? Do you want a guarantee for a year? We can certainly accommodate such a request."

"Not that type of security. War is on the horizon for the United States, and as an American in the spotlight and abroad, I'm naturally concerned for my safety. The time may come when it might be safer for me to return to the States."

"I understand your concerns, but war isn't certain for either of our countries. Having said that, what can I do to convince you to stay on with us?"

"I need to know I'm free to go if things look dicey. The contract wording that Mr. Costa has proposed stipulates that you may terminate our agree-ment for any reason. You must also give me two weeks' notice or provide the equivalent pay. It also stipulates that if I wish to leave, I must buy out the remainder of my contract at half of what I would have earned."

"Yes, that is standard in Brazil."

"Since world circumstances are not in our control, I would like the termination clause to be equitable. I want the freedom to leave for any reason as long as I give you two weeks' notice, forfeiting my final check without further penalty."

The Secret War

"I can live with that, Miss James, and won't force you to stay if you fear for your safety."

Hattie stood and extended her hand. "We have an agreement, Mr. Guinle."

The owner came to his feet and shook her hand. "I'll have our lawyers draw it up and send the contract to Mr. Marquez for your signature."

"It's a pleasure doing business with you." Hattie walked out, getting precisely what she wanted—a steady paycheck until she was ready to focus on her recording career and the Halo Club.

Once in the busy lobby, where the drone of conversations would drown their exchange, Hector said, "You didn't need me at all. You're an excellent negotiator."

"I need you to ensure the agreed-upon terms are codified on paper."

"I'll see to it," Hector said. "And what about Miss Moore's contract?"

"Hold on to it. I'll let you know." After saying goodbye, Hattie walked through the registration area to the entrance of the Golden Room.

The host glowed with recognition. "Hello, Miss James. This is an unexpected pleasure."

"Thank you. I had a meeting at the hotel. I'll be in my dressing room for a while. If you see Miss Reyes, can you tell her I'm here?"

"Yes, of course. Shall I send anything from the kitchen or bar?"

She declined and continued through the dining room, turning head after head of the guests enjoying their meals, as well as that of the assistant manager, Maya Reyes. Hattie James, the American songbird, only appeared for the evening show four nights a week, Thursday through Sunday. Seeing her in the club during the day on a Tuesday was therefore a rare treat. She took care to stop, shake hands, sign autographs, and take photographs with the patrons. At each table, she positioned herself so as to be able to keep an eye on Maya. The smiles and stolen glances they shared turned into a seductive dance. Memories stirred of last night's passion-filled sleepover and how special it was to have Maya in her arms until sunrise.

Finishing with the last guest, Hattie continued to her dressing room and poured a glass of water from the bathroom faucet to quench a throat parched from all those greetings. She fished a business card from her purse and dialed the embassy number on her dressing room phone.

"Security," a woman answered.

Hattie had expected Leo to pick up on his private line and was momentarily taken aback. "Um, yes. Is Commander Bell there?"

"I'm sorry, miss, but he's not in the office. May I take a message?"

"Please, can you tell him—"

"Hold on, miss. He just walked in."

Moments later, Leo's voice came over the phone. "Commander Bell."

Hattie giggled. "So formal. We see each other so much that sometimes I forget you're in the navy because you always wear a suit or something casual."

Leo laughed. "Comes with the territory in this job. When not on official duty, we're encouraged to wear civilian clothes outside the embassy to make us less of a target. Hate to cut this short, but I only have a moment. Why did you call?"

"It's urgent that I meet with you. Can you come to our favorite out-of-the-way bar?"

"I'm swamped, Hattie. Can this wait?"

"No, it can't. I wouldn't ask unless this was vital."

Leo let out a breathy exhale. "I can break away for a few hours around lunchtime tomorrow. I'm sorry, but things are crazy here today and tonight."

"Thank you, Leo. I'll be there by noon. Oh, and no unwanted guests."

"I expected as much. See you then, Hattie."

After hanging up, Hattie flipped off her shoes and waited for Maya on the couch. She leaned back, her mind drifting between Maya, her mother, her father, David, and Agent Knight.

It had been several weeks since Knight had asked her to talk up a customer to find out their purpose in town. But if that was the extent of the FBI's manipulations, she could live with him hovering.

Living under the same roof with David was a different story. He and Eva had gotten along fine after Hattie told her the truth about their lavender relationship. However, after finding the logbook in the steamer trunk, things had turned awkward for Hattie. Anytime David could not account for his time, she became suspicious, thinking he was hiding something.

The Secret War   35

The book had remained untouched for six months, however, and Hattie wondered if she was wrong to suspect him.

Training with her father had become something she reveled in, second only to being with Maya. Beyond today's surveillance lesson and extensive weapons instruction, she had learned ways to alter her physical appearance using makeup, wigs, and changes in clothing to blend into different settings. How to pick locks and bypass security systems. Hand-to-hand combat techniques and methods for silently neutralizing enemies. Methods for extracting information from captives and resisting enemy interrogation. Skills for surviving and operating in hostile environments, including navigation, camouflage, and survival tips. She was looking forward to learning how to use codes, ciphers, and clandestine radios.

The one thing he was not going to have to teach her was how to develop and maintain believable cover identities and backstories to avoid detection. She had been doing it all her adult life to hide her attraction to women.

Which brought her to Maya, the woman who had healed her broken heart and made her want to love again. She was sure Maya loved her too, but Maya had yet to say as much. However, she showed it while sharing bodies, in the care she took preparing meals, and how she was protective of Hattie at the Golden Room. She felt Maya's love down to her bones, but she wanted, needed, to hear her say she loved her at least once.

A shake on Hattie's shoulder forced her to open her eyes. Maya was there with her beautiful smile.

"Sorry to wake you, but we should get going to your mother's soon for dinner."

"I wasn't sleeping. I was thinking of you." Hattie sat straighter.

"I hope it was something good." Maya kissed her.

"Trust me, it was."

"Before I forget," Maya said, "I confirmed your backup performer for Friday so you can attend the president's special event."

"Thank you." Hattie rolled her eyes. "Being a national hero comes with obligations."

Maya laughed. "How did your meeting with the owner go?"

"Well. He agreed to my terms, so I can walk without a penalty."

"I knew you would get your way, but maybe you should think about staying on here until we're sure the Halo Club will make a profit."

"After you quit"—Hattie caressed Maya's cheek—"I'll have little reason to stay. Besides, your business plan is sound, and with my mother's influence, the nightclub will be an instant hit."

"I hope so." Maya sucked in an unsteady breath.

"I know so."

"What about Maggie's offer? You still haven't signed."

"I'm still considering it." Hattie stood, the topic hitting a nerve. "I definitely want to rerecord our duets, but committing to the twelve songs needed to compile two albums and the touring time to promote them would take a year. I don't want to be away from you for that long."

Maya's eyes turned sad. "I don't either."

"Which is why I'm stalling," Hattie said before thinking, *and why I'm waiting for you to finally say I love you.*

"You can't hold Maggie off forever. She deserves an answer."

"Yes, she does." And so did Hattie.

5

Hattie drove the coupe into the garage and entered her mother's house through the breezeway private entrance. Music and the savory aroma of Eva's cooking flowed from the front of the house. Slipping into her bedroom, she closed the door to the hallway and the one to the bathroom she shared with David. She dumped her purse on the dresser, as she did every time after returning home. After pulling some clothing from the steamer trunk, she checked on the logbook hidden in the lining. Her hand traced the book's outline, confirming it was still there. Removing it from its hiding place, she gasped.

"What the hell?"

The ledger was oriented differently. She should have pulled it out from the top using her right hand. However, her hand was around its bottom. It had been moved. In the six months she had been checking it day and night, this was the first time she had discovered someone had tampered with it. Her senses were up, and as her father had taught her, she discarded the idea of coincidence.

The first question that came to mind was why now? Did its movement have anything to do with the arrival of the American vice president? Or the Professor's son?

After replacing the book and clothes, careful to position them precisely as she had found them, she washed up in the bathroom and changed into another blouse and slacks. She put on her happy face and went toward the living room for the first family dinner with her parents and Maya. The mix of spices and a distinct seafood aroma grew headier the closer she got to the kitchen.

Eva and David were preparing the meal, as they had done together many times before, bobbing their heads occasionally to the beat of one of Hattie's recorded songs. They had become good friends once Eva stopped treating David like a future son-in-law. They seemed to enjoy occupying the same house, with Eva giving him some pointers on the piano and David helping her prepare most of the meals.

"It smells wonderful, you two, but you shouldn't have gone to so much trouble."

"Hi, Hattie." David briefly glanced up from his vegetable chopping.

Eva looked up from her concoctions at the stove and smiled. "Of course we should have. Maya is important to you, and it's high time I welcomed her and got to know her better."

Hattie walked closer and kissed Eva on the cheek. "Thank you, Mother. I'm sure Maya will love your cooking and appreciate the effort."

"I hope so." Eva's voice cracked a fraction with emotion...perhaps regret. "Yes, well, how about you start setting the table? Put out the good china from the hutch and the crystal glasses from the top shelf."

"I'm on it." Hattie went to her task, elated over Eva's endeavor to impress Maya. The attempt to go the extra step was noteworthy. It compared to how her mother had prepared for diplomats and dignitaries before one of her father's many parties when they were married.

David quietly watched as Hattie pulled out the right place settings and arranged the dining table. She stole glances at him, wondering if he had moved the book and why. Her mother had equal opportunity, but Eva had no reason to be in her trunk unless she had been snooping.

Her father appeared at the kitchen entrance, holding a pair of shears in one hand and a bouquet of freshly cut flowers in the other. He seemed to be relaxed, but with the FBI and the Nazis looking for him, he was perpetually on his guard. The neighbor's pass-through gate into Eva's back garden was still his preferred method of coming here and avoiding detection.

The Secret War 39

"Is this what you wanted?" he asked.

Eva glanced at the bright mix of colors and varieties. "It's perfect, Karl." She smiled before gesturing toward Hattie. "The vase is on the table."

Karl grinned and stepped deeper into the room.

Hattie noticed two things. First, her father had been there long enough to rummage through Eva's garden, which was sufficient time to access the logbook. Second, the smiles between him and Eva contained an undeniable, underlying attraction—a development Hattie was happy to see.

For years, she had deemed her mother unworthy of her father for cheating on him, but only months ago, the truth had come out. Eva had considered him vile, having believed he had become a Nazi. However, Karl's persona of a German spy had been a mission for his true identity as an agent for the State and War Departments. It was a secret he had to keep, but it came with epic consequences that Hattie was sure her parents regretted.

And so did Hattie. She lamented despising her mother for so many years, not realizing Eva had kept her suspicions about Karl to herself to preserve his daughters' image of him. She had sacrificed as much as he had. Seeing them being civil to each other and perhaps on the precipice of rekindling their romance made Hattie surprisingly happy.

Karl kissed Hattie on the cheek. "Hello, sweetheart." He turned his back to Eva and David and whispered, "Any luck with Leo?"

"Noon tomorrow."

"Good." He placed the flowers in the vase and arranged them in a pleasing pattern. "Are you coming?"

"I'll be there. We need to talk later."

"What are you two whispering about?" Eva's question came out sounding playful. "You were always two peas in a pod." Her mother could not know how true that comparison had become, with Hattie walking in her father's shadowy footsteps, learning to be a spy as good as he was. Well, almost.

"Nothing important," Karl said.

The doorbell rang, and Hattie's heart raced a little faster. Maya had arrived and would soon step into Eva's home for the first time. The most significant aspect of tonight's visit was that she and Maya would not have to hide who they were and who they were to one another.

"I'll get it." Hattie went out the front door, walked the pathway in the long shadows of the evening sunset, and opened the heavy garden gate.

Maya stood there in a colorful cotton dress and raised two six-packs of Guaraná Antarctica, one in each hand. "I hope these are okay." Her showing up with a soft drink and not a distilled spirit, which was tradition, was beyond thoughtful.

"It's perfect." Hattie kissed her briefly out of view of any house windows to avoid being seen. An invitation to Eva's home did not equate to permission to flaunt their sexual relationship in front of her parents. "And you look amazing."

"And so do you. Always."

"Are you ready for this?" Hattie rubbed Maya's arm and took a pack of soda.

"Are you?" Maya stepped inside the gate and walked side by side with Hattie.

"I thought I was."

Maya pulled her to a stop at the door. "I hadn't been in my parents' lives for years when they were killed in that accident. They had shunned me after learning how I loved. So cherish this, Hattie. Tonight is a gift."

"I..." Hattie wanted to say that she loved her but stopped short and kissed her on the cheek. "You're right."

They walked in and found her parents awaiting them in the living room. Karl took the sodas from both women.

"Thank you for coming," Eva said, pulling Maya into a hug warmer than any she had given her before. "Welcome to my home."

"Thank you for inviting me," Maya said. "It smells wonderful in here. Please tell me that's moqueca cooking."

Eva nodded. "It is, but I used sea bass instead of shrimp for tonight's special occasion."

"It should be delicious." Maya turned to Hattie's father, acknowledging him with a nod. "Hello, Karl." The slight was anything but subtle, highlighting the fact that she still blamed him for her sister's death. However, he took it in stride.

"It's good to see you, Maya. The sodas are perfect."

"Come in, dear." Eva placed an arm across Maya's shoulder. "Dinner is ready."

Everyone sat around the table with the clay pot of moqueca in the center. Surrounding it were side dishes of cheesy bread rolls, rice, and a salsa made with chopped tomatoes, onions, bell peppers, and parsley, dressed with vinegar and olive oil.

The traditional Brazilian meal was delicious, and the conversation flowed naturally, void of awkward pauses until Eva steered it to Hattie's contracts. "I understand wanting a little more control in your career, but an escape clause like yours shows Octávio little respect or appreciation for taking a chance on you."

"Coloring it as an escape clause is harsh, don't you think?" Karl asked. "This puts her on equal footing with the owner."

"But it's not how things are done." Eva wiped the corners of her lips with a cloth napkin. "The hotel is shouldering all the risk."

"Well," Karl said, "I'm proud of her for leveling the playing field."

"As am I." Maya raised her soda glass. "Men have a stranglehold on the nightclub business in Rio, and I applaud any time a woman can get the upper hand. We women must stick together."

"Times are changing." Eva nodded as if conceding a point. "Like a woman running the Golden Room."

"Or building a first-class nightspot from the ground up," Hattie said, squeezing Maya's hand. "With Maya's management skills, the Halo Club will be a guaranteed success."

"I couldn't agree more," Karl said.

Maya turned to Eva. "And thank you for helping us find a head chef. Your name will certainly interest top-quality candidates."

"You're right, Maya. Women should band together, and I think what you and Hattie are creating is wonderful." Eva glanced at Hattie. "Especially if it means my daughter staying in Rio."

Hattie squeezed Maya's hand atop the table again, grateful their first family dinner had gone well. "Yes, a good thing." She let her grip linger long enough to send the message that she wanted to stay, but—

"That's assuming this arrangement with Maggie Moore doesn't

consume much of her time," Eva said. Of course her mother would bring up the pending contract with Maggie, the one commitment that could take Hattie from Brazil and Maya. "Have you decided anything, sweetheart?"

"Not yet," Hattie said.

After a creamy caramel flan dessert and coffee, Hattie took Maya to the patio to let her see the back garden while the others cleaned up.

"This place is lovely. It's sizeable and modern with lots of luxury but not over the top."

Hattie laughed. "You should see my mother's closet with all her gowns and stage dresses. It's wall-to-wall extravagance."

"Well, the rest of it is delightful."

"Let me show you the best part." Hattie guided Maya to the French doors next to the primary suite. She went inside the ample-sized former bedroom and flipped on the wall switch, revealing an extensive assortment of rare plants and flowers requiring a cooler climate.

"Air conditioning?" Maya said. "Maybe I was premature in her not being over the top."

"She had it shipped from the States so she could grow her favorite flowers."

Maya went up and down the rows, touching the vegetation of various shapes and colors. "This is quite the collection." She stopped at the edelweiss. Dozens of blooms, each with a cluster of five or six yellow star-shaped florets at the center, stood out among the woolly-haired leaves. Fuzzy white petals surrounded the florets, and the leaves gave the plant a soft, silvery appearance. "This is what you used to signal your father."

"I did, yes," Hattie said. She paused for a moment and decided to address the elephant in the room. "You're still angry at him."

"Can you blame me? Baumann took Anna while searching for your father."

"You should know that he didn't come to Rio by choice. German agents broke him out of federal custody and forced him onto a freighter. He had no idea that escaping Nazi clutches had endangered all those women. He feels horrible and carries the weight of their deaths on his shoulders every day."

"Feeling bad won't bring them back."

The Secret War   43

"Nothing will." Hattie caressed Maya's cheek. "You've forgiven me for my part in Anna's death. After all, if I hadn't walked into your club looking for a job, Baumann would never have taken her. I hope you can find it in your heart one day to forgive my father."

Maya's lips quivered. "I'm trying." She lowered her head.

"I know. Coming here tonight and having dinner with him tells me so." Hattie moved closer until their bodies touched. She raised Maya's head by the chin. "Thank you for that." She kissed Maya, letting it linger, perhaps too long for being in her mother's house. Sensing Maya melt into the kiss and unable to help herself, Hattie pressed a hand against the back of Maya's head to extend it even longer.

The door to the hallway opened, and Hattie instantly pulled away.

Eva cleared her throat and appeared uncomfortable. "I've made a fresh pot of coffee."

"Thank you," Hattie said. "We'll be right there."

When Eva turned to walk away, Maya called out, "Eva, wait."

Eva stopped but remained silent.

"I'm sorry," Maya said, "especially after you invited me to your home."

"Yes, Mother," Hattie said. "I apologize."

Eva let out a breathy sigh and stepped closer. "I can't say this is easy for me, but I can see how happy you make each other." She rubbed both their arms. "This is your home, Hattie, and it should be your safe space. I want you two to feel free to be yourselves while you're here."

Hattie threw her arms around her mother's neck and hugged her tightly. "I love you, Mother."

"I love you, too, sweetheart."

6

Hattie drove into town late the following morning, quickly spotting her usual tail. She was not sure if it was the Nazis or the FBI, but she shook him with minimal effort. After taking a series of turns to ensure no one else was following her, she continued north toward the docks. She parked a few blocks from the Boa Vita on the outskirts of the nearby favela.

The bar had become an occasional meeting spot for Hattie and her father whenever they needed a public location and a bucket of indifference from the other patrons. According to Karl, he had initially picked the place for its proximity to the shack he kept for those just-in-case moments. However, Hattie had come to appreciate its atmosphere and the clientele's attitude. It was similar to the dive bars where she'd performed after the FBI ruined her New York career. They had called her a traitor, just like they called her father after he escaped from federal custody, and no one else would hire her.

The establishment was run-down, smelling of stale beer, urine, and thick cigarette smoke. The fanciest item in the place was the Brahma Beer lighted sign behind the bar hung high on the wall. The cheap quality of the tables and chairs often led to them becoming casualties during the daily scuffles. The same people who cheered on the scrapes had not batted an eye when Hattie and her team had roughed up an Italian military diplomat

The Secret War 45

months before. They had even forced him out at gunpoint and into a car. That type of discretion would be needed today when they talked to Leo about the Professor's son.

Though the place was large, only four seating areas provided an excellent view of both entrances and would allow them to keep their backs against a wall. She knew her father never sat at the same table twice in a row, leaving her with three options. Once inside, she walked toward the one where she believed he would be. She was not disappointed.

As she came even with a booth a few tables before her father's, a man grabbed Hattie by the forearm and slurred in Portuguese. "Hi, doll. Can me and my friends buy you a drink?"

Her father rose a fraction from his seat as if to intercede, but Hattie waved him off with a shake of her head and a smile. She would have fun with this drunk.

"Now, grabbing a woman isn't very polite," she replied in Portuguese like she had been speaking it all her life. All the vocabulary lessons her mother had taught her as a child had come back to her since arriving in Rio. Being immersed in it daily helped her become more fluent and brought her closer to Maya by sharing two languages.

She tried to lose his grip, but he had too strong a hold. This would require a bit of her training. "I suggest you let go. Otherwise, in ten seconds, I'll be with my friend and you'll be gasping for air with your hands around your throat." She glanced at the other men at the table. Their grins suggested Hattie's feistiness was entertaining. She had to give them the full show. "And your buddies here will get a good laugh at your expense."

"I'd like to see you try." The man tugged, drawing her nearer, precisely what she wanted...to be within striking distance.

"Don't say I didn't warn you."

Hattie rotated her wrist toward the man's thumb, the weakest part of his grip. She used her free hand to push down on it to break his hold. However, he was too big and strong for her to create enough leverage, which she anticipated by allowing herself to be drawn closer. She raised her other hand and, using a sideways punch, struck him in the Adam's apple. The man instantly loosened his hold, and Hattie twisted her arm and broke free.

The other two at the table roared as the rude one brought his hands to his throat, gasping for air. Hattie turned to them. "He should be fine in a few minutes, but if he turns blue, I recommend calling for an ambulance."

"Yes, ma'am," one said, laughing, while the other shoved a beer closer to the choking man. Both acknowledged her with two-finger salutes filled with respect.

Hattie continued her route and smiled when she sat beside her father. "That was fun."

Karl laughed. "I think he'll think twice before grabbing a woman again, but don't get cocky. He was drunk. They're a lot stronger when they're sober."

"I know, Father." She elbowed him in the side. "By the way, you're becoming predictable to me. I guessed right today."

"That's good when working in the field with a partner. They should be able to anticipate your next move. However, I must caution myself to not get lazy and become readable to the enemy."

"I doubt that will happen."

"Still," Karl said. "You said you needed to talk last night. We never got the chance."

"It's the logbook." Hattie clearly caught his attention. "It's there but was in a different position. Did you check on it before I got home?"

"No, I didn't, and the timing couldn't be coincidental."

"I agree," Hattie said. "It's time to confront David."

"You're right, but not here and not alone. Let's do it tomorrow night in your dressing room after your show."

Hattie acknowledged with a nod. Several moments passed in silence, but one cardinal rule about surveillance her father had taught her was to blend in. Silently sitting in a bar booth together was not blending in. They needed to be talking about something. "Can I ask you something?"

"Anything."

"Tell me about the Professor. How did you meet? Why is she so important to you?"

"She was my section chief when I was assigned to..." He paused. "You know."

Hattie knew he had secretly worked for years at the Cipher Bureau, also

The Secret War 47

known as the Black Chamber. It was a joint clandestine operation between the US Army and the State Department that was primarily focused on breaking codes in diplomatic communications.

"She took me under her wing. Trained me to do a whole host of other things. I didn't understand why until our unit was shuttered and she recruited me into what she said was her real job. Though partially retired, she's the only one associated with the government I trust now."

"Why do you call her the Professor?"

"She taught political science at a university at one time. When we worked together, everything was a teaching moment for her, so it naturally became her codename."

"Do you have one?"

"She calls me Nightshade."

"Why Nightshade?"

"Because it's a family of plants that can be both edible and toxic. She says I appear safe to the world, but I can be quite deadly in the right quantity. The moniker never really took with the department, so she's the only one who used the name—"

"Nightshade," Hattie whispered.

Ten minutes later, Leo appeared at their booth and sat. "I figured you'd be here, Karl. What do you need?" he said in his unique Texan drawl.

"I know you have a VIP in town."

"Why am I not surprised?" Leo snickered.

"A young, thin man was with him yesterday. Was he expected or a last-minute addition?"

"Last minute." Leo cocked his head. "Why?"

"I want you to set up a meeting with him."

"Not until you tell me why."

"Besides Hattie, his mother, the Professor, is the one person in the world I trust with my life. She brought me into this business and is still my handler. That man being here can't be a coincidence."

"No, it can't," Leo said, darting his eyes as if processing the information. "The White House and State vetted him. He's been on the VP's staff for over a year."

"His job might be legitimate, but someone else sent him here, and I want to know who did it and why. Can you set up a private meeting?"

Leo ran a hand roughly down his face. "All right, but not alone. It will have to wait. Their group is out of pocket for several days, but they'll be back in time for the Brazilian president's reception."

"Yes, I know all about that event," Hattie said. "It's Friday evening. My mother and I are invited, and she's slated to perform."

"Let me think." Leo scratched the back of his head. "I scouted the party location last week. I could set up the meet near the perimeter fence, but you need to stay off the property. That place will be crawling with security."

"Thank you, Leo," Karl said. "I appreciate this."

"Don't thank me until after your meeting."

Karl looked over Leo's shoulder and squinted at a man who sat in a nearby booth. "Were you followed?"

"Of course not. I know how to spot and lose a tail."

"I recognized the man who came in after you as an SS agent from São Paulo. He's at your six, three booths down."

Hattie glanced at the target for no more than two seconds, noting as many details as she could before drifting her gaze elsewhere. "Blond hair. Gray shirt. Glasses. Clean shaven. Average build."

"Well, damn. I saw him pull into the parking lot when I arrived. My head must not be in the game. I have plenty on my plate this week."

"Laziness will get us all killed."

Leo gave Karl an intense stare, the type that needed no words to express his impatience with the remark.

"Do you think he recognized you, Father?" Hattie asked.

"If he's any good, he did."

"Wagner will know you're still here. He'll want—" Hattie stopped herself before mentioning her father's coded lists of spies in front of Leo. Only her mother and Maya knew the truth behind the sheet music.

"Want what?" Leo asked.

"Revenge," Hattie said, which was not a lie.

Hattie had met Wagner twice, first at the ransom demand for her mother and later at the exchange that resulted in several of Wagner's men being killed. Their first encounter at the Golden Room still haunted her. He had arranged the discussion to retrieve the documents and key Hattie had taken from Ziegler's office, items that were vital for their plan to assassinate the Brazilian president. His collateral was Eva, whom he had threatened to kill if Hattie did not come through.

When Wagner ended that meeting, he left a fresh glass of vodka in the center of the table as if offering it to Hattie. Cheap vodka was her weakness; it could take her down a sewer hole quicker than a hurricane. Her alcohol addiction was a well-kept secret, though, and very few knew about her unhealthy appetite for that particular alcohol. Wagner had known too much about her that night, and Hattie wanted to discover how he had learned it.

Wagner had disappeared after the failed assassination attempt. Most involved in the foiling of that plan—David, Leo, and Maya—thought he had returned to Germany to escape prosecution. However, her father believed he was behind whatever big project was going on in the jungle. Karl had overheard an SS agent mention it but could never track it down. Hattie supported her father's supposition. Wagner did not seem like the type to retreat and accept defeat. He came across as a man who would dig in and fight harder.

"What's our play?" Hattie asked.

"I say we split up to see who he follows," Leo said. "If he shadows me, that means he didn't recognize you, and we should let him go."

"I can't take that chance," Karl said.

They could not allow this Nazi to leave and report back that he had a bead on Karl James. The only thing keeping Hattie alive was the possibility that she would lead either side to him. There was no question as to the man's fate then. The only uncertainty was how to go about arranging it.

"I don't want this to end like it did with the Italian officer," Leo said.

Leo had lured the officer to this bar six months ago, at Hattie's urging, after Eva was kidnapped. He had also helped to overpower him and take him to Karl's shack to get information out of him. That had ended in disaster. A struggle ensued, and the Italian was shot and killed with Leo's gun.

Hattie was there and had witnessed the man's demise. The massacre and depravity she had seen at Baumann's plantation had numbed her to the horrors of death, but its ripple effect was something she still grappled with. Death might have been deserved for those she considered vile. Baumann, that Italian, Ziegler, and this Nazi agent who would kill her and her father to get those lists fit that category. However, the loss to loved ones like Baumann's daughter Elsa, who was now an orphan, was something she would never get used to.

"I have no choice, Leo," Karl said. "I'm the big fish Berlin has been looking for. But I like your idea about splitting up. I'm betting he'll follow me. You two act like Leo has picked you up, go out the front, and come around to the back. I'll slip out the back door near the bathrooms. We take him to the shack and find out where Wagner is lying low. I'll take care of him later."

Leo shook his head with a tinge of revulsion. "The cougars and jaguars will eat well today."

"Yes, they will," Hattie said, releasing a loud breath. She agreed with Leo. Eliminating the SS agent may be necessary, but it was still distasteful. "Let's go. Wait until we're outside, Father."

She urged Leo up, hooked her arm around his, and walked like she was three cocktails in, something with which she, unfortunately, had had too much experience. As she walked past the booth with the rude man who had grabbed her earlier, the man averted his eyes and took on a sheepish look. The man outweighed her by at least a hundred pounds and could crush her with little effort, yet he cowered like this was grade school and Hattie was the bully.

His table partners snickered.

Perhaps she should not have, but Hattie grinned as she passed, enjoying the satisfaction of having put him in his place. As she went past the next table with the suspected SS agent, she took particular care to vary her stare between the floor and straight forward. It was something a drunk would do and something she had real-life experience with, unfortunately.

Leo led her to the front, earning only a few stares from the men leering at her on her way by. Once outside, they turned toward the corner of the building nearest the back exit. After passing the large picture window, Hattie dropped the tipsy routine and straightened her gait.

As they prepared to speed up to beat her father outside, Leo suddenly slowed and rocked backward on his heels. Hattie looked over her shoulder,

The Secret War 51

discovering that the man whose Adam's apple she had clocked had grabbed Leo by the back of his collar, pulling him off-balance.

They did not have time for this. Her father should have already left through the back door.

"You are persistent. I'll give you that." She gritted her teeth to contain her anger, raised her foot knee high, and rammed the rigid heel of her shoe into the top of the man's soft sneaker.

The man yelped in pain and loosened his grip on the shirt, giving Leo the opening he needed. Leo cocked back his arm and pelted the man with a devastating punch square on the nose, sending him to the ground and onto his bottom with a loud thud.

While Leo gave him a few more punches to keep him down, Hattie turned and darted down the side alley to catch up with her father. Turning the corner, she discovered Karl and the agent in a struggle near the door, fighting for control over a gun in the agent's hand.

Leo still hadn't caught up, so she had to act fast. She sped up, counting the precious seconds in her head. Each second it took for her to reach her father was a moment longer he had to defend himself against a much younger and stronger adversary. Karl was strong and skilled, but he was also almost sixty. His stamina was no match when facing a man who appeared to be in excellent shape and half his age.

As she ran, Hattie tried to open her purse and retrieve her Baby Browning, a small .25 caliber semi-automatic pistol. Her concentration was thrown, and she stumbled. As she reached the two embroiled in a battle for their life, her father flipped the agent around so his back was to her. She lifted her foot and slammed it into the back of the man's knee, a crippling blow that sent him toward the ground.

The gun they'd been struggling over went off.

Hattie felt her heart stop.

The man continued to fall, but she could not be sure if it was because of her accurate kick or if he had been shot. She flicked her stare upward to her father, who held the pistol in his hand and swung it with all his might across the man's cheek, delivering a devastating strike. His clothes were still their original color of blue and white, so her fear of him having taken a bullet evaporated. She snapped her attention to the agent on the ground, noting the small but growing puddle of blood appearing beside him.

Karl kneeled beside him, lifting his head and shoulders by the shirt collar. "Where's Wagner?"

"We found you once. We'll find you again." The agent spat blood with each cough and fell limp.

Karl dropped him onto the pavement as Leo ran up, huffing short of breath. Karl tossed him his set of keys. "Bring up my car. It's the blue Ford Deluxe at the corner."

Leo nodded and sprinted toward the street while Karl patted the man's pockets and took everything he discovered in them.

The back door opened, and a curious bar patron stuck his head out.

Hattie approached him quickly and barked at him in Portuguese. "Mind your business unless you want some of the same."

The man slammed the door shut and disappeared inside.

Leo sped the car through the alley, coming to a stop a few feet from the dead man, jumping out, and unlocking the trunk. He and Karl picked up the man by his arms and legs. Hattie rushed to the car to prepare space for him but found it had already been cleared. It contained only a crowbar, shovel, and painter's tarp already spread out to cover every inch of the compartment.

After they secured the man and were heading north out of town, Leo finally spoke, "The body count increases whenever we're together."

"It comes with the territory," Karl said. "You should know that by now."

"Until I met you, I was a happy analyst, pushing papers and escorting bigwigs."

"So was I once upon a time, but my country needed me." Karl glanced at Leo in the front passenger seat. Hattie got the impression her father was trying to read him to determine whether he had some hidden motive and if he could still trust him.

"Yes," Leo said. "I can see that."

Karl drove on the main highway out of town and pulled off onto the dirt road that led to his tiny jungle cabin. After a half mile, he stopped at a gap in the safety barrier, where the road edge fell sharply down a hill over-grown with wild vegetation.

The Secret War 53

They got out, and the two men rolled the agent's body, wrapped in the bloodstained tarp, down the slope. The trees and shrubs swallowed it, keeping it safe from discovery until the cougars and jaguars feasted on it tonight. After they closed the trunk, the three of them sat inside the car and Karl went through the contents he had found in the man's pockets.

Hattie leaned forward to look over the back seat. Her father laid out the items, shoved the keys to the side, and went through the billfold.

"Anything of intelligence value?" Leo asked.

"His identification papers are fake," Karl said. He tested the lighter, crushed the cigarettes, unscrewed the pen, and inspected the coins. "That's about it." He held up the camera and asked Hattie, "Do you think Maya will develop the film for you?"

"I'm sure of it." Hattie noted how her father left himself out of the equation. It was a sad reality she hoped would change one day.

7

Hattie took a long sip of tea, the honey soothing the persistent throat tickle she had picked up since yesterday's series of events at the Boa Vita. She had walked away from that place irritated in so many ways. The cigarette smoke was particularly thick, the patrons were exceedingly disagreeable, and the Nazis had tracked Leo, leading them to her father. The only positive outcome of that meeting was Leo agreeing to arrange a meet-up with the Professor's son.

A knock on her door drew her attention, forcing her from her dressing room couch. She opened it and found Maya, who did not offer her usual smile when they saw each other for the first time during the day. Hattie ushered her inside. "I was concerned when you didn't deliver my tea earlier."

"I was nearly late for work because I had a hard time developing the pictures from the camera you gave me this morning. The roll of film was so small."

"Did you get anything?" Hattie gestured for her to sit on the couch.

Maya did and scooted next to her. "Yes, and I'm worried." She removed an envelope from her purse, pulled out two dozen photographs, and spread them on the coffee table. "This man has been following us for weeks."

"We knew that was a possibility after the failed yacht bombing." Hattie scanned the photos of her, Maya, and Leo on the street, in a car, or in the club, together and separately. These were expected, considering their involvement in thwarting the assassination attempt. Her gaze settled on a much more disturbing photo. She gasped, throwing a hand over her mouth. If this agent had taken one picture of Hattie and Maya making love in Maya's bedroom, the probability was strong that others had been taken. Hattie's face was clearly visible, but Maya's was hidden, thankfully.

"My God," she finally croaked, clutching Maya's hand. Horrid thoughts of photos of her and Maya splashed across the front page of the *New York Daily News* flashed in her head. The city tabloid was known for its sensational coverage of scandal and crime. She had forged through the last nine months of the FBI tanking her career on the prospect that once they cleared her father's name, she could rebuild her American stardom. But there would be no coming back from the press marking her as a sexual deviant. More frightening yet was discovering that someone had gotten into Maya's backyard and slithered close enough to invade their privacy. There was no place where they could feel safe to be themselves.

"I'm so sorry, Hattie." Maya squeezed her hand. "If this gets out." She shook her head, tearing up.

Hattie lifted the picture and studied it. She was in the throes of ecstasy with her face toward the window. Though she was unsure when this was taken, the unbridled passion in her expression was unforgettable...as it was every time they shared their bodies. However, the most satisfying feature of the photo was Maya looking on as she brought Hattie to the edge.

Hattie looked up and focused on Maya's fear. "I'm more concerned about them getting close enough to take this picture. I worry about your safety, especially when I'm not there."

"If they're so crazy to try coming in," Maya said, "I'll greet them with the business end of my .22, my .38, or my shotgun."

"I have no doubt you will. Still, these are trained operatives, and there's no telling how many there might be."

"I won't spend my life in hiding, Hattie."

"I don't expect you to, but I'd rest easier if I knew you were safe. If you'd like, I can speak to Mr. Guinle about moving you into a room in the hotel."

"I can't afford that." Maya pulled back, distancing herself from Hattie and her offer. Money was still a wedge between them and might always be.

"But *we* can." Hattie emphasized the pronoun, reminding her they were partners in every sense.

Maya shook her head. "I won't have you paying for my keep."

"Then we need to take more precautions. Maybe get a dog that will alert on intruders."

"I'll think about it." Maya gathered the photos, returned them to the envelope, and handed them to Hattie. "Before I go, two male guests are having dinner in the club, spending money like it's their last day on earth. They asked if you would stop by their table after the show for a drink and take pictures with them."

"Sure. Who are they?"

"Tourists. They arrived yesterday. I think they're Germans."

"Oh, hell no. Odds are they're Nazi sympathizers. I've had my fill of Nazis for a lifetime."

Maya grinned. "I won't tell them until after your performance. Gotta keep them laying out that wad of cash burning a hole in their pockets."

Hattie laughed and kissed Maya before she left.

After changing into her stage dress and fixing her hair and makeup, Hattie made her way down the hallway and to the wings. She waited for the band leader's voice to come over the sound system. When he announced, "...proud to present the American songbird, Hattie James," she stepped into the spotlights as the curtain retracted. She greeted David with a firm squeeze of his hand on her way by. Though she no longer pretended when she was with her parents, the public image of her in a happy relationship with a man was still necessary for audience consumption.

Hattie stopped in front of the microphone at the band's first note. She cupped it like it was Maya's cheek and sang every song like she was making love to her—soft and sensual. Near the end of the set, when she moved out of the blinding light, she caught a better view of the faces in the crowd. One stuck out to her. She nearly cursed in the middle of the song, recognizing Agent Knight. His overt presence meant he had business for her. Her gut told her it concerned the high spenders who wanted a personal meet-and-greet after the show.

The Secret War

Hattie harnessed her resentment of Agent Knight and his unyielding hounding to give up her father, using it to kick her performance up another notch. That fire in her belly lasted through her traditional closing song and two encores. She chose the unpublished duets she had recorded with Maggie Moore last year, the same songs they hoped to rerecord someday to kick off Maggie's new recording label.

Deafening applause accompanied her off the stage. A towel awaited her on the tray with the glass of ice water the waitstaff had placed there during her final song. After drying off, she downed her cold drink and marched straight to her dressing room, still fuming over Agent Knight being in the audience. Once she slammed the door, she called out in a raspy whisper, "Father?"

He stepped from her private bathroom, wiping his hands dry with a small hotel towel. "Great show." After returning the cloth to the counter, he patted the section of his suit coat over his interior breast pocket. "I picked up the logbook for our talk with David tonight."

"That might have to wait," she said. "I saw Knight in the club tonight. That usually means he wants me to chat up a guest to discover why they're in town."

"If that's all he has you doing, I feel pretty good about him using you, unlike Butler, who had you infiltrating Baumann's plantation."

"Given how he threatened Liv and tanked my career, I still despise the man." The threat of the FBI throwing her sister into jail for aiding their father still hung over Hattie like a dark shadow, bending her to Knight's will.

"I can't blame you. Do you want to do this with David tomorrow?"

"Let me find out why Knight is here first."

A knock on the door.

"Hattie, it's Maya." Her voice was muffled through the door. "I have someone here who wants to speak with you."

Hattie shooed her father back into the bathroom before opening the door. Maya was with Agent Knight.

"I need your help tonight," Knight said, holding a fedora.

Hattie released a breathy sigh and moved to the side to allow him in her dressing room.

"Thank you, Miss Reyes. You can go now," he said, stepping inside.

Maya turned to leave, but Hattie pulled her into the room. "She stays. I'm growing tired of your little jobs for me, Agent Knight."

He eyed her with suspicion, but Hattie had told him months ago that Maya knew all about her fugitive father and Knight's pressure to force Hattie into flushing him out. "Fine. There are two German men in the audience tonight. I need you to talk to them and learn their names and why they are in Rio."

"I've already declined their invitation to come to their table. It would look awkward if I went there now."

"I don't care how it looks. Tell them you find them attractive and want to share a drink with them."

"Look, Agent Knight. I'm tired and want to go home."

"Do I have to remind you that your sister is one phone call away from being arrested for aiding a fugitive?"

Hattie gritted her teeth because Olivia had done nothing to help her father. The FBI had found classified State Department documents in her house, a file that her father had in his briefcase that Olivia's son had hidden from the adults. Knight had refused to hear the truth and used that discovery as a hold over Hattie to force her into doing his bidding time and again.

"Fine, Agent Knight, but I want to know why this time. Why are these men so important to you?"

Knight rubbed the back of his neck. "All right, Miss James. I don't see the harm in telling you. Your sister gets arrested if you or Miss Reyes leak one word of this."

Hattie sneered at him.

"I received a classified intelligence report from Washington this week, saying that three top Nazi aviation and aeronautical engineers disappeared from Germany days apart. They are believed to be bound for Brazil. I believe one or both of the men out there might be among those missing engineers. I need to know who they are, what they are up to, and whether it has anything to do with Strom Wagner, the man you're worried might come after you."

"Fine." Hattie held open the door to the hallway. "But you're not staying here. I don't want you pawing through my underwear while I flirt for you." She locked the door behind her once they exited.

Knight peeked through the backstage door and pointed out the two men Hattie was to target. "I'll be at the bar watching."

Maya whispered into Hattie's ear, saying those were the same high spenders who had asked for a special visit after the show. She added that she had yet to tell them that would not happen.

Hattie nodded and turned to Knight. "Pay your bill this time. I'm not picking up your tab again."

Knight slipped into the dining room and took a seat at the bar. That was Hattie's cue. Maya guided her through the sea of tables. They stopped briefly several times to shake hands, sign autographs, and have photos taken with the guests. Finally, they reached the Germans' table. The men stood. They were both around forty, trim, of average height, easy on the eyes, and looked much alike.

Hattie put on her best smile and spoke in English, "Gentlemen, the manager tells me you're having quite the party tonight and asked if I would join you. I'd be honored." One pulled out a chair for her. She sat and turned to Maya. "Bring another of whatever these two are having, and I'll have a drink from my private stock." That was code for soda water on the rocks in a cocktail glass.

"I'll have it sent right away, Miss James," Maya said before walking to the bar.

"Thank you for joining us, Miss James," one man said in broken English, offering her his champagne, but Hattie waved him off.

"Thanks, but I'll wait." Hattie sat. "So, you two obviously know my name. What are yours?"

"I am Gunter Kessler, and this is my brother, Ernst."

A server arrived with the drinks and quietly left after dropping them off.

Hattie inspected her glass. It had the bartender's special garnishments, one slice of lemon and two green olives on a skewer. It was a combination used only for her drinks, signaling it contained no alcohol.

"It's a pleasure to meet you, Gunter and Ernst. Brothers? Are you twins?"

"No," Gunter said. "One year apart. Ernst is the baby of the family."

"Are you from Rio? I haven't seen you at my show before."

"No, no. We're from Germany."

"What brings you to Brazil besides seeing my singing?" Hattie sipped from her cocktail glass, confirming it was only soda water with a twist of lemon.

"Business," Gunter said. "We're engineers."

"Oh, I have an uncle who is an engineer. He designs roads and bridges." Hattie lied to get them talking. "Is that what you do?"

"No, we look at plane designs to make them better," Gunter said, swirling his fresh drink. Ernst whispered something to his brother, but Gunter said something in German, referencing Hattie's name. "We're here to consult on a project."

"You must be excellent engineers if you're brought all the way from Germany."

"We are." Gunter leaned back, crossing his legs with a sense of self-assuredness. "When Ernst and I were in university, we tied for the top of the class. Now we are Germany's top engineers."

"Is that correct, Ernst?" Hattie focused on the quiet brother, guessing he had lived in his brother's bright shadow all his life. "But you're a year younger. How did you graduate the same year?"

"Gunter had a bout of measles when he was younger and missed a year of school. Still, he likes to say we tied, but I beat him by a tenth of a point."

Hattie laughed. "It seems Gunter is prone to exaggeration."

"The school chancellor called it a tie." Gunter tipped his glass to her.

"I would say he has earned the right to claim top honors." Hattie turned to Ernst, sensing he had always lost out to his brother's boldness when it came to women. She stroked his hand lightly with a finger. "But I'm sure you never let titles come between you and your dear brother."

After the club photographer took several pictures of them, they talked about Hattie's singing in Rio for another fifteen minutes. She compared it to her experience in the United States and explained that her mother had been a tremendous help in the transition. That information was public knowledge, but it gave the impression she had revealed something more personal.

The Secret War 61

During their discussion, Hattie noticed Maya stopping David from approaching her table by whispering something in his ear. He glanced at the bar in Knight's direction and back at Hattie before sitting at the other end.

Ernst served as the gatekeeper for his brother, steering the conversation elsewhere whenever it appeared Gunter might reveal something of value about their purpose in Brazil. Hattie believed she would not learn anything more except for the length of their stay.

"Well, gentlemen, it's been a pleasure meeting you. If you decide to come to my show tomorrow night, I'll ensure you're seated closer to the stage."

"I'm afraid that's impossible. We leave for our worksite tonight, but if things go well, we should come back through Rio in a week or two."

"I'll pass along your names with the club manager and make sure you get those front-row seats." She stood when both men smiled.

They rose to their feet, gestured for their check, and thanked Hattie for her time and kindness.

Hattie walked straight toward the stage door, not stopping for other guests who tried to get her attention. She had to beat Agent Knight to her dressing room to warn her father to hide again in case he came back there. Once backstage, she used the key hidden nearby, stepped inside, and locked the door, discovering the room unoccupied.

"Father?" she whispered, but she received no answer. Maybe he had changed his mind and decided it would have been better to confront David about the logbook another day.

Someone pounded on the door.

"Hold on!" she shouted and unlocked the door.

Knight pushed his way in and stepped toward the walk-in closet. Hattie had become accustomed to his intrusiveness while looking for her father wherever they met. However, this time, he might actually be there. She held her breath. That space was one of his favorite hiding places. Knight looked inside and quickly shoved the bathroom door open. His calm reaction told her that her father was not there.

"What did they say?" His tone was overly demanding, showing no patience.

"You're right about them being plane engineers. Their names are Gunter and Ernst—"

"Kessler," Knight finished for her.

"Yes, the Kessler brothers. They said they came from Germany to consult on a project but didn't get too specific. One said they'll be leaving town tonight and should be back in Rio in a few weeks if things go well."

"They're leaving tonight?"

Hattie shrugged. "That's what they said."

Knight handed her a business card with only a phone number printed on it. "If you see them again, call me right away, or your sister will pay the price." He rushed out the door.

Hattie stuck her head into the hallway, enjoying the sight of Knight in a panic.

Maya appeared through the stage door and wagged her thumb in his direction. "What's got him in a rush?"

"He wants to follow those Germans. They're leaving town tonight."

"Then he's screwed." Maya laughed. "Those two are long gone."

8

Gunter threw an entire month's pay atop the table, but he would have paid ten times that for the evening he had with his brother. Last year, before the Battle of France, he and Ernst were in Paris for an engineering symposium. He had seen Hattie James's photo in a Parisian newspaper and heard her record. That was all it took to fall in love.

When they checked into the Palace Hotel the night before and saw on the marquee outside that Hattie James would perform in the Golden Room tonight, Gunter had to attend. The opportunity nearly passed him by when the manager said there was a waiting list to see the show. However, a hefty tip roughly equal to the dinner bill got him and his brother a table near the back.

On his way out of the dining room, Gunter fished two souvenir boxes of matches from the bowl at the reception area. He checked his watch, determining they had only a few minutes before their ride would pick them up at the hotel's main entrance. "Would you mind getting our luggage from the front desk while I get our photos?"

Ernst shook his head at his brother's infatuation with Hattie James. "Sure, brother. I'll meet you outside."

Armed with the claim number, Gunter approached the coat check counter. Thankfully, they had spent enough time with the gracious Hattie

James that no one else was in line. He greeted the clerk and handed her the photographer's card. The woman came back with an envelope with the pictures.

"Would you like to look at them first?"

"No," he said. "I don't have time, but I'll take them all." He tossed down significantly more money than was needed and walked away happy with the photos documenting his once-in-a-lifetime meeting. He had yet to look at them but already felt like he was floating in the air.

Gunter walked into the most lavish lobby he had ever visited and recognized Ernst waiting curbside with their suitcases. He stepped through the spotless glass doors and threw an arm around his brother's shoulder. "That was an incredible evening. Thank you for indulging me."

"I'm glad you enjoyed yourself."

"That I did." Gunter patted his brother's back as a dark four-door sedan pulled up in front of them.

A tall, brawny man with hair and a complexion like his own stepped from the car, popped open the trunk, and grabbed two of their bags without saying a word. They loaded the rest, and the man opened the rear passenger-side door. Gunter and Ernst boarded. As the driver pulled out from the curved driveway, they settled in for the ride.

They followed the famed Copacabana boardwalk for a few blocks. Its mosaic walkway was lit by a series of streetlamps, highlighting the tourists and vendors still dotting the scenic beach at midnight. They drove for several kilometers and pulled up to a gated home in an upscale part of Rio. A man appeared inside the gate and rolled it open. Their sedan moved about forty meters up a narrow paved path before stopping at the house. It was not a mansion, but the house clearly belonged to someone wealthy.

They all got out. The quiet man and the driver placed their luggage by the front door.

"Leave your bags here," the driver said. He directed the other man to search Gunter and Ernst, taking their wallets and the envelope of photographs. Gunter suspected their bags would be searched, too.

The driver led them inside to an entry room minimally furnished with modern furniture. The space was void of the decorations and a woman's touch that Gunter was accustomed to at his house. It resembled more of a

The Secret War 65

dormitory common area than a home. Three other men were there, but they did not get up. The driver took them into an office near the front, where a sophisticated-looking man in his fifties sat behind a wooden desk.

The man gestured for Gunter and Ernst to sit in the guest chairs. "Why were you talking to Hattie James? You were told to talk to no one before we picked you up."

Gunter thought this man was being overly cautious and glanced at his brother. Ernst appeared nervous, taking this situation more seriously than what Gunter thought it called for.

"You must be Eckert. The boat captain said a man named Eckert would take us to the airfield. This is a misunderstanding. We had dinner at the Golden Room tonight, following orders to not leave the hotel, and Hattie James was the entertainment. After the show, she greeted guests at the tables." Suddenly feeling nervous, Gunter rubbed the back of his neck. "It would have been rude and even suspicious of us to not welcome her visit. I didn't think she would accept my offer, but she stayed and had a drink with us."

"What did you tell her?"

"Only that we were engineers here to consult on a project." When the man tilted his head, a bit of his brother's worry crawled up Gunter's spine. Sensing that Eckert was an SS officer, he suddenly felt the need to make his revelation sound more innocent. "I figured a vague portion of the truth was better than telling a lie that I might trip on. German tourists lying about why they were there when directly asked would have raised unwanted attention. I thought I was doing the right thing, considering."

"Considering what?" the man asked.

"Considering why we were brought to Rio."

"And what do you know about your task?"

The urge to piss his pants hit Gunter hard. Eckert had questioned everything he had said, treating him like a traitor. And he had seen what the SS did to suspected traitors. When he and his brother were called into their supervisor's office last week, they were briefed that a Luftwaffe project had stalled. They were told Berlin needed the country's most brilliant minds to solve a critical problem. Gunter and Ernst gladly stepped up and were instructed to pack a bag that night, saying they would be gone for several weeks. They were on a train to France by morning, followed by a trip in a U-boat for six days. When they were transferred to a fishing boat two days ago, its captain told them that upon landing they were to catch a taxi and check into the Palace. They were supposed to wait for a note from the front desk. That message this afternoon said a sedan would pick them up at midnight at the hotel's main entrance.

"Nothing beyond what our supervisor explained and the note to meet with you, Herr Eckert." Gunter's hand shook a little.

The driver handed Eckert the envelope. "And what about these photos?"

"A souvenir. Miss James had the photographer come by our table. She's such a celebrity. I couldn't resist buying the pictures before leaving."

"I'll keep them for now," Eckert said. "You can get them back after you complete your task when you return to Rio."

"When will we leave?"

"Tonight."

"May I use the bathroom first?" The urge to pee had yet to leave Gunter since the start of this interrogation.

Eckert gestured to the driver. "Show them both."

The man walked them to the other side of the house and down one of two hallways. "Front door. Five minutes."

"Thank you," Gunter said before the driver retraced his steps toward the office.

Gunter went inside first. While conducting his business, he berated himself for getting so starstruck that he did not follow orders. For not listening to Ernst when he wanted to order room service. After finishing and washing up, he opened the door to let his brother in.

A year younger but an inch taller and twice as strong, Ernst shoved him against the door with an anger Gunter had never witnessed from him. "Your mouth is going to get us shot."

"I'm sorry, brother. I jabber when I'm nervous."

"Learn to be quiet and listen. You saw what they did to Roth."

"That's because they suspected him of being a Jew."

"Because he didn't know when to keep quiet. It doesn't matter how brilliant you are at designing airplanes. If they consider you a risk, they will

The Secret War   67

shoot you like a dog." Ernst slammed the door and came out a minute later, much calmer. "Let's go do our job."

They met the driver near the front door, noticing, as presumed, that someone had rifled through their luggage, leaving shirt sleeves and pant legs poking from the partially zipped bags. The car they arrived in was gone, and in its place was a rugged Kubelwagen. The canvas roof had been rolled out, which meant rain might have been expected during the trip. No one offered to load their bags, so the brothers heaved their suitcases into the open trunk compartment. One did not fit, so they placed it in the back seat between them. The seats did not have as much padding as the other sedan, foretelling this would be an uncomfortable ride.

The men who had picked them up at the hotel got into the front, keeping their previous positions as the driver and strong, silent passenger. Neither gave Gunter a sense of reassurance that their time in Brazil would be pleasant. It was the opposite. He predicted someone would be watching their every move with guns pointed at their heads, ready to pull the trigger on a single order. As they pulled from the gate, he mumbled, "What have we gotten ourselves into?"

His brother shot him a chiding side-eye.

The streets in the residential area were deserted. The only signs of life were the occasional lights from passing houses and dogs barking in the distance. They picked up traffic on a main road leading through town. Once they were on the highway going north past the city limits and out of the protective reach of streetlights, their surroundings went dark.

While they were still on pavement, they were in the lush tropical rainforest of southern Brazil. Thankfully, the animals within it remained hidden in the thick weave of brush and trees, leaving the humans to their nocturnal travels. The paved road offered a permanent, comforting dividing line between the wild and civilization. It was like traveling by boat. The seas were untamed and dangerous but thoroughly charted. As long as they stuck to the well-traveled path, Gunter knew they would be fine.

Hours into the trip, the driver turned off the main highway onto a dirt road without any signs. Gunter had no sense of how far they had come or had to go. The gravel path shrunk quickly on both sides, and the earthy smell of live foliage became more potent. The night stars disappeared overhead, and the jungle was suddenly on top of them, as was the possibility of a cougar or jaguar pouncing on their vehicle. A sinking feeling set in. The soft cloth of the retractable roof would be no defense if they faced the claws of the big cats hunting for a meal.

Gunter's heart thumped faster than the beat of their tires against the rough terrain. Beads of sweat formed on his brow, but a glance at Ernst in the other seat revealed he appeared unaffected by the change in direction. He was always the more pensive of the two of them, absorbed in serious thought, and he rarely showed emotion, which made his earlier outburst at the bathroom more significant. Until they reached their destination, Gunter would take his baby brother's cue and remain calm as long as he did.

After taking another turn onto an equally primitive dirt road half an hour later, the driver slowed the car. Its headlights illuminated a wall of vines. Once they came to a stop, two guards dressed in utility clothes and bearing military-style submachine guns appeared on either side of their vehicle. Their weapons were pointed at the car, and their fingers were on the trigger.

The guard to their left shined a flashlight in the driver's face with his free hand, and the driver held up a leather case. The guard checked the documents of everyone in the car, comparing their faces to the photos on the identification cards. Whatever this place was, the security was robust.

The guard issued a hand signal toward the wall of vines, and it rolled open like a cyclone gate on wheels. They pulled forward. The road turned left several meters inside and meandered for another hundred to a place where the vegetation suddenly ended. A few lonely lights resting atop poles shone sparsely in the clearing. Sitting in the middle of the Brazilian jungle was a large military compound with several buildings, including two plane hangars. Gunter supposed the airfield was beyond in the dark abyss.

The driver parked near a smaller structure and honked his horn twice. He and his partner opened their doors, the brothers' cue to open theirs and step out with them. Gunter and Ernst gathered their luggage, where their escorts had moved halfway to the building. The sound of gas generators hummed from somewhere close.

Moments later, the building's door opened, and light spilled out, high-

The Secret War 69

lighting the wood-slat walkway to a gravel road. A man appeared and took a few steps toward them, the planks beneath his boots creaking with each foot plant. He waved several meters away. "Bring them inside."

The brothers picked up their bags without waiting for help, which Gunter was sure would not come, and followed the men. The facility smacked of an administrative support building, resembling many Gunter had been in at military airfields. Once in the light, Gunter instantly recognized the man as Reinhart Hoffman, a genius at airplane design and the creator of most of the Luftwaffe's operational craft.

"Renny," Gunter said, adjusting the grip of his suitcases. "I didn't know they called you in, too."

Hoffman grunted and pointed down the corridor. "I have you two in the rooms at the end of the hall. The bathroom is halfway down. Get a few hours of sleep, freshen up, and come to my office, the first door on the left as you came in. Breakfast is at six. I'll show you. We meet with Herr Wagner right after." Hoffman faced the escorts. "The flight line manager set aside quarters for you in the next building."

The escorts walked outside without saying a word, leaving the Kessler brothers with their old acquaintance.

When Hoffman turned on his heel toward his office, Gunter placed a hand on his shoulder. "Renny, wait. Can you tell us why we're here? What is this design project that has stalled?"

Hoffman stopped and went rigid, clutching his fists as he focused on Gunter. He stepped closer, invading the brothers' personal space. His face became beet red with anger.

"The project has not stalled. I told Wagner there was no need to bring in help and I would fix the shimmy before the mission date." Hoffman sneered at both brothers with a look of disdain. "I doubt either of you Kesslers could get up to speed in time to meet the deadline, let alone understand the complexity of my creation."

"So, it's your work that needs fixing." Gunter was beyond surprised. Göring considered Hoffman the Luftwaffe's golden child, accepting a Hoffman concept over a Kessler at every turn. Yes, they had come in a close second most times and were always asked to submit their ideas for new projects. However, losing to Hoffman had become tiresome, even when they had been praised for their daring concepts.

Hoffman narrowed his eyes. "It requires no such thing. The design is flawless. The manufacturing had issues." He waved his hand dismissively as if shooing away a fly. "But I'm sure Herr Wagner will get into that in the morning." He grunted again and vanished into his office.

Gunter and Ernst walked silently down the hallway, glancing at each other with raised eyebrows at the odd conversation. They dared not speak about it until they knew who might be listening.

After choosing a room, Gunter said, "See you in a few hours, brother."

"Yes, a few hours." Ernst disappeared into his room.

Gunter laid down his bags and unpacked them into the three-drawer wooden dresser, placing a few items on the rod in the open alcove. He bounced his bottom on the bed twice to test its sturdiness. The squeak and lack of firmness said this would be a long, backbreaking stay.

The room was stuffy, and he considered opening the window to let in some fresh air, but he was unsure of the local mosquito population. He had read about outbreaks of malaria in Africa and South America and did not want to risk contracting the dreaded disease.

After using the bathroom, showering, and brushing his teeth, he returned to his room, stripped down to his boxers and sleeveless undershirt, and got into bed. He thought about Hoffman's appearance. He appeared tired and browbeaten, likely a result of the pressure regarding whatever secret project he had been working on...the design Berlin had tapped Gunter and Ernst to fix. Whatever this plane was, he was sure if the aircraft did not perform as needed by the deadline Hoffman had mentioned, he and Ernst would not make it home alive.

9

Hattie was at the dressing room door, laughing with Maya about Agent Knight dashing out in a rush to catch the elusive German aeronautical engineers. She heard a tap on the private entrance door and guessed it was her father returning to finish their business with David. Knowing how Maya still held on to her resentment regarding her father, Hattie decided against inviting her in.

"I don't mean to cut this short, but I must have that talk with David and my father." She paused at Maya's sigh. "Please don't leave alone tonight. I want to make sure you're safe."

Maya offered a slight nod. "I'll wait."

Hattie locked the hallway door and took a deep breath before opening the back door and finding her father on the private patio. She let him inside. "I assume you heard Knight take off. Why didn't you come in?"

"Maya was here." His expression turned sheepish. "I've learned to knock first."

"Thank you." Hattie blushed at the memory of her father sneaking into her dressing room last week while she and Maya were there. The intrusion did not interrupt something a parent should never witness their child doing, but it had come close. "That's very thoughtful."

"I saw you sitting with those Germans. Why did Knight target them?" he asked.

Hattie relayed what Knight had told her about aeronautical engineers disappearing from Germany in recent weeks. She said those men were two of the missing that Knight had thought might have been bound for Rio.

Her father perked up. "That makes sense. This has to be related to the top-secret project Wagner has been working on in the jungle. This is why he's still in the country."

"What do you know about it?"

"Nothing specific. I overheard that it would be a spear in the heart of the Americans and change the balance of power and perhaps guarantee a victory in the war." Karl rubbed his thinning hair with both hands. "I think Germany is planning to attack the United States by plane, so we need someone on our side on it."

"But can Knight be trusted?"

"I hope so." Karl patted his breast pocket. "Do you still want to approach David tonight or postpone until tomorrow?"

"Let's get this done. I've waited long enough to know how that book got there." Hattie went to the couch, picked up the phone, and dialed the club's reception desk. "Yes, Mr. Townsend should be at the bar. Can you send him to my dressing room? Thank you."

"You sure you're ready for answers?"

"Yes."

"Even if it's not what you want to hear?"

Karl had hit a nerve. Despite her lingering suspicions of David and the logbook, he had been a loyal friend since coming to Rio. He had kept up the charade of their engagement with the public, including band members. After Hattie had revealed the truth about her association with Maya to her parents, he could have left. He had chosen to stay and befriend Eva without the lie of a lavender relationship hanging over his head. If he had decided to do otherwise, rumors of her and Maya's friendship might have turned scandalous...accurate, but shocking all the same. Hattie hoped David had a reasonable explanation for the logbook because learning some awful fact about him tonight would hurt her deeply. However, she needed to know whatever it was and hopefully put all this doubt behind her.

The Secret War 73

"Even if."

Minutes later, the doorknob rattled, and David called out. "Hattie, the door is locked."

"Hold on a second," Hattie said. Once her father ducked into her closet, she opened the door. "Come in, David." She secured the door again to eliminate unwanted intrusions.

"What was that bit with Agent Knight? Were those Germans again?"

"That can wait." Hattie glanced up as her father appeared in the room. "We have something to discuss with you."

"We?" David looked over his shoulder. "What's going on?"

Karl positioned himself between David and the exit to the private patio, limiting avenues of escape.

"Please sit." Hattie gestured toward the couch, and David sat next to her. "I need to talk to you about something I found."

"What did you find?"

Karl pulled Baumann's original logbook from his inside breast pocket and placed it on the coffee table in front of him. "This." He stabbed its cover with an index finger.

"Wait. *You* found it?" David asked with a hint of confusion in his tone. "Didn't you put it in the steamer trunk?"

"You knew about this?"

"I've known for months but was afraid to ask about it."

Hattie shifted uncomfortably on the couch. "I'm confused. Are you saying you didn't put it there?"

"Me?" David pointed to himself. "Didn't you?"

Hattie opened her mouth to reply, but Karl interrupted, putting up a hand. "Tell us what you know about Baumann's logbook."

David ran a hand through his hair, signaling he was nervous. "A couple of weeks into my recuperation after being shot, I was going through the steamer trunk."

"What prompted this?" Karl asked.

"Since Hattie told you and Eva the truth about us and her and Maya, we didn't have to pretend anymore. I wanted to separate the rest of our clothes and get a few items from the trunk."

"What then?" Karl asked, his tone patient.

"I saw a cut in the lining and thought I'd ripped it, but when I felt around, I found the book and put it back."

"Why didn't you say anything to me?" Hattie asked.

"Because I was afraid of what it meant, figuring you had placed it there," David said.

"Why would you think that?"

"I thought you had changed your mind, thinking that something in that book might have implicated your father, so you wanted it back. There was no way in hell Butler would have given it up without a fight, so I thought you must have taken it by force. Two months later, we found out that Butler and Cohen had disappeared and were last seen around the time you gave them the book. I honestly thought you had killed them for it and faked your surprise when we learned they were missing."

"But I had the photographs and handed them to Leo after the bombing attempt."

"I had no idea about those photos. When you handed them over, I assumed you'd had time to pore over them and realized nothing was in them to put your father in danger."

"I thought essentially the same thing when I found the logbook. Either you had taken it to protect me, or someone else put it there to make me think you had." Everything David said made sense to Hattie. They both thought the other had placed the book there and were afraid to find out why.

"I never thought about it that way, but I don't get it," David said. "That book has sat there for six months. Why are you asking me about it now?"

"I've checked on it regularly since finding it. Tuesday night, it was in a different position for the first time. Did you move it?"

David cocked his head back. "No, that wasn't me. I haven't touched it since the day I discovered it."

"So you had nothing to do with this?" Karl asked.

"No, I didn't."

"And you kept your mouth shut out of loyalty to my daughter?"

"I was afraid to learn what she may have done to get that book back." David looked Karl straight in the eyes. "And, yes, I would do anything to protect Hattie."

The Secret War   75

"Including killing an FBI agent?" Karl asked, but it came out as more of an accusation than a question.

David stood, narrowing his eyes. "You're saying I'm lying."

"It wouldn't be the first time."

"If you're talking about my engagement to Hattie—"

"I'm talking about all those times you tangled with Ziegler's and Wagner's men. You walked away every time with only a few scrapes."

"I wouldn't call being shot in the leg a minor scrape."

"That man had you dead to rights, yet here you are, alive and well."

David pushed the coffee table out of the way, sending the logbook flying. His body went rigid, and his hands curled into fists. "What are you accusing me of?"

"It's all a little too convenient for me," Karl snarled.

David stepped closer, within striking range. "I could say the same thing about you. Nazi agents busting you out of custody and killing those FBI guys to leave no witnesses. Being forced onto a Rio-bound freighter. So was you working for Baumann. Hell, you could have taken that logbook back because you realized your name was all over it. It wouldn't surprise me if you had Hattie kill Butler to get it back."

"I would never put Hattie in danger to save my ass," Karl said, standing his ground with a firm stance. "Can you say the same thing?"

"Yes, I can."

"Well, one of us is lying, and I know it's not me."

David cocked back his arm to throw a punch at Karl, but Hattie called out, "Stop it, you two. We shouldn't fight each other. We need to figure out how that book got there and why."

Karl turned to Hattie while pointing at David. "It's clear as day."

David's face contorted in pure rage. Hattie expected a fistfight to break out, but he backed down. "I don't have to stand here and take this." David sneered at Karl before turning to Hattie. "Find your own damn way home tonight." He stormed out the back door to the private patio, and a minute later, tires screeched in the parking lot.

Hattie plopped on the couch, burying her face in her hands. "That was a disaster."

"I'd say we learned a bunch," Karl said. "We know he's willing to go to any length to protect you."

Hattie snapped her head up. "Stop, Father. Just stop. You're giving me a headache. This entire night has been a disaster, starting with those pictures Maya developed."

"What about the pictures? You never mentioned Maya had developed the film already. What did she find?"

Hattie retrieved the envelope she had stuffed under the couch cushion, removed the offending photo, and handed the rest to Karl. "Most show that man had followed Leo, me, and Maya for weeks."

He flipped through the images. "We expected that. What about—"

Hattie cut him off. "Trust me. You don't want to see it. He got into Maya's yard at night and—"

Karl put up his hand in a stopping motion. "I get the picture."

"I'm afraid for her, living there alone," Hattie said. "And we're not safe even when I'm there with her."

He sat beside her on the couch. "Between David and the Nazis, this is becoming a tangled mess. I don't think the sheet music is safe anymore. We need to alter the lists in them."

Karl had told Hattie that before the FBI arrested him for giving secrets to Germany, he had suspected there was a Nazi mole in the American government. He had received two requests, one from the War Department and another from his German handler, a day apart. Both had wanted lists of known spies the other had in their countries. The requests had been too similar and made too close together to be coincidental. The only explanation was someone high up in the government was working for the Germans. Karl had replied by compiling the lists, hiding them in code in a collection of sheet music. He had altered the original documents at the State Department so no one else could recreate them.

"But aren't those lists your insurance policy? Isn't the threat of them getting into the wrong hands the one thing keeping us alive?"

"Yes, they are, but I don't believe for one second that David discovered that logbook and thought you had put it there. If that was the case, why didn't he destroy it to protect you?"

Hattie paused for a moment, letting those words sink in. "I don't know."

The Secret War 77

"Does Maya still have the photos you took of the sheet music?"

"Yes, she hid them where no one would find them. And I have Mother's notes of the Morse code she found in them."

"Good. We need to keep them separate, and I have to turn the sheet music into a red herring."

"How do we do that?" Hattie asked.

"Doctor the code on the sheets, leaving the pictures and your note as the only accurate copies. I'll take care of it and talk to your mother about Maya. You two will be safer at Eva's until this blows over."

Hattie struggled to wrap her head around what her father had suggested. "Mother has come a long way toward accepting us, but she'll never let us stay in her house together."

"Trust me. She will." Karl put the coffee table back in its proper place.

"You're sure about this?" Hattie had to admit she would feel much more at ease having Maya with her in Eva's gated home.

"I am. Eva would rather know you two are safe than watch you grieve if something happened to Maya. Gather her things and come to the house an hour after closing." Karl kissed Hattie on the forehead and disappeared into the private patio with the photos.

She sank back on the couch, raking both hands down her face. While not storybook-idyllic for the last six months, her life had been calm and better than it had been in years. She had a good woman, and her parents knew the truth. The cherry on top was that her mother and father were no longer at odds, and when they were all together, it felt like they were a genuine family again.

She checked the clock on the wall. The club had already closed its doors, and Maya would soon complete her checklist to send everyone home. After changing out of her stage dress, she returned to the couch, waiting for Maya to finish and come to the dressing room as promised. Meanwhile, the photo face down on the coffee table taunted her. Easing her hand over it, she caressed the back, relishing what it represented—the love she and Maya shared for one another. She flipped it over and traced a finger over the image of Maya's body...her well-defined back and shoulder muscles on her lean frame. They were all hers whenever Hattie craved them. She took a ragged breath, imagining them recreating the moment captured in the image.

A knock drew her from her fantasy, and she turned the picture over and opened the door.

"Ready to go?" Maya asked, stepping inside. Her head pivoted. "Where's David?"

"He was upset and left."

"I take it things didn't go well. Did he explain why the logbook was in the trunk?"

Hattie detailed David's story, her father's accusations, and the two nearly coming to blows. "Then he stormed out."

"I tend to agree with Karl. David's excuses seem convenient."

"Not you, too." Hattie lowered her head, feeling like they were ganging up on her. "I hear you, but I'm not ready to believe he's been working for the Nazis."

Maya rubbed Hattie's arms. "All I'm saying is that it's getting hard to trust him. Things aren't adding up, and you need to be careful."

Hattie blew out a loud breath. "I will."

"I'll take you home." Maya turned toward the back door.

"Wait." Hattie explained her father's idea about them staying at Eva's until they were sure Wagner was no longer a threat.

Maya laughed. "She'll never agree."

"Yes, she will because she loves me." Hattie picked up the photograph. "I'll sleep much better knowing no one can take more of these or get to you when I'm not there."

"You're serious about this?"

"Very serious. My father is over there now, talking to her, so it won't be a surprise when I walk through the door with you and suitcases."

"I don't think Eva is ready for this."

Hattie let out a deep sigh, realizing Maya needed more convincing. "I didn't think she was ready to hear the truth about us. She didn't think I was ready to hear the truth about her believing my father was a Nazi. We were afraid the other would crumble, but telling our truths and reaching out to each other for help proved we were wrong. We remembered that we are Machado women and are stronger and more ready than anyone might

The Secret War 79

think. It might be awkward initially, but she will get used to us living under the same roof."

"Temporarily," Maya added.

"Yes, temporarily." Hattie ran a finger down Maya's cheek. "Let's pack up some of your things."

"Okay." Maya let out a long breath. "Can we stop at the Halo Club? I want to check on the kitchen flooring."

"Great idea. I'm dying to see how it turned out."

They went to Maya's house, packed several bags, and checked on the hidden photographs and negatives of the sheet music. An hour later, Maya parked on the street near the employee entrance of the rebuilt Halo Club. As they got out, Hattie caught movement in the light cone from the street-lamp across the alley. A shadow shifted again and came closer.

Maya kneeled and held out her hands. "Coco, come here, girl."

The cat that once made the garbage cans behind the club her home sauntered over and rubbed her side against Maya's palms.

"I thought she had found a new home after the site was cleared of debris." Hattie bent and stroked the cat's head. "It's great seeing her here."

"Yes, it is. Coco has been the club mascot for years." Maya gave her a good pet before standing straight. "I'll start leaving out food and water for her." She dangled the key in front of Hattie. "You do the honors."

Hattie waved her off. "This is your club."

Maya squeezed Hattie's hand, unlocked the door, and flipped on the wall switch. The temporary lights flickered on. In the old club, this hallway served a dual purpose. It had been the service entrance for deliveries and employee breaks, but it also had housed the bathrooms used by customers and employees. However, the floor plan had been transformed into a more modern configuration. This entry now led to the back section of the club, including the storage room, kitchen, utility room, and employee-only bath-room. The old wooden planks had been replaced with a high-quality vinyl composition tile laid in a checkered motif using three different colors.

"It's beautiful," Maya said as they entered the kitchen. "You were right to go with a pattern."

"The Copacabana in New York had something similar. VIPs frequently toured the kitchen, and the floor gave them a good first impression. It's easier to keep clean than the wood that was here before, and polishing it with a buffer is simple."

"Well, I love it, and it looks better than the Golden Room's back area."

"That's the idea." Hattie winked.

"You haven't been here in a while," Maya said. "They've finished the stage platform. Would you like to see it?"

"I'd love to."

Maya pushed through the double kitchen swing doors and turned on the main dining room lights. The walls had been plastered and painted, and temporary strands had been strung across the high ceiling until the light fixtures arrived from Texas. The bar had been framed, the wall behind it painted, and the shelves and mirrors had gone up since Hattie was last there.

"The bar is coming along nicely. Are you sure you'll have enough room for everything you need and three bartenders? We still have time to make changes."

"I'm ahead of you. I had them add another two feet to accommodate the second beer refrigerator."

Hattie laughed. "The Golden Room is going to be sorry to see you go. You're always on top of things."

"I've learned that running a club and restaurant, pricy or inexpensive, comes with essentially the same problems when dealing with staff, vendors, and the building. The fundamental difference is with the clientele. The rich are much more demanding and fussier."

Hattie laughed harder. "No truer statement."

"Present company excepted." Maya bowed.

"Thank you." Hattie scanned the rest of the room, envisioning how it might appear once it was finished, but she couldn't get a picture in her head. She was not looking at it from her most familiar perspective. "Can we go on the stage?"

"Of course. The subfloor is safe to walk on."

Maya took Hattie by the hand, leading her to the new stage door and up the steps through what would be the curtain wings. They stepped to the center of the platform, and Hattie felt instantly at home.

Maya pressed herself against Hattie's back, wrapped her arms around her waist, and rested her chin on her shoulder. "Is it odd being back here on this stage?"

"Not really." Hattie scanned the room, getting a feel for its size and configuration once the lights were installed, the floor laid, and the tables positioned. "It's more open and much bigger than the old place. It feels like the Copa."

"I'm glad." Maya squeezed her tighter. "I know you miss the States."

"Hmm. I do." Hattie swayed a little, thinking of her appearances at A-list clubs in the States, her hours in the recording studio, and the fans recognizing her on the street. It was exhilarating, but it did not compare to the feeling of being in love. "But I'm very happy here with you."

"What do you miss the most about your old life?"

"I miss recording and hearing the final product on the radio for the first time. It's an incredible feeling."

Maya stopped swaying and turned Hattie a fraction in her arms. "I want you to sign that contract with Maggie. I love you too much to keep you from that." She had said those words casually as if she said them to her a thousand times before...as if she had always loved Hattie and always would.

Hattie felt emotion building in her throat, hearing the words she had waited months for. The corners of her lips drew upward as she finally said them back, "I love you, too."

"You need to follow your heart and record again."

Hattie caressed Maya's cheek. "I'm not ready to leave you, even if it's only for a few weeks or months."

"I'll be waiting right here for you, Hattie."

Hattie pressed their lips together tenderly. This kiss felt different. Maybe it was that they had finally declared their love for one another, but it was more than that. Hattie was finally home.

10

Hattie woke to a mix of savory smells wafting into the room. It was odd because she had closed the door last night when she and Maya went to bed after settling into Hattie's room. Eva's reception had been somewhere between civil and warm, a sign that she was trying.

As he left last night, Karl had given Eva a kiss on the forehead and a reminder. "Until I put Wagner in a grave, my family is safer here," he had said. "Hattie considers Maya family, so that makes her part of mine and part of yours."

Eva had sniffed back several tears and welcomed Maya with a hug. "Stay as long as you need."

The smell of breakfast cooking meant Eva was up, and Hattie suspected Maya, the early riser in the couple, might be helping. The sound of water running in the next room made her rethink things. She slipped out of bed, wearing her silky pajama shorts and matching top, and opened the bathroom door. Steam poured from the shower, fogging the mirror.

"The sheets were cold. I thought you would have slept in a bit after our late night."

The water turned off, and the towel hanging over the rod disappeared. Moments later, the curtain opened, and David appeared with the towel wrapped around his waist.

The Secret War 83

"I wondered why Maya's car was in the driveway when I pulled in. You're getting bold, bringing her home to stay the night. I thought you had more respect for your mother."

"I didn't know it was you. And Maya is here at Mother's invitation."

He snorted. "That came quicker than I thought. She doesn't mind you two screwing in her house?"

"Don't be crass, David. I know you're angry about last night, but what did you expect?"

"I told you the truth, and you stood there, taking your father's side without trying to believe me. We've been friends for years, and I expected more support from you."

Hattie let out a weighty sigh. "I'm sorry, but some of what he said made sense, and I can't think of anyone who would want me to think that you had placed the book there."

"Your father, for one. He's a confessed spy. What is he? A double or a triple agent? No one knows for sure. His life is so convoluted it's hard to keep things straight."

"I don't know what to say, David, other than I need to find out who hid Baumann's logbook there and why."

He went to the counter and put on his eyeglasses. Their round shape complemented his features well. "I do, too, but you obviously don't trust me enough to include me in the search. That's the difference between you and me. I've always had faith in you, even when you've given me plenty of reasons not to."

"Like what?" she asked.

"Like you disappearing most of the day on Tuesdays. You've never told me where you go, and I've never asked because I trust you." He stepped toward his bedroom door but stopped, craning his head over his shoulder. "And I've always protected you. Since coming here, I've done everything I could to keep you safe from the world your father has dragged you into. I'm afraid that you don't fully understand its dangers." He turned again and walked away, shutting the door.

Hattie wanted to tell him that after all the harrowing experiences since arriving in Rio—being hunted for sport and nearly blown to pieces—her eyes were wide open. She knew danger lurked around every corner, and with her father's training, she was preparing to face it.

Instead, she brushed her teeth, fixed her hair, and returned to her room. After dressing in slacks and a blouse, she went into the kitchen, where Maya was pulling two hot pans from the oven. Hattie stepped closer and kissed Maya on the cheek without disrupting her concentration. "It smells great. Where's Mother?"

"Getting the newspaper."

"I'm surprised she let you cook. Normally, she does it all when she's home. The only time I get to use the stove is when she's at the studio late with a student."

"She's an excellent cook." Eva walked in with the morning paper, already dressed and with her makeup done. "And you aren't. That's why."

"You're up and going early," Hattie said.

"I took a message for you a bit ago. Hector said that your contract with the Golden Room is ready to sign. I thought I might come with you. It's been a while since I've seen him."

"Sure. I'm sure he'll enjoy seeing you again. You were his best client for decades."

"Now you hold that honor." Eva sat at the table and sipped her coffee.

Hattie poured a cup and positioned herself between Eva and Maya, leaning her bottom against the counter. "You should know that Maya and I discussed it last night, and I've decided to sign Maggie's contract. That will mean going to the States for a couple of weeks to record our album and a few months at a time to hit the nightclub circuit to promote it."

"Are you sure that's the wisest choice?" Eva asked. "Columbia has a rich history in the industry."

"I'm still considered the daughter of a traitor. RCA did a thorough hatchet job on me, and I doubt Columbia would be interested. Even if they are, this isn't about the money. This is about friendship. I owe my start to Maggie. She's asked for my help in starting her new label, and I'm going to give it."

"But what about the Halo Club?" Eva asked. "You still need to get it off the ground. I have a good feeling about your venture. It could become an important part of the South American nightclub scene."

"You're right. It will," Maya said, transferring the food to plates and walking it to the table. "But that's my job. Hattie plans to go to the States with you for Christmas to visit Olivia and the kids. Once she and Maggie record the songs, they'll come here for the opening and perform them, kicking off their tour. They still have much to figure out, but she'll likely be gone most of the autumn here, spring there."

"And you're okay with that?" Eva asked.

"Not with the separation, but Hattie misses recording." Maya squeezed Hattie's hand and looked Eva straight on. "I love your daughter and want Hattie to do whatever makes her happy."

Eva cleared her throat, pinching her expression like she was struggling not to cry. "I can see that you do, and I can see that Hattie loves you too."

"Yes, I do," Hattie said, squeezing Maya's hand in return.

Hector Marquez's outer office was modestly furnished with a receptionist's desk, a half dozen guest chairs, and a coffee station in the corner. The walls were decorated with framed photos of several Brazilian singers and movie stars. Eva's was the most prominent.

The secretary perked up as Hattie, Eva, and Maya entered. "Hello, Miss James. Mr. Marquez is expecting you." She turned to Eva. "This is quite the unexpected pleasure, Miss Machado."

"Thought I'd pop by and—"

Marquez's door flew open. "I thought I heard your name, Eva." He pulled her into a brief, friendly hug. "Here to support your daughter, I see."

"All part of being a mother, my dear Hector."

"Please, come in." He gestured for them to enter his office and closed the door after them.

"Hector," Eva said, "I'd like you to meet Maya Reyes. She is the Golden Room's assistant manager and Hattie's good friend." It was good to see Eva politely introducing Maya and leaving out the fact that Maya and Hattie were rebuilding the Halo Club. They still wanted that fact closely held.

"It's a pleasure, Miss Reyes." He shook hands with her, turned to Hattie, and gestured toward the desk. "Shall we?"

"Yes. I'd also like to sign Maggie's contract."

"Really? I thought you were still on the fence."

Hattie glanced at Maya. "Not anymore. I'm ready to record again."

"Well, the agreement with the Golden Room will give you the flexibility to leave whenever you need."

Marquez reached into his lower desk drawer, pulled out another folder, and placed Maggie's contract next to Mr. Guinle's. He had no idea how necessary that clause was and not just because of the recording contract with Maggie and singing at the new Halo Club. Hattie was never sure when business with the FBI or her father might take her elsewhere. She needed the freedom to keep her family safe, including Maya.

"Let's get this done." Hattie picked up the pen on the desktop and added her signature to both contracts. She was relieved to no longer have her future in limbo. "When will you get these out?"

"After making copies, I'll personally walk the contract to the Palace today. We'll drop Maggie Moore's at the post office this afternoon and have it couriered via airmail. She should get it in seven to ten days."

"Good. I have time to send Maggie a telegram, letting her know I've signed."

"We can do that on the way home if you want, sweetheart," Eva said. "We don't have to get ready for tonight's party with President Garza for several hours."

"If you don't mind."

Hattie shook Hector's hand and thanked him for his excellent services. The three walked outside to their cars, and Maya pulled Hattie aside.

"I wish I could kiss you right now," Maya said. "I'm so proud of you and glad you're going to record again."

"If I didn't have to go to this presidential event tonight with Mother, I'd take you home and make sure you're late for work."

Maya grinned. "Speaking of work, David looked angry this morning. Will he be a problem, or should I see if Zoya can play piano for tonight's show with your backup singer?"

"He and I talked a bit. He's still mad and could use the night off. I'd call in Zoya."

"I'm on it."

11

Hattie drove Eva to President Garza's private mansion near the waterfront. The line of newer cars waiting to drop their passengers there screamed money. There were also several men with rifles and handguns positioned outside the stone-and-iron fence fronting the house and lush, ample grounds. According to the newspaper, since the failed assassination on the yacht six months ago, his staff had doubled the president's security presence.

Hattie pulled the sedan slowly down the shrub-lined driveway, each bush manicured to perfection. President Garza had chosen to hold this event at his family's palatial home, not one of the government palaces designed for such purposes. Oddly, those facilities weren't as secure as this location. His family was well known for its desire for privacy and had built the fence decades earlier to keep robbers out. The two-story mansion was a fortress.

She pulled up to an area roped off with velvet stanchions, where valets dressed in black tuxedos waited to tend to the guests. She recognized one as Javier, the valet from the Palace Hotel, where she and Maya had helped him get a job. When she stopped, two men jogged to her car. She was disappointed that one was not Javier.

The attendants opened both front doors and offered their hands to help her and Eva out.

"Thank you," Hattie said, speaking in Portuguese and accepting the man's hand. "I left the key in." She slipped him a tip.

"Thank you, Miss James." His expression brightened with a look of recognition, and he handed her a claim check.

Hattie looked for Javier, hoping to speak with him, but he was busy tending to another guest. Perhaps she would get a chance on the way out. She met up with her mother on the passenger side of the car moments before the valet whisked it away. Eva took Hattie's arm and raised her glittering white gown a few inches with her free hand. She ascended the broad stairs to the main entrance, taking care not to drag the delicate fabric on the ground.

"Miss James. Miss James," a man called out in Portuguese.

Hattie looked over her shoulder, discovering Javier sprinting up the steps. She gave him a brief hug. "It's good to see you. Not working the hotel tonight?"

"Like you, it's my night off, but I still pick up odd jobs. We're saving up for a car. It will be our first."

Hattie rubbed his arm. "I'm happy for you."

"All because of you. That night, when you saw my wife and me at Mr. Ziegler's gala, it changed our lives. I can't thank you enough."

"You'll have to speak to Miss Reyes after the first of the year. She might have another opportunity for you and Monica."

When another valet called out his name, Javier shook Hattie's hand with both of his. "I will." He took off down the steps and helped the next guest from their car.

Hattie and Eva went inside. A guard dressed in a dark suit searched their handbags.

The interior was befitting of a president—spacious and elegant. People wearing gowns and tuxedos and holding champagne flutes or cocktail glasses lingered in the vestibule. A waiter carrying a tray of drinks offered one to Eva and Hattie. Eva accepted, but Hattie asked if someone could bring her a glass of soda water with a twist of lemon. The server said she would send one to her promptly.

The Secret War 89

Hattie and Eva continued forward.

"You certainly have a soft spot for that couple," Eva said.

"His wife was kind to me when I started at the Halo Club. I consider them friends."

"Well, it's very nice of you. You have a big heart, Hattie."

"As do you, Mother." Hattie leaned in and whispered. "Thank you for opening your home to Maya."

"She's important to you, and I want to know her better."

"Well, I'm very grateful."

They walked down the wide hallway toward the din of dozens of conversations and recorded classical music playing softly in the background. It brought them to a substantial ballroom brimming with guests and servers tending to their every need and want. A stage was at one end of the room, and a buffet table loaded with various fruits, vegetables, bread, cheese, meats, and prepared hors d'oeuvres was at the other. Tables ringed the room, leaving the center near the back open for dancing. Everyone in the room was of some importance. There were military generals and admirals, senior members of the government, filthy rich businessmen, foreign ambassadors, and Brazilian celebrities like her mother.

Eva steered them toward a larger crowd. When they got closer, President Garza and his wife, Sophia, came into view. They were speaking to several dignitaries, one of whom was quite animated as if telling a tall tale. When the first lady, Eva's old and dear friend, locked gazes with Eva and Hattie, she opened her arms wide and stepped in their direction.

"Eva. Hattie. It's wonderful seeing you." Sophia hugged them warmly. She waved her husband over, who left his other guests in mid-sentence.

"Ladies, it warms my heart that you two are here tonight." The president kissed each woman on the cheek.

The crowd had reassembled around them, sharing hushed whispers at the arrival of Eva Machado and Hattie James, Brazil's new national hero. In the wake of the failed assassination attempt, the media had homed in on Hattie. She had become the face of the event, labeled the person responsible for saving the president, his family, and the lives of hundreds of the guests on his yacht. However, whenever someone praised her bravery, she always credited David, Leo, Maya, and even Maggie Moore for their parts—and her father in her heart.

The group talked about Hattie's rise to stardom since becoming the main attraction at the Golden Room. "What's next for you, Miss James?" Sophia asked. "Any chance we might hear new music from you on the radio anytime soon?"

"Perhaps," Hattie said. She did not want to drop Maggie's name or build up expectations in case she and Maggie encountered bumps getting her recording label off the ground. "I'm looking into a few options."

"I understand from Octávio's wife that you extended your contract at the Palace Hotel."

"News certainly travels fast in Rio." Hattie laughed. "Yes, the contract extends my appearances up to six months."

"Wonderful." President Garza rubbed his hands together. "We'll have to make a point of seeing your show sometime soon."

Hattie bowed her head a fraction. "I'd be honored."

A server approached. "Your requested drink, Miss James."

"Thank you." Hattie sipped from the glass, confirming it was tonic water.

"It's a shame the American vice president objected to you performing with your mother this evening," Sophia said, adding a long pout. "I would have loved to have seen both of you perform. I understand those parties you two performed at for the Swiss ambassador, whatever his name was, were quite the sight to see."

"Ziegler," Eva said, pinching her expression as if fighting a sour taste in her mouth. "His name was Frederick Ziegler." She placed her hand on Sophia's arm briefly to get her attention. "You're saying you wanted Hattie to sing with me, but Henry Wallace vetoed her? Why would he do that?"

"Something about her father being a murderer and a traitor."

Eva's eyes narrowed, and her jaw set. She was angrier than Hattie had witnessed in years.

"It's a lie," Eva said, pursing her lips. "Karl is innocent, and Hattie has needlessly suffered for it."

Hattie rested her free hand on the small of Eva's back. "It's all right, Mother."

The Secret War 91

"No, it's not, sweetheart. Our family has been through too much because of this," Eva said softly to Sophia. "Thank you for letting me know."

As they discussed other social goings-on in Rio, Hattie noticed Leo Bell had arrived, dressed in a crisp black suit, not his naval uniform. He spoke to several men wearing similar suits and pointed in multiple directions as if issuing instructions. Everyone dispersed, taking up positions near the exits and windows. Hattie studied two of the closest men, and both had bulges under their jackets, suggesting they had pistols underneath. They were likely security from the US Embassy.

Minutes later, American Vice President Wallace entered the ballroom with two men following steps behind. Wallace clearly did not consider them his equal. He waved up one. The man jotted notes inside a leather folio and stepped back. Hattie recognized the man as the one her father had said was the Professor's son. If the meeting between her father and this man was going to happen, it needed to be soon.

As Wallace greeted several dignitaries, Hattie searched again for Leo, finding him directing security as the vice president moved. She kept one eye on him and the other on the people in her group discussing the damage from the heavy rainstorms in northern Brazil last week.

"Isn't that right, Hattie?" Eva asked.

Hattie was only half listening, but the question was about delayed trains in that area and the president sending military troops up there to help with the relief effort. "Yes, I'm sure you're doing all you can, President Garza."

Eva squinted in confusion, suggesting Hattie's response was not what she had expected.

"I'm sorry." Hattie noticed Leo was now standing alone, scanning the reception guests. "If you'll excuse me, I'd like to say hello to a friend."

"Of course, Miss James," President Garza said. "I look forward to seeing my personal lifesaver perform someday soon."

Eva lifted her glass to her lips and mumbled, "It might be sooner than you think."

Hattie let the president kiss her on the cheek and his wife hug her before stepping away to find Leo. She saw him in the same location. He was still alone, focused on the crowd, so she weaved through the elegantly dressed guests and sidled next to him, facing the room's center.

"You look bored," she said.

"My bowl of oatmeal this morning was more exciting than this party."

"You certainly have a way with words." Hattie chuckled but quickly turned serious. "My father should be in place by now. Is this a good time?"

"As good as any," he said. "Wallace doesn't plan to stay too long."

"Then you can get back to your oatmeal. My father said he needs five minutes, ten if he has to do some convincing. Is that doable?"

"I'll do the best I can."

"I'll do the introductions so he's not spooked," Hattie said.

"Go out the door near the stage. Follow the garden path to the back of the property. I told him to wait next to a tall tree at the third pillar from the corner. It should provide him cover while they talk."

"See you out there."

Leo walked toward the man shadowing the vice president while Hattie stepped close to the wall, crossed in front of the stage, and exited through the door. She opened it wide enough to slip through. The patio was lit, and tables were aligned for guests to sit and enjoy the lush tropical garden. A few were outside at the far end, but Hattie put to use her father's training on being seen as little as possible. She eased the door shut to avoid attracting their attention and walked casually.

Hattie followed the paver-lined path to the stone-and-iron fence marking the edge of the property. She was unsure which way to go for the rendezvous with her father. Right was the shorter option, so she went there, figuring Leo would not send her on a trek in heels. The landscaping lights did not cover the area along the perimeter, so Hattie made her way through the shadows.

Counting down the pillars, she stopped at the third one from the corner near a large shade tree on the other side. "Father?"

"I'm here, Songbird." Karl leaned his head around a pillar and looked at Hattie through the openings between the fence's metal bars. "Is he coming?"

Hattie saw movement at the spot where she turned off the stone pavers. There were two shadowy figures. "Leo is with him."

The Secret War 93

Karl disappeared behind the column again as Leo and the man approached.

"This certainly is an odd place for a meeting," the man said. "This had better be good."

Leo stopped a few feet away. "It will be. Hattie James, this is James Cooke, Vice President Wallace's aide. Mr. Cooke, this is Hattie James. She is—"

"I'm aware of who she is, Commander Bell. If this is about her not performing tonight, I'm afraid I can't do anything about that."

"This isn't about hurt feelings, Mr. Cooke," Hattie said. She bit back her irritation, keeping in mind that their time for this meeting was short. "Someone acquainted with your mother wants to speak with you."

"I don't have time for a trip down memory lane. I need to get back to the party." Cooke pivoted to walk away.

"He knows her as the Professor."

Cooke stopped and looked back. "How do you know that name?"

Hattie had gotten his attention.

"I told her, Jimmy." Karl stepped from his hiding position behind the pillar.

Cooke's body stiffened. "Karl James. The FBI has been looking for you for almost a year." He shifted his stare to Leo. "How long have you known he was here? And why haven't you turned him in?"

"I believe Karl was framed," Leo said. "Listen to what the man has to say. There's more at stake here than bringing in a fugitive."

Cooke looked at Hattie before returning his attention to Karl. "All right, convince me not to call security and have you all arrested."

"Your mother brought me into her world and taught me everything I know. Besides my daughter, I trust her more than anyone."

"But how do I know she trusts you?"

"Ask yourself. How many people did your mother allow into your house when you were growing up?"

"None."

"Think back. You were five or six. Your mother asked me to come to her house to show me something. Hattie was sick that day, so I had to pick her up from school and bring her with me. You two played in your room while your mother and I talked. Why would she have invited me into her house and into your life if she didn't trust me? She let no one into her real life other than me."

Cooke tilted his head several times, shifting his gaze from Hattie to Karl. He settled on Hattie. "We played with my train set."

A twenty-two-year-old memory surfaced of having a stomachache and her father getting her from school since her mother was in New York City for a performance. Her father had said he needed to make a quick stop for work before taking her home, and she ended up playing upstairs with a little boy in his room.

"You had a conductor's cap and wooden ducks on your dresser."

"That was you?" Cooke's mouth dropped open, and his expression took on a look of shock. "That was the only time Mother allowed anyone other than family inside the house."

"That's how much she trusted me, Jimmy," Karl said. "She showed me pictures of you over the years. She was so proud when you graduated from Georgetown and started your position at the White House, though she wished you had gone into private business."

"I always wondered why she was against me working for the government until she finally told me about her real job."

"She knows how wielding the power of the government can corrupt even the best souls."

Cooke shook his head as if knocking all the haphazard thoughts into place. "All right, Karl. Commander Bell said you needed to ask me something, so ask."

"Did your mother send you here?"

"No, she didn't," Cooke said, narrowing his eyes. "Why do you ask?"

"I understand you were a last-minute addition," Karl said. "Why were you assigned to this trip?"

"The VP's regular aide was struck by a car and is in the hospital. I'm his backup."

"Was the accident suspicious?"

"It was a hit and run."

"If your mother didn't send you, I bet somebody wanted you here to flush me out."

The Secret War 95

"You're thinking the FBI is behind this?" Cooke cocked his head back.

"No. They need me alive to get their hands on the lists."

"What lists? And if not the FBI, who?"

"Your mother and I believe there is a mole high up in the War Department. We think that person framed me for giving secrets to the Nazis. That mole wanted certain names that I had access to. So did Germany."

"Was that what you gave the Nazis?"

"No, that information is safe," Karl said. "The mole wants me dead. And since they know about my connection to the Professor, your mother can narrow the suspects. It has to be someone we both worked with or someone she talked to about me."

"What do you want me to do?"

"Get a message to your mother. Tell her exactly what I told you and that the lists are safe with Songbird. I'll need her help to clear passage for me back to the States to locate that mole."

"All right. She's in hiding, but I know how to find her."

"Wait," Karl said. "Why is she hiding?"

"Before I left for Brazil, she said both sides were after her for intel she didn't have," Cooke said. "I'm guessing she meant you."

"I think you're right."

"I'll talk to her. We leave here on Sunday and should be in Washington on Tuesday."

"Thank you, Jimmy. Until you go, I suggest you remain at the embassy. Whoever wanted you here may have sent someone to watch you."

"I'm with the vice president. We have security around us twenty-four seven. I'll be fine."

"I hope so, Jimmy, for everyone's sake."

12

Hattie, Leo, and Cooke retraced their steps along the fence in the shadows. After reaching the stone pathway and the landscaping lights, Cooke laughed and shook his head. "I can't believe I once played trains with Hattie James."

"When this is over and I'm back in the States, you'll have to be my guest at one of my shows."

"I'd like that." Cooke glanced at her. "So, you think your father was framed."

Hattie pulled Cooke to a stop before she could see the mansion in order to remain out of view of other guests. "You know what your mother really did for the government. She trained my father to do the same thing. You, of all people, know that things aren't always as they seem. Karl James is an honorable man who sacrificed much for his country. He would never betray it."

He looked her in the eye. "I believe you, Miss James."

"Thank you for helping, Mr. Cooke."

They came back to the ballroom and split up, acting like their meeting never happened. Cooke returned to his post, shadowing the vice president. Leo checked with the other members of his security team. And Hattie returned to the side of Eva, who had moved on to talking to a pair of hand-

The Secret War   97

some Brazilian admirals. She was controlling the conversation as she always did.

"Sweetheart, you're back." Eva introduced the officials.

Hattie shook their hands. "It's a pleasure."

"The pleasure is ours," one said. "We're excited to see Miss Machado perform tonight and had hoped to catch one of your shows before returning to Natal. Unfortunately, we've been called back and must return tomorrow."

Chimes sounded over the speaker system, signaling it was time for the guests to take their seats for the evening's entertainment. The band members ascended the stage and took their positions with their instruments.

"I think I have a solution, gentlemen. Excuse us." Eva hooked her arm around Hattie's, and the men nodded politely. "Come, sweetheart."

"What are you planning, Mother?"

"To support our military and make things right." Eva patted Hattie's hand. "Take your seat. Our table is next to President Garza's."

While Eva took a position at the side of the stage, Hattie found her assigned chair and introduced herself to her tablemates. She was seated with the country's most influential radio station owner, the country's top banker, and a Brazilian army general, each with their wives.

An announcer came to the microphone at center stage and welcomed everyone to President Garza's reception in honor of United States Vice President Henry Wallace's visit. He offered a few words in English, praising a strong Brazilian-American alliance. He added that nothing represented it more than tonight's featured entertainer, Brazil's greatest treasured international star, who had lived in the United States for decades, Miss Eva Machado.

As the crowd roared with applause, Eva took the stage and signaled the band not to start playing yet. She stepped up to the microphone and stood, poised in her gown, the picture of elegance, beauty, and sophistication.

Eva spoke in English. "President Garza and my dear friend Sophia, thank you for letting me entertain you tonight. However, this evening would not be complete without a true demonstration of the bond between Brazil and the United States and how, in our hearts, we are all one family."

What are you doing, Mother? Hattie thought.

Eva extended a hand toward Hattie. "I invite to the stage America's most treasured songbird, my daughter, Miss Hattie James."

The crowd came to their feet and applauded, except for the people at the president's table. President Garza went wide-eyed, Vice President Wallace fumed, and Sophia Garza grinned from ear to ear.

Hattie decided she could not disappoint the audience. Or pass up the opportunity to shove Wallace's disrespect back in his face. The general seated beside her pulled her chair out farther as she stood and waved to the cheering fans. As she approached the stage, Eva spoke to the musicians— the same ones who had played during their appearances at Ziegler's mansion. The members scurried, rearranging their sheet music and pulling out others from their satchels.

Hattie joined her mother, giving her a warm embrace and whispering, "You're going to be in so much trouble."

"So worth it," Eva said. "I'll deal with Narcisco and Sophia later. The band knows the set we've been working on."

For the next hour, Eva and Hattie, mother and daughter, Brazilian and American, put on a heartfelt, sometimes lighthearted performance. It combined the hits of both women and one song never heard before, one that Eva had written about the regret and wasted time between lovers. It was an evening the guests would remember for many years. When Hattie and Eva took their final bows, the crowd rattled the windows with cheers and whistles. Even Leo, still standing his security watch against the wall, applauded.

As they departed the stage, people left their tables, mingling again and dancing to the recorded music playing in the background. Hattie's tablemates surrounded her and Eva, congratulating them on an incredible performance. They shook hands and posed for pictures by the official photographer working the event.

Eva tugged Hattie's arm, telling her that Sophia was waving them over. "Better to face them now than let this fester."

Hattie laughed. "I love your rebellious side, Mother."

"Live and learn, sweetheart." Eva led Hattie to the president's group.

Sophia greeted them first with hugs. Before releasing her embrace, she whispered in English to Hattie, "Your mother is naughty, but that is why I love her so."

Hattie did not fight her smile. "I feel the same."

"This was a night to remember," Sophia said.

"I couldn't agree more." President Garza hugged Hattie and Eva. "Your daughter might be American by birth but is a Brazilian at heart."

"Brazil is part of me, President Garza," Hattie said.

He turned to his right. "I'd like to introduce American Vice President Henry Wallace."

For a brief second, Hattie considered extending her hand out of respect for the office, but the man's look of contempt for her buried that thought in a flash. Instead, she held his stare without flinching or tipping her head. "Mr. Vice President." Civility was all she could muster.

"Perhaps Brazil doesn't care that your father is a murderer and a traitor who gives away secrets to Nazi Germany. However, in the United States, we frown on such things, Miss James," he said in a Texas drawl similar to Leo's. "We don't take kindly to those who defend depravity and deception."

Hattie cocked her head back. "I defend my father because he is innocent, and I don't take kindly to rudeness and arrogance."

Eva grinned with motherly pride.

"One other thing, Mr. Vice President. You've lost my vote."

"I think it's time for you to leave, Miss James." He snapped his finger at Cooke, who waved over security.

Leo rushed over, meeting another of his men near Wallace. "What seems to be the problem, sir?"

"The problem, Commander Bell, is that someone forgot to take out the trash, and I can't stand the smell any longer. Please see to it."

"Excuse me?" Leo looked between Wallace and Hattie.

"How dare you, Mr. Wallace." Eva stiffened her stance. "I don't care what position you hold. You have no right to refer to my daughter as trash."

"Henry," President Garza said. "There's no need for this. Miss James is a sweet and talented young lady who saved my life earlier this year."

Wallace turned to Garza. "Either she goes, or I go, and we will see how much Lend Lease money we throw your way. We'll go to French Guiana, Barbados, or Puerto Rico before I let one dollar go to a nation that blatantly insults us by supporting its traitors." He shifted to Leo. "Escort her out of my sight."

"I will do no such thing, sir." Leo squared his shoulders. "Miss James has done nothing wrong. Besides, this is President Garza's shindig. He has the final say as to who stays and goes."

"Step lightly, Commander Bell. I know who you are, and I am not surprised by the son of a murderer standing by the daughter of one."

"Excuse me?" Leo formed his hands into fists but kept them down at his thighs.

Shortly after meeting Hattie and hearing her story of fleeing to Rio to escape the shadows cast by her father, he shared the story of his own father with her. That one night, in a drunken rage, the man had killed Leo's mother, and Leo had joined the navy to escape the finger-pointing. He clearly did not like that reminder.

"You are a loathsome man." Hattie stepped forward, going toe-to-toe with the vice president. Security came closer, but Wallace waved them off. Her petite frame apparently did not pose a big enough threat for him to take her seriously.

"You need to rethink your next move, little lady." Wallace's condescending tone was infuriating.

An international incident was brewing, which could land Hattie in jail, cost Leo his job, and alter the war's outcome. She had learned from the events with Ziegler that the United States had identified Natal as a choke point in the battle for the Atlantic shipping lanes against Nazi Germany. If the US entered the war, building a base there could tip the balance in their direction. Hattie could not let the animosity between her and the patronizing vice president impact that development. She had risked everything to prevent Ziegler from doing the same thing with his assassination attempt.

Hattie turned to Leo. "It's okay. I'll go. He's not worth it."

"Sweetheart, no," Eva said. "This bully should not force you out."

"She's right," Leo said. "You have done nothing wrong."

"Then both of you leave," Wallace said, his eyes narrowing with building rage.

Cooke stepped forward. "Listen to Miss James, Commander Bell. Let's

The Secret War 101

not make a scene and turn this into something bigger than it is. Please escort Miss James outside, and we can talk tomorrow."

Leo's chest puffed and dropped to a breathy sigh. "Fine. But I'm not happy about this."

Hattie grabbed her purse and thanked President Garza and his wife for their hospitality before turning to her mother, who was to the point of tears. "It's all right, Mother. I assume Commander Bell will arrange for me to get home. You take the car." She handed Eva the valet check and hugged her. "I'll see you at the house later tonight."

"We will discuss this." Eva kissed her on the cheek.

Hattie accepted Leo's arm and walked from the ballroom among whispers, holding her head high. Last year, a scene like that would have humiliated her. However, the FBI's hounding her, the hit pieces in the American press, and the sneers she endured before leaving the country had made her immune to such low-class attacks. She was both a James and a Machado, and no one could break her backbone.

Once outside, Leo calmed down enough to hand a valet the ticket for his car. Hattie told the man they would wait near the end of the building. She wanted Leo out of earshot of guests who might come out because he was still seething and might blow his top.

"Well, that was quite the turn of events," Hattie said.

"I'd heard Wallace was a jackass, but he takes first prize."

"I can't disagree, Leo. You looked ready to call him out after school for a beatdown behind the gym."

"And I would have." Leo puffed his chest. "I kinda feel like it's become my job to stick up for you."

"I appreciate that, but you shouldn't have, not with the vice president. If they don't boot you from the navy, they could demote you and send you to some awful place for the rest of your career."

"It was the right thing to do, and you know it. I hate bullies like him. Judgmental, heartless people should not have that much power."

The mansion door opened, and the vice president, Cooke, and two other men stepped out. Those two fanned out like they were guards while Cooke waited with Wallace after speaking with the attendant.

Leo started to storm off in their direction, but Hattie tugged on his jacket sleeve, pulling him to a stop. "You have every right to be upset."

"Aren't you?"

"I don't like what he said, but unlike you, I've had a lot of experience being judged for things I can't change. And when it comes to my father, I've grown a thick skin. Other people's opinions don't matter."

"That's because you know the truth. He's innocent. My father isn't." Leo let out a weighty sigh. "He's serving a life sentence, and I live with that knowledge each day."

Hattie noticed shadows moving among the parked vehicles, probably an attendant fetching Leo's or the vice president's car. That area was not lit well, so it was difficult to determine what or who was there. However, a limousine approached the valet area as Leo's sedan pulled up. Something felt off, and she suddenly wished she had brought her Baby Browning in her purse. She did not think she could have gotten it through security.

"Leo, at your six. Movement between the cars."

Leo went still, his anger transforming into alertness. His right hand went to the pistol hidden in a shoulder holster under his jacket. He turned, pulling out his gun. "Where?"

"Last two."

"You packing?"

"No."

"Stay here." He took off toward the motion.

Damn, Hattie thought. She might not have had her pistol, but she could be of some help, so she took a different angle to the automobiles.

A gunshot rang out.

A second.

Hattie flinched, not knowing where the shot was aimed. She ran to where Leo should have been. Yes, there was danger, but she willingly went toward it. Before the ordeal at the plantation, she would do anything for those she loved but was unsure how far she would go. Now, she was trained and more sure of herself and her capabilities. Her worry was more for Leo than herself. Unfortunately, her heels slowed her pace. Instinct told her that whoever fired that gun would have taken off immediately to evade the armed security around the grounds.

The Secret War

A thud.

Coming close to the vehicles, she crouched to pose a smaller target in case her supposition was wrong. She eased between the cars, discovering Leo on the ground, holding a semi-automatic pistol in one hand and rubbing the back of his head with the other.

"Leo, are you okay?"

He appeared stunned.

An army of footsteps approached rapidly, and a sickening feeling knotted Hattie's stomach. If they did not present themselves as nonthreatening, they would indeed be shot.

"Drop the gun and lay face down."

He shook his head, clearing the cobwebs. "What?"

"Get down." Hattie snatched the firearm from his hand, tossed it onto the pavement, and pushed him down along with herself until they were both on the asphalt between the sedans.

The steps got louder. The swoosh of pant legs scraping against one another at a rapid pace meant security was seconds away. Hattie's heart pounded harder at the thought that one of those guards could be the type to shoot and ask questions later.

"Hands up! Hands up!" one yelled in Portuguese.

"We're unarmed," Hattie shouted back, raising her hands a few inches to demonstrate she was not a threat.

Someone grabbed Hattie by both arms, yanked her to her feet, and shoved her into the open. She finally got her bearings and realized two Brazilian police officers had a hold of her, and another two were dragging Leo out from between the cars. One picked up the pistol Hattie had tossed. Handcuffs tightened around Hattie's wrists with her hands in front of her belly.

Leo's too.

The officers pulled and pushed them toward the mansion's main entrance, where a crowd formed near the steps. The area appeared chaotic, with armed men running about and one shouting orders and sirens sounding in the distance. As they got closer, the scene became apparent. A man was on the ground, lying motionless on his side.

Hattie gasped, realizing the man was the Professor's son, Jimmy Cooke.

He was going to get a message to the one other person her father trusted so he could return to the States and unearth the War Department mole.

A man in a black suit approached them, giving a hand signal for the guards to stop. "Commander?"

Hattie recognized him as a man Leo had spoken to in the ballroom.

"Is the vice president safe, Simmons?" Leo asked.

"Yes, he's inside." Simmons drifted his stare to Leo's and Hattie's hands. "Why are you two in cuffs?"

"This is a misunderstanding. I went after the gunman, but he hit me and knocked me out."

Jack Lynch, the head of security and deputy ambassador at the US Embassy, pushed through the crowd. Hattie felt a little relieved seeing Leo's boss, someone she knew, but Lynch was a by-the-book bureaucrat, which, given the circumstances, was not all that comforting.

"What the hell happened, Bell?" The confused look on Lynch's face suggested the situation had overwhelmed him.

While the Brazilian officers consulted with an older man in uniform, Leo explained to Lynch how he and Hattie had spotted something suspicious near the cars. He added that he went to investigate but was knocked out after hearing a shot.

"You can't keep your nose clean, can you, Bell?" Lynch growled.

"I was doing my job," Leo said.

"Not after the vice president told you and Hattie James to leave. Any time you two are together, that spells trouble."

The senior-looking man introduced himself to Lynch as the Rio police chief. He said that Leo and Hattie were under arrest for suspicion of the murder of James Cooke and that his officers had found the likely murder weapon with them.

Lynch showed the officer his identification, said Leo had diplomatic immunity, and demanded his immediate release. The forceful request was surprising and gave Hattie a sliver of hope that this would be sorted out promptly. The Brazilian argued back and forth with Lynch, citing rules and the need for an official application before he would let a suspect go, but Lynch stood his ground.

President Garza, Sophia, Eva, and Vice President Wallace emerged from

The Secret War 105

the mansion. Garza requested an update from the police chief, and the chief asked Wallace some questions.

"If I hadn't dropped my eyeglasses and bent to pick them up," Wallace said, "I'd be the one dead."

"We discovered the weapon," the chief said, producing the pistol his officers recovered. "It was near this man." He pointed toward Leo.

"That is not my gun," Leo said. "It must be the shooter's. Mine has a pearl handle."

"Yes, my officer found it under a sedan," the chief asked. "Why do you have two guns?"

"I'm telling you that doesn't belong to me."

More discussion and nodding transpired. Then Wallace announced, "There will be no official request. Keep them in custody until you complete your investigation."

One of Leo's men on the security team stepped up. "Excuse me, Mr. Vice President. Moments before the gunshots, I clearly saw Miss James standing near the car parked at the end of the building, and she took off running. If the shot came from where the police chief said the gun was found, there is no way Miss James could have been the attacker."

"Please, Narcisco," Eva pleaded. "Do something."

Wallace harrumphed.

"Release Miss James," President Garza ordered. "But I'm afraid Commander Bell must remain in custody until this is sorted out."

Hattie's emotions were a mix of relief and dread. Leo remained under arrest only because he had dared defend Hattie against Vice President Wallace's insults. This was her fault.

"Please," Hattie said. "I can vouch for Commander Bell. He was going after the shooter."

"Did you actually see this other man?" the police chief asked.

"No, but I know Commander Bell. He would never do what you've accused him of."

"If that is the case," the chief said, "it will all come out in the investigation. Until we corroborate the existence of a second man, Bell remains under arrest." He gestured for his men to place Leo in the back of a police unit that had pulled up.

Chief Inspector Silva emerged from the patrol car, and another sickening feeling overwhelmed Hattie. She had embarrassed him publically many times for his lazy way of investigating and feared he would do anything to pin this murder on Leo just to spite her. This was a mess, and she could do nothing to help.

"This is horrible," Eva said. "Commander Bell is a good man."

Horrible was right, but Hattie saw her father lurking near the mansion's corner. They locked eyes. She knew what she would do in this situation and guessed his next move.

Hattie leaned closer to Eva and whispered in her ear. "We need a distraction."

"What?" Eva mouthed.

"Faint, Mother. Faint."

13

When Karl left the fence line meeting, he had a bad feeling about Jimmy Cooke being in Rio. It was a suspicion that had manifested after spotting him at the dock on Tuesday. Sticking around the mansion was not in doubt. The only question was what would happen and when.

Hours later, the gunshots confirmed he was right.

He could not immediately get a better look, though, not with the guards still around the perimeter. The wait was killing him. Two people he loved were inside that building, but he remained patient through the chaos of shouting and men running in all directions. He waited for at least one guard to lose his discipline and leave his post, and his bet paid off. One close to the corner of the property took off toward the activity through the squeaky pedestrian gate, leaving a gap between the officers. Karl glided in behind him.

Crouching behind the shrubs, he inched along the edge of the stone driveway until he came to the last bush near the corner of the mansion. He was close enough to the crowd at the entrance to make out the people. His eyes roamed the area for the only two people who mattered. Relief rushed over him when his gaze settled on Eva and Hattie standing together on the steps, but it tempered when he saw Hattie was handcuffed. Leo was next to them, with his hands bound like Hattie's. They were in an animated discussion with Jack Lynch, President Garza, Vice President Wallace, and two other men. Their backs were to him, and he could not be sure who they were.

Correction.

The men turned. One was Chief Inspector Silva, a man Karl trusted to do one thing: hold a grudge against Hattie and Leo Bell. Silva had been exposed to the public as inept for his botched investigation into the missing women whom Baumann had kidnapped. The reputation was magnified after the yacht assassination attempt, where he failed to capture Strom Wagner, the bombing's mastermind. And Hattie had been at the center of both cases. Leo, a newcomer to Silva's crosshairs, was a convenient target, easily taken down by his position in the navy and requirement to keep out of trouble.

People shifted, revealing a man in a black suit lying on the stairs. The distance made it impossible to discern who it was, but the dark spot around his body and the chaotic scene confirmed he was the victim of the earlier gunshots.

A uniformed police officer removed Hattie's cuffs. Karl let out a relief-filled breath. His sense that everything would be all right evaporated when the man put Leo in the back of a nearby patrol car and returned to the group.

Whoever was lying dead on the ground, Leo was under arrest for it. Karl had not known him for that long, but he could tell Leo had a good heart. He was capable of killing a person, but only out of self-defense or defense of others. Karl was unsure what was happening, but from the distraught expressions on Hattie and Eva, it seemed his supposition about Silva was right. The inspector had Leo's neck virtually in a noose and was in the mood for a hanging.

Hattie looked in Karl's direction and momentarily froze. *Good girl*, he thought. She had spotted him. All he needed was a distraction to get close to the patrol unit and talk to Leo. "Come on, Hattie. Just like I taught you."

Eva buckled at the knees, and Hattie buoyed her before she fell to the ground. All eyes in the crowd went to Eva Machado, Brazil's distressed superstar, supported by her daughter, a rising national star. Several went to their aid while the others looked on.

The Secret War 109

Karl walked normally, as if he belonged there, and went to the side of the patrol car not facing the commotion. He jimmied the lock, opened the door, and slipped inside, remaining in the shadows. "What the hell is going on, Leo?"

"I'm being framed for Jimmy Cooke's murder."

Karl felt doubled over by a sucker punch to the gut. "Jimmy's dead?" He thought about how this would crush the life out of Victoria, and his heart broke for her. A parent should never outlive their child, particularly a mother.

"Yes, I went after the gunman but didn't get a good look at him."

"And Silva thinks you're good for it. What about your diplomatic immunity?"

"Long story short, Wallace hates me, especially after defending Hattie against his insults, so he pulled rank. Which means I'm on my own."

Karl wanted to know more about what happened, but this was not the time. "I owe you, so what's our play?"

"I'd rather try my luck proving my innocence than trust Silva to do it."

"All right. Let's go."

Karl eased open the back door and slipped out. Leo slid across the seat and joined him. After closing the door, Karl retraced his steps to the edge of the shrubs. Leo followed. Once safely hidden, they crouched and made their way to the pedestrian gate. Karl checked for the guards, discovering one had returned to the post. The man was either a police officer or in the military, so killing him was not an option.

Karl signaled for Leo to wait there. The officer was positioned a few yards in front of the gate, creating a problem. The squeaky hinges would give him away, so his best course of action was acting like he belonged. Sometimes, the easiest way to work in the shadows was to be in plain sight.

Approaching the metal bars, Karl called out, using his limited Portuguese in a normal tone so as to not seem suspicious. "Guard, come here." He opened the creaky gate and pointed inside, toward the bushes. Three more steps, and Karl would be within striking distance.

The man turned. His face was barely lit by the distant streetlamp, making it impossible to gauge his response. However, his stiff posture and the speed with which he swung the automatic machine gun slung over his shoulder suggested he was on alert. Catching a bullet was a strong possibility.

Karl stared down at the muzzle and gestured behind him again, this time with a sense of urgency to draw the man's attention. "Quick, come here." He hoped the man did not have hair-trigger nerves and a moment of confusion would play in his favor.

The guard stepped forward, lowering his weapon a fraction. Another step and another. He peeked around the stone fence, giving Karl his opening. In one swift move, he pushed the barrel end of the rifle toward the ground with one hand and struck the man in the Adam's apple with the other. The officer dropped to a knee and gasped for air, bringing a hand to his throat.

"I'm sorry about this, but you'll have a headache when you wake up," Karl said in English and hit the guard over the head with his pistol. He eased him down by the lapel of his uniform jacket before he could tumble to the dirt and create more of a ruckus.

Once outside the gate, they ducked off the main road, where an ambulance and other police cars were whizzing past, crossing the road at the corner. Other guards were positioned on this street, but Karl and Leo strolled slowly like tourists taking in the scenic waterfront area. Karl walked closest to the commotion to block Leo's cuffed hands from view. They spoke in English, talking about going to Copacabana Beach in the morning to enjoy the beautiful ladies in their swimsuits.

Karl stole enough glances to see a guard tracking them down the street with his stare. The man started toward them, speeding Karl's pulse. He did not want to hurt another officer but saw no other way. He brought his hand inside his coat flap, placing his palm on his pistol's butt. His breathing became ragged as he thought about the family the man might leave behind for merely being good at his job.

A barking dog ran loose down the road, and a man chased after it, calling the animal's name. The activity caught the guard's attention. This was their chance to get away cleanly.

Karl slipped down an alley, and Leo followed. They sprinted at top speed and veered left at the end of the building. Not hearing footsteps at their backs, Karl slowed to a jog. He would never admit it, but not having

The Secret War   III

run like this in years, he was feeling his age and sucking in too much air to compensate.

After another block, Karl turned onto a busy street and readied his keys. "My Ford." He got in, leaned over, and unlocked the passenger door.

Leo slid in and closed the door with his cuffed hands.

Karl drove, though not toward the old shack in the slums.

"Where are we going?" Leo asked.

"Somewhere safe. The favela is burned since you were followed to the bar there." Karl glanced at Leo as he tugged at his handcuffs. "Glove box."

Leo fumbled around inside, located a bobby pin, picked the lock, and removed his cuffs. "Thanks. That was uncomfortable."

A flicker of unease crept its way up Karl's neck. Leo certainly knew how to defeat a lock for a naval intelligence officer who spent his career behind a desk analyzing reports. Karl's experience with him at Eva's hostage exchange and the yacht had shown him that Leo was also skilled with weapons and explosives. It was well beyond the training he should have received as part of his job. That troubled sense said Leo needed watching, but deeper in Karl's gut was the sense Leo could be trusted.

As Karl weaved through town to ensure he was not followed, he could finally get some answers. "What happened back there?"

"Hattie and I were leaving and waiting for our car from the valet."

"Back it up a bit. You're in charge of the vice president's security. Why were you leaving?"

"VP Wallace is god-awful familiar with my background." Leo paused, and they briefly locked stares. "I assume Hattie told you about my father."

Karl nodded, keeping his eye on the road. "She did." He felt for the man. Leo had joined the navy to outrun the pain of it and the shame of being a murderer's son. Though Karl was innocent of having slain two federal agents during his escape from custody last year, the FBI and media had branded him a killer. Escaping that humiliation was something Leo and Hattie had in common.

"Well, after Hattie performed—"

"Wait. Hattie sang? How did that happen?"

"Eva happened. She heard from Sophia Garza that she and Hattie were initially supposed to perform tonight. But Wallace had said he wouldn't sit for the daughter of a traitor and murderer singing for him. Then Eva did what she does best."

Karl laughed, making a turn onto the main highway out of Rio. "Stir the pot by inviting Hattie to sing with her."

"Everyone loved the performance, but Wallace was a blowhard and insulted Hattie. I came to her defense and—"

"And Wallace told you two to leave." Imagining the barrage of verbal abuse Hattie must have taken because of him, Karl bit back his anger. He focused on the more pressing matter and glanced at Leo. "What's your take? Was the VP the target?"

Leo cocked his head. "Why would you think otherwise?"

"It's too coincidental that hours after Jimmy agreed to get a message to the Professor, he was shot. He could have been the objective, eliminated to keep me and the lists in Rio."

"You have a point, but I think this was about our trip to Natal. We're on the verge of signing an agreement with Brazil to build a navy base there. If the vice president was killed here, our deal could be set back for years. I'd bet my bottom dollar that Strom Wagner is behind this. Whoever he sent missed."

"There were two gunshots," Karl said. "Both could have been the focus."

"Maybe," Leo said.

They focused on the road in silence after that while Karl drove to his new jungle hideout.

When the patrol car door shut for the second time, Hattie was sure her father and Leo had made their escape. She held Eva as she lay prone on the ground and fanned her face with a hand. A doctor had come forward through the crowd around them and checked Eva's pulse. President Garza and his wife looked on with concern.

The ambulance arrived and took Jimmy Cooke's body away. Meanwhile, the doctor gave Eva some water, asked several questions, and had her follow his finger across her field of vision.

The Secret War

"I'm fine, Doctor," Eva said. "I didn't eat enough tonight, and seeing all that blood made me a little lightheaded."

"Let's see if you can stand." The doctor offered his hand and helped Eva to her feet.

Eva stood and sipped more water. "I'm feeling much better. The dizzy spell has passed."

The doctor retreated to his female companion, and the surrounding crowd thinned.

Sophia came over. "You must be exhausted after that incredible performance."

"I am," Eva said.

Several shouts came from the area around the patrol car. Inspector Silva rushed over and spoke to two officers, waving his hands like a madman. After pacing back and forth and rubbing his hair enough to make himself bald, he returned to the steps and the police chief.

Silva palmed the back of his neck. "It seems our suspect has escaped, sir."

The chief inhaled deeply and narrowed his eyes. "Then it seems you'll be up all night looking for him. I suggest you start."

"Yes, sir." Silva slinked off toward his vehicle.

Hattie put her arm around Eva's shoulder. "This has been a long night, Mother. Let's get you home and into bed."

"Yes, please do," Sophia said. She waved to a valet and had him bring up Eva's sedan. While they waited, she fussed over Eva, who put on a good act of still being weak.

"I'm fine," Eva said as her car arrived. She kissed Sophia on the cheek, got in the passenger seat, and rolled down the window. "We'll have coffee soon."

Hattie got in, adjusted the seat and mirror, and drove slowly along the curved driveway. Once outside the gate and on the main road, she turned to Eva. "Nicely played, Mother. You deserve an award for that performance."

"I thought fainting in your arms was a nice touch." Eva laughed briefly before turning serious. "I assume Leo had help with his escape."

"Yes, Father was there tonight." Hattie glanced at her mother.

Eva's expression went blank. "Tell me he wasn't involved with the shooting."

"No, he wasn't, but he knew the man who was killed. Leo, Father, and I met with him earlier in the evening." Hattie looked in her mirrors and thought a car might have been trailing them. She turned at the next block.

"Do I want to know why?" Eva asked.

"You might, but telling you is up to Father."

Eva looked at the passing streets. "Where are we going?"

"Somewhere safe."

Hattie drove around Rio until she was sure no one was following them. She was certain her father would not have gone to his favela shack. It was not safe there. She turned onto the highway going north out of town. Once on the dirt road, she slowed down when her father's cabin came into view, doused the car's headlights, and parked near the front steps. A light was on inside the house, but Karl's car was not there. He typically hid it around back out of view.

"What is this place?" Eva asked, surveying the area through the windshield.

"It's Father's."

"This is where you've been coming for the last few months?"

"Yes."

"Do I want to know what you've been doing here?"

Hattie thought about the skills her father taught her here to become as good a spy as him. While they were all important and made her more confident in situations like the one she now found herself in, she had also relished the time with him. "No, but it was time well spent. I've really gotten to know Father."

They got out of the car and ascended the steps. The front door opened before she could knock.

"I knew you'd come here," Hattie said.

"I did, too." Karl stepped aside, allowing Hattie and Eva to enter. He whispered to Hattie in the doorway, "Your mother?"

"After that award-winning diversion, she deserves answers." Hattie stepped past him.

"This should be interesting." Karl closed the door.

The Secret War   115

Leo got up from the couch and looked relieved Hattie had arrived. Eva was another story. She wiped a finger across the coffee table, assessing the level of dust, and placed a handkerchief from her purse on the cushion before joining Leo.

"I know you didn't shoot that man." Eva patted Leo's knee. "But escaping makes you look guilty."

"Inspector Silva doesn't exactly inspire confidence in his ability to unearth the truth," Leo said.

"Point taken," Eva said, "but what do you plan to do?"

"Karl and I believe that Strom Wagner is behind this. I trust the people in this room to help find him and clear my name."

Eva drifted her stare toward Karl. "So this has nothing to do with the meeting the three of you had with that poor man earlier tonight?"

Karl gave Hattie the side-eye before turning back to Eva. "It could be."

"Why did you meet the vice president's aide?" Eva asked.

Karl sighed. "He was Victoria's son."

Eva pursed her lips. "I'm sorry to hear that. A mother should never lose a child. I have to ask. Why would someone want to shoot him after he spoke with you?"

"To stop him from getting a message to her to get me and those lists back to the States."

"Who is she to you?" Eva asked. "Obviously, she's not simply a colleague."

Karl explained how they met at the Cipher Bureau. That when the State Department shuttered its piece of the operation, she recruited him into Army Intelligence and trained him to follow in her footsteps.

Eva harrumphed. "I knew there was a reason I never liked her. She got you into this mess."

"She didn't hold a gun to my head," Karl said. "I signed up for this life because it was the right thing to do."

Eva glanced at her before turning back to Karl. "The FBI held a virtual gun to Hattie's head, and now you're dragging her deeper into this life you love so much." She closed her eyes, shaking her head.

"No one is holding anything to my head to help Leo, Mother." Hattie sat next to Eva on the couch. "Helping him is the right thing to do. I won't turn my back on a friend in need."

"I worry about you, sweetheart." Eva squeezed Hattie's hand. "I know firsthand how dangerous these people are."

"And Father has trained me well." Hattie turned to Leo. "I'll start by talking to Agent Knight. He might have a bead on how to locate Wagner."

"We have to find out if Inspector Silva has found any witnesses who might have seen the shooter," Leo said. "Besides exonerating me, a witness could lead us to Wagner."

"I can help with that." Eva briefly placed a hand on his leg.

"I thought you wanted to steer clear of this life," Karl said.

Eva straightened her posture. "Like you both said. It's the right thing to do. I can call Sophia and ask for a meeting with Narcisco. He'll make sure Silva tells us anything we want to know."

"Thank you, Eva. I appreciate your help." Leo patted her hand and turned to Karl. "Now I know what you've been going through, being accused of betraying your country and a murder you didn't commit. It's maddening."

"Yes, it is," Karl said. "Which is why we'll all find out what really happened."

"Together," Eva said.

"Yes, together." Hattie was delighted at seeing her parents no longer at odds, and working toward the same goal.

14

The look of worry in Maya's eyes, while not entirely unwarranted considering the events of last evening, was misplaced. Hattie planned to meet with Agent Knight in an hour to ask for help, not gather intelligence from some suspected Nazi spy on his behalf.

"You shouldn't go alone." Maya folded her arms across her chest as her expression morphed into impatience. "It might not be safe."

"We're meeting at a public café. I'm sure it will be okay."

"A man you met with hours earlier was assassinated by a sniper inside a compound surrounded by security guards. That should teach you that nowhere is completely safe. I'm going with you, and that's final."

After getting ready and driving into town, Hattie and Maya got a street-side table at a café in the shopping district. The streets were bustling with wealthy locals and tourists from the northern hemisphere escaping their dreary cold weather. The restaurant was packed, and the wait staff hopped between tables, tending to the customers.

Hattie requested the spot against the wall for its location and orientation. No one could sneak up on her, which was a must. It was also near the last table for an easy escape, but not on the end, to make her and Maya less vulnerable to an attack from the street. She kept scanning the area and up and down the road, watching the people around her and keeping an eye out for Knight. No one stood out as suspicious, but one or two at the tables could have been one of his assets.

Maya sipped her coffee and spoke softly. "He's late. I think he does this on purpose to control you."

Hattie could not disagree. Agent Knight was late for nearly every meeting he arranged with her. She whispered back, "It's his way of letting me know who's in charge. That he can pull any string he wants."

"Why do you put up with it?"

"As long as he thinks I'm scared stiff of him, he won't look too hard for my father." Hattie shot up straighter in her seat. "He's here."

Knight approached their table and sat on the third chair. Hattie had removed the fourth, placing it several feet away to ensure he had his back to the street. If he turned his head to signal anyone at the other tables, she would know he had a plant in the crowd and could narrow down the suspects.

"You said it was urgent." He flipped over his coffee cup and waved over a server, who filled it and scurried away.

While he sweetened it to taste, Hattie said, "I'm guessing you know the vice president's aide was killed last night at President Garza's party. I was there."

"Yes, I read the dispatch from the US Embassy and the account in the newspaper. I know you were an unexpected part of the entertainment and that Leo Bell is a suspect and escaped custody."

"What didn't make the paper because of my mother's influence is that I was outside with Leo, waiting for his car when we heard the shots. He's being framed. I think the vice president was the target, and Wagner was behind the assassination attempt, just as he was in the yacht bombing. He's still trying to stop the United States from building a base in Natal."

"I'm sure you're right, and I'm sure you have no idea where Commander Bell is hiding." Knight leaned closer. "Or do you?"

"How would I know that? He escaped when I was with—"

Knight waved her off dismissively. "Yes, I have the report. A number of guests saw you with the president and vice president when Bell went missing. What do you want, Miss James?"

The Secret War 119

"If we can prove Wagner was behind the shooting, we can clear Leo. Do you know where Wagner is or how we can locate him?"

"If I knew that, I wouldn't have you talking up every suspected Nazi who waltzes into the Golden Room."

Frustration built. The FBI had turned Hattie's life upside down, all in search of an innocent man, and she had had enough of Knight's manipulations. "I have done everything you and Agent Butler asked. My father is very good at hiding and doesn't want to be found. Perhaps he's not even in Rio. If I can locate the women Baumann kidnapped and uncover a plot to assassinate the Brazilian president, maybe I can find Wagner. You have to know something. Give me somewhere to start."

"Okay, Miss James." Knight leaned back in his chair and looked to his right, Hattie's clue that his plant was seated in that direction. "Rio is still the primary transit point for Nazi spies in the country. Since Baumann's plantation is no longer an option, we believe Wagner set up a safe house in the city. We've tracked a few people coming off fishing boats, but every tail I put on a suspect loses them."

"That's because you send amateurs, and you're not very good at it. I am, however."

"Which begs the question why you find the need to evade me."

"Because it's fun." Hattie formed a self-satisfied half grin. "Do you know what part of town this safe house is?"

"Somewhere in or around the Santa Teresa neighborhood."

"That's a start, but you can do better, Agent Knight."

"There's still one missing engineer from Berlin. This one designs planes. He disappeared after the two brothers, so I'm guessing he'll pop up in Rio tonight."

"Now that's something."

～

Hattie did not bother to lose the tail Knight had following her from the café. Her and Maya's next stop was at the Itamaraty Palace to speak with the president's chief of staff. She pulled up to the guard shack at the palace's reserved parking lot. An armed police officer came out, and she rolled down the window.

"Hattie James to meet with Cesar Tavares," she said in Portuguese.

The sentry consulted a sheet of paper on his clipboard. "Yes, Miss James. Miss Machado is already here." He directed her to park in a specific slot and told her to use the president's private entrance, where a man would meet her and take her upstairs.

"May my friend come inside with me?"

"Of course, Miss James. Give her name to the aide."

After pulling in next to Eva's coupe, Hattie and Maya ascended the steps and were met by a young man in a dark suit. He introduced himself and asked them to follow him to the presidential suite. The special treatment— reserved parking and the private escort—made Hattie feel like royalty.

Once up a flight of stairs, they passed an ornate set of double doors marking the president's personal office and continued to the neighboring one. The aide opened the door, revealing a woman sitting at a desk in an outer waiting room.

The woman looked up and spoke in Portuguese. "Please go right in. They are waiting for you, Miss James."

Hattie gestured for Maya to lead the way without asking permission. She followed her inside and discovered Eva in a guest chair in front of the desk. Mr. Tavares sat behind it, wiping the sweat beads from his forehead with a handkerchief.

A memory surfaced of the first time Hattie met Tavares in the police station after she was detained following the failed yacht bombing. He had secured her release. During the drive to the hospital to check on David and her father, who had been shot, Eva's relentless flirting had made the man as nervous as a cat. He had that same terrified expression today.

Inspector Silva was in a seat next to Eva.

Tavares stood and circled his desk. "Welcome, Miss James." He brought up a fourth chair for Maya. "I wasn't expecting another guest. Please sit."

"Mother." Hattie hugged Eva before sitting.

"Sweetheart, I've been having a lovely conversation with Cesar and Inspector Silva."

"That's wonderful." Hattie made no attempt to hide her sarcasm and acknowledged Silva with a forced smile before turning to Tavares. "Thank you for meeting with us."

"I understand you have some information about last night's shooting," Tavares said.

"Despite Commander Bell's escape, I can confirm his innocence. I'm certain the tragic event is connected to the assassination attempt on President Garza and that Strom Wagner from the German Embassy is behind it. I know Eva filled you in on her harrowing kidnapping by the Nazis. That's how desperate Wagner was to prevent the US from building a naval base in Natal. I firmly believe the attempt on Vice President Wallace's life was another try to stop that agreement."

"You make a sound argument, Miss James, but until Commander Bell turns himself in, he remains our prime suspect," Silva said in a smug tone.

"I see you're still not interested in the truth, Inspector Silva, which is why I asked for this meeting here, not at police headquarters."

"The truth, Miss James, is that the shell casing and gun found next to Commander Bell is the same caliber taken out of the victim."

"And what about the other pistol he had on him?" Hattie shifted in her seat, thankful they were on neutral turf where Silva could not easily dismiss her concerns like he had done every time she met with him.

"We have that too."

"What is the logic of Commander Bell having two firearms on him, one American and one German-made? The German weapon belongs to the shooter."

"Unless we can find a witness to corroborate your story about Bell, he remains our suspect," Silva said. "Even if he's cleared, the man must still answer for his escape."

"Who have you questioned? Valets had gone out to retrieve Commander Bell's car and the vice president's limo. I'm sure one of them saw Leo before the first shot."

"We are still interviewing. Two attendants and several guests had left by the time we got there, so we're tracking down their names."

"Why do I get the feeling you're dragging your feet, hoping for Leo's quick conviction to redeem yourself? You blame me for making you look like a fool for not finding those missing women."

Maya and Eva struggled to hold back grins as Silva shifted uncomfortably on his chair.

"Yes, well," Tavares said. "It seems the investigation is still in its early stages."

"Cesar, I'd appreciate an update from you soon," Eva said. "I can't stress how important this is to us."

"Of course, Miss Machado. President Garza provided specific instructions to accommodate you in any way we can." Tavares focused on Silva. "I'll expect a daily report on my desk by five each evening."

"Well." Silva harrumphed and stood. "I better return to the case." He turned and walked out.

Walking toward their cars, Eva laughed. "Putting Silva in his place was magnificent, sweetheart."

"He deserved every scathing word," Maya said with a satisfied grin.

Hattie returned Maya's smile before facing Eva. "Thanks for arranging this, Mother. I hope this was enough to get Silva to do his job this time. I need to update Father. Can you take Maya home?"

"You can't get rid of me that easily." Eva adjusted her purse over her shoulder. "I'm invested now, and I'm coming with you."

"Me too," Maya said. This was the first time since the yacht incident that she'd wanted anything to do with Karl outside of dinner.

Baby steps, Hattie thought. One day, they would all be a family. "Okay, but first, we'll need to drop off Mother's car somewhere."

15

Hattie drove with Maya to the market nearest to Eva's house, where Eva left her coupe in the parking lot. Once Eva hopped in the other car and they were on the road again, Hattie started her evasive maneuvers, working to shake Agent Knight's and anyone else's tail. After pulling from the lot into traffic, it took Hattie less than a minute and four lane changes to spot the vehicle trailing them. The inertia from her first abrupt turn forced Eva against the door.

"What are you doing, sweetheart? Slow down," Eva said.

Hattie had gotten a good look at the driver right before the move. "Knight is following us. I need to lose him."

Maya remained quiet in the back seat. After each direction change, Hattie glanced at her in the rearview mirror, and Maya appeared unworried. If Hattie had to label the look on her face, she would call it impressed. That gave her a real charge, making her more focused on dodging the green sedan two cars back. She made her way to the steep hills of the Santa Teresa neighborhood.

"Now it gets fun." Hattie grinned, shifted gears as she crested a hill, and completed a sharp turn. She avoided a pedestrian without putting a scratch on Maya's sedan but drew whimpers from Eva, who had clutched onto the door handle for protection. A glance in the mirror confirmed Maya was still enjoying the ride.

Knight was not so lucky. He clipped the fender of a parked automobile before straightening his wheel but continued, earning angry shouts from a man on the street.

Hattie snickered. She had cost Knight hundreds of dollars in repair bills in recent months. After another quick turn, she entered a narrow, winding alley. Walls of weather-stained bricks whizzed past the windows faster as she floored the accelerator pedal. Eva stiffened her posture and covered her face with both palms.

"It's all right, Mother. I've done this dozens of times."

"In my car?" Eva croaked, peeking through her splayed fingers. "I better rethink lending it to you."

"I'm a careful driver." Hattie pursed her lips at the insult, shifting gears again as they neared the end of the alley. Knight had lost some distance between the buildings, as he always did. She thought he would have put in more practice at this point.

Emerging without stopping for cross-traffic was always the tricky part. It required skill and a good amount of luck to avoid confirming Eva's evaluation of her driving by collecting dents. She trusted her track record and blew into the lane while banking right.

A horn sounded, and an oncoming vehicle screeched its wheels, but Hattie shifted again and increased her speed. A loud crash of metal hitting metal came from behind. Glancing in the rearview, she confirmed Knight had collided with another car, and his sedan had been transformed into a steaming wreck.

Hattie drove straight for another two blocks and turned. No one was following them.

"Sweet Jesus," Eva mumbled.

Maya laughed from the back. "You've been practicing."

"A little." Hattie winked at her in the mirror and continued north out of town.

Soon, they were on the dirt road toward Karl's cabin, heading deep into the rainforest. The noon sun broke through the canopy several times before the jungle opened to a familiar clearing. No cars were out front like last

The Secret War 125

night, and there were no signs that anyone was inside. She reached under her seat, pulled out her hidden Baby Browning, and slipped it into her handbag.

They got out, and as they climbed the wooden steps to the porch, the recognizable pop of a semi-automatic pistol firing through a silencer joined the screech of the toucans. The sound was subtle but jarring all the same. Hattie retrieved her weapon, turned off the safety with a quick push of her thumb, and gestured for Maya and Eva to return to the security of the sedan.

Worried expressions took over, but they did not look panicked as they secured the car doors with them inside.

Hattie removed her low heels and stepped lightly to minimize the noise as she circled the structure. A second pop prickled the hair on the back of her neck. Her senses heightened. Pebbles felt sharper beneath her feet. Lush foliage looked greener and smelled more earthy. Toucans sounded closer than they did a moment ago.

Peeking around the corner, she knew what should have been there. There was a pile of wood for the stove and a fallen tree for target practice. The rain barrel was by the back door for washing clothes, and the outhouse was at the edge of the clearing. Karl's sedan was there. Everything was in place, with two additions. Karl and Leo were on the log, reloading their pistols.

Hattie lowered hers and stepped out. "You're getting soft, Father. If I were the enemy, you'd be dead."

Karl laughed. "The birds in the trees announced your arrival minutes ago. After we saw your car in the clearing, we returned to our fun."

Hattie rolled her eyes. "Of course you did. I better get Mother and Maya."

"Maya's here, too?" Karl's tone was more than questioning her. He doubted her judgment for bringing Maya here, and it hurt. But she thought he might have done so for Leo's sake. She had yet to welcome Leo completely into her inner circle by revealing her relationship with Maya. However, Maya had helped rescue Eva from the Nazis and foil the yacht bombing and opened her home to Leo during the ordeal. He had to know how much Hattie trusted her even though he was unaware she loved her. So, Hattie was back to being hurt. Her father *was* questioning her.

"Of course I would bring her." Hattie added a bit of sharpness to her reply. "After everything we've been through, she's family."

Karl offered a contrite nod. "I can't disagree."

Hattie turned on her heel and retraced her steps to the car. Maya gripped the steering wheel, twisting it hard enough to rip its molding if she continued. Eva rubbed her hands together, a sign that she was upset. The last time Hattie found her mother doing this, Eva had learned Hattie and Maya were lovers. She could tell her mother was worried her life was about to spin like a top again.

As Hattie walked closer, her eyes met Maya's, and Maya crumpled in relief. Eva did, too.

She waved them over when she got to the porch. They got out quickly.

Eva was the first to her and gave her a brief but firm hug. "You had me frightened, sweetheart."

"Father and Leo were having target practice out back. They're waiting for us inside." Hattie turned to Maya.

"Next time, don't go alone," Maya said. "Take me with you." She spun Hattie around and pulled her into a long, tight embrace filled with profound relief.

A moment later, the front door opened, forcing them apart. Hattie looked up, and Leo was in the doorway but said nothing before returning inside.

"I know, and I will," Hattie said. "Let's go in."

She led them to the main room, where Leo was filling glasses with water from a pitcher, and her father was placing a fresh towel on the cushion for Eva.

"I dusted for you, Eva," Karl said.

"He means I dusted, and he picked up." Leo laughed.

Eva sat and blushed. "Thank you, but you didn't have to."

Leo placed the drinks on the table in front of the couch. "Yes, he did."

Karl gave him a side-eye and focused on Eva. "You were right last night. The place was a mess."

Hattie and Maya joined Eva on the couch while the men brought out folding chairs.

"We came from a meeting with Narcisco's chief of staff and that dreadful man, Inspector Silva," Eva said. "Cesar has agreed to update me regularly on the investigation." She turned to Leo. "I'm sorry, but you're still their prime suspect."

"I expected as much when I escaped."

"I did learn," Hattie said, "that two valets and several guests left before the police could interview them. Any of them could be the shooter, but I'm betting one of the missing attendants saw something and might be afraid to talk."

"You might be right," Karl said.

"I know a valet who worked there last night. I'll speak to him before my show tonight."

"What about Knight?" Leo asked. "Did you meet with him?"

"I did. He agrees Wagner is likely behind the assassination attempt, but he still doesn't know where he's at. Since Baumann's plantation is no longer available, he thinks Wagner set up a safe house in Rio to ferry through people they smuggle into the country."

"That makes sense," Karl said. "It would need to be gated and well guarded. There aren't too many neighborhoods in Rio fitting that bill."

"They've tracked a few people from the docks, but they lose them in town."

Karl laughed. "You're right about Knight. He's not very good at surveillance."

Hattie grinned at the memory of dodging Knight on the way here. "Very much the amateur. However, he thinks the safe house is near Santa Teresa."

"That gives us a starting point."

"He also said that there's one more engineer from Berlin who disappeared two days after the other two I chatted up the other night. If his calculations are correct, that guy should be smuggled in on a fishing boat tonight."

"This is good, Hattie," Karl said. "The engineer will lead us to the safe house, and the safe house will lead us to Wagner."

"We need to stake out that dock tonight," Leo said. "If we link Wagner to the shooting, I can come out of hiding."

"Not 'we,'" Karl said. "You can't chance being seen. I'll go. I've done it plenty of times."

"If you think I'm gonna sit here and dust the furniture again, you're a few sandwiches shy of a picnic. We both know surveillance and tracking is a two-man job. You'll need backup since Hattie and Maya will be at the club, so I'm coming. And that's that."

"There's no talking you out of this, is there?" Karl sprouted a grin, his tell that he already knew the answer. Leo would work this op with him.

"Not on your life."

"I doubt this guy will go directly to the safe house," Hattie said. "If he received the same instructions as the first two, odds are he'll come to the Copacabana Hotel and be picked up later." She directed her attention to Maya. "If he does, can you get him a free ticket to my show?"

"Sure, but I'll need to know when he comes to the hotel." Maya turned to Karl and Leo. "I'll stay at the hostess station and check the registration desk every fifteen minutes until you give me the word."

"That will work," Karl said.

"After my performance," Hattie said, "I'll visit his table and chat him up."

"What if he wants to take the conversation to his room as so many men want from us?" Eva shook her head, a caution born from experience.

"I accommodate him."

"And what if he wants to take it to the bed?" Eva pressed.

"I won't let it get that far."

"You can't be sure."

"I can handle myself, Mother. You'd be surprised what I've learned in the last six months."

Eva snapped her stare at Karl and gave him the evil eye.

He shrugged. "She can take care of herself."

"It's too dangerous, Hattie." Maya pursed her lips. "I don't care how many self-defense techniques you know. If a strong man lands one good punch, he will overpower you." Her voice went to a fraction above a whisper. "Make you helpless."

The Secret War   129

"If he moves it up to the room," Karl said, "we can be right outside the door, seconds away."

Maya locked eyes with him in a hard, experience-filled stare. "Seconds is all it takes."

Hattie swallowed the emotion growing in her throat. When Hattie first saw Maya at the Halo Club last year, she easily handled an unruly customer by using leverage on his thumb. The strength and confidence displayed in that one maneuver were incredibly sexy. Hattie thought Maya had developed the ability to handle herself to keep the peace in her establishment and customers safe. However, her comments made Hattie believe it was out of something much more personal.

"Let's get in a little more training. Maya, you run Hattie through her paces." Karl wagged his thumb at Leo. "This one still pulls his shots to the left with the silencer."

"An inch, Karl. A whole inch." Leo rolled his eyes.

Hattie laughed, enjoying the playfulness between these two.

"Is your pantry stocked?" Eva stood at Karl's nod. "I'll make us lunch while the rest of you prepare to put my daughter in harm's way." She walked into the kitchen with her chin held high, a sign that she was incensed.

Karl sighed and stepped toward her. "Eva."

Hattie tugged him to a stop. "I'll talk to her. Show Maya the techniques you've taught me. I'll be right behind you." She turned to Maya. "You'll see I'm ready for this."

Once the others were outside, Hattie joined her mother at the counter. Eva had already dug out some rice to boil and was slicing vegetables to cook.

Hattie leaned her bottom against the lower cabinet, crossing her arms across her chest. "You're angry."

"Can you blame me? Haven't you been in enough danger between Heinz Baumann and Frederick Ziegler? Now, with Strom Wagner and these engineers, it seems you're looking for more."

"I don't welcome it, but trouble has found us. I believe Father when he tells me this all has to do with setting the playing field to the Nazis' advantage. They want to drag the United States into the war before the Americans are ready. It will be a long, bloody one we can't win unless we have a foothold in the Atlantic to strangle Germany's import of materials to continue their aggression."

Eva peeled a potato with the speed of a machine gun.

Hattie briefly touched Eva's arm to slow her down and continued. "Wagner is hell-bent on stopping an American navy base from being built. Father fears he already has a backup plan in motion in case he fails, and it concerns those aeronautical engineers. They are building something in the jungle that could determine the war's outcome. If I can prevent that by flirting with a Nazi tonight, I will. And if doing so helps clear Leo's name, all the better."

Eva stopped and stared at the mess of potato peelings. "You're so much like your father when he was your age, ready to do what was righteous. I presume that's why he became a spy."

"I suppose so, but spending time with him here for the last few months has shown me more of the man. I can tell you that the things he's had to do, the sacrifices he was forced to make, have hardened him. He is still loyal to his country, but he will move heaven and earth to do what is right for his family."

"You're speaking of the deaths at Baumann's plantation," Eva said.

"Yes, and more. I'm the same way." Hattie paused when Eva looked up at that comment as if looking for more explanation. However, this was not the time to detail the Nazi they shot the other day. "He and I will go to any length to protect the family, including Leo and Maya."

"But not David?" Eva cocked her head at the probing question.

"The jury still is out on him."

"Why?"

There was no better time to tell all to her mother. Hattie went on to explain about finding the logbook in the trunk after handing it over to Agent Butler and suspecting that he was killed for it.

"And you think David did it for some sinister reason," Eva said.

"Yes. Since you didn't do it, who else would have put it there?"

"Anyone who wants you to think he did."

"I thought the same thing. I finally asked David about it after discov-

The Secret War   131

ering it had moved this week. He knew about it but claimed he thought I had killed Butler and hid it there to protect Father."

"This is a mess. No wonder things have been strained with you two and why you didn't want him to come with you today."

"Until I figure out whether I can trust him, I need you to act normally around him."

"I think I can muster another performance." Eva patted her hand.

"That you can." Hattie's inner circle—Maya, her parents, and Leo—was growing stronger. She felt the energy when they were all together, and the trust between them was firming up.

16

Gunter and his brother had been at the airfield buried deep in the Brazilian jungle for thirty-six hours. They had slept for four of those and spent the rest addressing flaws in the schematics, which Reinhart Hoffman insisted was sound and required only minor tweaks. Hermann Göring's golden child of airplane design was either delusional or in denial. Whichever was the case, his mindset spelled doom for everyone involved.

Hoffman sat at his engineering table, poring over schematics, tables, and data collected from the previous test flights, comparing them against Gunter's and Ernst's calculations for the new modifications. His hair was unkempt from hours of pulling at it. He stabbed at his coffee mug again, bringing it to his lips, only to snap back and stare at its contents. His irritation surfaced with a loud grunt. He stomped to the percolator, refilled his cup, and marched back, gulping half the brew by the time he returned to his seat. The man was running on sugary, caffeinated fumes, on the verge of collapse.

There was no talking sense into Gunter's old rival. With the looming deadline only a week away, he and Ernst were on their own to solve the flaws until real help arrived tonight or tomorrow. Armand Klein was a friend and every bit as talented a designer as Hoffman. Privately, Gunter considered Klein better; Armand's arrogance was the only reason he was not Göring's favorite. The man rarely took no for an answer and did not know when to hold his tongue when faced with criticism. If not for his genius and ability to see things more quickly than he and Ernst could, Gunter would have written him off years ago.

Two hours after he and his brother started reviewing the designs, they had isolated the problem to the wing, not the welds and bolts connecting it to the fuselage. It was simply too damn thick and long. The thickness was needed to accommodate the added fuel bladders essential for the extended trip, and the length was required for the larger engines to generate enough power to compensate for the increased load.

The laws of physics would not change. Longer wings created more stress and flexed more, especially under heavy aerodynamic loads like the requirement for the bombing run. Structural failure was a high probability. Short of designing an entirely different engine that was lighter and could produce the same amount of power, they would need to shorten the wings. This would increase their rigidity and ability to handle the pressure during the tight climbing turns more effectively. But Hoffman refused to listen.

Ernst had checked the calculations over and over for hours. He showed Hoffman yesterday that removing a two-meter section from the base of each wing would decrease the load by a quarter. However, Hoffmann insisted that space was needed for fuel storage for the return trip to the airfield. The mission required flying over enemy territory and that of unfriendly countries, so there was no opportunity to refuel.

"Herr Wagner might not care about getting those pilots home safely, but I do," Hoffman had said hours ago during the last tantrum that sent him to his corner.

"What about changing the parameters to fly on to Germany, not Brazil?" Gunter had replied. "That would shave over a thousand kilometers off the longest mission."

"Don't you think I've suggested that?" Hoffman had thrown his hand in the air in frustration. "Wagner said that's not possible. The planes are required to return to Brazil."

"What about staging the aircraft farther north? We could delay the mission and build a refueling field at Brazil's northern border."

"Again, that is impossible." Hoffman had slumped in his chair. "There simply isn't time. Wagner's order is that the mission must commence just after midnight on December 7th. Otherwise, the entire project is a failure. We would have had to start such an airfield months ago for it to be an option. So we must work with what we have. There has to be a way to stabilize the wings."

Gunter and Ernst had concentrated on the dilemma from a macro level, thereafter, not on the weak point where the wing and fuselage met, which was Hoffman's focus. They had looked at the issue as a problem of scale—how to get the extended wing to perform aerodynamically like a shorter one. Running the math over and over, they had adjusted the requirements for each weld and bolt length and width along the entire wing to increase its load capacity.

Welders and machinists had been working for the last eight hours, making the modifications, and should have been nearing completion. Gunter left his workstation and approached Hoffman, putting an arm around his shoulder. "Come on, Renny. Let's go to the hangar and check on the crew. We'll need to inspect every bolt and weld."

The three engineers retrieved their notes and prepared clipboards to mark off each inspected item as they went. As they stepped from the administration hut, the odor of aviation fuel was strong, but it was mixed with the smell of fresh rain on the tarmac and surrounding jungle. The tail end of the storm that had unloaded its fill of water during the lunch hour partially blocked the sun high in the late spring sky. The humid air had their clothes sticking to their bodies from sweat by the time they reached the hangar.

The absence of hammering and the sound of machinist tools was a good sign...hopefully. Half the crew was cleaning the equipment, and the others were on a break at the bench, drinking water and smoking cigarettes. They all looked tired from working since dawn.

Hoffman waved over the foreman, who reported his men had made all the changes.

"Very good," Hoffman said. "Accompany us on the inspection."

The man's shoulders sagged, but he nodded.

A close examination revealed the work was impeccable. They had finished scrutinizing the left wing and were halfway done with the right when Wagner entered the hangar, demanding his daily update. Hoffman and Gunter broke away while Ernst and the foreman continued the examination. Hoffman detailed their new strategy of increasing the wings' stress capacity and explained they were now assessing the modifications.

Wagner appeared pleased with their progress. "Schedule a test flight for sunset. We are running out of time."

"I understand we're down to only one spare plane," Gunter said. "We should wait until Armand Klein arrives to check our work."

"I took you at your word when you assured me you were on the right track." Wagner drew back the flaps of his coat, exposing a holstered Luger on his side. He cocked his head and eyed him. "Have I misplaced my trust?"

The claws of fear grabbed hold, knotting Gunter's stomach into an acidic mess. "No, you haven't. Based on my knowledge and expertise, I stand by our collaboration, but Berlin saw fit to bring in Armand. I agree with that decision. His mind operates like no other, and he spots things even the best of us might miss. I think it's prudent to wait."

"That will mean another day wasted. We're not scheduled to ferry him out here until tomorrow. But I suppose we can speed up the timeline and pick him up tonight." Wagner rubbed his chin. "Tell me, Mr. Kessler. Do you require Mr. Klein's keen eye for all the tests?"

"I think—" Gunter started.

Hoffman cut him off. "No. I would want his assessment before we conduct the mission's maximum stress test."

"Then, until he arrives, you can run the others," Wagner said. "Set it up for sunset. I'll arrange to have Mr. Klein brought here by sunrise."

"Excellent, sir. I'll see to it." Hoffman wiped the sweat from the back of his neck with a handkerchief as Wagner walked away. He was as nervous as a cat, and it was becoming contagious.

Gunter felt Wagner's cold, steely grip around his throat even as he disappeared through an office door. "What have you gotten us into, Renny? And why is the deadline fixed? What is happening on December 7th?"

"If you want to go home when this is over, don't ask questions, and work with the parameters you've been given."

Fear crept up Gunter's spine. "All right. Let's finish their examination and set up for the test flight."

Orange stripes had replaced the earlier rain clouds in the evening sky, and the oppressive humidity had dropped from fractional cooling. The plane passed inspection, was fueled, and rolled from the hangar. The pilots had changed into their flight suits and equipment and were in the midst of a lengthy, thorough examination of the wings.

Gunter appreciated their diligence. He was a student of aeronautics, an expert in the physics of flying and the mechanics of an aircraft, including its materials and propulsion systems. The scientific aspect was a constant. It was loyal like a dog. The right amount of lift, thrust, drag, and gravity would allow a plane of any size and weight to overcome gravitational pull and maintain controlled motion through the air. The only variable on his end was the mechanics. Flaws in the design or materials could result in tragedy. Gunter was sure they had addressed those deficiencies, but he would have been more comfortable with that stance with Armand Klein's confirming assessment.

The pilots, however, had no basis for such confidence. They were trained to operate what the designers and builders produced. In training and combat, they had to rely blindly on the soundness of their craft, but this bomber was a different animal. The design and construction in its current state were untested. Sitting in that pilot's chair took courage most men did not possess, including Gunter, despite his expertise and trust in the laws of physics.

On the other hand, Hoffman had visibly grown impatient with the pilots' attention to detail. His breathy sighs and toe-tapping had become irritating. "Come now, fellas. Let's hurry this along," he shouted.

"Let them be, Renny. They need to believe in her."

"They can believe on schedule."

"Do you want to get behind that yoke?"

Renny remained quiet.

"I thought so," Gunter jeered.

They filed into the operations room. Hoffman's assistant was ready with the radio. Ernst reviewed their design notes at a desk. Wagner was in a chair near the panoramic window facing the flight line.

Once the plane was in the air, it passed all the basic tests regarding speed, elevation, and gradual banking without a single issue. Hoffman moved on to the second phase, which increased the stress on the wings but came short of the maximum mission requirements. He and his associate appeared pleased, but Wagner seemed bored with the pilots' slow, deliberate methods. Gunter remained patient and in awe.

After entering the final higher-speed banking maneuver for this evening's test, the captain reported over the radio, "Minor vibrations but much improved."

A smile formed on Hoffman's lips as he signaled for his subordinate to relay their acknowledgment and to order the plane to return to base.

Wagner rose to his feet, buttoning his coat. "I'll send a runner to wake you when Mr. Klein arrives. Make sure the pilots get some rest."

"Yes, sir," Hoffman replied.

Once Wagner was gone, Hoffman opened a lower desk drawer and pulled out a bottle of premium aged whiskey and four tumblers. "This deserves a toast, gentlemen."

"I think it's a little premature for celebrations," Ernst said. "We still have one more test."

"Suit yourself, but I'm not letting this go to waste." Hoffman filled each cup with a generous pour. "I might not get another opportunity to savor this."

Ernst relented and picked up a drink along with Gunter and the assistant.

Hoffman put the bottle down and raised his glass. "I know we were never friends, but I always admired the work of the Kessler brothers. Here's to a successful collaboration."

"And to a flawless test later tonight," Gunter added.

He downed the amber liquid, expecting a harsh burn with a sharp alcohol bite, as had been his experience with cheaper whiskey. However, the initial warmth spread through his chest as the complex layers of flavors unfolded. The rich, smooth tastes lingered on his palate, leaving him with a deep appreciation for the craftsmanship behind each sip. It reminded him of the Führer's private plane, for which he and Ernst spearheaded structural modifications. Like this prized liquor, it was a well-earned luxury.

They indulged in one more drink before heading to the mess hall for dinner with the crewmen once they landed. The conversation was upbeat about the test results and the pilots' improved confidence in the aircraft.

"I felt a significant difference on this run," the captain said. "She handled beautifully in the turn, like I was in control, not the other way around."

"I have a good feeling about the improvements," Gunter said. "She should get you there and back."

"I hope so. The other pilots are getting antsy. They feel like it's a suicide mission or a one-way trip, and they'll have to ditch in the Gulf of Mexico or somewhere in Central America."

"Not here, Captain," Hoffman said.

The pilot had clearly revealed too much about his orders. He had likely assumed Gunter and Ernst had been fully briefed.

Now Gunter's curiosity was piqued. The ditching locations confirmed his suspicion of the target. The plane they were working on was designed to bomb the United States. He sat in silence for a moment, letting the significance of a strike of such magnitude sink in. If this mission was successful, the war was about to get bigger. A lot bigger.

17

Once the sun set behind the mountains and the sky darkened, Karl loaded the sedan with jackets and hats for them to wear in order to avoid being recognized. He added binoculars to observe from a distance, a jug of water and some bread for the potentially long night, and pistols and extra ammunition in case something went wrong. Standing by the car, he tried one more time to talk Leo out of coming, but the man was as stubborn as a mule.

"Clearing my name is one thing," Leo said, "but there's too much at stake. You said the Germans plan on attacking the United States on our soil. If there's even a remote possibility of that being true, we need to stop them."

"All right. Every cop in Rio is looking for you." Karl tossed him a fedora. "Hide that mug of yours."

Though Karl was accustomed to working alone, he had to admit he was relieved Leo had insisted on coming. His daughter would be at the center of this operation, and Karl could not leave anything to chance. More eyes and guns on the target were never a bad thing.

Driving through town with the streetlights all turned on, Karl carefully ensured they did not pick up a tail by checking his mirrors, changing lanes, and making frequent turns. Once satisfied they were not followed, he found a corner parking spot close enough to the docks for an easy getaway. Down the street, he recognized a familiar car. Before getting out, he used his binoculars to scan the area. After dark, the wharf mainly attracted fishermen cleaning up after a day on the ocean and wealthy boat owners taking a beautiful woman onto the bay for a romantic dinner. Anyone else would stand out.

"There you are." Karl spotted Agent Knight in the shadows near a closed store with a good view of the marina's only pedestrian gate.

"Who?" Leo asked.

Karl handed him the binoculars. "Tackle shop doorway."

Leo peered through the field glasses. "What's our play? He might help me, but we both know what he would do if he saw you."

"We need to put him on ice until morning. His car is down the street. By the time anyone finds him, we should be long gone."

"I can live with that." Leo tipped back his hat a fraction, exposing his face.

They got out of the sedan and devised a plan on the fly after grabbing some rope from the trunk. While Leo approached Knight from the front of the shop, Karl went around the side and came up behind the agent. They timed their arrival to coincide.

"Hi, Sam," Leo said.

"I figured you'd come after Hattie met with me today," Knight said. "You're hoping to clear your name."

"More than that. We both know something is up with those missing engineers. I have reason to believe the Germans are planning to attack the United States."

"My thoughts exactly," Knight said.

"Which is why I don't like having to do this."

Knight made a move like he was reaching for his service weapon, but Karl slammed his pistol against the back of his head, sending him to the ground. Knight's body was dead weight, and Karl feared he might have struck him too hard. True, he despised the man for dogging Hattie. Knight had forced her into the spy world by threatening to jail his other daughter, but Karl had only killed because he had to and never someone on his side.

He laid him on the concrete and checked for breathing by placing a hand on his chest. To his relief, it rose up and down. He grabbed Knight by one arm and lifted him until he could sling it over his neck. Leo did the same, and they carried Knight to his vehicle, his oxfords dragging along the asphalt path.

Leo patted Knight's pockets, located his car keys, and unlocked the trunk.

They tossed Knight inside it. Once they bound his hands and feet together, they stuffed a handkerchief into his mouth and tied a section of rope around his head to hold it in place. After placing the keys on the floorboard by the gas pedal, Karl led Leo across the street from the tackle shop. They climbed the metal stairs to the rooftop at the back of the building, the perfect perch for a stakeout.

They set up with an eye on the entire marina and the pedestrian gate. Karl hoped the target would show up in time to entice him to Hattie's show before it was over. Otherwise, they would have to wait another night. If that happened, they could miss their one opportunity to get information out of this man, find the safe house, and locate Wagner and whatever plane he was likely building.

After they agreed on shifts, Leo took the first and asked, "How do you know about the docks and this lookout spot?"

Karl unloaded the water bottle and the bread, placed the food atop his satchel, and started eating. "When I worked for Baumann at the plantation, I was assigned once to pick up a man at the Palace who was smuggled into Rio via U-boat. I got several useful bits of intel out of him while making him prove his identity. He was young, and he never realized I was working him. I learned a fishing boat had met the sub offshore and took him here. The fisherman told him to check into the hotel under a specific name and wait until contacted by one of Baumann's men."

"Very efficient," Leo said, staring through the binoculars. "Do you think someone at the Palace is working for the Nazis?"

"I'm not sure. The process could have been carried out without an insider at the hotel."

"Interesting. What about this lookout spot?"

"Baumann had me doing surveillance here a few times. Another SS agent suggested this was a good location to watch and go undetected. He was right. This is unobstructed high ground, the ledge provides great concealment and cover, and there are two egress points."

Leo released a soft breath. "Got to hand it to the Nazis. They're excellent tacticians."

And so was Leo. Karl could tell he had been holding back during target practice and was more skilled than he had let on. When asked, Leo had claimed he had done a lot of hunting while growing up in Texas. Karl had assumed as much after learning his background, but that only explained his rifle expertise. Leo's skill with handguns and explosives suggested he had had expert instruction.

Leo did not wear an academy ring, so he must have been a college man and got his commission through the Naval Reserve Officer Training Corps. Karl was familiar with the curriculum, and it did not include courses beyond basic knowledge. Neither did the Naval Intelligence School for an analyst, as Leo claimed to be. There was more to Commander Leo Bell than he let the world see, but something in Karl's gut still told him Leo was a standup guy. That he was precisely the type of man Karl wanted to watch his back in a firefight.

"Yes, they are," Karl said. "I spent enough time embedded with the SS to know to never underestimate them. Germany has leaders with brilliant, albeit sadistic minds, and their scientists and engineers are some of the most gifted on the globe. If we get into a war with them again, it will be one of attrition. We will have to choke off their supplies to negate their technological advantage."

"You've thought this through," Leo said, maintaining his watch of the marina. "I've come to the same conclusion." He asked for a drink of water. After sipping it, he asked, "So when should this guy be brought in?"

"Anytime from sunset to sunrise," Karl said.

"This could be a long night."

"Not as long as you might think. The fishing boat isn't in its slip. Look about halfway down on the right."

Leo shifted and angled the binoculars. "Got it. One empty slot."

"The captain receives a coded radio message and leaves about an hour in advance of the rendezvous time. He's gone, so the U-boat is already in the area. My guess is that he'll be here any time."

The Secret War 143

Leo pulled his stare away briefly to shake his head at Karl. "That's why you had me take the first watch."

"You're catching on quickly." Karl laughed.

Leo gave him a quick grin and returned to his task. For the next thirty minutes, they did not speak except for Leo's request for a drink and a chunk of bread to chew on. Karl kept his eye on the street, ensuring no one sneaked up on them.

"I got something." Leo straightened and went on high alert. "A boat has entered the marina."

Karl moved to the water side of the rooftop and asked for the binoculars. He focused the device and located the vessel motoring in. "That's him. We better reposition to the ground level."

It would take the vessel about ten minutes to motor to the slip and tie off, so Karl and Leo did not have to hurry. They picked up their area, leaving nothing behind to indicate someone had been on the roof, and climbed down the metal stairs to the street alley.

Agent Knight had been in an excellent position earlier. It offered a perfect view of the marina's pedestrian gate, but anyone lurking in the shadows under the awning would be hard to spot unless they moved. It also provided a direct route to their car down the street for a quick getaway. They set up in the same location and waited.

The boat's engine whined lower, signaling it was nearing its slip. It cut off and roared again for a few seconds, indicating the captain was lining up. The rumble stopped, leaving only the distant sound of city traffic and waves lapping against the docks.

Minutes later, footsteps on the wooden gangway slats announced someone approaching the paved area. Karl and Leo remained still, blending in with the darkness. Moments later, a white man dressed in a dark suit and homburg hat appeared through the pedestrian gate. The man's choice of hat was very telling. Similar to a fedora, it had a stiffer brim and was more formal in appearance—a sign the man was rich or of some status. He also carried an expensive-looking leather suitcase. A man who could afford such luxuries during wartime was privileged or had the ear of someone senior in the Nazi Party.

The man stopped at the curb and scanned left and right down the street as if searching for a coming car. *Interesting*, Karl thought. As far as he knew, the process of ferrying in smuggled passengers did not include being picked up directly from the marina. That would have been too dangerous. Anyone staking out this location could easily follow them and discover the next stop in the smuggling chain. Something had changed, and Karl wanted to know why.

The man waited for a while, pacing up and down the sidewalk. Remaining still in the shadows had become more difficult with each passing minute. Karl's back had stiffened fifteen minutes in, making him realize he was getting too old for this line of work. When this was over and he cleared his name, he would officially retire from both his jobs with the State Department and military intelligence.

After another five minutes, the man crossed the street, walking in Karl and Leo's direction. Karl eased his hand to his jacket opening, ready to pull his handgun. The man angled toward the building across from them, the one from where they staked out the marina from the rooftop. He went to the payphone on the corner, put in a few coins, and spoke slowly in English, presumably to the operator. His tone was heavily accented, making it obvious he was German. The conversation was hard to make out from that distance, but Karl distinctly heard the man say, "Taxi."

The man hung up the phone and retraced his steps to the pedestrian gate with his back toward Karl and Leo. Karl took the opportunity to slide across the front of the building, and Leo followed. Within moments, they were around the corner and out of view of their target. They walked at a fast pace but did not run, to avoid thumping their shoes against the pavement. In seconds, they were in Karl's sedan. This spot was on the route a cab would take to pick up a passenger at the gate and take him to the hotel, so they remained in the car.

Minutes later, headlights appeared a few blocks down. Karl and Leo leaned lower in their seats to avoid being seen in the bright beams. As the vehicle passed in the opposite direction, traveling toward the center of town, Karl confirmed it was a taxi. He fired up the engine and followed without turning on his lights, keeping his vehicle dark until the cab turned onto a main road with more traffic. After flicking on his lights, he stayed

The Secret War 145

back far enough to not be obvious he was tailing the cab but close enough to not lose it.

When the cab merged onto Avenida Atlantica, Karl knew they were headed to the Palace and chanced a bold move by passing them. If it continued past the hotel, which Karl doubted, he could zip back into traffic. However, he could not chance the engineer checking in before they could valet the car and signal Maya to get him a ticket to Hattie's show.

After Karl returned to the far-right lane a few cars ahead, Leo kept an eye on the taxi in the side mirror. The tricky part was next. Karl turned on his blinker, preparing to pull into the hotel's curved driveway. Traffic had thickened since he decided on his risky move. If he had to resume his tail, catching up might prove difficult.

Karl slowed, drifting into the turn lane. "Please tell me they're following."

"I'm not sure," Leo said, squinting to get a better look in the mirror.

Karl braked more and started his turn. "It's now or never."

"Wait, they're turning."

After blowing out a loud breath, Karl eased his car to the valet stand, where a young man greeted him and took his keys. He thanked and tipped the man and hurried inside with Leo without acknowledging the attendants opening the glass doors for them. There simply was no time for pleasantries. As Brazil's most wanted fugitive, Leo donned his cap to avoid being recognized.

The grand scale of the lobby always amazed Karl, especially the crystal chandelier hanging from the ceiling. The light it cast bounced off the exquisite marble floor to illuminate the entire space evenly.

Several elegantly dressed guests dotted the lobby. Men wore dark suits, a few wore tuxedos, and women wore fashionable dresses. Several matched their partner's tux accents with formal gowns made from delicate silk. The bulk of the foot traffic flowed toward the north end of the hotel, where the Golden Room was preparing its dinner service for Hattie's show. It would start in half an hour, so they would have to hurry to pull off this operation.

Karl scanned the interior, but Maya was nowhere to be found. She had said she would bounce between the lobby and her duties at the club's hostess station, and they had likely caught her at the other end of that cycle. He whispered to Leo, "Get Maya. I'll stay with the target."

Leo offered a confirming nod and walked swiftly among the slow-moving flow of guests.

Karl went to the seating area and chose a plush, velvety chair with an unobstructed view of the hotel's main doors and the registration desk. He did not like having his back unprotected, but such was planning on the fly. It came with a higher risk.

A minute later, the man entered through the double glass doors. He also ignored the helpful staff members at the entrance. However, he did not seem in a hurry, merely rude, and he carried himself with a hint of arrogance, which sparked a sense of uneasiness in Karl. Arrogant men—particularly privileged ones—did not understand the meaning of no, and the plan was for Hattie to butter him up and skim intelligence. This operation had just gotten dicier.

The man queued in the short line at the registration desk, placed his status-symbol suitcase on the floor, and looked about the room. If he had brought his gaze to eye level, Karl would have been concerned that he was on the lookout for someone suspicious following him. However, the man had angled his head upward as if inspecting the cavernous two-story-high room and the grandeur of the space. Karl did not look away. Doing so would have drawn the attention he hoped to avoid.

The line at the desk moved as clerks attended to the arriving guests, and Karl's patience was growing thin. The target was next, and their window of opportunity was closing.

Something touched Karl's shoulder, causing his muscles to stiffen. His vulnerable backside may have gotten him caught. He had been so focused on the target that he had not been scanning the area for FBI or Nazi agents who wanted him captured.

Whoever was behind him leaned lower to Karl's ear. "She's here," came the whisper in a voice he recognized as friendly. Leo sat beside him and added, "And she knows which one."

Karl relaxed and shifted his stare until he located Maya. She got the worker's attention at the registration desk from a distance and gestured toward the man at the head of the line. The clerk nodded. Thankfully, the

The Secret War

147

target was checking his pocket watch, and Maya's signal passed unnoticed.

The worker finished with his customer and called the next in line. The target walked up and spoke pleasantly at first. However, after a minute of the clerk sifting through a stack of papers, the target appeared agitated. He raised his voice loud enough to draw the curiosity of everyone in the lobby.

"Check again," he barked in English.

That was Maya's signal. Karl and Leo queued to hear the conversation as she approached the desk.

"I'm a manager in the hotel, sir," Maya said in English. "What seems to be the problem?"

"This dunce can't find my reservation."

"I'm sure it's simply a clerical error." Maya circled the counter and sidled up to the clerk. They talked briefly in Portuguese before Maya turned to the target. "I'm afraid several reservation slips were damaged in a water leak this afternoon."

The man was a textbook example of pompous arrogance. "The Aldon would never allow this level of incompetence. No wonder this is such a primitive country."

"I apologize for the inconvenience, sir, but I'm happy to upgrade your stay to a suite at no extra charge. I'm sure it will meet the standards of Berlin's finest hotel. I can also provide a complimentary dinner and a seat at tonight's Hattie James performance in the Golden Room."

"That's a tempting offer, but I won't occupy a corner in the back along the thoroughfare to the restroom."

"I'll personally seat you in the center with an excellent view of the stage. If you'd like, I can have Miss James stop by after the show, which starts in thirty minutes."

"I won't have time to take my bags to my room."

Maya waved over a porter. "I'll have your things brought up and send a warm, wet towel to your table so you can freshen up."

The target smoothed the flap of his jacket. "That will be acceptable."

After consulting the clerk, Maya returned to the public side of the registration desk. "Please follow me, sir."

Karl and Leo followed when she led the man from the lobby. Maya stopped at the hostess station, spoke to a server, and grabbed a leather-bound menu. She escorted the target to a table three rows back from the stage in the center, a premium location she had held aside for tonight's operation.

When Karl and Leo stepped up, the hostess said Miss Reyes had cleared them to enter. They headed to the bar, removed their hats, and sat along the short side at the end with a good view of the target. The room was nearly at capacity, with servers rushing between tables with trays of food and drinks. The hotel photographer was making her rounds, snapping posed pictures of the guests and handing them claim checks for the photos.

Maya stopped by several tables, speaking to the customers and nodding her approval. At one, she waved over a server who jotted something on her notepad before scurrying away. Maya walked to the back of the room and stepped up to the end of the bar near Karl and Leo.

"Room 234 under the name Franz Mueller." She then spoke to the bartender, telling him to send a bottle of champagne to the target's table on her tab.

Everything was in place. The ball was now in Hattie's court.

18

Tonight marked the first time Hattie and David would return to the stage since their Thursday night confrontation. Her meetings with Agent Knight, Cesar Tavares, and her father had kept her from seeing him until an hour before they had to leave for the show. Dinner with Eva was oddly quiet, but Hattie was relieved she had finally clued in her mother to her doubts about him. Having a second ally in the house who knew everything was reassuring.

David's mood was surly in the car to work, and his brief interaction with Hattie was brusque. He was still annoyed with her about the logbook and her lingering lack of trust.

"I need to know we're okay," Hattie said.

"Let's concentrate on tonight's show. We can talk later. Do you want any changes to the set?"

"No, the current lineup is fine for tonight. And, yes, we will discuss this. I don't like this tension between us."

"Maybe I should return to the States. I'm sure I can find work on the West Coast since you're the focus of the media frenzy, not me."

"Okay, wow." Hattie shifted uncomfortably in the front seat. His anger ran deeper than she had thought.

Part of her wanted to trust the friend who had had her back and saw the good in her when she could not. They had met when Hattie was still reeling after Helen Reed broke her heart. If not for a fortuitously placed fire escape, she would have fallen to her death in a drunken stupor. That had been her wake-up call, and meeting David in the recording studio the next day was a sign of needed change.

She could tell that first day, when he had eyed the male drummer, that he was like her, and they would make the ideal lavender couple. He had helped her through to sobriety, buoying her whenever she felt weak. If he had not been her friend, she doubted her career would have recovered. In fact, without his friendship, she might be in a casket six feet deep. All of that history, however, might not be enough to salvage their relationship now.

When they neared the Palace, she remembered Inspector Silva saying they had yet to track down and interview two valets from last night's party. What she had in mind was a long shot, but she had to try.

"Can you drop me off at the front of the hotel and park in my reserved spot? I need to talk to someone."

"Sure, why not? Another thing you're keeping from me."

Hattie sighed. "I want to speak to Javier. He was working at the event at the president's home last night, and I want to know if he saw anything. He's not the type to talk to the police, but he trusts me."

David glanced at her, briefly locking stares. His eyes said he appreciated the honesty. "Okay."

He turned into the driveway but kept in the through lane instead of lining up in the valet queue. Stopping even with the main door, he said. "I'll check on you a few minutes before we go on."

Hattie patted his hand and said in an earnest tone, "Thank you."

Once he drove away, she scanned the area for Javier. He was a short, unassuming man, so he never stood out. Not seeing him, she walked toward the attendant stand. Another staff member was there.

He took a second look when she approached. "Good evening, Miss James. How may I help you?" he asked in Portuguese.

"I'm looking for Javier," Hattie replied in kind. "Is he working tonight?"

"Yes, miss. He's pulling a car around and should return soon."

Hattie did not have much time to get ready for her show. "I need to ask him a question about my car. Could you tell him to come to my dressing room immediately?"

"Of course, Miss James."

Hattie entered the hotel through the double doors and thanked the porters for opening them. People dressed in expensive suits and gowns murmured in hushed conversations when she walked through the lobby. The star of Rio was in their midst. Despite several movements in her direction, she did not stop for autographs.

After passing the indoor café and walking the length of the long corridor, she came upon the Golden Room's entrance, where the hostess greeted her.

"Where is Miss Reyes?" Hattie asked.

"She was tending to a grumpy guest and went to the kitchen, I believe."

Hattie laughed. "Can you have tea and honey sent to my dressing room and ask Miss Reyes to see me before my show?"

"Yes, miss."

Hattie walked inside, knowing she would draw guests' attention and have to stop for some pictures. She glanced at the bar. At first, she did not see who she was looking for, but focusing on the shadows in the corner, she spotted her father and Leo. Karl gave her an affirming nod.

The operation was on.

Hattie made her way through the dining room, stopping three times for autographs and once for a photo. Getting the crowd excited before a performance typically resulted in more roaring applause, hoots, and hollers, so she did not mind this part of the job. However, tonight, she wondered which man sitting alone was the missing engineer and how much information she could draw from him.

Once behind the stage door, she passed the band members donning their bow ties and tuxedo jackets for the show. They greeted her with friendly hellos, and she thanked each one by name.

Finally in her dressing room, Hattie leaned her back against the door, thinking that between David's moodiness and buttering up the German, this could be a long night.

A knock startled her.

"Who is it?" she called out in English and sighed.

"It's Javier. You wanted to see me, Miss James." His voice and the possibility of helping Leo gave her a surge of energy.

She opened the door. "Please come in." He looked up and down the corridor, nervously clutching his valet cap. "It's okay, Javier." She pulled him in by his coat sleeve.

He kept his head down, clearly uncomfortable being there.

"I want to know if you were still at the event last night when the gunfire started."

He did not answer.

"You won't get in trouble, Javier. Why don't we sit?" She gestured for them to move to the couch. Once seated, she continued, "A dear friend of mine has been accused of shooting that man. I know for a fact that he didn't do it, but the police won't believe me unless someone else saw what happened. I'd hoped you might have seen something, but if you weren't there..."

"I was there, Miss James, but you can't tell my employers."

"I'm confused. Did you do something wrong?"

"You see, I was tired last night from taking extra shifts at the hotel. And when I was told to take my break, well, I took a key from the valet box and—"

"And you took a nap in a vehicle, right?"

"Yes, miss. That is forbidden. We're only allowed in the cars to move them back and forth. I swear that was the first time I've broken the rules."

"I understand, Javier, and I can't blame you. I promise not to say anything, but I need to know what you saw."

"I was woken by a gunshot. When I sat up, your friend, the navy man, came running. There was another shot, and a second man hit your friend over the head with something and ran away. I'm sorry I didn't get a good look at him."

"It's all right. What did you do next?"

"I got out, hid in the bushes until guests came out, and left with them. I feel bad that I didn't stay to talk to the police, but I was afraid of losing my jobs."

"Don't worry, Javier. No one has to know you were in the car, but I need you to tell Chief Inspector Silva at police headquarters what you told me.

The Secret War 153

You can tell them that you were wiping down the cars with a polish rag when you heard the shots, were afraid after you saw what happened, and ran."

He did not look convinced, and Hattie understood his reticence. Good-paying positions like his were difficult to come by in Rio, and he was rightly afraid of losing his.

"I know why you're scared, but do you remember I mentioned you should see me and Miss Reyes about an opportunity after the first of the year?"

"Yes, I do."

"This stays strictly between us, okay?"

He nodded.

"She and I have become business partners and are rebuilding the Halo Club. It will be a place of luxury and attract clientele like the Golden Room. I guarantee you and your wife Monica will have jobs there for as long as we own the place because we are family." Hattie clutched his hands and gave them a firm squeeze.

He offered a polite smile filled with gratitude. "Yes, Miss James. Tomorrow, I will tell the police what I know because we are family."

"Thank you, Javier." Hattie hugged him. Her attention was drawn to another knock on the door.

"Hattie," Maya's muffled voice came through the door. "I have your tea."

Javier's eyes got extra round. His body tensed. "I shouldn't be in here."

"It's all right. She won't mind." Hattie opened the door and let Maya in, who paused when her gaze drifted toward the couch. "Javier was just leaving."

He stood, went to the doorway, and stopped. "I'll see to it first thing in the morning, Miss James."

"Thank you, Javier." Once he left, Hattie closed the door and waited for Maya to put the tray on the coffee table. "I have good news." She relayed her discussion with Javier, omitting that he had been asleep inside the car. That part was his story to tell. "And he's going to see Silva tomorrow." She returned to the couch and prepared her tea.

"That's wonderful. Leo will be cleared soon and can come out of hiding." Maya sat beside her. "Did you see Karl and Leo at the bar?"

"I did." Hattie sipped her drink. The warm liquid and sweet honey coated her vocal cords.

"The engineer is here. I seated him in the center of the room and will point him out to you. I told him I'll have you stop by his table after your show."

"You're getting good at this sneaky stuff."

"I guess I am." Maya laughed. "I had him put in room 234. It's at the end of the hall facing the back near the stairwell, so we can set up right outside if he asks you to go to his room."

"What do you mean by 'we'?"

"You're nuts if you think I'm going to sit on my hands while you're in a hotel room with a man you just met. Or any man, for that matter. I'll be there with your father."

"I don't want—"

Maya placed her index finger over her lips. "No arguing. We're partners in every sense. You're not doing this without me."

"Okay." Hattie did not like the idea of Maya being in danger if something went wrong, but she supposed Maya felt the same way about her. Hattie would not fight it because it was how partners should treat one another equally in all things.

Half an hour later, Hattie stepped onto the stage after the band leader announced her name. She expected David to reach out his hand so she could grab it as she passed, but he remained focused on his piano. *Stubborn*, she thought. Hattie gave his shoulder a quick rub and continued to her mark at the microphone.

Hattie went through her set. Maya had disappeared for a while but returned halfway through. She spoke briefly to a man sitting alone at a table. When she left his company, she turned to the stage, locked gazes with Hattie, and nodded twice. Hattie was sure the man was their target. During the remainder of the show, she made eye contact with him three times to make a connection and possibly spark some hope in him.

After the last note was sung and the curtains closed, she and David walked down the backstage corridor. She said, "I need to visit a table. He's a suspected Nazi who Agent Knight is interested in, so I should butter him up by myself." That part was not a lie. She simply left out Leo's and her father's involvement.

"I get it. Does Maya know? I noticed her talking to a guy during the show. Was that him?"

"Yes, that's him. I need to change and get out there."

"All right. I'll be at the bar."

Damn, Hattie thought. David might see Leo and her father if he took his usual spot. She had to think of something fast to keep them as far apart as possible. "I'd like you a little closer tonight. Would you mind staying in the wings and keeping an eye on our table through the curtains?"

"That's actually a good idea. He won't know he's being watched."

"I'll see you out there." Hattie hoped her suggestion did not backfire.

After freshening up and changing into comfortable slacks, a blouse, and a pair of flats trendy enough for the Golden Room, Hattie emerged from the stage door. Patrons stopped her twice for autographs and photos before she reached the target's table.

"Good evening," Hattie said. The man stood, and she continued, "The club manager tells me you're a very important hotel guest and asked if I would stop by your table. Would you mind if I joined you?"

"Please do." He pulled out the other chair for her.

Hattie sat and looked at the cocktail glass of amber liquid on the table. "Can I buy you another drink?"

"No, but I'd love to offer you one." The man spoke with a heavy accent, suggesting he did not use English often. He waved over a server. "I'll take another Chivas, and Miss James will have...?" He looked at her with questioning eyes.

"My usual," Hattie said. Monica had served her in the club several times and knew her order meant tonic water garnished to resemble a cocktail.

"Of course, Miss James." Monica took off toward the bar.

Hattie turned to her tablemate and extended her hand. "Hattie James. And you are?"

"Armand Klein." He cringed as if he had misspoken, giving her the impression that he had given her his actual name, not the one he had been told to use.

"What brings you to Rio, Mr. Klein?"

"Work."

"What type of work?"

"I design airplanes and am here to consult on a project."

"I've always found it mindboggling that something so heavy can fly in the air."

"It's a matter of physics," Klein said.

Over the next hour and three drinks later, Hattie put on her best performance of the evening, pretending to enjoy the conversation, be half-drunk, and be attracted to him. Though he was easy on the eyes, he came across as pompous, which was the ultimate turnoff.

The crowd had thinned since Hattie sat with Klein, and she was growing anxious to get more information from him. He had been more guarded than the two brothers were a few days ago, but she thought maneuvering him into a more private environment might loosen his lips.

"The club will close soon," Hattie said, "but I'm not ready to call it a night. Are you?"

He adjusted his necktie like the conquering hero. "Would you like to join me for a nightcap in my room?"

"I would," Hattie said, hoping she would not come to regret those two words.

19

For the last hour, Karl worked hard to remain calm and appear unaffected on the outside while his daughter flirted, laughed, and drank with their target. The first two activities did not bother him as much as the imbibing did. Hattie had opened up to him about her drinking problem and how hard she struggled at times to maintain her sobriety. He suspected she had been served water and was an excellent actor at playing drunk, but a part of him worried that might not have been the case. It was always possible the server had messed up the order or that, despite his scrutiny, the target had put something in her drink like Baumann had.

The dwindling crowd meant the club would close soon. If Hattie had gotten information from him that would lead them to Wagner or the safe house, she would say goodbye and go backstage. However, if she failed, she would have to continue the operation in his hotel room. Perhaps Maya had had some luck while searching his luggage during the show.

Hattie stood, and so did the target.

"Come on, Hattie. Turn in the other direction," he mumbled softly. "Go back to your dressing room."

To Karl's dismay, Hattie let the man put his hand on the small of her back and guide her toward the club's entrance. "She can handle herself," he whispered and sighed. He hated going to Plan B but reminded himself that he had spent the last six months training Hattie so she would be prepared for such situations.

"I hope so," Leo said. He had been standing silently beside Karl until now. Saying something now meant he was as concerned as Karl.

They were climbing down from their stools and starting their tail when David entered the dining room through the stage door and made a beeline to Hattie. He was walking too fast to not be noticed. Karl and Leo continued, increasing their pace but not enough to create a spectacle.

Hattie and the target disappeared out the club door, and David followed...too closely. He was so close that it seemed he wanted the man to notice him, and Karl could think of only three explanations.

It was possible David was jealous and was intent on stopping Hattie from making a mistake with that man. That only made sense if David believed her romantic interests extended to include men. Karl supposed Hattie might have told him she was interested in both sexes to seem more like him, but that scenario was unlikely.

Or David could have been trying to perpetuate the public image that he and Hattie were a couple. It would have appeared odd to passersby if he had seen Hattie with the man and done nothing to intervene.

Another possibility was that David did not want the man telling Hattie what he knew. That was something Karl would never discount. During his years of experience in the covert world, he had learned to expect the unexpected. Considering that Baumann's logbook had surfaced and David was the primary suspect for its appearance, this supposition was not a giant leap. It also informed Karl that David needed more scrutiny.

Karl and Leo passed the hostess station and entered the wide corridor leading to the front of the hotel. David had slowed a fraction, but Karl caught up and grabbed him by the fabric of his jacket to slow him even more. David nearly stumbled, but Karl steadied him and shushed him with a finger to his lips before he could create a ruckus.

"You're too close," Karl said in a hushed tone. "Stay with us."

David looked at him and Leo and nodded.

They continued past the indoor café, blending into the crowd and keeping a reasonable distance between them and Hattie without losing

The Secret War 159

sight of her. Once they reached the lobby and saw Hattie heading toward the elevator, they peeled off and slipped into the stairwell. Karl and Leo sprinted up. David lagged behind, but Karl knew he still struggled a bit with his leg.

Upon reaching the second floor, Karl discovered Maya at the door, peering out the tiny glass window of the stairwell door leading to the hallway. "What are you doing here?" he asked.

"What do you think?" She gave him a look that said he could not talk her out of being there and dangled a hotel room key in front of his face.

Karl grabbed it and asked, "Did you find anything in his luggage?"

"A book written in German, but it appeared to be a novel. He had some papers, so I took pictures of them. I can develop the film when I get home."

David caught up. "Looks like I'm a little late to the party. What's going on? Where's Agent Knight?"

"He's tied up at the moment," Karl said.

David acknowledged Leo with a nod. "Who is this guy with Hattie? Why are you and Knight interested in him?"

"We think he can lead us to Wagner and, in the process, clear Leo from that shooting at the president's gala."

"Shh," Maya said. "The elevator is here."

She moved to the side with her back against the wall to make herself less visible through the window. Karl did the same.

Hattie's voice got louder, and so did her laugh. She sounded drunk.

"What was in her drinks?" Karl said in a muted tone.

"Water," Maya mouthed, placing an index finger to her lips.

Hattie and the man stopped at the last door in the hallway. They got quiet. He pulled the key from his pants pocket, opened the door, and went into the room. A light turned on.

Hattie glanced at the stairwell door, locked stares with Karl, and winked. He nodded, replying to her signal.

The target's hand appeared through the doorway. It was extended toward Hattie. She took it and disappeared inside.

The door shut.

Maya visibly gulped.

So did Karl. Until now, he had been confident Hattie could handle herself. He had taught her various techniques to extract information from a subject without getting into a compromising situation. However, here his beloved daughter was, behind a closed door with a man she had just met. It did not get riskier than this. If things got dicey, she would have to rely on her training. And with the possibility that her skills might not save her, that door between Hattie and Karl suddenly looked formidable.

Maya put her hand on the knob and pulled the stairwell door open a quarter of the way before Karl grabbed her hand and eased the door shut. He knew what he was about to say would sound strange to Leo, but urgency required it. He would deal with the fallout from violating Hattie's privacy later.

He spoke softly, "I know you want to be out there as much as I do, but you need to leave this to Leo and me."

Her chest heaved from the pressure of the situation. Karl knew how hard it was to put a person he loved in harm's way. Relying on someone else when Hattie's life might hang in the balance was something he knew he could never do. He was her father. He had brought her into this world, and it was his responsibility to protect her or die trying. That burden extended as well to Maya as Hattie's chosen life partner, and he would not endanger her either.

Karl clutched her by both arms. "Trust me."

Her jaw clenched, but she nodded. "Okay."

"Stay here with David." When he said those words, he realized he was glad Maya was there. He wanted someone to keep an eye on David and make sure he did not do anything stupid to jeopardize the operation. Having seen Maya in action at the old Halo Club with unruly customers, he was confident she could handle or slow him down.

Karl and Leo took a position outside the door to better hear what was happening in the room. If Hattie called for help or they heard a commotion inside, Karl would barge in using the room key, gun blazing.

There were voices—a good sign. If things escalated, he would know instantly.

Then...

Music started. It took him a moment to discern its origination since it drowned out the conversation in Hattie's room.

The Secret War 161

"It's never easy," he whispered. He and Leo returned to the stairwell and closed the door. Turning to Maya, he said, "There's a racket coming from the room next door. I can't hear. Can you handle it?"

"I'm on it." Maya straightened her posture, assuming her manager's look. She entered the corridor and knocked on the neighboring door loud enough to be heard over the radio. Moments later, the door opened. Karl could not see who answered, but Maya spoke to someone. "We've had a noise complaint, sir. I have to ask that you turn it down...Please don't make me call security."

The door to Hattie's room opened, and the target stuck his head into the hallway. The operation was falling apart quickly. Karl placed his hand on the butt of his pistol, ready to act.

"I'm happy to send up something from the kitchen for the inconvenience," Maya continued. "Thank you, sir. I'll have room service bring that right up." She turned toward Hattie's room without skipping a beat and walked to the door.

"What seems to be the problem?" the target asked.

"I apologize, Mr. Mueller. We had a noise complaint. The Palace prides itself on providing a pleasant experience."

"Thank you for your prompt attention. It's much appreciated."

"If there's anything we can do to make your stay more enjoyable, please don't hesitate to call the front desk."

"I won't."

When the door closed, Maya slumped her shoulders and went back to the stairwell. She blew out a breath of relief. "I think he bought it. I saw Hattie, and she looked fine."

"Great job, Maya." Karl rubbed her arms, thinking she would make a brilliant agent. She was calm and creative under pressure.

Karl gestured for Leo to follow him into the hallway but stopped when a server stepped off the elevator with a tray of drinks and continued toward Hattie's room. "Trouble," he said, waving Maya forward for a better view. "Who ordered those?"

"He did before he left the club," she whispered.

"Real?" Karl asked, meaning he wanted to know about Hattie's drink.

"Water. I made sure."

"I hope so."

The waiter knocked, announcing, "Room service."

The door opened. The target tossed a few coins on the tray, grabbed the glasses, and disappeared inside again. Karl waited impatiently for the elevator door to close and take the server away.

20

Hattie was relieved to hear Maya's voice at the door. That meant backup was steps away, so she could push Klein harder for information on why he was there and where he was going. She stepped near the dresser in line with the short hallway in the room and the open door. Klein blocked most of the view, but she saw a sliver of Maya's shoulder and head between him and the doorjamb.

"Thank you for your prompt attention. It's much appreciated," Klein said to Maya and shifted to close the door, revealing a better perspective of her.

"If there's anything we can do to make your stay more enjoyable, please don't hesitate to call the front desk." Maya looked past the man directly at Hattie for a brief second, but it was long enough for Hattie to communicate that she was fine and did not feel threatened.

"I won't." He closed the door.

Before he turned, Hattie fumbled with the room service menu on the dresser. "Who was that?" she asked as he approached.

"The manager handling the loud music next door."

"They're extremely efficient around here." Hattie spun on her heel, holding the menu. "How about a Cobb salad? I haven't eaten since this afternoon, and those drinks have gone to my head."

"How about some water?"

"You're very attentive." Hattie went to the couch. "Are you this way with your wife?"

"Who says I'm married?" He filled a glass from a pitcher on the dresser and brought it to her.

"Thank you." Hattie accepted the drink and pointed to the indentation on the man's empty finger. "Your wedding ring has left a mark."

"Does that bother you?" He removed his suit jacket and placed it over the chair beside the dresser.

"Not in the least." She crossed her legs and pretended to sip, remembering a hard-learned lesson—never eat or drink anything she or a trusted friend did not prepare. The last time she was careless, she ended up drugged as one of Baumann's animals and hunted for sport. "Tell me about home. You sound Dutch or German. Maybe Swiss."

"German, actually. You can't trust the Dutch to design an airworthy craft."

"I've heard the Germans are—"

A knock on the door drew Klein's attention. "What now?"

"Room service," a male voice announced through the door.

He raised an index finger. "Wait a minute. That's our cocktails from the club."

Hattie shifted uncomfortably on the couch. She could easily fake a single sip, but the target would expect her to imbibe with him. Tricking him into thinking she had would require creativity.

At the slam of the door, Klein returned with two cocktails. One looked like his Chivas on the rocks. The other contained special garnishments on a skewer reserved for Hattie's virgin concoction, which the bartender typically prepared for her. Still, she would play it safe.

He sat beside her on the couch, exchanging the cup in Hattie's hand for her cocktail and placing the water glass on the table. "Now, where were we?" He drank a generous portion and placed his cocktail down.

"You were about to tell me how Germans design superior planes. Is that why you're in Rio?" She pretended to sip.

"You certainly ask a lot of questions." He scooted nearer.

The Secret War 165

"I want to know if this will be a one-night stand or if you'll be available for a repeat performance."

"Direct, right to the point." He continued closer. "I like that." He kissed Hattie on the neck.

She pushed him back. "Well?"

"Why do you want to know?"

"We have much to fit in if this is a one-nighter. I prefer to go slow and savor things, so if there's a chance of—"

"There is." He took her drink from her hand, placed it on the table, went in for another kiss, and pressed his thigh against hers. "If the work goes well, I should come through Rio again in a week."

"So you're leaving." Hattie pretended to enjoy the attention by offering a little moan. "How much time do we have?"

"I wish the plans hadn't changed. Otherwise, we would have all night. Unfortunately, we have only a few hours."

Hattie moaned again. "What happens then?"

"I get picked up and taken to wherever this plane is I'm supposed to fix."

He became more insistent and used both hands to urge Hattie to lie on the couch. He outweighed her by seventy or more pounds. If she allowed him to get on top of her, she might not have a window of leverage to force him off.

Hattie had noted in the club that he was left-handed. She turned the tables and pushed him backward onto the cushion with his left arm pinned to the back of the sofa. He seemed to enjoy the aggressive move, and if he liked it too much, Hattie could more easily control his non-dominant hand.

"I like men who fix things. They're good with their hands. Do you fix these planes with your hands?" Hattie ran a finger down his chest through the fabric of his white dress shirt, swallowing the urge to shudder.

He brushed his right hand against her leg, starting at the knee and working his way up. "With my own designs, yes. I inspect the first construction, but this is Reinhart's nightmare. I'll leave the hands-on task to him."

Hattie added a second finger and a third to her stomach-churning caress. "Who is this Reinhart? Is he picking you up? Would he be interested in joining us?"

He grinned and yanked her closer with a firm grip on her arm. "You are a tease." He kissed her on the lips, but she still had leverage and pulled back. His eyes narrowed, a sign his impatience had peaked.

"I have only begun to tease," she said in her most seductive voice. "Tell me about Reinhart. Is he smarter than you? Does he make bigger and better planes than you?"

Klein laughed. "This plane might be bigger and fly farther than anything we have, but it is by no means better. That's why Berlin called me here. They are in a rush to fix the damn thing." He clutched her arm again, tighter this time. "Enough about Reinhart Hoffman. We do not have much time."

That bit of information set off bells in Hattie's head. The Germans were building a big aircraft with a long range, and they were in a hurry to get it airworthy. Her father was right to suspect a strike against the United States. They needed to stop whatever this man was in Brazil to repair.

"Like I said, I take things slow to titillate."

He forced her hand to his crotch. "I am more than titillated." He was erect and ready for a lot more than talking.

Hattie felt violated and wanted to puke. She pulled back, but he had a tight grip on her hand. On instinct, she reached around with her free hand, grabbed his thumb, and bent it backward against the natural motion of the joint.

Klein instantly loosened his hold and screamed in agony. He shifted in a way to relieve the pressure on his thumb, but Hattie sat on his chest and twisted harder. He yelped again, sounding more like a little girl on the playground than a fully grown man who clearly considered himself of some importance.

A loud bang at the door announced an intrusion. Hattie snapped her stare toward the commotion. Karl emerged from the interior corridor with his gun drawn, pointed in her direction. He looked rattled but determined and stopped a few steps in. Leo was right behind him with his pistol.

Both lowered their weapons and laughed.

"Looks like you don't need a big brother to beat down the bullies behind the gym," Leo said.

"At least not this one." Hattie focused on the man beneath her, who was still writhing in pain. "If I let go, do you promise to behave?"

The Secret War 167

Maya entered the room.

He shook his head between grunts. Hattie released her hold.

Klein looked at Maya. "You." He grunted louder and pushed her off, sending her tumbling into the coffee table. She struck her head there and felt dazed. Her vision was blurred, but the continuing scuffle concerned her. The commotion got more intense, and Hattie struggled to get her eyes to focus.

The piercing sound of breaking glass rushed her effort to focus and hoist herself to her feet with the aid of the table. Maya stood with her mouth agape. Hattie turned to look behind her, discovering David standing near a broken window and Klein missing. "What the hell happened?"

"David happened," Leo said.

David put his hands on his hips and lowered his head. "I was protecting you."

Maya went to the opening.

Karl sucked in a rattled breath. "We had him. Now, our only lead is splattered on the pavement outside."

"He's not dead yet," Maya said, "but he's not going anywhere."

Everyone went to the windows. It was dark, but there was enough light from the service entrance to see Klein writhing in pain on the ground among the garbage bins. His left leg was in an unnatural position, and it was clearly broken.

"We need to get him back up here and question him," Karl said.

"Not here," Maya said. "There are too many guests on this floor."

Karl ran a hand roughly down his face. "Okay, you and David stay here, clean up, and make sure no one from the hotel gets in. Hattie, Leo, and I will take care of him." He threw Maya the room key.

"We have to act fast. His contact will be here in a few hours to collect him." Hattie asked David to give Karl the keys to Eva's car. "We'll take our car. It's the closest. I'll be right behind you."

Karl acknowledged with a nod. He clearly understood she wanted a moment alone with Maya. "Come on, Leo. David, wait in the hallway."

Once they departed, Hattie clutched Maya's arms and looked her in the eyes. "Someone is coming to pick up Klein soon."

"Klein? He registered under Mueller."

"That follows," Hattie said. "If anyone asks for his room number, you have to stall them. We believe they are planning an attack against the US, and we need to find out what he knows. Don't tell David."

"I understand. I'll take care of things."

Hattie kissed her deeply but briefly and left the room. In the hallway, she focused on David. "We will talk later about this."

Without waiting for a reply, she darted down the stairs and went out the hotel's back door. Karl was nowhere in sight, but Leo was with Klein, muffling his screams with a hand over his mouth.

Hattie stood over the man and sneered. "You shouldn't have made me feel your crotch."

Leo narrowed his eyes at the man, looking like he had retaliation in mind.

"He's not worth it, Leo." Hattie returned her attention to the man on the ground. "I must say the experience was quite lacking."

Leo snickered.

Headlights approached the trash area. Hattie peeked around a large bin and recognized her car. Karl parked and opened the trunk. After retrieving a length of rope, he and Leo tied Klein's hands together, put a gag over his mouth, and loaded him amid more muffled screams.

Karl drove from the hotel and away from the beach, taking precautions as usual to ensure they were not followed. Hattie asked him to hurry since the clock was working against them. Once they were out of town, traffic in their direction became nonexistent. Her father relaxed his concentration, cutting the frequency of his mirror-glancing pattern in half.

Hattie used the lull in the activity to relay what she had learned from Klein to Leo and her father. She told them about Armand Klein being called to Rio to fix a flaw in an aircraft design by Reinhart Hoffman. That the plane was big and had a longer range than anything Germany had built before. She also said that the Nazis were in a rush to get it fixed. "He seemed to know much more than the other two engineers who came through the club."

"It sounds like you were right about an attack on the United States," Leo said.

"Which is why we need to pump him for more information." Karl

The Secret War   169

twisted the steering wheel harder in his grip before turning off the highway
and onto a gravel road.

The jungle at night always humbled Hattie. The wilderness, untouched
by mankind, went on for hundreds of miles. It was one of the few areas left
on earth where any sign of civilization was still primitive, like her father's
cabin. It was a world apart from the concrete jungles of Rio and New York
City that had spoiled Hattie. This jungle was ruled by cougars, jaguars, and
venomous snakes, not power-hungry politicians, greedy businessmen, and
crime bosses. And it was a reminder of how tenuous society was and how
they were only one step away from returning to the chaos of the
wilderness.

Karl doused the car's headlights when his cabin came into view and
coasted toward the back, parking out of sight from the access road. They
opened the trunk, discovering Klein had weakened during the trip.

After getting Klein on the couch and he called for Ingrid, Hattie real-
ized he must have sustained internal injuries or a concussion from the fall.
He was delirious and fading fast. She huddled in the corner with Leo and
Karl in the dim light of three lanterns around the room.

"He's pretty far gone." Karl glanced at Klein on the sofa.

"I don't think we'll get anything more out of him," Leo said, shaking his
head.

Hattie remembered their conversation in the Golden Room. He had
mentioned that it was a shame the club did not have a dance floor. "Let me
try. Get a glass of water and a damp towel."

After Karl and Leo retrieved the items, they observed from the corner.

Hattie sat sideways on the cushion and offered Klein the drink, which
he sipped with her help. "Armand, you need to tell me where that airfield is
and how much time we have before that plane becomes operational."

"You know I can't talk about work, Ingrid. It is forbidden."

Hattie dabbed his forehead and face with a wet cloth to make him
comfortable. "I know, sweetheart, but you promised to take me dancing.
When can we go?"

"I told you, I have only a week to fix things when I get there." He patted
her hand weakly. "I will take you when I get back."

"From where? Where in Brazil is this plane you're supposed to fix?"

"Somewhere in the jungle. The SS will take me, but that's not important. We will dance soon."

"Why do you have to leave me, Armand? Why is this plane more important than me?"

"It's the silly Japanese." He struggled to keep his eyes open. "Why we are friends with them, I'll never understand."

"What about the Japanese?"

"They are dragging the Americans into the war."

"How?"

Klein closed his eyes and thrashed in pain. "I don't know."

"Why do we need that plane? I want to go dancing."

His voice was weaker, and his breathing was more labored. "Don't worry, Ingrid. I will make sure America is focused on them, not us. We will go dancing in Paris soon. Now kiss me."

Hattie sensed his end was nearing, and as much as it turned her stomach, she could not deny him his dying wish. She leaned in, pressing her lips against his in a tender kiss. Feeling his muscles go lax, she pulled back; he was gone. His chest no longer rose with the intake of a ragged breath. His eyes remained open, still and lifeless, and Hattie felt a twinge of sadness. She was relieved this Nazi was not alive to make the final fixes for a plane that might attack her country, but her heart went out to Ingrid. The woman did not know it, but she had lost a husband today.

Hattie stood, pushing back on the lump in her throat to concentrate on their task. "The Japanese are planning something."

"In a week," Leo added.

"Whatever it is, it will drag us into the war," Karl said, "and Germany intends to magnify it in such a way that we will focus on Japan, not them. The Nazis are betting the United States won't have the resources or willpower to fight a two-theater war, freeing Germany to continue its march across Eastern Europe. The Axis powers will get their world dominance more quickly than anyone imagined." He turned to Hattie. "You said someone is supposed to pick up Klein in a few hours. We need that to happen."

"But he's dead." Hattie was unsure where her father was going with this.

The Secret War 171

"But they don't know that." Karl shifted to Leo. "You're about his size and age."

Leo pointed at himself. "Me? What about you? You speak German, unlike me."

"Every Nazi agent in this country knows my face by now. You're the obvious choice."

Leo released a long, loud breath. "Okay, but what do we do with him?"

"Like what we've done with the others...let the animals have him."

After taking everything from his pockets, including his room key, wallet, and identification papers, they dropped his body down the jungle ravine, providing the big cats with another feast. The drive back to town was quick, and no one spoke. They had but one chance to stop the attack.

21

Karl parked Hattie's car in the employee area, positioning it for a good view of the rear entrance. He, Leo, and Hattie returned to the hotel, climbing the stairs in silence to the second floor. They entered the suite using the recovered room key and discovered Maya and David inside on the couch. They had rearranged the furniture in the room, but the most crucial alteration was placing an armoire to block the broken window. The new configuration looked natural, as if the designers had intended this layout.

"Nice change." Hattie peeked her head behind it, noting some additions. "You've been busy."

"We put the ironing board there first and stuffed the bedspread around the opening to muffle the outdoor noise."

"Good thinking," Karl said. He tossed David the car keys. "We'll need to cover both the front and back exits, so I parked the car in the lot across from the back stairs. I'll take the front."

Hattie knew her father had deliberately assigned David to surveil the least likely exit the agents would use. If Leo pulled off his deception well, the SS agents picking him up would have no reason to conceal their departure and should leave through the lobby.

"Did Klein give you anything else?" Maya asked. "Did you take him to a hospital?"

The Secret War   173

Hattie considered detailing what they had inferred from the intel she had gleaned, but with David in the room, she decided to keep it vague. "Not much more than we already know, but I got the impression whatever he was supposed to work on would be used soon."

Maya narrowed her eyes at Karl. "He died, or did—"

"No, Maya," Karl said. "I didn't kill him. He was delirious and must have had internal injuries from the fall." He shifted his stare to David and kept it there for several beats, laying blame for the man's death at his feet. "We should set up. Maya, can you stay in the lobby and ring the room when the agents enter the hotel?"

"I can do that," she said. "What about Hattie?"

"We agreed she should be in here," Karl said. "If the SS saw Klein leave with Hattie from the club, she should be in the suite."

"But she'll remain in the bedroom and come out only if they become curious," Leo said.

"Besides," Hattie said, "we need another pair of ears in there to hear where they might take him."

Maya kept quiet, offering only a muted nod and a blank expression. She was absorbing the danger Hattie could face inside that room.

Karl patted Leo on the shoulder and kissed Hattie on the forehead. "See you soon."

After he and David left, Hattie said to Maya, "I'll walk you out." She went to the door and ensured no one was in the hallway before exiting. Once in the stairwell, she pulled Maya into a reassuring embrace. "I need to do this," she said, pulling back. "We learned something disturbing, and now we have to stop them."

"Just be careful." Maya caressed Hattie's arm and looked less worried.

"I will."

They kissed briefly but passionately. Hattie spent those few seconds memorizing the smoothness of her lips, the faint smell of her perfume, and the taste of her soft tongue. In case something went wrong, she wanted to remember that moment and replay it over and over again.

Maya disappeared down the stairs, and Hattie returned to the suite.

Leo walked into the outer room from the bedroom. He had changed into a different pair of pants and was slipping on a white button-down. His sleeveless T-shirt highlighted the definition of his muscular arms. "Not a terrible fit on the slacks, but his shoes were too small."

"Did you try the suit jacket?"

"A little tight in the shoulders, but it should be fine." He buttoned the shirt, tucked it into his pants, and worked on his tie but fumbled with it. "It feels strange wearing another man's clothes."

"Let me help." Hattie stepped closer and tied a perfect half Windsor, classy but not too bulky. She patted his chest when she was done and moved back to take in his appearance. "You look nice, but you need to act arrogant. Klein came across as pompous."

"I think I can pull that off."

Hattie went to the dresser and poured a glass of water. "Would you like some?"

"Please."

She brought the glasses to the couch and sat after handing him one. "By the way, I have some good news."

"I could use something positive about now."

"I spoke to Javier. He's a valet at the Palace who also worked at President Garza's reception." She considered what to reveal about their conversation, but keeping her word was more important than providing irrelevant details. "Long story short, he saw what happened and will make a statement to Inspector Silva in the morning. He can corroborate that another man was the shooter."

"That is good news."

"Why don't we practice those German phrases my father taught you?

"I'd rather talk to you about Maya."

Hattie expected him to be curious after tonight's events. Maya had shown too much concern for it to be mistaken as stemming from only their friendship. She was concerned about opening up to him. Although she trusted him, she was unsure of his moral upbringing and whether he would be as understanding as her father.

"What do you want to know?" she asked.

"I take it you two are more than friends."

"What if we are?" Hattie inhaled deeply and held it. Besides her parents, she had never wanted anyone in her life more than Leo to know the truth and accept her.

"I would say it explains a lot and that I'm okay with it or at least I want to be."

She let out that anxiety-filled breath. His response was not the ideal one she was looking for, but it was more than what her mother had offered at the revelation. "Thank you."

"You and David never seemed like a good fit. I assume he's in on it."

"He is. We've been friends for years."

"Karl obviously knows. Does Eva?"

"Yes, and she's growing to accept us."

He leaned forward, rubbing the back of his neck. "I won't lie and say, 'Hey, good for you,' but I've never been around people like you. It's well... different."

"Trust me, there are people like me everywhere. You've been around us plenty but never realized it. You're correct about me being different. I love differently than society expects, but it's not wrong."

"I can't disagree with you." Leo rested his elbows atop his legs. "I saw it tons growing up in Texas and in the service. Whites can't marry blacks, Hispanics, or Indians. Sometimes it just ain't right." He downed his water.

"No, it's not." Hattie leaned forward, resting her arms like him. "Are we okay? Still friends?"

He turned his head and locked stares with her. "You're like my little sister, Hattie. That hasn't changed. I will always feel like I have to protect you." He laughed. "Though, this does explain why you were never on my radar."

"Your what?"

"Radar. It's a new navy term for detecting planes and surface ships. You were never on the scope of romantic attraction."

"I get it." Hattie chuckled with him. "Mother thought otherwise. She called you the third wheel in my engagement."

"Knowing what I do now, that sounds absurd."

"Imagine what I went through, having to defend both of us." Hattie patted his leg. "Thanks for not turning your back on me and our friendship. I'm glad you know and that there are no more lies between us."

"Yeah." He went to the dresser, refilled his water glass, and stayed there drinking it with his face to her. Whether his stance was intentional, Hattie appreciated it.

"Until you're comfortable with the idea of Maya and me, I won't press the issue."

He slumped his shoulders and looked at her again. "Look, I know how hard it is to bury part of yourself. Living a lie isn't easy. I'm glad you told me, but I don't want you to feel you have to hide it from me. You love her, right?"

"I do, and she loves me."

"That's all that matters." He cocked a half smile. "But if she breaks your heart, she'll have to answer to me."

"I'll tell her as much." She winked, feeling better about their friendship and the chances of her and Maya making it work in the long run. Secret relationships were always doomed to fail. However, this one was finally in the open among those Hattie cared about.

Hattie woke from a nap on the bed and checked the alarm clock on the nightstand. It was nearing one o'clock. She stretched and went into the sitting area. Leo was sitting on the couch, looking at a small photograph.

"Did you get any sleep?" she asked.

"A little."

"What did you find?" She gestured toward the image.

"I found it in Klein's billfold. I'm guessing it's his wife."

A tinge of sadness crept through her. "She doesn't even know she's a widow. She still thinks he's coming home in a week or two and will go dancing with her in Paris."

"I hate war." He returned the photo to the man's wallet and slipped it into his hip pocket.

Hattie sat beside him. "You're afraid a serviceman like you might look at your wife's picture that you keep in your wallet."

"Making Beverly a widow is my greatest fear."

"And that makes you a great sailor and an even better husband. The navy needs more men like you."

The Secret War 177

The room phone rang, and Hattie's breath hitched. They snapped both their stares toward the dresser. On the second ring, Leo picked up the handset. "Hello?" he said in German.

"Thanks, Maya." He hung up and turned. "Two are coming. She said they might have been in the club tonight, so they could know you came up with him."

This was it.

"It's good that I'm the one here. My being here won't surprise them." She hugged him and said, "You got this."

"Don't come out. If they intend to search the suite, I'll try to warn you, okay?"

"I trust you."

After returning the water glasses to their proper place, Hattie went into the bedroom and unbuttoned her blouse to make it appear they had a romantic encounter earlier that evening. She kept her shoes close in case she had to make a quick move. Her Baby Browning pistol was in a hidden compartment in her handbag.

A knock. It sounded like it came from the outer door.

This was the tricky part. During the drive to the hotel, Karl taught Leo a few basic German phrases that could get him through the initial meeting with the SS agents. Karl, Hattie, and David would follow, and they would wait until Leo was taken to the airfield and Wagner.

The plan had several gaping holes, but it was the best they could devise on the fly. What if the agents suspected Leo was not Klein? What if they found Hattie? Or what if they exited the hotel without Karl or David spotting them? Any number of things could go wrong, but they had to try to stop this plane from going operational.

Hattie discerned two male voices besides Leo's. She understood only a few words and phrases in German from her childhood with her father and could not make out most of what was said in the other room. She heard *Klein*, *suitcase*, *glasses*, *wet*, and *woman*. Leo replied with *yes*, *no*, or *I don't know* to the questions. Hattie cringed, doubting whether they had disposed of the room service drinks, but a glance over her shoulder confirmed they were on the nightstand. The men must have been talking about the two water cups and noticed that both had been used. It was an easily overlooked detail, but these agents had caught it. They had been trained well.

Leo raised his voice, speaking in German, "Yes, a woman."

That was Hattie's warning that an agent was about to enter her room. She put on her shoes, hung her purse over her shoulder, and opened the door while pretending to fumble with the buttons of her blouse.

"Armand, I don't think I have another round in me." She looked up and saw a man two steps from the bedroom and another holding Leo by the arm. Both were tall and muscular like Leo but perhaps a bit younger, in their thirties. "My, my. I know I mentioned inviting someone to join us, but I'm afraid four makes a crowd. It's really not my thing."

The man pulled Hattie further into the outer room.

"Armand? What's going on? Who are these men?"

Leo spoke with his best German accent, which had a hint of a Texas drawl. "Colleagues. I must leave for work."

Hattie jerked her arm to break free, but the man had too firm of a grip. "This isn't funny, Armand. They're scaring me."

"What are you doing here, Miss James?" the one holding Leo asked in broken English.

"How do you know my name?"

"Everyone in Rio knows who you are. Why are you here?"

"I would think that is rather obvious. Do I have to spell it out?" When he did not reply, Hattie continued. "S-E-X. We had sex."

He cocked his head, but his expression remained the same...unmoved. "What did he tell you about why he's in town?"

"That he's here on business."

"What else did he say?"

"That he finds me attractive, and he thanked me for doing those things his wife doesn't do to him anymore."

The man grinned. "I'm confused, Miss James. I must have been misinformed."

"About what?"

"About your...predilections." His response was disturbing. It more than hinted he knew about her sex life. A chill traveled through her as she remembered the photo of her and Maya in bed together that she had recovered from the dead SS agent a few days ago. The man clearly knew about her interest in women, which suggested more photos might be floating out there.

"I'm not sure what you mean."

"I think you do." He focused on his partner. "Take her. She's coming with us. We need to learn what he might have told her."

"I told her nothing. Let her go." Leo struggled less to maintain his German accent. "Das ist ein Befehl."

Hattie did not understand what he said. Her father had tried to cram in several phrases while preparing Leo for this operation, but she did not remember that one. It did, however, catch the agents' attention. They paused and stared at Leo with curiosity.

The same man repeated, "Take her."

"Nein. It was just sex." Leo spat the words in English, staring down the SS as if they were about to commence a duel. He threw off the man's grip and stepped toward the other agent. Both men drew pistols from their jackets, and the one holding Hattie held his against her temple.

"Halt," the one in charge barked, "unless you want her shot."

Leo stopped mid-stride. The anguish in his eyes said he regretted having failed her.

"Thank you, Herr Klein," the agent said, tying Leo's hands together with a section of rope from his jacket pocket. "This is until we can confirm who you are. I'm sure you understand."

The other agent tied Hattie's hands at her belly and used a tight grip on her arm to pull her out the door. Leo followed, forced out the door and down the back stairs a few steps behind her. The agents led them to the door David was covering. Her old skepticism of him reared its head again, only much more magnified. She had no choice but to trust he would spot them and alert her father. That thought came with a sickening sensation of doom. That she and Leo were on their own.

The first agent pushed the door open. Vents to the laundry facility were on the right, spewing warmed, fresh-smelling air. The odor of dinner scraps and guest garbage coming from the collection of trash bins on the left behind a cement block wall countered that tranquil scent. Hattie glanced at where Klein had fallen, half-hoping to see David or her father there, ready to pounce, but no one was there but two cats rummaging for food.

Once past the refuse area, the employee parking section came into view. Cars belonging to the overnight staff were in the partially filled lot. They were faintly illuminated by the streetlamps on the perimeter and a waxing gibbous moon partially obscured by the passing rain clouds. Despite the low light, Hattie recognized Eva's sedan, but she could not tell whether David was inside, which was the point of surveillance: to go undetected. The sinking feeling she had earlier twisted Hattie's stomach tighter. What if the SS had found David and killed him?

Hattie's breath caught when she spotted Maya's car and saw the silhouette of a woman's head and hair in the driver's seat. Maya must have gone directly to the back entrance after calling the room. Her belly unknotted as a wave of relief washed through her. Maya was there. Maya would see to her and Leo's safety and alert her father.

The men walked them through a similarly lit guest parking area and forced them into the back of a dark sedan. Hattie started working at her restraints the instant the door closed, and she suspected Leo was doing the same.

Once the agents boarded and drove from the lot onto the hotel access road leading to the main boulevard, Hattie knew they would be okay. Maya and her father would be there. And she had Leo beside her.

Last year in New York, Hattie blindly trusted only two people: Karl James and David Townsend. She knew they would always have her back and protect her. Her father was on that list for obvious reasons, but David had made the cut because he had protected her secret for years. However, jealousy or something deeper had developed since coming to Rio and had become his motivation, bouncing him from her trusted circle. In his stead, she had placed Maya. The trust Hattie felt for her ran deep and unshakeable.

Tonight, she added to that exclusive list the man sitting beside her with his hands tied. She studied him as they traveled through the city. Between Eva's kidnapping, the yacht bombing attempt, not turning in her father, and

The Secret War 181

arranging a meeting with Jimmy Cooke, Leo Bell repeatedly had proven himself trustworthy. And after their talk about Maya in that hotel room, she firmly believed everything he had done for her and her father was for the right reason.

22

Minutes earlier

The more Karl thought about this plan, the more he hated it. Ideally, they needed a second pair of ears in that suite to learn the location of Wagner or the safe house if the SS agents let slip the information. So many things could go wrong, but Hattie had already established a reason for her being there by leaving the club with Klein. Even if the agents found her, he had learned Hattie was adept at telling lies. She had hidden her relationships with women all her adult life, after all.

Yes, Hattie was the obvious choice to be the ears up there, but Karl still did not like putting his daughter in harm's way. If he had been a nail biter, he would have chewed them to their nubs long before his wristwatch read midnight, waiting for this operation to kick into gear. He had been in this position at the yacht months ago. Hattie's life had rested in Leo's hands while he disarmed the bomb. Tonight, her life relied on Leo's undercover skills. While Leo would have him believe he was merely an analyst who had spent his career behind a desk, Karl suspected he had field training and experience. No matter how this went down, he was relieved Leo was with her and not him. He was equally skilled, or so Karl hoped, but he was also younger, stronger, more agile, and had more stamina. Karl rested more

The Secret War

183

assured that Leo would be the closest to Hattie and get to her first if things went haywire.

He shifted uneasily in his seat. His bottom had started to ache an hour earlier from sitting so long, and now his right leg cramped from not being able to stretch it out.

He had noted a handful of taxis dropping off guests. Those did not interest him as much as the sedan that had pulled into the driveway two minutes ago. It had passed the valet stand and turned toward the free guest parking on the side of the building. It was the only non-commercial vehicle to enter the hotel grounds in the last half hour. There were only two ways out. The front, where Karl was staked out, and the service entrance for delivery trucks in the back. However, the gate for the rear area David was covering was locked after regular business hours. That meant Karl's location offered the only view of the way in and out of the lot at night.

Karl wished they had another team member who could have covered the back. Taking risks with Hattie's safety was against his nature, and David was a giant gamble. His actions had added up to the conclusion that he could not be trusted. That stunt he pulled tonight, bulldozing Klein out of the window, took the prize. Karl did not buy for one second that he had thought the man was going after Hattie and had acted out of instinct to protect her. It made sense, though, if he did not want the engineer telling them what he knew.

That was why he assigned David to the back, the least likely avenue of departure if things went smoothly with Leo and Hattie, which was the probable outcome. It was a crapshoot as to which way the agents would leave, but he went with the odds since the front was the only way in after midnight. Nonetheless, Maya would serve as his safety valve and dart to the back once the agents arrived.

The Palace lobby looked quiet through the glass. Besides the people dropped off by taxi, Karl had seen only one guest strolling through in the last fifteen minutes.

Moments later, two men on foot dressed in suits appeared around the corner of the hotel. Karl sat up straighter, picked up his binoculars, and tracked their path. They walked toward the unoccupied valet stand and entered the lobby through the double glass doors. Once inside, they went to the registration desk.

Maya had been sitting in an armchair for hours, sipping on a drink, presumably water, while reading. She straightened in her seat but remained in character, tilting her head at the book in her lap.

The men spoke to the clerk, and one handed something to the junior employee behind the counter. It was likely a payoff for Klein's room number. They turned and walked toward the elevator.

Once they disappeared around the corner, Maya went to the bank of house phones along the lobby's far wall and lifted the first handset. She was alerting Hattie and Leo.

This was it. SS agents were on their way to the room.

The pain in Karl's bottom and leg suddenly vanished, replaced by a sense of anxiousness. The humid night air did not help. Beads of sweat soon formed on his forehead, and his armpits grew damp, but he could do nothing to control or mitigate the uncomfortable feeling. The operation was underway; all he could do was wait.

Time crawled by, but after only seventeen minutes, a pair of headlights appeared on the hotel access road. Karl could not be sure, but they could have been from the sedan the Nazis were driving. The vehicle followed the curve in the pavement and stopped at the curb, where it met the main boulevard. It turned left, which led north out of the beachfront area.

Karl started the engine and prepared to pull onto the street but stopped when a second set of headlights came into view on the access road. It could have been David in Eva's sedan, but its shape was smaller than hers. It could have been Maya's car. The lights flashed three times, their signal that the target had come out through the back exit.

"Thank you, Maya."

Karl pulled into the empty traffic lane. After Maya and another automobile joined his direction of travel and he was comfortable that he would blend in, Karl flicked on his lights. He kept a reasonable separation between him and the agents' car to avoid being spotted.

At the end of the oceanfront street, the SS went north into the city. Karl followed. A glance at his side mirror confirmed Maya had also turned. He felt at ease at this distance since other vehicles were on the road.

After a mile and only one turn, traffic became nonexistent. He did not expect it to pick up again at this time of night. At the next corner, he doused his headlights before the agents' sedan came into view again. He rechecked his mirror. Maya had done the same, but not before she had completed the turn. He hoped the SS did not spot her.

A silence cloaked Rio's empty streets, in stark contrast to the city's vibrant nature during the day. The shadows cast by sporadic streetlamps and the moonlight breaking through the thin clouds played tricks, making each passing corner seem like a potential threat. He remained alert for the possibility of another Nazi T-boning his sedan to knock him off the hunt.

He gripped the wheel tighter, his eyes straining to follow the agents' car in the upscale residential Santa Teresa neighborhood. Every twist in the road was a gamble in the dim light, but the danger of losing them electrified the air and magnified his focus.

The car reduced speed, as it did for each turn, but this time, they were on a straightaway. Karl slowed more abruptly than before, but not enough to screech his brakes. When the sedan drove into a driveway, he knew this was the place and coasted his vehicle to a stop.

The property appeared to belong to someone wealthy. Like Eva's, it was walled off from the street; the back probably was too. The gate was not visible from this position, but the compound likely had one. Getting inside would be challenging.

Maya's darkened sedan pulled in behind him. Once the agents' vehicle disappeared from view, the doors to Maya's car opened. Maya emerged from the driver's side and David from the passenger's. Karl kept his eye on the vehicle in the mirror, expecting Hattie to slide out if things had gone right. However, when both doors closed without her appearing, he knew they had not. He fought off a wave of lightheadedness. His daughter was now in the safe house, and she would need him.

Maya got into the front seat on the passenger side and David into the back. Karl did not have to ask what happened. Maya's silent, terrified stare said Hattie was taken. Only one question remained.

"Was she hurt?"

"I don't think so," Maya said, "but her hands were tied. Leo's were, too."

"Was he okay?"

"Yes, he looked fine."

A blown cover was one of the worst things that could happen during an operation. It typically ended in deadly consequences. The fact that Hattie and Leo were both alive and unhurt was a good sign. It meant they had some time to plan their attack and did not have to go in with guns blazing.

"What are we waiting for?" David asked. "They'll interrogate her. If they think she knows anything, they'll kill her."

"I know that." Karl bit his tongue, holding back a sharper reply. "But we're no good to her dead. We should think this through."

"How many people do you think are there?" Maya asked.

"An SS safe house has a keeper and usually three or four agents assigned. If the ones with Hattie and Leo are passing through, there could be six or more."

"But it's gated," David said. "How do we get inside?"

"I have an idea," Maya said, "but we need to find an all-night café in the nightclub district."

When the driver turned west and did not stay on a northern path out of town, Hattie rested a little easier. If the Nazis intended to dispose of her, they would have gone toward the jungle, where countless deaths had been hidden from the authorities. Instead, they had gone west into the hills and the Santa Teresa neighborhood. It was the area where Agent Knight had said he tracked the SS but without identifying the precise location of their safe house.

Tied up and abducted was not how Hattie hoped to get on the trail of Strom Wagner, but she was sure that Maya and her father were following. Though the light on the roads was scant and, at times, nonexistent, she thought she had seen the glimmer of a vehicle traveling without headlights behind them at a turn. Her father had her practice this tactic while navigating the streets in the middle of a surveillance operation to go undetected. It must have been him. That knowledge made her less afraid, but she also had to do her part. She had worked on the rope around her wrists

The Secret War

during the trip from the hotel and had achieved some progress. Given time, she was confident she could loosen it.

Their car slowed in a residential area and turned into a driveway. They stopped at a wrought-iron gate. The driver got out and pressed a button resembling a doorbell on the pillar at the entrance. Two men emerged from a house and walked through the fenced-off courtyard toward the gate. One of them swung it open. The driver pulled the sedan inside about thirty feet and parked it near the house.

The agents from the hotel got out, yanked Hattie and Leo from the back seat, and led them to the front door. The one holding Hattie by the arm had an extra tight grip and seemed to take joy in forcing her to bend to his will. He took long strides, one to every two of Hattie's, and did not slow to let her keep up. Instead, he pulled her as she shuffled along the concrete at nearly a jog.

The men who had tended to the gate followed them inside to a sparsely decorated living room. Two lamps were on, but the couch and easy chair were unoccupied, and the radio set was off. There were two corridors. The SS men pushed them down one, past a kitchen on the left and a smaller room with a desk on the right. She lost her footing in the narrow space, but the ruffian refused to stop. He dragged her, facing backward with her feet scraping across the tile. Pain shot through her shoulder as her arms stretched to their maximum at an odd angle.

Leo shouted something in German and thrashed against the grip his captor had on him. He elbowed him in the ribs, bouncing him into the wall and sending him to the floor. Lunging forward, Leo threw his bound hands over the head of the guy handling Hattie like a rag doll and locked his forearm against the man's throat. The agent stopped and gasped for air, but his hand clamped harder on her arm. Leo was choking the life out of him, and the agent was determined to hold on to her.

Leo's captor shook off his daze, hurried to stand, and sprang toward Leo. He pulled on Leo's collar to break his chokehold, but Leo grunted and wrenched tighter until Hattie was free. She thumped into the wall.

The men from outside rushed the hallway, which was too narrow for six. Hattie slithered a few feet down to get clear of the scuffle. Each agent fought for space and leverage. They took turns whaling punches at Leo's kidneys and ribs until he lay limp, and they forced his arms from around the ruffian's neck.

Hattie felt useless on the tile, hands bound, while four men pounded her friend. All she could do was watch in horror until they stopped. Two of them dragged Leo into a room at the end of the hallway. Another man clutched Hattie's arm and pulled her into the room across from Leo's. He threw her onto the bed and slammed the door on his way out.

Frustration kicked in the moment she was alone. She doubted those men were done with Leo. Eventually, they would beat the truth from him about why he felt compelled to rescue a one-night stand. Once they did, they would have their turn with her.

She did not want to learn how far they were prepared to take their interrogation. It was clear now why her father had been so insistent on her learning several self-defense techniques. She would not have a chance four-on-one, but if one got her alone, the prospect of her getting away was much better.

Multiple footsteps sounded from the hallway, as did the telltale sign of a continued beating in the next room. Hattie did not understand what was being said in German, but their voices were loud.

She assessed her surroundings. The room had the iron-frame bed with a mattress she was sitting on, a small table serving as a nightstand, a luggage stand, and one boarded-up window. The uncovered ceiling light was reachable if she stood on the table, but she doubted it would hold her weight. She checked the door, but it was locked from the other side.

Her father had taught her that any everyday item could be a tool to aid in escaping or subduing an attacker. She just had to find it. Prying off the wooden planks covering the window would make too much noise and draw the attention of her captors. A broken bulb could be a weapon, but first, she needed to free herself from her bindings.

Pulling back the mattress revealed the spring frame and metal slats underneath the woven metal platform holding it in place. Each length was thin with a sharp edge, so she tossed the flimsy, worn cushion to the floor and flipped the frame onto its side using both hands. Straddling it, she positioned the bottom section of rope around her wrists above one slat and rubbed against it hard and fast, fraying several layers of hemp.

The Secret War 189

Beads of sweat built as a result of her furious pace. Finally, some of the hemp split, and her restraints loosened, freeing her hands. One spring on the frame was loose, so she bent the other end back and forth until it broke off. That edge was sharp and ragged and would make an excellent weapon.

Hattie flipped over the wooden table and stomped on a leg, snapping it off. The break made a loud sound, which could have been heard from the hallway. She put the bed in place and fluffed it with the pillow under the blanket to make it appear she was in it. After hiding the broken table behind the bed, she picked up the table leg and the spring, one in each hand. One would act as a club to stun her captor and the other as a knife to jab out an eye.

She waited to make her move.

23

After thirty minutes, Maya, Karl, and David were set up for entry, armed with a takeout order, pistols with suppressors, and extra ammunition. Karl and David flanked the gate on each side, ready with weapons and their backs against the brick wall. Maya walked up to the gate, carrying the bag of food, and pressed the buzzer by the opening.

Moments later, footsteps sounded, and Maya signaled behind her back with two fingers, indicating two men were coming. She shifted the load in her hands, turned slightly, and motioned David on the other side.

The clicking of loafers against concrete stopped, and one man asked in German, "What do you want?"

Maya spoke in Portuguese. "Eu não entendo. Você fala português?"

The man replied in German that he did not understand.

Maya said, "Do you speak English? I have a food delivery."

"No, go away," the man said in English.

"Look, somebody called in an order, saying they would be here at two. It's two. If someone doesn't pay, it comes out of my paycheck. I don't care who, but one of you has to come up with six reals."

"Six?" He scoffed at the hefty price tag for takeout. "What the hell did they order?"

"Doubles of feijoada, pão de queijo, and brigadeiro."

The Secret War 191

"I don't know what that is."

"Look, it doesn't matter what it is." Maya flapped her hands wildly while ranting loud enough in Portuguese for neighborhood dogs to begin barking.

"Fine, fine, but be quiet." The man's voice was filled with agitation.

The gate creaked open with the panel sliding inward.

Maya took a step backward.

Karl and David emerged from the concealment of the wall as two men stepped forward. They fired. Karl aimed center mass at the man on the left and hit him twice in the chest. His target jerked and fell to the ground. The other man turned at the waist like he had been shot in the shoulder. Karl pivoted and shot twice again, sending him to the pavement as well. He did not have time to analyze how David could have missed from that short distance, even for someone without proper training. However, the man had been moving, so he let it go.

Maya put the food down, drew her pistol, and attached the silencer.

Karl and David slipped inside the compound and dragged the bodies of the guards against the wall beyond the cone of light illuminating the gate. Stashing them behind some bushes would have been better, but the area had been paved for parking, and the nearest building was thirty feet away. Only one car was in the courtyard, close to the house. Out in the open would have to do.

The compound had two buildings—the main house and a smaller structure resembling a storage shed, which was dark. However, the lights were on in the house. They pushed forward. At the door, Karl took point and tested the knob. It was unlocked. He counted down with his fingers. *Three. Two. One.*

He opened the door smoothly so as not to draw attention, as if he were an agent returning from the courtyard. He entered the living area. One man was in the room, sitting on a couch. Karl shot him with two rounds to the chest. He reloaded.

David went left to what looked like a study. Maya went right toward the kitchen. Muffled pops said they both fired their weapons twice. That made three down with possibly three remaining.

A hallway led deeper into the house, likely to bedrooms and bathrooms. Karl retook point. He turned down the lit corridor and came face-to-face with an SS agent. He recognized the man as one he had met once when he came through Rio from São Paulo. The man yelled, "Intruder," in German before Karl could get a shot off. He pulled the trigger, but the man had pivoted. The bullets hit him in the back near his kidneys. He thumped against the wall and tumbled to the floor as blood spread on his white shirt.

There was no hiding their presence now. Whoever held Hattie and Leo knew they were in the house.

A gunshot sounded from one of the back rooms.

A gut-wrenching feeling of dread ripped Karl's insides wide open. He stood frozen. "Hattie!"

Hattie heard shouts. Footsteps came down the corridor again, more rapid this time. She positioned herself against the wall beside the door, prepared to attack. The latch outside the door creaked. The knob turned. She anticipated that whoever entered would have their pistol drawn, aimed, and ready to fire. Hattie raised her club, knowing Leo was hurt and would not last much longer from the brutal beating he was getting. Her heart pounded, and her breathing labored in short inhales at the possibility of missing her captor with her first strike and failing her friend.

The door quickly swung on its hinges into the room as it was pushed open. The thin, distinctive muzzle of a Luger appeared a second later. Hattie swatted at the wrist of the hand holding it, forcing its aim toward the floor and tilting the gunman off-balance.

The gun fired. A bullet pierced a wooden slat, splintering it.

Hattie saw a fraction of his profile, but it was insufficient to be sure who it was. She wheeled her hand with the spring level with the man's face, hoping to take out an eye. At the last moment, the man straightened a fraction, and her strike landed directly below his Adam's apple. Droplets of blood spattered on her hand. He gurgled and reached for his throat, but it was too late. She had delivered an incapacitating, if not deadly, blow. He fell to his knees, revealing his face. It was her captor. He collapsed on the floor.

Hattie had killed a man with her bare hands, but she did not have the time to dwell on the fact that she had taken a life. She grabbed his gun and stepped into the hallway. Motion to her left caught her attention. She swiveled with her finger on the trigger, ready to fire.

Long black hair made her pause.

Maya.

Maya had come to save her. Karl was beside her, and David was behind him. All three had their pistols with silencers drawn. No one said a word, but Maya sagged against the wall in palpable relief.

Hattie pointed at the door across the corridor and mouthed, "Leo." The latch was not locked, suggesting the room was either unoccupied or an agent was in there with Leo.

Karl moved forward and glanced at the open room with the dead man lying on the floor. He offered a nod. The sad look in his eyes said he had guessed what she had done and was grateful she was unhurt.

Maya squeezed her hand, her chest still heaving with relief.

Karl focused on the other door, turned the knob, and pushed it with all his might. Instead of rushing in, he stayed back, crouched, and readied his pistol with both hands.

Two gunshots rang out, splintering the wooden doorframe.

Karl called out something in German. A man from inside the room shouted something back.

"Hattie!" Leo yelled, followed by a loud thwack and a grunt.

This had become a standoff, with Leo caught in the middle, which meant they required a distraction.

Hattie raised her makeshift club and signaled to Karl that she would throw it in the room. The resulting noise should provide what they needed. After his nod acknowledging her plan, she stepped even with the door, wound up, and let the table leg fly. It clanked against the wall and bounced off the tile in a repeating pattern.

Karl launched himself toward the room, leading with his gun. His feet left the ground, and he went in sideways, firing his weapon rapidly. He landed with a loud thump and moaned.

Hattie rushed inside with the recovered Luger. Unlike the other room, there was no bed. Besides the chair Leo was tied to near the far corner, the space was without furnishings. An agent lay, shot in the arm, with blood spreading on his sleeve. He raised his hand with a pistol, aiming it at her. She had no time to think, only react. She fired at him twice and twice again until he slumped lifelessly to the floor.

"It's clear," she said.

Maya hurried in and looked from Hattie to Karl, from the dead man to Leo, and back at Hattie.

David came in behind her.

"David, tend to my father," Hattie said. "Is the rest of the house clear?"

"Yeah."

"Good. Maya and I will get Leo."

While David helped Karl stand, Hattie and Maya focused on Leo.

"Did they hurt you?" Leo asked Hattie as both women worked on loosening the ropes around his wrists and ankles.

Hattie's arm still ached from the agent manhandling her in the hallway, but her injury paled in comparison to what had been done to Leo. His face was bloody and swollen, and one eye was barely visible under the blood-streaked, puffy eyelid. "Don't worry about me. We have to get you medical attention. You might need stitches."

"I can't chance going to a hospital. Someone might recognize me."

"Let's get him to Eva's," Karl said, rubbing the small of his back. Hattie guessed he had aggravated his old injury while doing his Captain America imitation. "But first, we need to search this place for intel. Something here might lead us to Wagner."

And the airfield, Hattie thought, but that was something they had yet to share with David and would not unless they had no other choice.

She and Maya helped Leo to stand. He wobbled but got his balance after a few moments. "Can you walk?" Hattie asked.

"Yeah, I'm a little slow."

Karl faced Maya. "Can you locate a pillowcase or a shopping bag? We need to gather everything of intelligence value we can find."

Hattie grabbed Maya by the arm as she turned to leave. "There are pillows in the room across the hall."

"I'm on it." Maya nodded and left.

Karl went to the dead agent on the floor. He rummaged through his pockets, retrieving his wallet, identification, several slips of paper, a pack of cigarettes, a lighter, some coins, and his weapon. When Maya returned with two pillowcases, he dumped the items in one.

"Search everyone, every drawer, and every cabinet. It's too dangerous to stay here, so take anything that looks personal. Work in teams so you don't miss anything. Maya, you go with Hattie. David, you're with me."

"I can help." Leo struggled to take a few steps.

"You should rest," Hattie said. "Let us do it."

Karl and David searched the back.

Hattie and Maya led Leo to the entry room, sat him on the chair, and retrieved some hand towels to stem the bleeding on his face. She pointed at Leo and said, "Stay."

She and Maya went through the pockets of the dead man on the couch and did the same to the ones in the front part of the house. They piled their personal effects on the coffee table next to the magazines and newspapers they would take. The kitchen revealed only food, cooking items, dishes, and utensils. Hattie grabbed the takeout containers from the trash, thinking their eating habits could yield helpful information. She placed them in a grocery sack from the kitchen and toted the bag into the entry room.

She and Maya turned their focus to the study. Shelves along the wall housed a dozen paperbacks. She ran them over to the table near Leo and rejoined Maya to go through the desk. In the top middle drawer, she had found pens, blank paper, a stack of notecards with numbers written on them, and a collection of keys. The lower drawers revealed some files and a black notebook smaller than Baumann's infamous logbook. They grabbed the items without inspecting them and returned to the entry room.

David and Karl came from the back, carrying a partially full pillowcase. They dumped everything from the coffee table into it.

"We need to search the shed and car before we go," Karl said after Hattie relayed they had finished going through the front of the house.

Hattie helped Leo up. "You and David get him to your car. Maya and I will take care of the rest." When David reached for the pillowcases, she said, "Wait. There was a set of keys. Let me have them. The shed might be locked."

Once the others were through the gate, Hattie and Maya went to the agents' vehicle. It was clean except for a few maps in the glove box. She took them. They moved on to the shed. Its door had a padlock. Hattie tried the keys on the ring until she found one that unlocked it. Inside, she noted the lightbulb protruding from a wall socket and pulled the string to turn it on. The area had hand tools, gardening implements, and four crates. She popped the top of the first one with a crowbar from the small workbench.

"Holy moly." Hattie had discovered a cache of German hand grenades.

Maya looked over her shoulder. "Holy moly is right."

They opened all the wooden containers and found explosives, machine guns, and ammunition.

"We have to take these," Hattie said, "but we'll need to get David and my father."

"We can carry one together," Maya said.

They replaced the lids, grabbed the lightest box by the rope handles, and walked it out of the gate to Karl's sedan.

Karl hopped out of the driver's seat and opened the trunk. "What did you find?"

"A cache of weapons and explosives. There are three more crates, but they're heavy. You and David will have to get them."

Karl waved David up from the other vehicle. Hattie and Maya searched the dead agents near the stone wall, taking everything from their pockets while Karl and David retrieved the munitions and firearms from the shed. Within minutes, they had everything stowed in both trunks and were back on the road to Eva's. Hattie was in the front seat of Maya's car, glancing at her from the passenger side. Tonight had been a wild ride. And it was still not over, not by a long shot.

24

When the group arrived at Eva's home, Karl and David rearranged the cars, pulling theirs into the garage to secure the firearms and explosives in the trunks. Hattie and Maya helped Leo through the garden courtyard and into the house, using Hattie's key.

"Mother," Hattie shouted. "We're back." She guided Leo to the couch. "Bring a wet towel and your first aid kit."

"What?" Eva appeared in the doorway from the kitchen. "My Lord. What happened to Leo?"

"It's a long story." Hattie loosened Leo's tie to make him more comfortable. "First aid kit and towels. Get some water so we can clean him up."

While Eva was in the kitchen, Maya shifted cushions to help him sit upright and changed the blood-soaked towel out with another from the safe house. She tossed the old one on the back patio and rejoined Hattie on the sofa.

"How are you feeling?" Maya asked.

"Like I've been run over by a truck." Leo groaned.

Eva returned with the supplies, including a bowl of water to rinse the towel. "I take it things didn't go as planned."

"It got complicated, but now eight men are dead, and we've lost our only lead to Wagner." Hattie dabbed at Leo's wound with the damp towel.

The bleeding had slowed, but he still had deep gashes above and below the swollen eye.

Eva's head swiveled in every direction. Her voice became brittle with fear. "Where is your father? And David?"

"They're—"

"We're right here, Eva," Karl said. He stepped through the front door, carrying one of the pillowcases of items from the safe house. He moved stiffly, likely due to lingering aches from the night's earlier ill-advised lunge. David came in behind him, lugging the other case. They placed their loads on the floor.

Eva rushed over and wrapped her arms around his midsection, giving him a relief-filled embrace. "I'm so glad you're okay."

Karl groaned softly and hugged her back. "I'm fine, Eva, but we need to get Leo patched up. Do you know anyone who can help and show discretion? We think he needs stitches."

"Yes, but you won't like it."

"Who?"

"Joaquim Navarro." Eva let out a little sigh.

"Is he still practicing medicine? I would have thought he lost that privilege a long time ago."

"He has helped many young women when their options were limited. Some were the daughters of powerful and influential families. You, of all people, know that." Eva raised her nose at Karl. "The government won't dare strip him of his license, though Lord knows they should have. I'll call him." She went to her study.

Karl stood arms akimbo, lowering his head in the wake of Eva's verbal browbeating. "I'll check the perimeter." He went out the patio door.

"Leo," Hattie said, "I think you would be more comfortable lying down while we wait for the doctor. I'll take you to my room."

"Put him in mine," David said. "I can sleep on the couch. Let me grab a few things first."

"That's very kind. Thank you." Hattie gave him a gratitude-filled smile before he disappeared into his room. When he returned, she and Maya took Leo and the supplies to David's room. They settled him into the bed.

The Secret War   199

"We should get you out of these bloody clothes." Hattie grabbed a T-shirt from David's dresser.

"I'll do it," Maya said.

"Thanks." Hattie handed her the clean shirt. "I'm going to check on Father." She was concerned about his back and was perplexed by his and Eva's spat moments earlier.

After exiting through the breezeway door, she sat at the patio table. She waited in the dark for her father to return from checking Eva's stone fence and the pass-through gate with the neighbor. She also needed a moment alone to catch her breath. So much had happened in the last few hours, not to mention days, from Baumann's logbook to Leo being on the run to a plot to attack the United States. The weight of it all was crushing her.

She and Leo came close tonight to becoming two more bodies for the animals to devour for dinner, another secret for the jungle to hold. Leo had taken the brunt of the fallout, but a portion of Hattie's sympathy fell on Ingrid, the widow of the engineer killed earlier. She even felt a little sympathy for Klein. Despite his philandering ways, in his delirious state, he had clung to the one thing that likely had brought him joy—a loving wife. In that respect, despite his arrogance, she was glad to have made his last moments a little more bearable.

Karl appeared through the garage door leading to the breezeway and walked toward the house.

Hattie called out softly, "Father."

He detoured and joined her at the table. "Everything okay in there?"

"Yeah. I needed a moment to myself. How's the perimeter?"

"All my trips are still in place, so no one has sneaked in."

"Good. What was that with you and Mother? Do you have a history with this doctor?"

He sighed. "He used to be Eva's family physician. I met him during my return assignment here when you were a toddler. An embassy staff member had gotten a girl in trouble, if you know what I mean."

Hattie nodded. "He got her pregnant."

"Right. Since I was married to a local and had been in the country years earlier, he asked if I knew a doctor who could take care of it. I introduced him to Navarro, who had a private practice." Karl wiped the back of his neck. "Well, he got paid well for his services. A few months later, another aide came to me with the same problem. Before I knew it, I'd aided in six abortions in two years. I regret it to this day."

"And naturally, being a good Catholic, Mother was upset with you."

"When she found out, yes." He leaned back in his chair. "But she's right. Throw enough money at him, and he's very discreet."

"But can you trust him to not turn you and Leo in?"

"I'll make it clear he won't want to betray either of us."

"I can do that, Father. What leverage can I use?"

"Part of the payment he insisted on from the ladies was... how should I put it? A personal service. I didn't know it until years later, which is why I regret it so much."

Hattie cringed, sucking in her rage.

"He's married, so I'm guessing he doesn't want his wife to know how he was paid for illegal abortions." He shifted in his chair. "Enough about that. Did they hurt you?"

"Just a little arm twisting, but I'll be fine." Hattie rolled her shoulder to loosen the strained muscles.

"With everything going on, I'm concerned about the sheet music and the lists," he said.

"Did you take care of them like you said?" He told Hattie he was going to change the Morse code. That meant her photos of them and Eva's summary sheet would be the only remaining copies of the encoded spy lists. Even if the Nazis got their hands on the actual lists, the names and locations were useless without the cipher. Only the Professor had that.

"I fixed them, but I still think we should check on them," Karl replied.

"I'll do that," Hattie said.

"Are the pictures safe?"

"Yes, they're well hidden." Hattie pushed up from the chair when she heard the doorbell. "That must be Navarro."

Karl said he would wait at the patio table in the shadows of the roof overhang until the doctor was in the bedroom. The prudent move was to postpone an uneasy meeting between him and the doctor until Leo was patched up.

Hattie went inside.

The Secret War 201

David had let in Doctor Navarro.

Eva greeted him with an awkward hug. "I'm sorry to call you so early, but a friend is hurt, and I require your discretion in treating him."

"I see. Who is this friend?"

"He's an American and a good friend of my daughter's." Eva gestured toward Hattie. "Joaquim, this is Hattie James."

"It's a pleasure, Miss James."

"Thank you for coming, Doctor. My friend was badly beaten and might need stitches on his face. Can you help him?"

"I brought what I might need, but I must know what this man has done that he can't go to a hospital for treatment." Navarro appeared unconvinced and not yet willing to give aid.

"He's been accused of a crime he didn't commit. I can vouch for that because I was there. I found a man who can clear his name later today, but my friend needs help now."

"You're talking about the American who shot and killed that man at the president's home and tried to assassinate the US vice president."

"Like I said, I know he didn't do it. Will you help him?"

He glanced at Eva and back at Hattie. "For Eva, yes. I will help him."

"Thank you, Doctor." Hattie gestured down the hallway. "I'll take you to him."

She led him to David's room, where Leo was sitting in bed with a wet towel pressed against his eye. "This is Dr. Navarro. He's here to look at your wounds."

"Thanks, Doc," Leo said in his charming Texan drawl. "They worked me over pretty good."

Navarro looked over his shoulder at Hattie. "If you'll give us some privacy, Miss James."

"Of course. Call me back here when you're done." She looked at Leo. "You're in excellent hands. Holler if you need anything."

Hattie returned to the living room but found Maya, David, and her parents in the kitchen, sifting through the stuff from the safe house.

"Find anything?" Hattie asked.

"We just started," Maya said.

Hattie approached the table and eyed the pile of personal effects. It was unsettling to think that hours earlier, their owners had been alive, and these were some of the last things they had touched before taking their final breaths.

They piled like items, wallets with wallets, cigarettes with cigarettes, books with books, and so on, until everything was neatly organized and ready to analyze. Karl read the little black book while David emptied the billfolds and arranged what he found on the table in piles. Maya looked at the notecards. Eva grabbed the manila files.

Hattie looked at the miscellaneous pieces and noticed an odd connection. "This is strange. Many of these things are American. The paperbacks are all dime-store novels. The smokes are Lucky Strikes. Their money and change include American currency."

David picked up the identification cards. "They had Texas and Florida driver's licenses, which look real."

"What were they planning?" Hattie asked.

"The traditional method of getting spies into the US on merchant vessels has been cut off," Karl said. "Maybe those planes won't carry only bombs. Maybe they plan to dump SS agents along the route."

"Why would they do that?" David asked.

"Germany has been looking for my lists," Karl said. "They must assume the identity and location of every German spy on that list is compromised. This might be their way of refilling the well."

"Lord." Eva gasped, threw a hand over her mouth, and slammed a manila folder shut.

"What is it?" Karl reached for the file.

Eva slapped his hand. "Trust me. You don't want to see." She gave her daughter a peek.

"Can I have those, Mother?" An awkwardness hung in the air. "I was afraid more were floating out there."

"You need to destroy them. I hope these are the only ones, because if the press ever got hold of them, your career would be dead at the very least. And the police." Eva threw her hand to her mouth again. "Dear God. You could go to prison for what's in those photos."

Her mother's reaction bordered on a lecture, which was the last thing

Hattie needed today. She had graver issues to worry about. Hattie stuck her hand out for the file. "Thanks for the ugly reminder, Mother."

Eva's eyes filled with tears as she handed over the folder. "I'm sorry, sweetheart. Telling me about your relationship is one thing. I wasn't expecting to see...I mean, it was...I don't know—"

"Immoral? Illegal? Flat out wrong?" Hattie barked.

Maya squeezed Hattie's hand and whispered, "It's all right. We have the pictures now."

Hattie knew Maya intended to calm her, but the caress had the opposite effect. It made her angrier to think that touching this way in public would stir gossip and prompt the media or a power-hungry cop to dig into her personal life. It infuriated her that a government could criminalize the act of physical love between two consenting adults.

"No, it's not. As long as we have to hide who we are, it will never be all right."

"You won't have to hide here and never with us again," Eva croaked. "This is your safe place."

Hattie sucked in a calming breath. She should not have snapped at her mother when they had more important things to do. "I'm sorry, Mother. I know that. Stress must be getting the best of me tonight."

"Let's focus on what needs doing," Maya said. "These cards have phone numbers and a letter, sometimes two, but no names."

"Let me see." Karl looked at a card. "The letters refer to an agent's designation in Rio. The closer to the start of the alphabet, the higher they are in the organization. This is great intel. Finding the corresponding address would unearth the entire Nazi spy ring in Brazil."

"What about the black book?" Hattie asked.

"Names and dates, so it's a logbook of sorts," Karl said. "It looks like they tracked whoever came through the safe house."

"You have to love German recordkeeping," Eva said. "It will be their downfall during this war."

"I'm done with your friend," a voice behind her said.

Everyone turned their attention to the kitchen doorway. The doctor was there, and his stare was fixed on Karl.

"How is he?" Hattie asked.

"I cleaned his wounds and gave him fourteen stitches. I used dissolvable sutures since I doubted he would be available for a follow-up to remove them."

"Prudent," Hattie said.

"I gave him something for the pain, but make sure he gets plenty of fluids and rest."

"We will." Eva got up and handed him an envelope filled with money. "Thank you, Joaquim. I appreciate your help."

"I'll walk him out," Hattie said, handing Maya the folder with the intrusive photos of them. She guided him to the front door and walked him into Eva's garden as the first slivers of daylight kissed the morning sky. She stopped halfway to the courtyard door to the driveway.

He paused, too.

Hattie touched his arm. "I trust you will tell no one about what you did and saw here tonight."

"Of course," he said.

"Because I would hate to read a story in the newspaper about those women to whom you gave abortions and forced into servicing you in the exam room. Your wife would be devastated."

His eyes got extra round, illuminated by the single light along the path.

"So, we have an understanding?" She opened the gate.

"Yes, we do." He clutched his medical bag close to his chest.

"Good, because I know where you live, Doctor." She closed the gate and walked inside without a second thought of issuing her threat. He was despicable.

Returning to the kitchen, she discovered Leo at the table and her mother filling his plate with food she had cooked before they got there. He appeared tired and resembled a boxer who had gone fifteen rounds in a hard fight. However, he looked much more alert than when they arrived.

"How are you feeling?" she asked.

"A little loopy from the pain meds, but the doc said that will last only a few hours." Leo took another bite of the cheese rolls and washed it down with acai juice. "Karl said you guys have been going through the items we took from the safe house. He has an interesting theory about the Nazis using the long-range bomber to drop spies into the States."

The Secret War

"Yes, but there's nothing that leads us to Wagner or the airfield. We're at a standstill." Karl patted Leo's back between the shoulders. "At least Javier will provide his statement later today. That should clear you."

"That's not very comforting while whoever killed Jimmy Cooke might still be out there, and Germany is about to escalate things." Leo had another mouthful of food.

"As much as I hate the man," Hattie said, "we should take what we know to Agent Knight. He has access to more resources. Maybe the FBI can send in more agents."

"Even if they did," Karl said, "it wouldn't be in time. Klein mentioned he only had a week here."

"What else can we do?" Leo asked. "We're out of leads."

"We use me as bait."

Eva snapped her head in Karl's direction. "Absolutely not."

Hattie closed her eyes at the hard truth. Leo likely would be cleared today, so that was no longer the issue. However, her father was right if they wanted to stop the Nazi attack on US soil. They had come to the end of their rope, and time was running out.

She opened her eyes and asked, "What are you proposing?"

Karl looked at her squarely in the eye. "I surrender myself to the German Embassy and offer to give up the lists but only to Strom Wagner in person. That will either draw Wagner to me or me to him. Whichever way, he will lead the rest of you to the airfield so you can stop that plane from becoming operational."

Hattie tightened her jaw. His proposal was too hard to swallow. "Sacrificing yourself is not an option, Father. There has to be another way."

"I'm open to suggestions, but like Leo said, we've exhausted our last lead. The Nazis are desperate to get their hands on those lists. Even if Wagner suspects a trap, he won't pass up an opportunity to get them."

"This is too risky." Hattie shook her head, fighting the inevitable.

"So was you and Leo in that hotel room with him posing as the engineer. Now it's my turn to play the hero." The determination in Karl's eyes suggested he was set on this dangerous course.

"We don't have to decide this right now," Hattie said. "There's still a little time. Can we table this until we've gotten some sleep?"

"Sure, sweetheart."

Eva offered the other side of her bed to Karl. "It's not like we haven't shared one before."

"Thanks," Karl said. "Couches and my back aren't getting along these days."

Eva's offer was made and accepted a bit too quickly to be mistaken for anything but something brewing between them. And that wisp of something warmed Hattie's heart. The sense of them becoming a family again was stronger than ever.

David told Leo he could take his room so he could sleep more comfortably and he would stretch out on the couch.

Hattie and Maya went to her room and changed into night clothes. While Maya was in the bathroom, Hattie checked the steamer trunk for the logbook as she did most nights. It was still there and had not altered position. She wanted to check the sheet music in David's bag, but it was in his bedroom, so she knocked on the door.

Leo called out, "Come in."

Hattie opened the door. "Sorry to bother you, but I need to get something for work."

"Sure, come in."

She located the satchel on the floor near the dresser, picked it up, and turned to leave but stopped. "I'm so glad you're okay, Leo. I was afraid they were going to kill you."

"That thought crossed my mind, too, but I wish we'd found something to lead us to Wagner."

"Me too." She chuckled, inspecting his face. "Huh, I think it's an improvement. Beverly might like it."

Leo laughed but then grimaced in pain. "Thanks a lot."

Hattie felt terrible but could not help herself and snickered. "I'm sorry. You get some sleep. Goodnight, Leo."

"Goodnight, Hattie." He laughed and closed the door.

She went back to her room.

Maya had finished in the bathroom and was brushing her hair.

Hattie opened the case on the bed and looked for the bundle of sheet music her father had gifted her. The sheets with the secret lists of spies embedded in the stanzas were not there. She looked again through each sheet of paper, but the bundle was gone. Every sheet with a coded message was missing. Another wave of dread washed through her. Six people had had access to that room since Hattie last checked on the music. Eva had no reason to take it, nor did her father. Maya had been in the room, but Hattie trusted her with her life and ruled her out. The others were Leo, David, and Navarro. Any of the three could have taken the sheet music, but the doctor made no sense as a suspect. Which left only Leo and David.

Yes, Hattie was angry that one of her friends had betrayed her deeply, but she was also frustrated with herself. She had once trusted David with all her secrets and had done the same with Leo. Now, she doubted her ability to read people. Was she so naïve that she blindly trusted anyone who showed her kindness? She had to be more careful. Which meant becoming more cynical, more suspicious of people...more jaded.

"Is everything okay?" Maya asked.

"No, the sheet music has disappeared."

"David had his satchel in the car with him tonight. There's a chance someone could have taken it when we were in the safe house."

"Wouldn't they swipe the entire case, thinking they didn't have time to sift through it?"

"You have a point," Maya said.

"I'll be right back. I have to tell my father."

Hattie entered the hallway, eased her door shut, and went to the other end of the house while David used the bathroom. She knocked softly on Eva's bedroom door. "Father, I need a word with you."

Moments later, the door opened, and her father appeared in his boxers and undershirt. "What's up?"

She leaned in and whispered, "The sheet music is missing."

"They're getting closer, or think they are. Those lists might not serve as viable leverage for much longer." His eyes looked distant as if he were weighing his options.

"There's still time."

"Get some sleep, sweetheart." He closed the door.

Hattie returned to her room, confused by her father's reaction, but she was too tired to go back and get to the bottom of it. She turned off the light and slid into bed. Maya wrapped an arm around her. Her mind wandered between the sheet music and the photos. Between the secret plane and the widow sitting somewhere in Germany, expecting to go dancing with her husband in Paris. She finally settled on the man whose life she had taken with her makeshift weapons. Stabbing him in the throat had disturbed her more than she had anticipated, and she muffled a sob.

"Are you okay?" Maya asked.

"I killed a man with my bare hands."

"You did what you had to do," Maya whispered.

Yes, slaying that man had been necessary for her survival, but killing, no matter how justified, was ugly. "It doesn't make it less disturbing."

"I know." Maya kissed her shoulder. "I sometimes have nightmares about the man we beat to death with rocks on Baumann's plantation. I remind myself I wouldn't be alive and holding you today if we hadn't."

Hattie finally let a tear fall, squeezed Maya's comforting arms, and gave in to her exhaustion, hoping the bad dreams would wait.

25

When Karl shut the door on Hattie, he knew what he had to do. Once whoever took the sheet music handed it over to the German Embassy, it would not have the allure it had now. He had to act before his only leverage for staying alive and flushing out Strom Wagner was gone.

"What did Hattie want?" Eva stepped out of the bathroom, rubbing lotion on her hands.

"The sheet music is missing." Karl returned to bed, leaning against the headboard on top of the covers.

She stopped mid-stride and gasped. "The lists."

"They're safe. Hattie took pictures of them, and I doctored the sheets, so the Morse code is gibberish. We're more concerned about who might have taken them. Were you home all day?"

"No, I gave two lessons at the studio."

"How about the doors? Was everything locked when you came back?"

"Yes, nothing was out of the ordinary."

"That means someone in the house took them. The question is who."

Eva slipped into the bed on the other side, sitting beside Karl and pulling the covers to her waist. "Who is your money on?"

"Any of them."

"You can't really think Maya did this?"

"I've learned to never rule anyone out, but this escalates things. I need to use our only avenue left to find Wagner before it's too late."

"What do you mean?"

"Like I offered earlier, I have to dangle the lists as bait while he still wants them."

"But that means offering yourself up." She took Karl's hand and laced her fingers with his.

"I have to." He was not turning himself in as some grand gesture of sacrifice to his country. Sure, he wanted to stop the attack, but this was the only way he knew to keep his family safe. The Nazis had to focus on him, not Hattie or Eva.

"I know you do."

"Hattie will know what to do."

"Have you told her?" Eva asked.

"I'll leave her a note before I go." Karl lifted his arm, inviting Eva to his side. "Come here."

She scooted over and rested her head against his chest. "I suppose I can't talk you out of this."

He rested his hand on her shoulder and pulled her in more snugly. "How long have you known me?"

"Too long."

"Can you promise me something?"

"It depends," Eva said, and Karl could almost hear her smirk.

"It's important that you help Hattie locate the Professor if I can't."

She squeezed him tight around his midsection. "Don't say that. Plus, I have no idea where she is."

"You know more than you think." He lifted her chin to look her in the eye. "Promise, Eva."

Her eyes moistened with tears. "I promise."

They fell asleep in each other's arms. Karl had dreamed of being this close to Eva for years but had thought the possibility of it coming true was about as likely as hell freezing over. Though Eva now knew the truth, that he had not become a Nazi, the hatred she had harbored for him for over a decade must surely have erased the love she once felt for him. But tonight, having her next to him again gave him hope that they could rekindle what they used to share. For now, he would settle for her kindness and this embrace.

After a few hours, Karl slipped out of bed and kissed Eva on the forehead without waking her. He dressed, snatched a bobby pin from her bathroom, and went to her study. He jotted down a message there for Hattie, telling her of his plan to give himself up at the German Embassy. She and the others were to follow and get Wagner. Next, he penned letters to the three women he loved more than life itself—Eva, Hattie, and Olivia. Each emotional goodbye expressed what he cherished most about them and what he wished for them. He sealed the letters into envelopes and slipped them and Hattie's note under her door.

Karl placed his hand on the door to Hattie's bedroom, where she lay sleeping with Maya. He hoped his suspicious mind was simply that, and Maya did not betray her. It would break his daughter's heart. "See you soon, sweetheart."

After loading the weapons and explosives and what Hattie and the others would need into Maya's trunk, he drove away. Three people in that house would go with Hattie after she found his note. Two deserved her trust, and one did not. Karl had a feeling he would know which one before this operation was over.

Hattie woke to the afternoon sun pouring through the window, and Maya was still asleep beside her. The alarm clock on the nightstand said it was nearly three. She pulled back the blanket and swung her legs over the edge of the mattress. Shaking off the fog of sleep, she noticed a piece of paper and three envelopes on the floor next to the door. She stretched, padded over, and picked up the items. The letters were individually addressed to Hattie, Eva, and Olivia. The loose paper was a note in her father's handwriting.

She gasped.

The message read, "Hattie, time is running out. We have a small window to use the sheet music as leverage. I'm turning myself into the German Embassy at four o'clock this afternoon. The offices are closed, so the only ones coming in and out of the building will be for me. If Wagner doesn't come to me, they will take me to him. Either way, this move will lead you to the airfield. I packed Maya's trunk with the explosives and weapons you'll need. Take her sedan with the others and stake out the embassy. There is only one way out with a car. Follow whoever comes and goes. You're ready for this. I know you'll get me out of this, sweetheart. No matter what happens, I need you to get the lists to the Professor, so make sure Eva stays home. Your mother can help you find her if I can't."

Hattie threw a hand over her mouth to muffle a sob.

Maya wrapped her arms around Hattie from behind, pressing their bodies together and looking over her shoulder. "Is everything all right?"

"Far from it."

Hattie hurried to Eva's bedroom to confirm that her father had left. She rushed in without knocking, discovering Eva was in tears on her side of the bed.

"Why didn't you stop him?" Hattie's tone was sharp.

"I woke, and he was gone, but I knew what he had planned."

"Why didn't you tell me? I could have stopped him."

"You know that's not true. He's stubborn, much like you."

David appeared in the doorway. "What's going on? Where's Karl?"

"He left to give himself up as bait." Hattie craned her neck toward him. "We're supposed to follow him."

"When?"

Hattie opened her mouth to answer, but with the sheet music missing, her gut told her David could not be trusted. "At ten tonight."

"That gives us time to find him," he said. "Should I have Maya call in your replacement?"

"She's already working on it. We can cover more ground if we spread out. Leo needs to rest, but Maya and I can check my dressing room at the Golden Room, the Halo Club, and her house. Can you canvas his shack in the favela and the bar and stake out the safe house from last night?"

"Sure."

"You take Eva's coupe. We'll take Maya's car and pick up Eva's sedan. Return here by seven."

Hattie had misdirected David and hopefully bought her, Maya, and Leo enough time to get on Karl's trail before he figured it out.

Karl parked two streets away where there were no cars. He wanted to approach the German Embassy on foot and not give Hattie an opportunity to stop him. Armand Klein had made it clear that a military assault on the United States was imminent. They had run out of leads. It would take drastic measures to lead them to Wagner and the airfield. His plan had gaping holes. Any number of things could go wrong, but he could not live with himself if the attack happened and he did not try to thwart it.

After hiding the car keys in the rear wheel well, he walked toward the embassy. He had emptied his pockets, leaving only a passport and the watch on his wrist for the Nazis to find. The timepiece, he hoped, would not be taken in a search, allowing him to track the hours in the Germans' custody.

At the second corner, he stopped for passing automobiles before crossing. He looked up and down the street and spotted Maya's sedan a block down and across from the embassy's main gate. It was the ideal spot from which to surveil comings and goings. His brief glance only made out two heads in the car, but he was confident there were more. The only question was whether the number totaled three or four, with David rounding out their numbers.

Traffic cleared, and Karl swiftly traversed the road. His stare went to the bright red Nazi flag towering over the buildings in the compound. It billowed in the gentle breeze like a blowing trumpet of strength and power the world should bow to. The last time he was at the embassy, he had come in with Heinz Baumann and gone by the name of Joseph Fuller. This was the name of the SS agent he had killed on the Rio-bound freighter from Baltimore. Assuming his identity was easy since they were similar in appearance, but it was not enough to get Baumann off the mission of finding Karl James. Karl had eluded capture for more than nine months now, but today, he was going to give up the chase and turn himself in.

The Brazilian sentry perked up first as he approached the shack at the gate. The Germans always hired civilian guards who could translate the local language to work alongside an SS officer.

Karl handed the Brazilian Fuller's passport and spoke in German to get the attention of the other guard. "Contact Strom Wagner. He will want to meet with me."

The SS officer put down his newspaper and got to his feet. He inspected the passport and looked at Karl. His eyes rounded with recognition, and he jumped on the phone, telling someone that Karl James was at the gate and wanted to speak to Wagner. He offered several "jawohl" replies before completing the call.

"Follow me," he said in German before opening the pedestrian gate.

Karl took a deep breath and stepped inside, onto sovereign German soil. There was no going back.

The SS man held the Joseph Fuller passport and led Karl down the curved driveway to the main building.

Two men in enlisted SS uniforms, armed with MP 40 submachine guns, emerged from the front doors and charged toward Karl. Each grabbed him by the arm, and the gate guard turned over his passport to one of them. Using firm grips, they led Karl into the lobby. The area was unoccupied. Karl expected as much for a Sunday afternoon.

The SS escorts walked him past the dozen chairs in the middle for visitors and the clerk's check-in desk. They paralleled the service counter along the back wall, going past the opulent German statuary around the perimeter and the prominently displayed framed photos of Adolf Hitler and Heinrich Himmler. They took him through a door, deeper into the nonpublic part of the embassy. If they escorted him to a room with windows, he knew the odds were better that the initial interrogation might be on the friendly side. However, they took him to the center of the building and into a room with a solid steel door and walls and a ceiling reinforced with sheet metal. Not only would escape be challenging, but the room was also soundproof.

After searching Karl and finding nothing, the guards left, locking the door.

The room had no decorations and was furnished with a five-foot-long table and two upright chairs made of steel. This was the embassy's version of an interrogation room, which was quite robust. Its only weakness was the tile floor, but burrowing through would take some time.

Karl positioned the desk lengthwise parallel to the door and far enough away from either wall so he would not be easily pinned in. He chose the chair facing the door to reduce the chance of being surprised and settled in for a lengthy wait. It was Sunday, and personnel would have to be called in and others notified before they received instructions on how to proceed.

He folded his arms across his chest and remained upright but struggled not to let the warm, stagnant air lull him to sleep. His thoughts, oddly, went to Hattie, and he wondered whether she had arranged for her backup performer to sing at the Golden Room tonight. He knew how much joy she took performing in front of an audience; he didn't want his plan to put her in breach of contract.

He nodded off a few times but woke whenever his head leaned abruptly to one side. Each time, he glanced at his watch. Two hours had passed, and sunset was nearing. His hosts were likely waiting for darkness to cloak whatever they had in mind.

The door finally opened.

"You've got to be kidding." Karl laughed. He recognized the man as the coward who had tried to flee from President Garza's yacht after Karl and Leo had taken out his fellow attackers. The man, however, had been stopped by Brazilian police. His diplomatic status and trading of Karl's name to the authorities obviously had gotten him out of prosecution but gotten him demoted to weekend standby duty.

"Why are you here, Herr James?" the agent asked in English.

"I want to meet with Strom Wagner to exchange the lists for leaving my family alone. I will remain in the shadows, but my wife, grandchildren, daughters, and their significant others are off-limits. The American vice president is considering the same offer. Both expire at midnight. The first one to agree to my terms gets the lists. And if they go back on their word, the lists will be released worldwide."

"I could beat their location out of you," the agent said.

Karl snickered to show the threat did not scare him. "What shall I call you? Because you won't like the ones I'm floating in my head."

"Klaus."

"Look, Klaus. You could try, but if I don't check in every twenty-four hours, the lists will be sent to every newspaper in Washington, DC, Rio, London, Berlin, and Paris. I don't believe Herr Wagner would want that to happen." Karl checked his watch. "We're already three hours in."

"I will get a message to him." The agent let out a loud breath filled with frustration.

"I suggest you do, but I will only accept a deal if I speak to him in person like I did with the Americans. I know he is still in the country and at the airfield, so bring him here or me to him." Karl had guessed that last part, but he was good at bluffing. "You've already wasted two hours, so you had better be quick about it."

The agent's eyebrows rose, signaling Karl was on the right track. "I'll be back." He left and locked the door.

Another hour passed, and Karl was getting antsy. He was thirsty and had to pee, and doubted the wisdom of his strategy of boxing in the Germans. He was betting the airfield was out of radio range, which meant the embassy would have to send a messenger to its location to courier Wagner back. That would waste too much time with a midnight deadline looming, and they would have to bring Karl to Wagner.

The door finally opened again. Klaus entered with a man dressed smartly in a double-breasted suit. Karl recognized him as the new German ambassador in Rio.

"I see he brought in the big guns, Herr Falkenberg." Karl spoke in German.

Falkenberg sat in the chair across from Karl and unbuttoned his jacket. "I am prepared to offer what you have requested in exchange for the lists tonight. You have my word that we will leave you and your family alone."

"Your word means nothing to me, so I'm afraid your man has wasted another hour. I have a history with Strom. If he says we have a deal, I will believe him. Either way, the lists will go public if I'm not released and back in Rio by three o'clock tomorrow." It was all a lie, but Karl had on his best poker face. "The choice is yours."

"All right, Mr. James." Falkenberg switched to English, perhaps as a reminder that he surmised Karl's loyalty lay with the United States. "We will take you to Herr Wagner."

"You better let me pee first. Otherwise, I'll make a mess of your charming accommodations."

Falkenberg stood, re-buttoned his jacket, and turned to Klaus. "See to it and leave immediately." He left without another word.

Klaus waved Karl to the door and walked him down the hallway to the bathroom. "Two minutes."

"When you're my age, it takes as long as it takes." Karl went inside, slamming the door in his face.

With limited time, he scanned the room while conducting his business, looking for anything that could serve as a weapon. The bobby pin he had taken from Eva's this morning and hid in his shoe would serve as a lock pick if the agent handcuffed him for the drive. All he needed was something more substantial to incapacitate the man.

The pedestal sink had no stopper, and the mirror above was intact. He would be heard if he broke it to use a large shard as a shiv. The wooden toilet paper roll was a potential choice, but it was too small and soft to do much damage. That left the toilet tank.

He finished, zipped his pants, and opened the faucet to run the water. Meanwhile, he lifted the tank lid and pried up the metal arm connecting the flush handle. When it was about to snap, he coughed hard to mask the noise. He tried to stop it, but his hand slipped, with the rod, into the tank.

"Great."

He shook off the rod and slid it into a calf-high sock. Its wetness made him cringe, but it would stay in place unless he broke into a full run.

Klaus pounded on the door and shouted. "Hurry up in there."

"Just finishing up." After replacing the tank lid, he washed his hands, dried them with a paper towel, and opened the door. "Hold your horses. My plumbing doesn't work like it used to."

Klaus led him to an exit that fed to a fenced-off area with five automobiles. Three were sedans, and two were Kubelwagens with their cloth tops down. One Kubel had its engine running and a driver in the front seat.

"Great," Karl said. This two-door utility vehicle was designed for rugged terrain and maneuverability, not comfort. "This is going to be a long night," he whispered.

"Give me your hands," Klaus said, holding a pair of handcuffs.

After being cuffed, Karl climbed into the back seat. Klaus sat in the front passenger seat, and they drove toward the gate. Last year, he would have been worried about getting out of this situation alive. He worked alone then and relied solely on his training and ingenuity. However, Hattie was waiting outside the fence tonight. She still had much to learn, but he did not doubt her loyalty and love for him. Together, they would get through this.

26

Hours earlier

Parked down the street from the German Embassy, Maya scooted closer on the bench seat beside Hattie and touched her shoulder as Karl disappeared inside the guarded compound. "Your father knows what he's doing."

"Still." Hattie leaned back and swallowed against the uneasiness manifesting in her throat. "So much could go wrong."

Hattie agreed with her father's strategy but was put off by his decision to set the plan in motion before discussing it further with the rest of the group. If she had known what tactic he planned to take once inside, his offer as the sacrificial lamb might have been easier to accept. She felt blindfolded and had to rely on the knowledge that Karl was a master at leveraging information and things to his advantage. However, this was not an ordinary intelligence-gathering operation. If he failed, there would not be a second chance to get it right. He would never be found.

Leo craned his neck from his spot in the driver's seat to look at her more clearly. "When you told me he'd gone off alone, I thought he was a few cards shy of a full deck. But Karl has been at this a long time and can manipulate any situation better than anyone I know. He'll lead us to Wagner and that airfield."

"Thanks, Leo."

"I'd be more worried about the pissy mood David will be in when he realizes you sent him on a wild goose chase." He picked up the binoculars beside him on the bench.

"It was the right call." That was the one thing Hattie was sure about today.

"I'll take the first watch." Leo lifted the binoculars to his eyes and focused steadily on the embassy gate, which was a block down.

Maya leaned back and closed her eyes. Napping was the wise choice, but Hattie was too amped to rest. She reread her father's note, concentrating on the last sentence. "*No matter what happens tonight, I need you to get the lists to the Professor, so make sure Eva stays behind. Your mother can help lead you to her if I can't.*" It almost sounded like he expected to fail, and that was not like him. He never gave up hope.

Maybe that sliver of doubt was why she had brought the letter he left for her, leaving the other two in the study for Eva to find. She folded his note, returned it to her handbag, and dug out the envelope. After sliding open the flap, she pulled out and unfolded the sheet of paper and read it in silence.

To my songbird. The day you were born, the center of my world forever shifted. From the moment I first held you, everything I did was for you. Like your mother was, I knew you were destined for great things. I was already proud of the woman I knew you would become. Those seven years when it was the three of us before your sister arrived were magical. Your mother and I were never more in love, and Eva was never happier. Music may have been her passion, but motherhood was her calling. By the time Olivia was born, you were so much like Eva, beautiful inside and out. You both had a heart of gold and a voice that could bring a smile to millions.

I'm ashamed to say that, as my career took a turn, I lost sight of what was most important. My choice to do what I thought was for the greater good strained your relationship with her, and that is my greatest regret. I can't undo the past, but hopefully, you can learn from my mistake. Never lose sight of family, whether blood or chosen. Maya is your chosen partner. Regardless of whose path you choose to follow, there will be times when you'll have to choose between what is right and what is best for you. Choose neither, sweetheart. Choose what is best for Maya, and you will never have to live with regret. Today, I choose what is best for you and Eva. I choose to bring my exile to an end. I choose to no longer live in the shadows. I love you with all my heart. Father.

Hattie covered her mouth with her hand and whimpered. He planned for this to be his final mission and wanted to come back to her...to Eva ...to their family. He had sacrificed for his country, and this message was his twenty-twenty hindsight. An admission that what his government had asked of him was too much. And Hattie loved him more for it. If she had half his strength, courage, and wisdom, she could never fail Maya.

Hattie wept silently for the man her father was, for the pain her family had endured, and for the partner she hoped to be for Maya. When she settled and grabbed her handbag, she caught Leo watching her in the rearview mirror. He said nothing, but his look of concern said everything.

When he returned his focus to the embassy gate, Hattie stuffed the letter into the envelope, the envelope into her purse, and her bag onto the floorboard. She scooted closer to Maya, leaned her head against her shoulder, and closed her eyes.

Yes, a nap was the wise choice.

It was Hattie's watch. It was seven o'clock with the evening sun fading over the western mountains. Maya sat in the passenger seat beside her, and Leo lay in the back asleep. She and Maya sipped from their corked water bottle sparingly to preclude the need to use the bathroom. Between checks with the binoculars, Hattie held Maya's hand. It was the first time she had been alone with Leo without Nazi guards since revealing her and Maya's relationship. It was also the first time she did not have to hide such an intimate act from him. Having everyone in her inner circle know her truth felt freeing.

She checked her mirrors, looking for signs of anyone surveilling them, but found nothing suspicious. Traffic remained light in this government-office-dominated part of town.

A luxury car passed their vehicle, carrying the driver and one passenger in the back. Hattie focused on it when it slowed approaching the embassy. It stopped for passing automobiles in front of the gate, preparing to make a turn. She sat straighter in her seat. "Someone has arrived."

Maya reached into the back and tapped Leo's leg. "Leo."

"What?" He popped up, grimacing in pain. He was still sore from his beating.

"A sedan is here."

He leaned his head forward between the headrests. Hattie handed him the binoculars.

"It's the German Ambassador's car. Karl has gotten their attention." He passed the field glasses back. "Do you want to switch and let me drive?"

The sentry saluted the vehicle and rolled open the gate with great speed. The auto disappeared inside the compound.

"Not on your life." Hattie sensed things would happen quickly now. She trusted her reaction time more than his tonight. "You have a swollen eye and might have a concussion. I'm driving."

Fifteen minutes later, the SS guard bolted from the shack and pushed open the gate. He stood at the side of the driveway and saluted smartly again. Hattie started their engine, shifted the transmission into first gear, and turned the wheels when the ambassador's staff car reappeared. She gripped the wheel, asking herself whether the ambassador would personally transport Karl to the airfield. Berlin would consider her father's capture a monumental success, so whoever brought him in would be held in good favor. She doubted, however, that an ambassador would take on such a time-consuming task, so she put the gear in neutral, set the brake, and killed the engine.

Maya snapped her stare at Hattie. "Aren't we going to follow?"

"No."

"We're going to lose him," Maya said.

"Be patient." As each minute passed, Hattie twisted the steering wheel with both hands tighter and tighter. She hoped she had made the right decision. If she guessed wrong, they would lose her father's trail.

The Secret War 223

Sweat beads dripped from her brow and trickled down her cheeks as doubt overtook her. She ran in her head all of her horrible choices over the years. Dating John Hamilton during her senior year to appear normal. Opening her heart to Helen Reed. Blaming her mother for breaking up their family. Drinking herself into oblivion to numb her heartache. And trusting David with her secrets. She feared not following the ambassador would surpass them all.

Then...

The guard opened the gate again. She brought the engine to life, holding her breath. A German utility vehicle with its retractable top folded down rolled through, and she let a grin form. When the car stopped at the curb, she grabbed the binoculars. Three men were inside. Her father was in the back. He looked in her direction when the Kubel turned onto the street, sending a wave of relief through her.

"We're in business." Hattie shifted into gear and followed at a distance.

"Good instinct." Leo patted her shoulder and leaned back, settling in for the ride, wherever it took them.

Hattie blended into the Sunday evening traffic, easily tailing the Kubel through the city. Their steady direction of travel was very telling. Either the driver was not trained in evading surveillance, he was not expecting it, or he was luring Hattie in. No matter the reason, she maintained her spacing to minimize the chance of being seen. The same held true on the main highway, which cut a wide path north through the jungle. Occasional passing traffic gave credence to traveling behind Karl's vehicle. The waxing gibbous moon remained out, showing three-quarters of its light side. It provided enough illumination for her to douse her headlights if she needed to follow closer in the winding hills.

The turn west an hour later proved trickier. The two-lane road was still paved but much less traveled and narrower. The tropical forest closed in, creating the sense that they were wedged between two giant walls of trees and shrubs. Clouds started to form, dimming their route, and the many curves along the path became dangerous with their lights off, so Hattie increased her traveling separation. Periodically, she upped her speed before a turn until lights appeared, ensuring she did not lose them on a side road.

The clouds darkened another hour into the drive, threatening to release their fill of water. They cut off the only illumination source besides her headlights, which meant staying close was imperative. She was closer than her training had informed her was a safe distance to remain unseen, but the conditions made it necessary.

At the first raindrops, Hattie slowed and doused her lights, expecting the Kubel to pull over. She crept to a stop at the turn's apex, discovering she had guessed right. The vehicle was idling on the shoulder. Its front and back lights were still on, and exhaust fumes billowed from the tailpipe in a shimmery cloud rising against the backdrop of the foliage.

Karl's escorts got out, requiring her to cut the engine to avoid being heard. The Germans briefly looked down the road in the direction of Maya's car but quickly shifted their attention to their task when more raindrops fell. They unlatched the front and rear roof bindings and unfolded the car's top until it was in place, cocooning the passenger compartment. After securing the windshield latches, they climbed back inside the vehicle. The Kubel lurched forward like the driver had ground the gears. They resumed their route.

Hattie turned on the engine and put the sedan in gear, leaving her headlights off. She wanted to be a reasonable distance back before turning them on. She followed but slowed suddenly, watching the car ahead turn right and its lights disappear into the vegetation. Moments later, she completed the turn, too, discovering that they were on a rocky dirt road where the jungle formed a narrow tunnel around them. Fear tingled the back of her neck. The German utility vehicle was designed for rough terrain with heavy-duty tires, but Maya's sedan was made for the city. Her tires might not stand up under these rough conditions.

Twenty minutes in, Hattie's fear became a gut-wrenching reality. The car pulled dramatically to the left. They had developed a flat.

27

An hour into the trip, Karl's back began to ache. He doubted his escorts would answer if he asked how much longer he would have to endure the pain. Consequently, he remained quiet and shifted in his seat for another hour. When he saw signs for Tres Rios, he was confident these men were taking him to the secret airfield.

Nine months ago, when he was still working for Baumann on his plantation, he had overheard visiting SS agents mention something big under construction in the jungle past the rivers. They had made it sound as if it could change the trajectory of the war. He had tried for weeks to find what was being built without success. Everyone had been tight-lipped, and he never picked the right agent to follow. He had an inkling at the time that whatever was going on would be used against the United States. Why else would it have been located in the Western Hemisphere? But the bomber, combined with his theory about the new crop of spies to replenish what his lists had endangered, made this the most critical mission of his career. Turning himself in had set the bomb ticking regarding those lists; Ambassador Falkenberg had likely already sent a coded telegraph to Germany, telling them of Karl's capture and his ultimatum. He had only so much time to stop the attack now, get the information to the Professor, and get his life back.

During the drive, he had noticed Hattie behind them several times, though she had done an excellent job hiding her presence. Then again, he was on the lookout for her.

The night sky darkened with rain clouds. When he felt the first drops on his head, he knew it would not be long before an entire store of water was unleashed on them. The jacket he had on would begin to cling to him like a wet rag in the first minute of a jungle deluge.

The driver quickly pulled their Kubel to a stop to raise the roof. As soon as his escorts got out of the vehicle, he reached inside his shoe and retrieved Eva's bobby pin. As the men worked on the roof, he focused on picking the lock of his handcuffs, using the noise of the latches to mask his activity. By the time they were done, he had the cuffs loosened enough to slip out of them easily and the pin had been returned to its hiding place.

"Thanks. I thought I was going to show up looking like a drenched mutt," Karl said when they got back in. He chanced a question he knew they would not answer with any accuracy. "How much longer?"

"A while," the driver said.

Once they were moving again, Karl looked through the small square opening in the back of the canvas covering. It was hard to tell, but he thought he spotted the fender of Maya's car glistening in the light drizzle. His shoulders relaxed with the knowledge that Hattie was right behind them.

They turned onto a narrow dirt road, which changed the conditions of the game entirely. Fears that Maya's auto might not keep up on the rocky terrain crept in. Karl peeked through the opening as frequently as he thought safe as the rain came down harder, but he never caught the glimmer of Maya's sedan again.

The storm passed quickly, which was Karl's chance to let Hattie catch up if she had car trouble. "I need you to pull over," he said in German.

"Why?"

"I have to pee again."

"It can wait," the agent in the passenger seat said.

"No, it can't." Karl needed to make a fuss they could not ignore, so he unzipped his pants and shifted. "You can explain to Wagner why the vehicle smells like piss."

The Secret War 227

"Wait! You are more trouble than you're worth," the agent said, ordering the driver to stop again. When he did, he added, "Make it quick."

Karl used his cuffed hands to open the rear door. He walked on the muddy road, staying in the ruts created by their tires until he was about five feet behind their Kubel. He stepped to the edge of the shrubs and pretended to conduct his business. A minute later, he heard another door open and close and glanced over his shoulder. The driver had gotten out to relieve himself, too.

Karl stalled. Finally, the other agent yelled at him to hurry up. He zipped and shifted to step toward their vehicle when he saw a faint glow above the tree line. It must have been the headlights from Maya's sedan, or so he hoped. He returned to the Kubel, satisfied he had done some good. Maybe.

Klaus held the door and sneered. "No more delays."

Karl sneered back. "You are in no position to make demands of me. And when the time comes, I will take great pleasure in killing you." He slid in the open rear door and slammed it shut. "Let's go."

They resumed their trek toward what Karl assumed was the secret airfield. The route was slow on this road, and he saw the glow above the trees several times, but his escorts seemed oblivious to its presence. Or so he hoped.

His mind drifted to the letters he wrote before leaving the house that morning. He intended the recipients to read them in the event of his death, so he had poured his heart into each one.

The one to Olivia came easily. No matter how old she turned and how many children she had with Frank, she would always be his baby. Frank put a roof over her head and food on the table, as a good husband should, but Karl doted on her and bought her trinkets to show his love. His little girl was smart, kind, and as loving a mother as Eva was, and she was raising her son and daughter to be the same. The kindness he saw in those kids every time he visited was a legacy he was proud of.

Eva's letter came harder because of the pain he had caused her. All those years of concealing his real job tore him up inside. However, it paled in comparison to the agony Eva went through, thinking he had turned into a Jew-hating Nazi, particularly since she had Jewish blood running through her veins. His lies drove her into another man's arms, and the only one he could blame for her moment of weakness was himself. He was in her debt for hiding what she believed to be the truth from their girls and not turning them against him. Despite thirteen rocky years of her misguided hatred of him, she was the only woman he would ever love. He was sure they would have stayed together to this day if he had not gone down the rabbit hole of undercover work.

Hattie's letter was the hardest to write because his life in the shadows had scarred her deeply. While Eva turned her pain into hatred, Hattie was stuck in the middle. She was barely out of high school when his marriage to Eva fell apart, and she was left holding the pieces. At the same time Eva did not tell the girls about him, Hattie did not tell Olivia about finding Eva with another man. Protecting the ones they loved was a trait Hattie and Eva shared, but he regretted being the underlying reason that either of them felt the need to exercise it. However, his most profound regret was ruining the special bond Hattie and Eva once had. Their relationship was on the mend, but they had lost thirteen years together. That was a consequence for which he would never forgive himself.

About twenty minutes later, they slowed and came to a stop where the road ended at a thick growth of vines. The driver honked the car horn. A small section of vegetation shaped like a pedestrian gate opened inward. A man in civilian clothes and armed with an MP 40 submachine gun appeared.

They had arrived.

Hattie eased off the gas and gripped the wheel tighter, making adjustments to steer the sedan straight until it coasted to a stop. She allowed enough room on the passenger side in case Maya had to get out.

"What's wrong?" Maya asked.

"I think we have a flat. It's pulling hard to the left." Hattie turned off the engine and stepped into the rain. The front left tire was down, but the muddy conditions would make changing it challenging. It would take too many precious minutes to fix, time they could not afford to lose.

Maya and Leo got out and inspected the tire with her.

"Do you have a jack and a spare?" he asked.

"I do," Maya said, extending her hand. "Key, Hattie."

Maya and Leo rushed to the trunk and emptied it enough to remove the tools and the spare. They worked at a feverish pace. While Maya positioned and operated the jack to raise the car, Leo loosened the lug nuts. Lifting the spare into place, he grunted in pain. In less than ten minutes, they had on a fresh tire and the old one in the trunk, along with the tools and weapons.

The second the doors closed with everyone back inside, Hattie shifted into gear and pulled out. Maya and Leo were filthy from head to toe. They had completed the repair in record time. However, Hattie feared they had not worked fast enough to catch up with her father if there was more than one side road ahead.

She pushed the boundary between speed and safety, and it required every bit of skill she learned from her father to keep from fishtailing. The rain had stopped, but hope had left her after fifteen minutes, and tears trickled down her cheeks.

Suddenly, a wall of vines appeared where the road should have continued. She slammed on her brakes, rocks crunching beneath the tires. Unsure what to think of the obstacle, she put the gear shifter in neutral and idled the engine.

"What do you think it is?" Maya asked.

"I have no idea, but all of us shouldn't be in the car when we check it out."

"Give me the trunk key," Leo said. "I'll come up by foot from the tree line."

Hattie reversed several yards, positioning the sedan out of view of the obstruction. She had a bad feeling and did not want to chance losing their armament. "Take the explosives."

"I'll hide the automatic weapons under the flat tire." He hopped out, popped open the trunk, and returned to the driver's side, carrying a submachine gun and two knapsacks crisscrossed over his shoulders.

Hattie rolled down the window, taking the keys back. "I'll give you a minute to get into position."

He looked weak from the beating he took last night but also determined to provide her with backup. "I'm going in blind, so I'm not sure what I'll come across in the brush."

"Either way, we're going in," Hattie said. They had not come all this way only to turn around when her father had risked so much. No. She knew what had to be done.

He patted her arm through the opening and disappeared into the trees.

Hattie and Maya checked their sidearms, thumbed off their safeties, and placed them in their waistbands at the small of their backs. They said nothing, focusing on the road ahead, and clutched the other's hand. That touch said everything that needed saying between them. They would do anything for the other, as Hattie would do anything for her father.

Her pulse thumped her impatience as she counted down the seconds to give Leo time to move into a tactical position. At ninety, giving him an extra thirty, she squeezed Maya's hand and let go. "Lost tourist again."

If the vines hid a fence, they hoped to entice out whatever guard might be on the other side. And when he spoke to one of them, the other would subdue or shoot him.

Maya pulled a folded road map from the glove box and partially unfurled it, preparing for their performance.

Hattie turned on her headlights and moved forward slowly. The wall of vegetation came into view, and she continued toward it, stopping ten feet short of it. She and Maya exited the car, putting on their act of lost and confused travelers while standing in front of the beams.

They spoke in Portuguese.

"You took the wrong turn off the highway," Maya said, waving and pointing her index finger on the map.

"You said it was three kilometers past the last intersection. I drove exactly that distance. The cabin should be on this road. Either the map is wrong or your mother's directions are."

A man with a machine gun emerged from the vegetation five feet away, behind Maya, aiming his weapon at her. Hattie moved to draw her firearm, and Maya did the same at the precise time, suggesting another armed guard was likely sneaking up on her.

Two voices shouted something in German, and Hattie felt something hard pressed against her back.

Hattie and Maya were too slow. The Germans were too quick. Her first approach to the wall had blown the element of surprise, and waiting for Leo had given the enemy time to set up. She had blown it, but Leo was still out there. Or was he? He could have passed out from his concussion or been captured by a German guard. Hattie pushed that last thought out of her head. She trusted his strength and ability to escape a one-on-one pickle.

The men continued to shout.

Maya raised her arms, but Hattie kept hers down. She glanced over her shoulder, determining her attacker held his gun with both hands on his right side. Her training kicked in.

She pivoted on her right heel. Spinning left, she lunged toward him, taking herself out of the line of fire. He yanked his weapon back to aim again and fired a burst into the gravel. Hattie flung her right elbow into the man's face, causing him to stumble backward and stop firing. She sent him to the ground with a swift knee to the groin and drew her pistol, but before she could wheel around, the other guard shouted something behind her.

"Hattie," Maya called out.

Hattie turned. The German had swapped his machine gun for a Luger and was holding it against Maya's temple.

Hattie would find a way out of this if it were only her, but she could not risk Maya being hurt. She dropped her weapon and raised her hands in surrender.

Her attacker climbed to his knees and struggled to his feet. He stood, bent slightly at the waist, grimacing in pain, before grabbing Hattie by the arm. Both men ushered her and Maya toward the dense vegetation. A small section similar in size to a pedestrian door opened inward, and they took them inside. A third guard closed it. Hattie glanced back and determined the wall was a cyclone fence and gate covered with wild vines.

After tying Hattie's and Maya's hands with rope, the sentries yanked their arms, forcing them deeper into whatever this place was. Shadows from the moonlight played tricks in the dark, but Hattie eventually made out a vast clearing in the jungle. Several buildings were on the left, and the flat open area on the right must have been an airstrip.

They had arrived.

28

Karl's escorts drove him farther into the airfield, angling toward the structures on the left. The tires on their utility vehicle crunched the gravel on the path along their route. They were deep in the heart of the Brazilian jungle, yet they were not. An expansive section had been cleared, an airstrip and taxi aprons paved, and support buildings raised. This space was an operational airfield in the middle of the wilderness.

The entrance to each building was lit by a single porch light. The constant whine of gas generators explained the availability of electricity this far from civilization. They stopped in front of a support building, sitting just shy of two massive airplane hangars.

Karl exited the vehicle with his hands still loosely cuffed. He focused on the area near the taxi apron. More than a dozen large bombers were parked in the shadows there, sending a chill through him. He had thought the attack might involve five or six planes, but the plan was obviously more extensive than he first thought. If this strike got off the ground, Germany could deliver a devastating blow against the United States.

Klaus yanked Karl's arm, but Karl threw off his grip. He considered escaping his restraints, overpowering these two, and finding Wagner on his own, but that came with too much risk. He first needed to assess the threats lurking in and around the buildings.

Knowing Klaus had orders to get him to Wagner alive, he replied boldly to the rough treatment. "Careful. You might meet your demise sooner than you think."

"Inside." The other agent gestured toward a support building made of corrugated sheet metal that was connected to the first hangar.

Karl walked with his hands at his belly, making it appear as if they were bound securely. He stretched the kinks from his back as he passed through the threshold. The sterile interior resembled many military facilities he had encountered during his career, hastily constructed with painted plywood.

His escorts led him down the corridor, past an office. Glancing through the open door, Karl saw four men. Two were sitting behind desks, and two were standing at a chalkboard on the far wall, studying a hand-drawn schematic. Karl surmised two must have been the aeronautical engineers Hattie had met with three nights ago.

They made it to the hangar. The area smelled of machine oil and aviation fuel. Various tools and equipment lined the walls, but a plane was not there, the one thing he had hoped to see up close. If it was still there, then maybe he was not too late. Both sides of the hangar had glass windows and four doors, suggesting each led to more offices.

They went left through the middle door and entered a generously sized office. The multiple tables and chairs suggested it was a briefing room.

"Sit," Klaus said before leaving with the driver.

Karl suspected one stayed nearby to guard the door while the other went to brief Wagner. He sat at a table across the room, facing the door he had come through with a good view of a second door at the head of the room. A scan of his surroundings did not reveal any better item to serve as a weapon than the one he already had. He then slipped one hand from the cuffs and retrieved the metal toilet handle arm. He stuffed it in his sleeve far enough so he could palm an end to keep it in place and returned his hand to the cuff. He considered what tactic to take once Wagner arrived and decided it would depend on who else was in the room. No matter how many there were, taking out Wagner was the priority.

According to his watch, ten minutes had passed when the door opened again, Wagner walked inside, and Klaus returned. That was much quicker than he had expected, so fast that Karl suspected Wagner had been waiting for him. The question was how he knew to expect him when this location was out of military radio range. He supposed the embassy might have sent a messenger to the airfield while he had been waiting in the interrogation room.

Wagner was dressed in a pristinely pressed single-breasted dark pinstriped suit over a white button-down shirt and a tasteful blue tie. He had worn something similar nearly every time Karl had seen him, making him think it had become Wagner's uniform of sorts.

Karl remained in his seat, forcing Wagner to come to him. "Hello, Strom," he said in English.

Klaus stayed at the door.

"Hello, Karl." Wagner came closer but not within striking distance. "That incident with Eva was purely business, not personal."

"You should have let her go, Strom. We once swore to each other that our families were off-limits."

"Taking her was Ziegler's doing. I was cleaning up his mess."

"By using her as a pawn. That is unforgivable."

"I can't change the past, Karl. She survived with no harm done." Wagner adjusted his tie, a sign he was anxious. "Coming here was a mistake."

"It may seem that way."

"I will get those lists and you." Wagner looked confident. However, appearing to have the upper hand, even when the opposite was true, was his style, and that would be his downfall.

"I hate to disappoint you, but that won't happen tonight," Karl said. "Did your man brief you?"

"Yes, he did."

"Then you know if I don't check in tomorrow, those lists will go public. I want your word that my family, including their significant others, are off-limits, as it has always been. If you do that, I will give you what you want and fade into the shadows."

"Herr Himmler is not happy with you. When I left Berlin, he told me not to consider coming home unless I bring you in. Your disappearance embarrassed him, Karl."

"His ego is not my greatest worry."

The Secret War   235

"It should be. He won't let this go." Wagner released an uncharacteristic sigh, which likely meant his last point was not a bluff. Karl's old acquaintance was caught in the middle.

"You need to convince him. You know I love only one thing more than country."

"Family," Wagner said the term with reverence.

When Karl knew him in Germany, that once meant something to him, and from the resolute look in his eyes, it still did. Protecting family was why both of them did horrible deeds.

"After what happened with Eva, you realize I'll do whatever it takes to keep them safe."

"You must reconsider, Karl, and tell me where those lists are."

"Not until I have your word."

"I'm afraid that won't happen." Wagner snapped his fingers.

Klaus opened the door and moved to the side.

Karl's stomach twisted into a massive knot. Hattie and Maya entered under guard with Lugers pressed against their temples and their hands bound by rope. They both looked unhurt, which was the only reason he did not spear Wagner in the neck.

"I'm sorry, Father," Hattie said. "We couldn't let you do this alone. I thought the *three* of us were in this together?"

The way Hattie emphasized the word *three*, he was sure she was telling him that a third person had come with her and Maya. Considering their lingering doubts about David, it must have been Leo. His absence provided a sliver of hope. He needed to stall to give him time to infiltrate, find them, and assess what they were up against.

"You've made a grave error, Strom." Karl bit back his anger to remain calm. He swallowed it, letting the raw emotion fuel his determination to get out of this with everyone alive. "You have broken all the rules."

"They came here armed, making themselves a target. They changed the rules, not me." Wagner took a step closer. One more, and he would be within striking range. "If you don't give me the lists, I must treat them as combatants."

"I promise, if you hurt either of them, your wife and four children will not be safe." Karl sneered. "I won't stop until they are all dead. And, if for some reason I don't kill you tonight, there will be no place you can hide. I will find you."

"Enough grandstanding, Karl. The lists' location or they die."

"I don't think you want to be why those lists go public. Himmler will have your head."

"He'll have my head if I let you go." Wagner craned his neck to look at the others behind him. "Kill the other one."

"Nooo!" Hattie shouted and squirmed to break free of her captor's hold, but he was too big and too strong.

Karl raised his leg to step forward and get within arm's length of Wagner but stopped when the door at the head of the room flew open.

"I told you not to hurt her." The third person on Hattie's team appeared in the doorway, but it was not the person Karl expected. The man walked into the room without a guard forcing him in.

Hattie's stunned expression signaled she was processing this turn of events. Karl was, too. He had expected duplicity from this man but did not expect Hattie to trust him enough to bring him with her on this operation.

"David?" Hattie finally said, but the confusion in her voice was surprising. She was not expecting him, not at all.

Every suspicion Karl had had about David since shaking his hand for the first time on Christmas Eve last year in New York was just confirmed. He was a spy. The only thing he was not sure about was for how long. David had been friends with Hattie for two years. If the SS recruited him after Karl fled to Brazil, that meant he was weak, greedy, or both. But Karl had sensed for some time Himmler's growing doubt regarding Karl's loyalty to Germany over the United States. David Townsend could have been Himmler's safety valve, assigned years ago as a deep mole to get close to Hattie and keep an eye on him.

"What are you doing here?" Hattie said, tears building in her eyes.

"Protecting you." David's worried expression appeared genuine, but Karl was still skeptical.

"But how did you know to come here?"

"How is not the important question, sweetheart. The question is when," Karl said. He turned to David. "When did you know to come here, and when did the SS recruit you?"

David kept his stare on Hattie. "It was Wagner not long after we arrived in Rio, but everything I've done was to protect you. The rest does not matter." He shifted his focus to Wagner. "Like I told you before, I know where he hid the lists. I'll make sure they stay here and will tell you where when I know Hattie is safe and back in the United States."

The wounded look on Hattie's face said reality had sunk in. David had betrayed her deeply. He had gained her trust and learned her secrets, only to get to those lists. "David, how could you?" she called out, her voice tainted with the pain and anger stemming from his treachery.

"It's all right, Hattie. I'll protect you." David turned to Wagner again. "I hadn't realized it until yesterday, but I've had them all this time. The lists for Hattie's life."

"You see, Karl. I can get what I want another way." Wagner dismissively waved his hand at David. "I can torture him. His kind always breaks."

"But the lists alone do you no good without the cipher." Continuing the dialogue was Karl's goal. He needed to give Leo time to get in place.

"I know you, Karl James. Family above all else. We will break your code. The important thing is to get my hands on those lists. And you."

"David may have figured out where I originally hid the lists," Karl said, "but who's to say I wasn't onto him and altered them?"

"He's right." Another voice came from the open doorway leading to the hangar. Leo Bell appeared. A German guard held him at gunpoint. "He was onto David. Hattie too. It makes sense that he would have altered the lists."

Hattie closed her eyes briefly and slumped her shoulders in palpable disappointment. She clearly had expected him to rescue them, not get captured. But was he? Leo's hands were not bound like Karl's, Hattie's, and Maya's were. Neither were David's.

Something was off, and Karl's intuition told him the situation had just become more unstable...more dangerous. It was reasonable for David to not be restrained, given the SS had recruited him. But Leo not being tied up was perplexing. The Germans were trained to control their captives, and restraining them would have been the first step. No Nazi guard assigned to a clandestine facility would have been so careless without a good reason.

"We know he did that to the originals compiled by his War and State Departments, so no one had both lists but him." Wagner turned to Karl.

"But you would not chance destroying the only copy. You are too smart for that."

"That's the first thing you've gotten right tonight, Strom. I am too smart for you, which is why you will never find the correct lists."

Leo stepped forward and spoke in perfect German. "I can help with that, Herr Wagner."

29

Hattie's mind reeled from the revelations inside that room. Despite the underlying doubts she had had for months, she was having a hard time coming to terms with the realization that David was an SS asset. Now, she had to understand why Leo appeared to be helping and could speak German flawlessly. Her world turned upside down in the last few minutes.

"Leo?" Hattie's heart sank. She was unsure what he had said, but the smile on Wagner's lips meant it was not good for her or her father. Or Maya.

Leo switched to English. "Karl embedded the lists in sheet music that your man over there"—he jutted his chin toward David—"has carried around for months. I have that sheet music now, but you need the photographs of them that depict the original markings. I'll have to show you where I've hidden them...in the nightshade."

Her father cocked his head at Leo, but Hattie's brain went into a tailspin. This was betrayal stacked upon betrayal, threatening to swallow her whole. The only thing keeping her from drowning in it was her seething hatred for Leo and David at the moment. She had let them both into her inner circle, trusting them with her secrets, and they repaid her with duplicity.

A mountain of questions formed regarding David. She could almost swallow David's betrayal since the Germans had approached him in Brazil and likely threatened to harm him or Hattie unless he recovered the lists. After all, it had been a crazy nine months. Both the Nazis and Americans had been desperate to get their hands on them to protect their covert agents and unearth enemy spies in their own country. But David had claimed that everything he had done was to protect Hattie. How far had he gone? Did he kill Nala Cohen and FBI Agent Butler to obtain Baumann's logbook? If he did, why did he hide it in their steamer trunk and not just burn it?

There were probably many other questions, but Hattie's head was already hurting from looking at past events through a new lens.

The most perplexing twist was Leo. Nothing he had said or done would make her think he would help the Germans. He came across as an honorable man loyal to the United States. The job of a spy, though, was to con people into thinking he or she was something he or she was not. Hattie had dismissed too quickly the possibility of Leo taking the sheet music. But why would he do such a thing? Was he really a German? Or were the Nazis holding something over him, too? And how did he learn about the photographs?

She might never get answers to her questions, and in truth, that did not matter right now. She had to figure out how to get her, Maya, and her father out of there.

Wagner snapped his fingers at the guards. "Take care of the rest. We don't need them."

"Wait." Leo put up a hand in a stopping motion. "You'll need them alive if you can't break the code without the cipher."

"That might be true, Mr. Weiss." Wagner unbuttoned his double-breasted suit coat and turned his attention to David. "But you, Mr. Townsend, have overplayed your hand. Your services are no longer required." He opened his jacket flap and drew a Luger pistol from a hidden holster.

"Whoa." David raised his hands chest high with his palms out. "I've done everything you asked. I killed those agents to get Baumann's logbook back."

"But a copy still made it to the American government."

The Secret War 241

"I had no idea she'd taken those pictures. You told me to get and hide the book if it showed up. I did that. You told me to keep you apprised of Karl's movements. I did that, too."

"But you never gave up the lists. It's a shame." Wagner grunted…a sound of disgust. "We expected more of a backbone from the grandson of Friedrich Ebert, something to prove you weren't like your father."

"You promised if I helped, you would leave my parents alone." David formed his hands into fists and tensed his arms and shoulders. He was ready for a fight.

"You're Friedrich Ebert's grandson?" Karl raised both eyebrows.

"Who is that?" Hattie asked.

"Only Germany's first elected president in 1919."

"Yes," Wagner said, "but like his father, he can't be trusted. He's more loyal to your daughter than to the country of his birth."

"What do you expect?" David sneered. "You hold my brother hostage and threaten to kill my parents unless I do your bidding. Fear never instills loyalty."

"Which is why we no longer need you." Wagner aimed and fired.

The loud crack was deafening, causing everyone in the room to flinch.

"Nooo!" Hattie shouted. Her lungs constricted, making it hard to breathe, as David clutched his gut, blood oozing between his fingers.

His shocked expression was terrifying and said he knew death was coming for him. He dropped to the floor on his knees, his head wobbling like a child's toy until his body thumped onto the concrete.

Hattie broke her captor's hold and rushed toward him. David may have been willing to sell out her father by turning over those lists, but she wanted to believe it was all to protect her. He deserved to be punished, but not shot to death. She pressed her bound hands against his abdomen to stop the bleeding, but the damage was too severe. Wet, warm liquid coated her fingers, and a distinct metallic smell wafted up from where the bullet struck him. She had been around enough death to expect the odor, but it still turned her stomach. Every death did.

"Let me help," Maya cried out. Seconds later, she was at Hattie's side, helping put pressure on the wound, but the blood was still coming too fast.

"Take Weiss to get the photos," Wagner said, "and bring him to my office. James is to stay alive until I return."

Footsteps and a slamming door sounded behind her, but Hattie could not take her eyes off David. He only wanted to protect her. "I'm so sorry, David."

He coughed up blood and weakly placed a hand on Hattie's arm. "It was all for you. Butler. Cohen. Cooke." He spewed more red, and his words came out splintered. "The logbook. I couldn't do what they asked. Couldn't kill you."

"It's all right, David. I understand." Her throat thickened from fighting the swell of agony. "You were protecting me."

"All for you." He gurgled once, turned quiet, and stopped moving. His chest remained still, and the room was silent as life left his body.

Damp tears trailed down Hattie's cheeks. Wailing sobs came at the thought he had been her friend through his dying breath. He had kept her secrets, kept her walking toward the light when the darkness of a broken heart nearly consumed her, and kept her safe when she ran into danger.

Maya scooted closer, pressing against Hattie's shoulder.

Hattie stared at her blood-soaked hands. She had seen too much blood in the past nine months, some from Maya's sister, some from her father, and too much from David. A tidal wave of regret crashed over her and left her wondering if all this bloodshed was worth the results.

She snapped her gaze toward her father and barked through her tears, "I wish you had never given me those damn lists. He needed to pay for what he did, but not like this."

"No, he didn't," Karl said. The muscles in his jaw quivered, but his rush of emotion failed to make up for David's death. Not even close.

Hattie pushed back a few strands of David's hair from his face, gently closed his eyelids with her hand, and sobbed. "Goodbye, my friend."

"Let's sit, Hattie." Maya wiped the blood from her hands on her pant legs before offering them to her.

Hattie dried her hands on her trousers, too, and accepted Maya's gesture. She rose to her feet and fell into Maya's tender embrace.

Maya moved her to a nearby table and offered her an upright chair. They both sat, with Maya's arm around Hattie's shoulder. Hattie looked up and realized Leo, Wagner, and an agent had left, leaving only two guards near the door they had come through. The odds were in their favor at three-to-one, but their bound hands and the distance between them and their captors put them at a disadvantage. Besides, she was still reeling from the death of her friend and placed a portion of the blame squarely at her father's feet. Helping him at the moment required energy she did not possess.

She stared at her father again, wondering what he was feeling. Was it regret? Sadness? Anger at the man who had pulled the trigger? She could not tell through his blank expression, and that frustrated her. "Are you happy? Now, you don't have to worry about not trusting him."

"Hattie," Maya said softly, rubbing her back in broad circles. "I know you're hurting, but that's not fair."

Hattie met Maya's eyes. "What's not fair is so many people, including your sister, dying for lists that may mean nothing right now. Both countries have likely recalled their operatives."

"Not all," Karl said. "Some are in so deep they can't be reached. If I hadn't censored those lists, one of those names would have been mine. That's why I'm willing to risk so much to protect them."

"Tell that to his mother." Hattie pointed at David's body and cried again.

"I will see to it when this is over." Karl swallowed hard. "Like I've done for all the others I knew personally who perished under my watch."

Hattie paused at seeing the anguish in her father's eyes. She had not considered the operations he had completed before and the people who had died because of something he had done or failed to do. It must have been a burden that weighed heavily on him every night when the voices of the dead called out to him. She would not wish that load on anyone.

Hattie stood, walked over to her father, and rested her head against his chest. It rose and fell in unmistakable sadness.

He nuzzled her hair with his chin in a virtual, touching embrace. "I'm so sorry, sweetheart."

"I know, Father."

"We need to spread out if we hope to get out of here," Karl whispered. He shed the loose cuffs before working on the binding around Hattie's wrists until she was free. "I'll create a scene to lure the guards closer. Use this."

Hattie clutched the rope to make it appear her hands were still tied and accepted whatever her father had slipped her from his sleeve. She returned to Maya's side at the table and said softly, "Diversion time. Follow my lead. Ask for water."

Maya offered a furtive nod.

Hattie hoped to divide and conquer. She needed to get one guard out of the room and draw the other close enough to attack him with the metal rod her father had passed to her discreetly. She waited for her father to begin his ruse so she could create a commotion.

Moments later, Karl raised his hands to his neck, pretending they were still bound, and loosened his tie. He drifted his head back and forth slowly like he was disoriented and began laboring his breathing. After wiping his brow, he swayed and called out, "Hattie." His voice sounded weak and brittle with confusion. He clutched his chest, dropped to one knee, then the other, and repeated, "Hattie?" This time, he said it more as a question before falling to the floor next to David's body.

"Father!" Hattie rushed to him and knelt, acting frantic. "Are you all right? Did you bring your nitro pills?"

"They took them in town." He croaked his words.

Maya came beside her. "He's dehydrated and needs water."

Hattie snapped her focus to the guard at the door. "Help him." The captors did not move, so she continued. "Wagner gave you an order to keep him alive. Water or he will die." She knew a few terms in German and said, "Wasser. Krank."

The men looked at each other, and the older one gestured for the other to go outside. Hattie remembered passing a large jug with a spigot in the hangar and suspected he was going there. That would not give her much time to act.

Hattie loosened her father's tie more and whispered to Maya, "Stay here." She ran a hand through her hair roughly and pursed her lips. "He needs his pills. Maybe someone brought them." Approaching the guard and steepling both hands at chest level, she put on her most distraught expression. "Please, you have to find his medicine."

She stepped closer. Three steps away. "Pills. Bitte."

Another stride. "I'm begging you."

The man raised his empty hand while keeping his pistol pointed at her. "Halt. Komm zurück."

Hattie knew he had ordered her to stop, but time was short and options were few, so she continued. "It's his heart." She took the last step and thrust the jagged edge of the rod into his gut. She pushed hard until the four inches of metal beyond her fist penetrated his abdomen and her hand was flush with his shirt.

The guard jerked as he crumpled into the wound, and his mouth fell agape. Only a grunt and a wheezing gasp for air escaped his lips.

Hattie pulled back the rod and stabbed him in the throat.

His eyes closed, and he dropped limp on the ground, blocking the door.

Karl poked his head up. "Get his gun."

Maya rushed forward and helped drag his body against the wall so it would be out of view when the door opened. She handed Hattie the Luger and returned to her position, kneeling in front of Karl.

Hattie heard footsteps outside the door and raised an index finger to her lips to shush Maya and her father. She positioned herself to hide behind the door when it swung open.

The knob turned.

Hattie considered her next move. She had a pistol in one hand and a metal rod in the other. A gunshot would alert others, and they had no idea how many more guards might be inside the compound. Being quiet was a must.

The door opened, swinging toward her. When the guard's hand carrying a paper cup appeared, she slid around the door. His bent arm came into view, and she sprang into action. She lunged forward, shivved him in the kidney, and, in the next second, whacked him on the back of the head with the firearm. The strike was decisive, and the crack was sharp. The guard would not recover from her blows. He collapsed instantly, dropping the water and splashing it in an oblong puddle, mixing with his blood.

Hattie scrambled and shut the door. They had overpowered and disposed of two of their captors. She had seen a third but suspected there was a compound full of Nazi mechanics and pilots, and all they had was two Lugers and a shiv. Searching both men, she discovered two extra clips of ammunition on each. She had no way of gauging the opposing force, but she surmised forty-eight rounds between them would not be enough.

Hattie went to her father and, with Maya's assistance, helped him up. She handed him a gun and two magazines. "What now?"

"Where are the weapons and explosives?"

Hattie gritted her teeth as another wave of anger tensed her muscles. "I gave them to Leo."

"Then we still have a chance."

Hattie cocked her head back in confusion. "What do you mean?"

The door flew open.

Hattie, Karl, and Maya shot their heads in its direction. Leo appeared in the doorway, aiming a pistol toward them.

30

Karl and Hattie raised their guns simultaneously, but neither fired. He hesitated because Leo had spoken a single important word before leaving the conference room. However, he suspected that Hattie hesitated out of the friendship she once had shared with him. Nevertheless, he drifted his aim over Leo's shoulder in case he was wrong and there was an armed guard following him. He was pleasantly surprised that no one else came.

"Whoa!" Leo's eyes got extra round, and he raised his hands in surrender. "I thought I would have to shoot my way in here to rescue you guys."

"Rescue?" Hattie spat her words. "You betrayed us. Tell me why I shouldn't kill you right now."

"Because Wagner thinks I'm Erik Weiss."

"How do you know that name?" Karl said, firming his grip on the Luger. There were only two ways he would know that information; one meant he was a traitor. Karl would not let his guard down until he was sure. "And it better be the correct answer."

"Weiss was one of the agents who extracted you from federal custody when you were transported for arraignment. He should have been on your list. Weiss is a naval officer living in Silver Spring, Maryland. The Professor had me capture and interrogate him. I broke him. Now, as far as the Germans are concerned, I am him."

Hattie kept her aim at Leo. "From the look of things, you really are him. Wagner knew who you were."

"He was supposed to," Leo said. "I spent weeks learning everything about Erik Weiss and how to speak German." He turned to Karl. "The vocabulary was easy enough, but I gotta say, the word order rules are confusing as hell. I felt more mixed up than a squirrel in a yo-yo factory."

An hour ago, Hattie would have laughed at Leo's way with colorful expressions, but Karl could tell that Leo had drop-kicked her sense of humor to the curb.

"Stop with the nonsense, Leo, or Erik, or whatever your name is." Hattie sneered at him.

"I don't know how else to convince you." Leo shook his head, lowering his hands more and placing his empty one on his hip.

Karl thought of one definitive test. "You said a word before you left?"

A grin formed on Leo's lips. "I thought you might catch on. Nightshade. The Professor said she used to call you that."

"Other people have heard her use that term," Karl said, "but only two people know why."

Leo's smile got bigger. "The genesis of her codename for you told me everything I needed to know about the man I was supposed to keep an eye on. She said that you appear safe to the world but can be deadly in the right quantity. She also said to tell you to trust no one until you have eaten much salt with him."

Karl snorted and lowered his pistol, never happier that his instincts about a man were correct. "How is the old woman?"

"Testy."

"She hasn't changed."

Hattie looked confused and still had her weapon trained on Leo. "What the hell is going on?"

"It's okay, sweetheart. The Professor is the only person I know with a Cicero quote for anything."

"So he's been working with her?" Hattie asked.

"No one works *with* the Professor, only *for* her," Leo said.

"Nothing truer." Karl snickered once. "Where did you put the weapons and explosives?"

Hattie lowered her gun but still looked leery.

"In a barrel in the hangar."

"How many did you neutralize?"

"Two," Leo said, "but there have to be more." He faced Hattie. "I'm sorry about David, but I had doubts about him from day one. Weiss said the SS had embedded someone in the James family in Rio. It had to be him or Maya." He craned his neck to look at Maya. "I'm glad it wasn't you." Leo refocused his attention on Karl. "What's the plan?"

"Destroy the hangars, aircraft, and designs to build them." Karl's expression turned stony. "And kill Wagner."

"And take David with us." Hattie appeared incensed that Karl did not include retrieving David's body.

Karl let out a deep sigh. "I'm afraid that's impossible, sweetheart."

"We have to bring him home," Hattie pleaded.

Karl placed his hands on Hattie's shoulders. It broke his heart to tell her this, but they had no choice. "His real home is likely Heidelberg. We can't take him there. There's no one waiting for him in the States."

Hattie muffled a sob. Reality did nothing to ease the heartache of leaving her friend behind. Nodding, she asked, "What do you need us to do?"

"Leo is the explosives expert." Karl turned to him. "I saw about a dozen planes out there. How should we do this?"

"The pencil timers all have thirty-minute delay capsules, but we don't have enough to go around." Leo rubbed the back of his neck. "Though, if the aircraft are close together, we can place the charges in each wing."

"Right." Karl nodded. "The explosion from one will set off its neighbor. Genius. You, Hattie, and Maya rig the planes and the other hangar. I'll find Wagner and drop some in here and the admin areas to destroy the plans. How quickly can you be done?"

"A dozen craft with three people? Ten or twelve minutes."

Karl checked his wristwatch. "We meet in the parking lot in fifteen. Where did they take Maya's car?"

Leo dangled Maya's keys. "One building down from the Kubel."

Maya snatched the keys. "Thank you."

Karl peeked his head out the door, confirming that no one was inside the hangar, and waved the group forward.

Leo jogged to a corner, removed the lid from a barrel, and retrieved the satchels of explosives containing TNT, pencil detonators, and a few grenades. He dug out two of each and a small pair of crimpers and handed them to Karl.

Karl stuffed them into his suit coat pockets.

Leo held up an explosive and detonator. "All right, ladies. Place the TNT on every wing wheel. Push a detonator in the top of the block in the left wing, like this. I don't have enough pliers to go around, so I'll crimp the detonator to start the timers."

"Got it," Hattie and Maya said, almost as one.

Once everyone grabbed a military submachine gun and ammo, Karl squeezed Hattie's and Maya's hands. The nagging feeling that he might fail or never see his daughter again hit him like a lead weight and constricted his throat with emotion. Karl pulled Hattie into a brief hug. "See you soon, sweetheart."

It was odd to think it, but witnessing Hattie overpower those two guards had him simultaneously proud and terrified. The killing aspect was awful. Any unnatural death always was. However, seeing her take to her training and come into her own as a covert operative made him think she was becoming more like him every day. She had always been like her mother in beauty, talent, and temperament, but her skills and abilities now mirrored his. As much as that filled his heart, it also frightened him. When others ran from danger, she rushed toward it like him. She had been dragged into his perilous world but had chosen to stay. To do whatever was needed for family and country.

He took off across the hangar. While the others jogged along the flight line to place the devices on the aircraft, his first order of business was to find Wagner. Killing him would set back Germany's secret long-range bomber production for years but also give him satisfaction. More importantly, though, Wagner had kept his wife hostage and could have killed Hattie in that yacht explosion. Anyone who threatened his family had to die.

Karl knew Wagner was not the type to inconvenience himself by walking far every day to work. He figured his office was near the conference room where he and the others had been held. He veered toward the support offices, planting a pencil timer, explosive charge, and grenade in such a way as to bring down the hangar doors and west wall.

He had his MP 40 slung over his chest but held the recovered Luger as he weaved his way down a short corridor. Bursting through the door closest to the hangar opening, he discovered a radio control room with a large picture window view of the airfield. He placed a TNT block with a timer there and crimped the tip of the detonator. Glancing outside through the glass, he spotted three figures darting across the apron to where the aircraft were parked virtually wingtip to wingtip. Despite the limited supply of timers, it was clear that the first blast would easily set off the explosive on the next and so on, down the line.

He returned to the central part of the hangar and retraced the route his escort had taken him through the attached building. The empty hallway was lit and silent. Going from doorway to doorway, he cleared each room quietly so as to not alert Wagner to his approach.

Upon reaching the room where he had noticed men by a blackboard, he scrutinized its contents more closely. The formulas on the board and diagrams on the desks suggested this was the engineers' room. He set another charge and timer. For added assurance, he piled a bunch of papers on the floor and set fire to them with a lighter he found on a desk. He wanted to leave nothing behind for the Germans to use to recreate the bomber any time soon.

Karl continued down the corridor, wondering where the men he had seen earlier had gone. They were likely the Nazis' brain trust for building warplanes; he would need to dispose of them too.

He stood to the side and pushed open the next door as smoke floated into the hallway. A gunshot rang out, and a splintered hole appeared in the plywood wall across from the door. The element of surprise had been lost. Karl slipped the Luger into his waistband at the small of his back and slung the submachine gun into the ready position. Taking a deep breath and releasing it halfway, he lunged into the doorway and sprayed the room with rapid fire. Papers and blood flew as bullets riddled two flailing bodies.

Karl let go of the trigger and inspected the victims. Neither was Wagner.

They resembled two of the men he had observed previously. He sensed he was getting close. He released the magazine of his MP 40, letting it clink off the concrete floor, and loaded a fresh clip of ammunition. As he continued deeper into the structure, a distant crackle and the pungent smell of burning wood, paint, and plastics reminded him that time was not his friend tonight.

He tested the next door gently, discovering the knob was locked. With little real estate left in the building, his pulse raced at the thought Wagner could be behind that door. He gave the lock a quick burst from his automatic rifle, sending wooden chunks and small splinters into the air. Raising his leg, he kicked the door open, generating a loud crack. Pistol fire immediately followed. Karl crouched near the frame and waited for a break in the barrage.

Silence.

Holding the machine gun outstretched into the doorway, he fired blindly into the room and dashed inside, not allowing whoever was there time to recover. The lone man was dead. Still no sign of Wagner.

A door slammed.

The exterior door at the end of the hallway bounced against the doorframe, telling Karl where to go. He rushed to it and charged through the exit to the parking area. He had Strom Wagner in his sights. The man was hurrying toward his staff car, but his progress was bogged down by the items he carried in his arms. He appeared to be hauling document cases.

Karl fired a burst in the air. "Strom, stop!" Before he shot him he wanted to face the man who nearly succeeded in killing his wife and daughter.

Wagner stopped. The satchels fell to the ground, and several sheets of paper found their way out and spilled onto the gravel. He raised his hands over his head, holding a distinctive bottle in his left as he turned. Wagner always had a soft spot for fine brandy and kept a stock of it wherever he was posted. It figured that his one weakness would be his downfall. Going back for those documents was one thing, but taking the time to scoop up his prized possession had cost him his life.

"It was never personal, Karl."

"It's funny, Strom. In our business, we often say that killing to accomplish the mission is never personal, but I've realized it always is. Ending a life or threatening one is its definition. The ripple effect on loved ones left behind is deeply profound, which is why I am done. You will be my last kill."

"I suppose I should be honored, but—"

Karl fired, hitting Wagner in the gut. The brandy dropped to the ground, the bottle shattering into pieces and splattering its contents on Wagner's wingtips. His body jerked and slumped against the car. The man who almost killed his family was dead.

It was personal. It was done.

31

Gunshots sounded in the distance, amplifying the danger lurking at the darkened secret airfield. Hattie turned in their direction, hoping her father was unhurt.

"He'll be fine. Come on," Maya said, hurrying past her. She had rushed her words, which came out more forcefully than Hattie was accustomed to hearing from her.

Hattie shook off her worry and concentrated on setting the next explosive. She shifted the submachine gun slung over her back so it would not slip off. Her new worry became completing her task without getting bogged down by her weapon and the explosives satchel. She reached into the wheel well of the plane. The craft was massive, nearly seventy feet long and half of a football field wide from wingtip to wingtip. It meant they had to sprint between planes after placing each device.

Hattie's chest heaved from the exertion as she stopped at the neighboring wing. She pulled the TNT and a pencil timer from the satchel draped across her shoulder. After gently pushing the end closest to the red plastic ring of the detonator into the top of the explosive, she carefully placed the block atop the tire. Once the task was complete, she crouched to exit the well. Leo came behind her to crimp the tip of the detonator and start the timer.

The Secret War 255

"We're doing good on time," he said. "One more plane."

She squeezed his hand in an apology for doubting him earlier. "One more." She took off running toward the last aircraft, where Maya was rigging the explosive on the closest wing. When Hattie approached and was about to run past, they acknowledged each other with brief stares in the bright moonlight. They said nothing because that glance said everything, but there was no time to dwell on the fear and worry.

Hattie arrived at the last wheel, placed the TNT and detonator, and waited for Maya and Leo to join her.

Footsteps came up rapidly behind her.

Hattie turned and discovered a German guard was advancing quickly on her. He carried a firearm like Hattie's, and it was aimed at her. Hattie's machine gun was hung crisscross at her back. She had no time to drop the cloth satchel with the two extra explosive blocks, swing her machine gun around, and defend herself against the attacker.

Hattie focused on the barrel of his weapon. The tip glistened in the moonlight, announcing its lethality. The only thing standing between her and death was the pressure needed to pull the trigger.

She closed her eyes and thought of Maya, wishing she could have kissed her lips one more time. She thought of her sister Olivia, wishing she could have lived to see her nephew Matthew and niece Sarah grow up. Thought of her mother, wishing she could have sung with her once on the Golden Room stage, not just at smaller, private events. And thought of her father, wishing she could have told him how proud she was of him. How she respected the sacrifices he had made for his country despite deep misgiving over his choices and the wise counsel he gave so she could learn from his mistakes. But none of that would happen.

Death was one trigger pull away.

Gunshots rang out.

Hattie jerked, expecting a searing, all-consuming pain or nothing if the shot was to her head, but the nothing she felt perplexed her. She was still standing, still breathing. She opened her eyes, discovering Maya rushing toward the guard with her weapon pointed at him, but he lay lifeless on the asphalt. Hattie's chest heaved with relief and confusion.

Maya kicked his machine gun out of his reach while holding her own weapon and darted to Hattie with panic in her eyes. She clutched Hattie's arms. "Are you okay? Were you hit?"

Hattie cleared her head and took inventory. "No, I'm fine." Maya had saved her again. It was eerily reminiscent of the final confrontation with Baumann at the plantation after he had shot and killed Maya's sister. When Baumann was about to shoot Hattie and her father was too far away to stop him, Maya had protected her. And tonight, when the guard had Hattie in his crosshairs, Maya had safeguarded her again.

"We need to hurry. More guards might come." Leo came around the nose of the plane, crimped the last detonator, and pocketed his tool before readying his automatic rifle. "Let's go."

Gunshots sounded in the distance again.

The three ran the length of the apron but gave the hangar a wide berth to avoid an ambush and to steer clear if the detonators went off too early. Performing on stage had given Hattie leg strength and stamina, but she was not accustomed to running.

More gunfire sent a panic racing through Hattie, but she slowed at the disturbing smell of smoke. She gasped as they passed the end of the structure. Flames poked out from the seams in the corrugated metal roof, and smoke billowed from windows and other minute crevasses in the siding.

"Father!" she called out.

"Right here, Songbird." Her father emerged from the other side of an automobile, holding his weapon.

Hattie went to him and felt relief when he wrapped a strong arm around her shoulder. She glanced behind her. Wagner was on the ground, not moving. "You got him."

"I got him," he said. "Let's go."

"Maya's car caught a flat on the way here, and we had to change it," Leo said. "The sedan might not make it back to the main highway."

"We can't leave it here," Karl said. "If the Germans find it, they will come looking for her. Let's take hers and the Kubel I came in. If she breaks down, I can use it to push the sedan and dump it in the jungle."

"I'll hot-wire it," Leo said.

They hurried toward the vehicles.

The Secret War 257

Leo stopped when he got even with the rear seat of the sedan. He leveled his machine gun.

The others readied their weapons and covered him.

"Don't shoot." The voice came from inside the vehicle.

"Get out," Leo ordered.

A head popped up from the back, and then a second one. Hattie recognized the two as Gunter and Ernst Kessler, the engineers she met at the Golden Room a few days ago. They opened the door and scooted out with their hands raised.

"Please don't shoot us," Gunter said. "We were here to consult, not build." His tone was timid, and his hands shook like a lost dog, a far cry from the confident, flirty man she had encountered at the club.

Hattie lowered her weapon. "What can you tell us about the aircraft and what Wagner planned to do with it?"

"My brother and I know the schematics inside and out. We know it's designed to be a long-range bomber. Wagner called it Operation Amerika."

"We don't have time for this," Leo said. "The first explosives will detonate soon."

"Take us with you," Ernst said. "There is nothing for us in Germany now. We can tell your government everything we know about the plane."

Hattie turned to her father and whispered, "Maybe we *should* take them with us. We have room since we're taking both cars."

Karl ran a hand down his face. "Fine, but we tie them up. Leo and I will take them in the Kubel. Hattie, you and Maya go in her sedan."

While Leo got the Kubel running, Karl retrieved some rope from Maya's trunk. He ushered the brothers into the utility vehicle's back seat and bound their hands together.

Maya started her engine, and Hattie stood near the back door on the driver's side with her father. Karl explained that she and Maya were to lead the way. If they had car trouble, Leo would push her to the highway.

Karl pulled her into a brief hug. "I'll see you at home, sweetheart."

A gunshot.

Karl slumped against the back door and dropped to his knees.

Without time to fall apart, Hattie processed the situation quickly. Her father had been shot in the back. Her weapon was in the sedan and out of reach, so she grabbed the Luger in her father's waistband. Wheeling it behind him, she saw Wagner, still lying on the ground, but with a pistol in his hand. Hattie fired and dashed toward him, continuing her attack until his gun fell to the pavement, and his arm fell limp on the gravel.

Hattie surveyed her surroundings with her weapon, but no one else appeared. She focused on her father. He was still on his knees, and Maya and Leo were at his side. Panic ripped through her as the worst flashed through her head. He could have taken a bullet to a vital organ, and they were hours from the city and medical assistance.

"How bad is it?" she asked.

Karl looked weak, unable to hold himself up, and grimaced in agony.

"He has to get to a hospital," Leo said.

Hattie turned to Maya. "Is there anywhere close we can take him?"

"I'm not sure. This far out, local doctors only have basic first aid."

"We can't stay here," Leo said. "This place will explode in a few minutes."

"We need to get him to Rio," Hattie said, hoping he could last that long. "Let's put him in the back of your car, Maya. I'll sit with him."

After some effort, they sat Karl in the back seat. Maya sped out the gate first, and Leo followed in the utility vehicle with the tied-up Kessler brothers. As the Kubel cleared the perimeter, the first explosion went off. Then another, and another, and another. Hattie craned her neck, looking out the back window. The horizon was aglow in a bright, yellowish-orange, rising wall of flames. The explosions repeated. The planes had been destroyed, and the plans for them were now ash.

Removing Karl's jacket, Hattie discovered the bullet wound was in the back of the shoulder. "It will be all right, Father." She forced herself to sound more optimistic than she was. He was losing blood quickly, and without proper medical attention, the odds of him surviving the rough, winding trip to Rio were slim. His only hope was for her to stop the bleeding.

She unbuckled his belt with one hand and slid it through the loops of his pants in one swift motion. "Lean on the door," she told him. She balled up his jacket and rested it against the wound. Holding it steady with one hand, she strung the strap over his shoulder and arm and pulled it tight. He grimaced in pain, but she needed to apply pressure. There were no notches in the leather deep enough into the belt to secure it. She improvised by wrapping the strap's end around her hand and holding it in place. The compression, she hoped, would slow the bleeding long enough for them to make it to Rio.

"Rest, Father. I've got you. We'll get you to the doctor." Hattie surprised herself by sounding so confident they would make it in time. It was hope talking, she knew, but that and the strength to grip that compress firmly were the only things between her father and death. She had to hold on to both. No matter what.

Maya was an expert driver and could sling her car through Rio's narrow, hilly streets like a professional, but this was not the city. This was the jungle. The dirt road to the main highway was the challenge. If they could make it through the twists without catching another flat or getting stuck in the mud and rocks, they had a good chance of making it in time.

Maya kept her speed up and steady, slowing only for the turns. The trick was not jerking the wheel to prevent a rock from digging into the tread and puncturing the tire. And Maya handled each one with deftness. However, with each twist of the road, inertia flung Hattie about. She braced herself with one arm against the back of the front seat while keeping a tight hold on the belt over her father's shoulder with the other. He groaned in pain at every turn, but it could not have been helped. The clock was as much of an enemy as the road.

Hattie kept her focus on her father to monitor his condition and not fret about how long the trip would take. His alertness dwindled with each cry of pain. So did Hattie's optimism, but when their tires hit the smooth pavement and the car stopped rattling, a burst of hope filled her.

"We're going to make it, Father. You have to hold on."

He clutched her forearm, which was straining to keep the compress in place. "We're about to be dragged into the war. The Japanese are planning an attack, and the Nazis want us focused on Japan, not Germany. We need to root out their spies." His voice got weaker with every succeeding word.

"Save your strength." Hattie rested her free hand over his. "We'll arrive in Rio soon."

"No." He gripped her arm tighter. "Promise you'll get the lists to the Professor. She will help you root out the mole. We can't win if you don't."

"But she's in hiding. Where can I find her?"

His hold loosened, and his head slumped to one side.

"Father?" She touched his face, but he refused to wake. Her heart thumped at the thought he had taken an irreversible turn. Instead of panicking, she moved her free hand to his chest, searching for evidence of life. It was rising up and down but too faintly to be mistaken as anything but a bad sign. He was fading fast.

32

Hattie switched arms throughout the ride to keep pressure on her father's wound, but both ached after hours without a break. She checked his breathing and felt his temperature by pressing a hand against his forehead. Nothing had changed. He was weak but holding on. Hattie had to decide where to take him now that they had hit the city limits.

It was nearly three o'clock in the morning.

The same quandary had presented itself when they had to address Leo's injuries from the safe house. Karl James, too, could not be brought to a hospital, let alone seen. The Germans and Americans were both after him. The Brazilian authorities already knew he was in the country following the attempted presidential assassination on the yacht. They would capture him and turn him over to whichever side made the best argument for his extradition.

"There's a hospital about ten minutes from here," Maya said.

"Not there. Go to Eva's. We'll call Dr. Navarro and have him come to the house." Hattie knew she could control him.

"Are you sure?"

Hattie was not confident about much tonight, but she was certain her father would not have wanted to be taken into custody. "Yes, take him home."

Minutes later, they were coasting to a stop on Eva's driveway. Leo pulled in right behind them in the Kubel. Maya exited the sedan quickly, unlocked the garden gate, and opened the car door to get Karl out.

Leo rushed to them. He struggled to remove Hattie's father from the back because Karl was unconscious and too heavy for him.

"Let us help!" one of the Kessler brothers called out from the back seat of the utility vehicle.

Hattie looked at Leo and pleaded with her eyes. "We have to get him inside."

Leo nodded his concurrence.

Maya dashed to the Kubel and untied their hands. The brothers went to Leo's side.

Ernst, the younger brother, appeared to be the strongest of the three. "I'll carry him." He crouched in front of Leo, facing him. "Lay him over my shoulder." He let Leo fold Karl over him so he was crisscrossed. It was similar to the way Hattie had once seen a fireman lift a man from a burning building in New York City. Her father's head was at Ernst's back, and his feet were suspended at knee level. Ernst steadied Karl's uninjured arm against Karl's dangling legs.

"This way," Hattie told him before turning to Maya. "Take him to David's old room."

She hurried through the gate, down the garden path, and through Eva's front door. The house was dark. Hattie expected her mother to be sleeping in her room at this hour, so she called out, "Mother! Wake up!" She turned on the lights and ran down the hallway toward Eva's bedroom. "Mother!" she repeated.

Reaching the open door, she hit the switch for the overhead light, causing Eva to stir. Hattie rushed to the bed and shook her mother by the shoulder. "Mother. Wake up. Father is hurt."

Eva sprang up. "Karl's hurt?" She flipped back the covers and swung her feet to the floor. "Where is he? Which hospital?"

"We couldn't risk the authorities recognizing him, so we brought him here."

"Let me see him." Eva slipped on her robe.

"You need to get Dr. Navarro first. We're taking him to David's room."

"I'll call from my office." Eva walked swiftly down the corridor. "What happened?"

"He's been shot in the back and has lost a lot of blood."

Eva paused. She turned to face Hattie. "How bad is it?"

Hattie's throat thickened from the truth. "Bad."

Thank goodness Maya and Ernst had entered the other hallway toward the guest rooms as Eva and Hattie came into view of the living room. Her mother needed to focus for a few minutes, and seeing Karl bleeding and unconscious would break her.

They got to the office. Eva went to her desk, found the doctor's business card in the drawer, and had the operator dial his number. A moment later, she said, "Joaquim, it's Eva. Something horrible has happened. I need you at the house immediately." Her harried voice left no doubt that she had been shaken to her core. "Someone's been shot...No, we couldn't take him to the hospital...Yes, come right now...We'll get everything you need... Thank you, Joaquim."

Eva hung up the phone and turned to Hattie. She was pale, and her hands shook. "We need to start boiling lots of water and find clean towels and a wash basin."

"I'll have Maya or Leo gather everything."

Eva nodded and straightened her posture, which was her way to keep from falling apart. "Take me to him."

Hattie walked her mother to David's old room. Karl lay on his back in the center of the mattress atop the covers. Leo was seated beside him, applying pressure to the gunshot wound. Maya stood by the dresser.

Eva gasped, placing her hand over her mouth. "Karl." She glanced at the Kessler brothers standing close to the window but did not question who they were or why they were there. Instead, she sat on the near side of the bed. "He looks so pale."

"I did what I could to stop the bleeding." Hattie's lips quivered as memories of that gut-wrenching ride from the airfield flashed in her head. Whenever her arm weakened or her hand slipped a fraction, she reminded herself that his life rested in her hands and on her determination to save it.

"She was incredible, Eva," Maya said. "We drove for three hours, and she kept pressure on his wound the entire time. Anyone else would have tired out, but Hattie stayed strong."

Eva held Karl's hand and squeezed it. "That's because she's Karl James's daughter. They don't know how to give up."

Hattie placed a hand on Eva's shoulder. "Which is why I know he'll get through this." She shifted her focus to Maya, explained that the doctor was on the way, and listed the things he had asked to gather before his arrival.

Maya left, taking the Kessler brothers with her.

Eva caressed Karl's hand and said, "Tell me what happened."

Hattie took a deep breath. "Father's plan worked. The Germans took him inside the embassy. A while later, after the ambassador came and went, two men took Father by car into the jungle. We followed them to the airfield. We tried to get in, but Maya and I were captured. A lot of stuff went down, but Leo helped us overpower the guards. We blew up the planes, and Wagner shot Father before we could get away."

"Is Wagner dead?" Eva asked.

"Yes, Mother." Hattie gritted her teeth. "He's dead."

"What about those two men? Who are they?"

"They're aeronautical engineers," Hattie said.

Eva kept her focus on Karl, not once diverting her attention. "Why did you bring them?"

Hattie shook her head. "They know they will be killed if they return to Germany, so they asked to come with us. We'll turn them over to Agent Knight."

"And David? Where is he?"

Hattie muffled a sob, glancing at Leo. His sad eyes told her he was sorry. "He's dead, Mother. Wagner killed him."

Eva's breath hitched, and she finally looked at Hattie. "Was he working for them?"

"They were blackmailing him, but, in the end, he only wanted to protect me."

Eva lowered her head and cried, covering her mouth with her free hand.

Soon, Maya returned with Navarro and the items he had asked for.

Eva stood and stared Navarro straight in the eyes. "You save him, Joaquim, or so help me God, I will haunt you through eternity."

"I will do my best, Eva, but I will need someone to assist."

"I will," Maya said.

Navarro acknowledged her with a nod. "Give us the room. You won't want to see this."

Maya took over for Leo, and Leo and Eva exited into the hallway.

Hattie went to Maya and caressed her back. "Thank you." She turned her attention to Navarro. She stared at him for several beats, effectively renewing her threat to expose him if he failed to do his job. "Do everything you can, Doctor."

"I will." He swallowed hard.

When Hattie left the room, she was confident Maya would ensure Navarro patched up her father and did whatever was needed to save him. She joined the others in the living room and sat beside her mother on the couch. "He's going to pull through, Mother. I'm sure of it."

"He's too stubborn to die, at least not until he's needled me for another thirty years." Eva focused on Leo. "You should know, Leo. I heard from Cesar Tavares from President Garza's office. A witness came forward, and you've been cleared of all charges."

"What about my escape from custody?" he asked.

"Yes, that too. Narcisco has seen to it as a personal favor."

Leo let out a loud breath. "That's a relief. Thank you, Eva. I'm not cut out to be a fugitive."

"Not many are," Eva said.

Hattie was sure her mother was referring to Karl. He had been on the run for almost a year, wanted by Americans and Germans. Few people would have had the skill or fortitude to go undetected for so long, but her father had done it with ease.

Leo stood. "Would you mind if I borrowed a car? I need to drop these two off at the embassy, and it's not a good idea to traipse through town in a stolen German diplomatic vehicle."

"Take Maya's. It's blocking the garage," Hattie said. "Take my house key and let yourself in when you come back."

Once Leo and the Kessler brothers left, Hattie started some coffee and poured her mother a glass of wine. "Here. Drink this. It will help you relax."

Eva accepted the cup, gulped it down in seconds, and placed it on the table. "Thank you. Funny how you never realize how much you care for a person until you think you might lose them."

Hattie sat beside her. "You still love him."

Eva sighed. "Yes, I do."

"The last thing he told me in the car was that I had to promise to get the lists to the Professor. He passed out before telling me how to find her but had said earlier that you could help."

"I don't know what your father thought I could do to locate that woman. I only met her a few times."

"Think, Mother. This is very important. She's gone into hiding, and according to her son, he was the only one who knew her location. I doubt Leo will know where she's at."

"What does Leo have to do with the Professor?" Eva asked.

Hattie took in a rattled breath, remembering how hurt she felt when she believed Leo was working for the Nazis. "It's a long story, but he works for her like Father does."

Eva shook her head and mumbled, "So many damn spies."

"Where did you meet the Professor? When?"

"She came to the house a few times for your father's parties." Eva let out a single laugh. "I'm starting to think your father held all those get-togethers so he could watch people and learn their secrets."

"I'm sure he did." Hattie thought about this. What a perfect situation her father had created, hosting hordes of diplomatic social gatherings, to which everyone who was anyone jockeyed for an invitation. Those events at their house must have been a gold mine of intelligence gathering. "What can you tell me about her?"

"Victoria said she sometimes went by Vicky and that she taught political science at Georgetown."

"There has to be something else. Do you remember where she lived?"

"I did run into her once at Montrose Park. She said she had a place a few blocks away. Wait." Eva shifted on the couch cushion. "I recall Karl and I talking to her at our Christmas party. Both times she wore this god-awful

The Secret War   267

pearl necklace and cat-eye glasses. She said she was going for a weekend getaway at her family's cabin on the Eastern Shore."

"Virginia or Maryland?"

"Maryland, I think. I might have a picture of her, but I think Olivia has those photo albums."

"This is a big help, Mother. Thank you."

Soon, Dr. Navarro entered the living room, carrying his medical bag.

Hattie and Eva stood, clutching each other's hands.

"How is he, Joaquim?" Eva asked.

"I removed the bullet, cleaned up his wound, and stitched him up. He suffered significant blood loss and should have a transfusion, but he would need to go to a hospital for that."

"Will he recover?" Eva clutched Hattie's hands harder.

"The odds are good, but the next few days will be critical. I started him on an IV to build up his fluids and maintain his blood pressure. I left two more bags for Maya to change out, but I will return with more and bring more sulfa to prevent an infection."

"Can we see him now?" Eva's hand shook, but Hattie squeezed it, and she calmed a little.

"He's still unconscious and will remain that way for some time. His body must produce more blood."

"Are you saying he's in a coma?" Hattie asked.

Eva muffled a sob.

"Yes. There's no telling when he might come around. Maya tells me you compressed his wound for hours until you brought him here." He paused at Hattie's nod. "That likely saved his life. I've done everything I could. Now, we wait. I'll come by every day to check on him."

"Thank you, Dr. Navarro," Hattie said.

She walked him out and returned, finding Eva sitting on the bed next to Karl. Maya was in a chair near the window. She looked exhausted. She went to Maya and wrapped an arm around her shoulder. "Thank you for helping the doctor. Was my father ever in pain?"

Maya shook her head. "No. He never woke."

"There's coffee if you want some."

"I'd rather get something to eat, shower, and go to sleep."

"Yes," Eva said. "The sun is coming up. You two should rest. I'll sit with Karl."

Hattie kissed her mother on the head and went to the kitchen with Maya. They whipped up some scrambled eggs, cut up a batch of fresh fruit, and sliced a few pieces off a loaf of homemade bread.

After taking her mother a plate, some juice, and coffee, Hattie rejoined Maya, discovering she had moved the food to the table. Before sitting next to Maya, she kissed her on the lips, grateful to have been alive to do it again.

"You saved my life," Hattie said.

Maya sighed. "And you saved your father's. We all did what we had to."

Hattie heard the front door open. Moments later, Leo appeared at the entranceway.

"Hungry?" Hattie asked. "We made plenty."

"Starved. I'll dump the Kubel in town after I eat." He entered and sat across from Hattie. "How's Karl?"

"The doctor patched him up," Maya said. "He lost a lot of blood, and it might be some time before he wakes."

"If he wakes." Hattie finally voiced her fear that her father, the man she had looked up to all her life, might remain in a coma and never recover.

Maya squeezed Hattie's hand. "You have to stay positive. He'll come to."

"Maybe." Hattie pushed away her fright. She had to focus on what needed doing and turned her attention to Leo. "How did it go?"

"I got the Kessler brothers into the US Embassy and called in Agent Knight. I told Knight and my boss, Jack Lynch, about what happened at the airfield but did not mention Karl. I said I shot and killed Wagner and grabbed the Kessler brothers on the way out."

"Did Knight buy it?" Hattie asked.

"Probably not, but he mentioned that the Germans covered up the events at the safe house. The local police were never called in. Anyway, the ambassador is arranging a military transport to take them to the United States. It should be here tomorrow afternoon and depart Wednesday morning."

"I must get on that plane," Hattie said. "I have to find the Professor and give her the lists. My father said she'll need help finding the mole in the War Department."

"I'm coming with you," Leo said. "I met the Professor a few times in DC. We can start there."

"I am, too," Maya said. "And don't argue."

"But what about your job at the Golden Room and the construction of the Halo Club?" Hattie asked. "We don't know how long we'll be there."

"I was going to quit soon, anyway. I trust your mother to oversee things while we're gone."

And that was precisely why Hattie loved Maya.

December 3, 1941, two days later

Hattie closed her suitcase. She had packed enough clothes and personal items to last her two weeks into two bags. If she needed anything else, she would buy it in DC and leave whatever she could not fit in her luggage in her apartment in New York City or at her sister's house. In June, she had had her banker send her landlady another six months of rent and prepay the utilities, taking her through February. When she was in the States, she would have to decide whether to keep the place.

Hattie lifted her final suitcase and headed to the neighboring bedroom. She kissed her father on the forehead. He had yet to wake up, but his color had improved, and his body had stopped sweating. She was cautiously optimistic about him waking. Giving up hope was not in her blood.

"I'll find the Professor, Father, and we will find that mole. I promise."

She went into the living room. Eva and Maya had returned from taking the rest of the luggage to the driveway.

A car horn honked outside.

"Our taxi is here," Maya said. "Is that it?"

"Yes, last one, I swear."

"I'll take it out," Maya said. "I'll see you out there."

Hattie approached her mother and rubbed her arms. "You're certain about handling things at the Halo Club on top of filling in at the Golden Room until Mr. Guinle can replace me full-time?" She hated to leave the hotel on such short notice but was grateful to have had the termination clause in place to free her to continue her father's mission.

"I'm sure. For now, Octávio only needs me at the Palace one night a week, and you and Maya left excellent notes about the Halo Club. The nurse I hired starts today, so she'll stay with your father when I have to go out."

"I'll check in regularly with Olivia. I want you to call her if there's any change in his condition."

Eva wiped a tear from her cheek. "I will, and you have to promise to be careful."

"I will." Hattie drew her mother into an emotion-filled hug. If everything went well, she and Maya would return to Rio in two or three weeks, and her father would be awake and driving her mother crazy. Any other outcome was unthinkable.

Twenty minutes later, the taxi pulled up to the main entrance of Camp Afonsos on the northwestern edge of the city. Leo Bell stood at the gate next to a Brazilian military guard. The cabby helped transfer their luggage into a waiting official sedan. Hattie paid for the fare and tipped the man well.

Leo held the sedan's door open for them. "We're all set."

They got in, and the driver took them to the flight line, where an airliner with United States government markings roared its two engines. The propellors generated a robust wind, and the smell of fuel and fumes was strong.

Two American servicemen unloaded their suitcases and carried them up the stairs near the back of the plane.

Leo opened the car's rear door and gestured for Hattie and Maya to follow him up the steps. "You'll be happy to know the FBI is working with the Brazilian authorities to comb through the airfield. All the planes were destroyed, and several German mechanics and pilots were taken into custody. They hope to learn more from the survivors."

"At least some good has come out of this." Hattie's unconscious father tempered her gratification of having thwarted an attack on the US.

Once inside, Leo pointed toward a door opposite the passenger hatch. "That's the lavatory. Instructions are taped to the wall."

Hattie scanned her surroundings. The cabin had seven rows of seats, two seats to the left of the aisle and one to the right. Open cubby holes were above them, and several contained luggage, including hers and Maya's. Six men sat closer to the front, facing the nose of the plane. Two were the ones who had retrieved the suitcases from the sedan. It was hard to tell by the backs of their heads, but two resembled the Kessler brothers. The opening to the cockpit allowed her to see two American military pilots fumbling with switches and dials on the dashboard.

"Where should we sit?" Hattie asked.

"Anywhere on the left side of the craft with two seats."

"Thanks, Leo," Maya said, turning to Hattie. "Window or aisle?"

"You choose."

The passenger hatch closed as Leo went forward and spoke to the pilots.

Maya slipped in first, taking the seat nearest the hull in the second to the last row. Hattie sat beside her. They placed their handbags on the floor under the seat in front of them.

Leo came back. "We take off in a few minutes. If you have to use the lavatory, I suggest you use it now."

"We're fine," Hattie said after checking with Maya.

Leo nodded and returned up the aisle, making way for a man who had gotten up to go aft, presumably to use the bathroom. The man's face became apparent when Leo took his seat. Hattie's stomach twisted into knots.

"Hello, Miss James," the man said.

"Agent Knight, what are you doing here?"

"Escorting our defectors and keeping an eye on you." Knight narrowed his eyes. "Our business with your father is far from over."

"I suppose not." She closed her eyes and settled in for the thirty-six-hour trip.

The stakes were high, and time was Hattie's enemy. The lists tucked away in a hidden compartment in her purse had to find their way to the Professor. If she failed...Strike that. Failure was not in Hattie's lexicon.

AUTHOR'S NOTE

Nazi Germany's Amerikabomber project inspired the long-range heavy bomber in this story. During WWII, Germany's Aviation Ministry sought to create a long-range bomber to attack the US, aiming for New York City. Though the idea surfaced in 1938, concrete proposals did not emerge until early 1942. This ambitious project received proposals from several aircraft manufacturers, including Messerschmitt, Junkers, Focke-Wulf, and Heinkel. Among the noteworthy candidates was the Messerschmitt Me 264, a long-range strategic bomber boasting an impressive 9,500-mile range, with three prototypes produced. The Amerikabomber project, while innovatively designed, struggled with high costs, scarce resources, and technical problems. Ultimately, none of the proposed planes went into mass production, and the project was scrapped by July 1944.

While plotting this story, I wondered, What if the project was ready to go into operation earlier than history suggests, and Germany built and planned to launch a fleet from the jungles of Brazil? I took the story plot further, wondering, What if the Axis powers collaborated on the Pearl Harbor attack to weaken the US military, but Germany's involvement was thwarted?

Historical records show Japan started planning the Pearl Harbor attack in early 1941, yet I found no proof of German knowledge of these plans before November 1941. However, it is possible, even probable, that Hitler's regime was aware of the situation well before then.

THE NIGHTSHADE
Hattie James #4

Her voice enchants crowds. Her secrets will expose conspiracies. One mistake could cost her everything.

December 1941: As bombs fall on Pearl Harbor, singer Hattie James faces a personal nightmare when her sister Olivia vanishes. The kidnappers demand an impossible price—her father's classified list of undercover American and Nazi spies.

Wartime paranoia and family loyalty take Hattie to Washington D.C. with Maya and Commander Leo Bell to hunt an elusive, high-ranking mole in the War Department who is after those lists. Leo, a military intelligence officer with access to classified operations, becomes their crucial inside man, navigating the treacherous corridors of power. Meanwhile in Rio de Janeiro, Hattie's father Karl slowly recovers from near-fatal wounds under her mother's watchful care as Nazi agents close in on his location.

As war declarations echo across radio waves, these fragile alliances become Hattie's only hope of untangling a conspiracy that threatens both nations. As Hattie inches closer to the truth, she discovers that exposing the traitor might save her sister—or destroy them both.

**Get your copy today at
severnriverbooks.com**

ACKNOWLEDGMENTS

Thank you, Barbara Gould, my plotting partner in crime. She is still the best sounding board I could ever ask for.

Thank you, Kristianne and Nancy, for reading my rough, rough, rough first draft, providing your unfiltered thoughts, and pushing me to be a better writer.

Thank you, Jacquelin Cangro, my amazing developmental editor, for helping me whip this story into shape.

Finally, to my family. Thank you for loving me...and keeping the pantry stocked with popcorn.

ABOUT THE AUTHOR

A late bloomer, award-winning author Stacy Lynn Miller took up writing after retiring from the Air Force. Her twenty years of toting a gun and police badge, tinkering with computers, and sleuthing for clues as an investigator form the foundation of her Lexi Mills thriller series, as well as her Manhattan Sloane novels. She is visually impaired, a proud stroke survivor, mother of two, tech nerd, chocolate lover, and terrible golfer with a hole-in-one. When you can't find her writing, she'll be golfing or drinking wine (sometimes both) with friends and family in Northern California.

Sign up for the reader list at
severnriverbooks.com

Printed in the United States
by Baker & Taylor Publisher Services